also by
Rona Jaffe

The Best of Everything

away from home

a novel by

RONA JAFFE

1960

Simon and Schuster   New York

ALL RIGHTS RESERVED
INCLUDING THE RIGHT OF REPRODUCTION
IN WHOLE OR IN PART IN ANY FORM
COPYRIGHT © 1960 BY RONA JAFFE
PUBLISHED BY SIMON AND SCHUSTER, INC.
ROCKEFELLER CENTER, 630 FIFTH AVENUE
NEW YORK 20, N. Y.

FIRST PRINTING

LIBRARY OF CONGRESS CATALOG CARD NUMBER: 60-6722
MANUFACTURED IN THE UNITED STATES OF AMERICA
BY AMERICAN BOOK-STRATFORD PRESS, INC., N. Y.

for my grandfather

O que o Brazileiro destroi de dia,
cresce de noite.

What the Brazilian destroys during
the day grows back at night.

CHAPTER *1*

RIO. At this hour the beach was not usually so deserted. But now only a few lingering bathers remained, and a group of boys playing their daily soccer game at Posto Six. The sky was streaked with the pink and blue beginnings of sunset. If you looked straight out to sea you could see only the incredible blueness of the water for miles and miles and then the striated sky. A little to the right you could see an island with a lighthouse on top of it, just beginning to blink its man-made star into the evening. Farther to the right was the five-mile curving crescent of pale sand—the beach of Copacabana. On the far left, mountains, green, brown, gray, starting to fade into blue and purple in the setting sun. It was Christmas Eve.

On the small traffic island in front of the Copacabana Palace Hotel they had just lighted up the Christmas tree for the first time, and it looked a little strange and out of place: northern fir and luminescent globes in a hot tropical night. In front of the tree was the mosaic sidewalk, swirls of gray and white tiles in the manner of old Portugal. It was getting darker.

On the beach that edged the sidewalk in front of the hotel the man who sold kites had laid them to rest. They were bird-shaped kites made of cloth, great eagles, red and blue and black and white, that flew above the beach during the day in the blue sky like real birds, and in the evening perched in the sand supported by thin wooden poles. All day another man had been

1

working too, dressed in shabby khakis, crouched in front of a giant sand castle he had built and finishing the last exquisite details of the windows with a tiny pointed stick. Now it was complete, just as the sky turned black and filled with stars. Carefully he set candles all around the sand castle and lighted them, so that from across the street it looked like a mysterious shrine, all glowing. He put a painfully lettered sign in the sand in front of it: *Exact Replica of the Taj Mahal.* He had never seen the Taj Mahal except on picture postcards. There was a string of lights now all along the curve of beach, the lights that some people call The Queen's Necklace. They were street lights, lights of hotels, of sidewalk cafés, of apartment buildings, of Copacabana and Ipanema and Leblon.

In one of the great modern apartment buildings overlooking Copacabana Beach an American couple named Helen and Bert Sinclair were sitting in their library waiting for a long-distance telephone call he had put in to the States an hour before. They were a good-looking couple, he very dark, she fair, both young, with the look of settled Americans in a foreign country: healthy, sleek, privileged, proud, and vulnerable.

Helen had lighted only one lamp as the room had slowly darkened. Under the lamp on the desk the telephone rang; the long-drawn-out ring of Long Distance. "That's it," Bert said. "You take it first."

"Hello?" Helen said into the receiver, not quite sure whether or not she should shout. This was the first time they had spoken to New York.

"Helen?" her mother said. "How are you? Are you all right?"

"I'm fine. We're all fine. Can you hear me?"

"Yes, I can hear. Are you sure you're all right?"

"I'm *fine*, Mother. We called to say Merry Christmas."

"Merry Christmas, darling. Merry Christmas." She could hear her mother begin to weep. "How are Roger and Julie? I read in the papers that there's a smallpox epidemic in Brazil."

"That's the first I ever heard of it," Helen said. "The children are fine. Please stop crying, Mother, I can't hear you."

"Does Julie still have allergies?"

2

"No, they've gone. I wrote you that. *Please* stop crying, Mother. I can't hear *anything*." It gave Helen a sick feeling to hear her mother cry on the telephone; it was like going down too rapidly in an elevator. And in a way, she felt angry at her mother, too, for crying now when all she and Bert had wanted was to call and make tonight a happier Christmas Eve. "How's Daddy?"

"He's fine. He's here, grabbing the receiver out of my hand. Take care of yourself, Helen. Take care of yourself, darling. Don't let the children drink that milk. They never pasteurize it. I'll send you some more powdered milk by air mail."

"Mother, that costs a *fortune*. Please don't. They *do* pasteurize some of the milk. Don't send me any more milk. Please stop crying."

"Hello, Helen!" her father said happily. "Merry Christmas!" He sounded so hearty and cheerful and genuinely glad to speak to her that it almost made Helen start to cry herself.

"Daddy, how are you?"

"Fine. We're all fine."

"Is it cold in New York? Is it snowing?"

"It's nice and invigorating. Eight above zero. You would like it."

He wants me to come home, too, Helen thought. He knows how much I hate cold weather. "It sounds lovely," she said.

"I went ice skating this morning in the park. Your old man can still do a figure eight. I wish I could take Roger ice skating."

"And *we* wish you could come here and lie on the beach with us," Helen said cheerfully. But she was beginning to feel depressed and homesick, and she was wondering if it would have been better after all if they had not called. They could have sent a cable and avoided the pang of sensing all the unsaid things that came through those familiar voices.

"Do you still like Rio?"

"Yes."

"How's Bert?"

"He's fine. I'll let you speak to him." She held the receiver out to Bert, mouthing "Hurry."

"Hello," Bert said. "Merry Christmas. Fine. We're all fine.

3

Thank you, same to you, sir. Hello, Mother. Merry Christmas. We're all wonderful. Thank you. Yes . . . just a minute." He cupped his hand over the mouthpiece. "Your mother wants to say goodbye."

"Oh, Mother," Helen said. "Goodbye. Have a wonderful, wonderful New Year. Kiss Daddy for me." What she wanted, really, at that moment, was to ask to speak to her father again; but she thought of how long they had spoken on this transatlantic call already and of the money it would cost, and how none of them had actually said anything that mattered, and her throat closed with the beginning of tears. It occurred to her suddenly that her father might die, that she might never see him again or hear his voice. Her father was always so reassuring and comfortable about everything, even when she knew that he was as worried as her mother about some imaginary South American epidemic. He could say, "I miss you," and they were two people missing each other and it was honest and natural. Of course they missed each other. But then her mother would say, "I miss you," and sob, and suddenly Helen would find herself obliged to feel so sorry for her mother's bereavement that she did not miss her mother at all.

"Is Daddy all right, Mother? Are you sure?"

"He's all right. But he misses you and the children. Do you really have to stay there for three years?"

"Bert *has* to stay. We're going to say goodbye now. The children send love. Give Daddy a kiss for me. Goodbye, darling."

When she replaced the receiver her hand was shaking. *I wish we hadn't called.*

Bert smiled at her, looking a little satanic in the dark at this moment. "My God," he said. "It's a good thing we decided not to put the children on. We wait here an hour and a half for the call to come through and it costs four contos, and then everybody cries so much you can't hear anything anyway. You look like you could use a very small Scotch and water."

It was exactly what she had been thinking, but for some reason, perhaps because she felt guilty at hearing her thoughts expressed

4

aloud, she felt annoyed at him. "You don't have to make fun of them," she said, more vehemently than she had intended.

"I'm not. I think your father's wonderful."

"And you can't stand my mother. You never could."

"I just think you ought to tell her a few things," Bert said coolly. "You're a big girl now. You have two big children."

"And I'll *always* worry about my children, even when they're grown up. That's the way mothers are built. If you're a mother, you're a mother in your head too. Otherwise you shouldn't be one."

"All right," he said. "Excuse me. Do you want a Scotch?"

"No, thank you."

"Well, I do." He walked to the door, not looking back.

"Please!"

He turned then, and when she looked at his face that was so beautiful to her, and remembered that this man would belong to her forever, no matter what ridiculous things they might say to each other in anger, she almost hated herself. "I do want a Scotch," Helen said, very softly. "Wait and I'll come with you."

They walked to the living room hand in hand, and Bert made two very stiff Scotches at the bar. "What's that silly thing they always say here?" she asked.

"*Chin-chin.*"

"Yes. It sounds Chinese, not Brazilian." They touched their glasses together. The first taste of Scotch and water was good and Helen drank it all quickly, feeling herself beginning to unwind. It had been stupid to get upset. Relatives always wept at things like long-distance calls on holidays, and weddings, and christenings, because of the whole fabric of emotion that has been woven about these events, not because anyone is genuinely moved. It was a mild form of hysteria. It was stupid to get upset about it. They had been alone here for almost a year and they would remain here over two years more, and there was nothing to be done about it. No one had put a gun at hers or Bert's head and said, "You *must* go to Brazil." They had come here by choice, for the money, for the adventure, for the chances Bert would have when he eventually returned to the States. They had wanted to come. And when they finished the three years here they would probably go to another country, like Colombia, for another three years, and only then would they go home.

She put her arms around her husband's waist. "Do you love me?"

"Yes."

"*Muito?*"

"Yes."

"*Demais?*"

He smiled. "Yes."

"Do you think I'm an old, boring mother of two—what you said —two *big* children?"

He put his hands on the small of her back and then slid them lower, pulling her to him. "No, I think you're the young, beautiful mother of two little, tiny, midget children."

"Hold me there. I like that."

"Hold me too. Just for a minute."

Just for a minute, Helen thought; like two guilty teen-agers necking in the parlor. She looked into his eyes and knew that he was thinking the same thing. It's very nice to tell children about sex but you mustn't act it out for them. The children will finish their dinners and run in any minute. When you have children you *are* a Mother, you *are*, with a capital *M;* and you have to make love at night when they're sleeping, or when they're away, and things are never just the same.

"I'm thinking of something I'm going to do to you tonight," Bert said.

"We have to go to that damned party," she whispered against his mouth.

"After the party."

I hate it, Helen thought; I hate it, I hate it. Eat on schedule, sleep on schedule, play with the children on schedule, even make love on schedule. Not when you *want* to, but when everything else is neatly disposed of and it's time. Is that all life has turned into for us?

"What's the matter?" Bert asked when she drew away slightly.

"Nothing, darling," she said gently. She kissed him and drew

6

away farther, pretending to look for a cigarette. "I thought it was supposed to be the *men* who don't like to begin things they can't finish. I think it's the women too."

He lighted cigarettes for them both and gave her one. "Do you think we ought to eat something before this dinner tonight?"

"Not unless you're hungry now. They're Americans, so they'll serve early. I figured out a whole timetable. There are the Americans who say, 'We always eat at six-thirty, just like at home,' with that tiny bit of comfortable smugness in their voices; and then of course they have to serve a whole buffet at midnight anyway. And then there are the Embassy people and the others who've semi-adapted, and they have dinner at eight or eight-thirty. And then there are the Brazilians, who have dinner at ten."

"Or twelve or one," Bert said wryly.

"All right, love, I can take a hint. I'll have Maria make you a sandwich. Margie and Neil are coming over for a drink first, and then we'll drive to the party in their car, if you want. It's sport shirts tonight."

"Good."

She went into the kitchen to talk to the maids, and then into Julie's room where the children were finishing their supper with the governess. It occurred to her fleetingly as she walked down the hall, pressing a light switch, picking up a book that Roger had left on the hall chair, that she had turned into a kind of major-domo. Menus, lists, social schedules, clothes, orders to servants—she sometimes felt as if she were running a small hotel. During the years in their apartment in Riverdale, and then in the house in Westport when the children were older, she had done her own work with only a twice-weekly cleaning woman to do the heavy jobs. Looking back, she realized she had probably done the work of five, but all her friends had done the same so none of them had really thought it was extraordinary. And now she was only the giver of orders to others, and she felt ten years older.

Margie and Neil Davidow came at seven, wearing that polished, brushed look of people who have just dressed for a party. She was a smallish, dark girl, with an excellent figure and an even more spectacular clothes sense, and an incredible neatness and femininity of person that passed for beauty and actually managed to substitute very well for it. Many people said she was beautiful. Very quietly, Margie was a typical product of the twentieth century. She had had her teeth straightened while she was in high school, and her nose shortened a year later, and she wore invisible contact lenses for her nearsightedness. She had no children, and her husband had money, so she spent most of her time taking care of herself and her husband; choosing soft material to have his suits made, finding an obscure Italian tailor to cut them better than anybody else. She was twenty-five and Neil was thirty-one, the same age as Bert Sinclair. But Neil Davidow looked much older than Bert, not because of his features but because he had a kind of settled look. He was tall, with large features and dark straight hair. Until Margie had told her, Helen had never been able to guess how old Neil actually was. Neil and Margie had been married for five years, three of them spent in Brazil, and Margie Davidow was Helen Sinclair's best friend.

As soon as greetings had been exchanged the two couples separated; the men to the bar to make fresh drinks, the women to the corner of the sofa.

"Look at us," Helen said, laughing. "The men on one side of the room and the women on the other. God forbid someone should flirt with someone else's wife."

"I'll tell Neil to come over and flirt with you," Margie said cozily. "He'll love it." She waved at her husband. "Come here, darling, we need you."

"What are you talking about anyway?" Helen said. "Money or women?"

"Money," said Neil.

"Women," said Bert. "Be quiet, you'll have them too sure of us."

"Well, at least give Bert some good tips on the market, Neil," Helen said.

"That's what I'm doing," said Neil.

How he lights up when he talks about business, Helen thought.

8

And look at my husband. They look as if they're off on a treasure hunt. "Don't you want a drink, Margie?"

"No. No, thank you. We'll have to drink at the party, and it's too hot tonight."

"Listen," Helen said, "Roger is going to flip tomorrow when he sees that train you and Neil gave him. You shouldn't have spent so much money. I never saw a train like that in Brazil."

"I sent to F.A.O. Schwarz for it," Margie said. "Why not, anyway? By the time you all go back to live in the States he'll be too old for trains. And I adore him."

"Oh, how he adores you, too!"

"I really ought to have children," Margie said vaguely. She turned her gold bracelet around on her wrist and looked at it as if she had never seen it before. "I can, you know. There's nothing wrong with me. I just . . . never decided to." She lowered her voice. "I had two martinis in the kitchen before we came here. You might have gathered."

"You look fine," Helen said.

"Neil got a letter from his mother today and she made another one of those awful coy remarks about how nice it would be to be a grandmother. I hate it."

"I hate it too. Luckily for me I had Julie right away, so all I had to put up with was 'Oh, you're too young, too young, what a *shame!*'" She and Margie grinned at each other companionably. Then Margie's smile faded.

"There are limits to everything," she whispered vehemently. "I don't care what anyone tells me. You can tell me my shoes clash with my dress, or my new tablecloth is ugly, or I ought to learn more about politics. All right. Okay. I'm not a brilliant person, I'm just an ordinary person, and I'll thank anyone who wants to tell me something if it's going to help me improve. But there's one thing I can't stand. Nobody is going to tell me when I'm going to do my screwing with my husband, *nobody!*"

Helen looked at Margie, troubled. She had never seen her so excited. She covered Margie's hand, where it lay on the couch, with her own. "Of course not."

"I'm just drunk," Margie said lightly. She smiled, and she

looked the same as before her outburst—unruffled, serene, lady-like, not even a bit of face powder beginning to wear off. "You know," she said quietly, "Sometimes, like this evening before we got here, I wish I were dead."

Neil Davidow was looking at his watch. He came over to the sofa and smiled at Margie, reaching out to pull her to her feet. "Come on," he said. "We have to go. We'll be late."

"We'll all take our car," Margie said. "All right?"

Helen looked at both of them, Margie encircled lightly by her husband's arm, looking up at him with an expression that could only be honest affection, warmth and pleasure, Neil with his before-party look that showed he *knew* he was going to have a good time no matter what happened. In many ways, except for being childless, they were the most conventional couple Helen knew. And yet there was sorrow there, and suffering, and something worse, she suddenly realized, some kind of secret that one held away from the other. "Come and say goodnight to your brats," Helen said, taking Bert by the hand. "I promised them."

Margie and Neil came too, and as she watched Margie kissing Roger and Julie, Helen wondered briefly if she herself were the kind of unpleasant mother who showed off the delights of mother-hood to her less fortunate friends. She hoped it wouldn't look that way to Margie. She felt a kind of wariness for a moment in the presence of her friend who was dear to her and could be hurt by something completely unwitting and innocent. But Margie seemed perfectly happy, and when they all went down in the elevator she was already fussing with the back of her hair to be sure the humidity had not spoiled her set and you would not think she had another thought in her head. God, Helen thought, I'm glad I have a happy marriage. I'm glad I can know that it's always going to be there, that it's always going to be the same.

The party they went to was given by an American couple named Mildred and Phil Burns, who were both in their mid-thirties and came from Chicago. They were known to their friends as Mil and Phil. Mil was the sort of woman, as Margie Davidow had once put it, who always walked into a room where there were

10

strangers and said, "I'm Mil Burns and this is my husband." When she was eighteen years old she had been Corn Queen at Iowa State College, and she had been allowed to sit on a float surrounded by her handmaidens in white dresses. Her husband sometimes mentioned this when talking about old times back in the States, but Mil never talked about it. She had gained twenty pounds and a husband and three children, and the past was rather silly, but when she walked she held her head up stiffly, partly to show her handsome profile, partly to minimize her double chin, and partly so that her invisible crown would not slide off.

Phil Burns had arrived in Rio six months before his wife, and had rented their apartment, arranged for the necessities, set up his business, and then sent for his family. Mil had arrived protestingly, hating the apartment, hating the climate, hating the cockroaches, hating the telephone system, hating the tan bath water. They had been in Brazil now for more than a year, and Phil loved it as much as Mil did not. He was one of those enthusiastically overassimilated Americans who say things like "I know a wonderful little bar where you can go if you don't want to meet anyone you know—because only American tourists go there." He always carried a copy of the South American edition of *Time* magazine, and he said, "No?" at the end of questions that he asked in English.

Mildred met them at the door. The living room was already filled with people, talking and smoking, and a white-coated butler walked about with a tray of highballs. "You don't mind if you have to introduce yourselves?" Mil said. "I'm hoarse. I've been yelling at the maids all day. They're so stupid. I tried to tell them how to make a decent-looking *hors d'oeuvre*, but they can't learn."

"I think they look beautiful," Helen said, taking an infinitesimal pie filled with hot-flavored shrimps from a tray on the coffee table.

"You're crazy, Mil," Margie said. "You always worry too much."

"Heleninha!" Phil Burns said, putting an arm around Helen's waist. He pronounced it *Eleneenya*. He was a little shorter than

11

his wife, and he had a boyish, Ivy League look, a crewcut graying at the temples, and earnest, sad eyes. Helen liked him. "There are some people here you don't know," Phil said. "There's a Brazilian—see—over by the window talking to the woman in the flowered dress. His name is Nestor and he's extremely interesting, you ought to talk to him. And there's Trainer Wilkes, from the Embassy. He's not really *with* the Embassy; he's just here on a temporary exchange mission to bring Little League Baseball to Brazil. The gal in the flowered dress is his wife." Phil had his other arm around Bert's shoulders, Brazilian style, and he patted Bert's upper arm as he spoke.

"I'd like a drink," Bert said. "Do you want one, Helen?"

"Yes, please, darling."

Phil waved at the butler, who came over immediately with his tray of drinks. "Here. Scotch, gin, or rye. I didn't want to make martinis; it's too hot. But if you want one, I'll sneak you one in the kitchen."

"No, no," said Bert. "Scotch is fine, thank you."

"I found the first Carnival records for fifty-nine," Phil said happily. "I'll play them later and we can dance. Maybe things will get wild."

"Somebody will drop dead of a heat stroke," Mil said. "That's the wild thing that will happen."

"I've got all the windows open," Phil said, beginning to look less happy. "It will get cooler later. Do you want me to bring the fan in from our room?"

"It doesn't do any good in *our* room," Mil said, "so what makes you think it will help with this mob in here?" She walked to the front door to greet other arriving guests, holding her head high, her emerald pendant earrings swinging against her tanned neck.

"She hates the heat," Phil murmured apologetically.

"Don't we all," said Helen. "The front of our apartment is unbearable during the day. I have to stay in the back when I'm home. But at night it's cool."

"It's only the crowd," said Phil. "This is a very cool apartment. Listen, this is Trainer Wilkes. Trainer, Helen and Bert Sinclair."

Trainer Wilkes was a tall, good-looking man in his late thirties.

He had curly brown hair and horn-rimmed glasses and a suntan. When he shook hands with Helen he took her hand gently, almost gingerly, as if for years his forceful handshake had made ladies wince and he had finally learned. He was wearing a black silk suit and he looked hot. "How do you do," he said.

"I'm glad to meet you," Helen said. Phil Burns had pulled Bert away to meet someone else, and she found herself alone with Trainer Wilkes. They looked at each other for a minute, trying to think of something to say, and Helen smiled. "Have you been in Brazil long?"

"Few weeks."

"How long are you staying?"

"A year."

"Do you like it? I guess everybody asks you that and you must be sick of hearing it."

"Oh, I like it," Trainer Wilkes said, not too enthusiastically. "Getting to like it. It's interesting. Wouldn't like to live here, but it's all right."

"Where are you from in the States?"

"Garnerville College in Pennsylvania. It's a small school; you've probably never heard of it. But we have one of the best baseball teams in the country."

"I'm afraid I don't know much about baseball," Helen admitted. "My son was too young to play when we left the States. Is that what you do there, teach baseball?" She smiled at him. "I guess that's why they call you 'Trainer.'"

"I teach English history," he said. "English history and baseball."

"And Phil said you're here for the government."

"More or less. I'm with the Cultural Division. We bring our ideas, our culture, over here, and it makes friends. I'm here to teach Little League Baseball. That's my job. And I'll tell you something." He raised his glass and drank thirstily, as if the effort of such a long speech were too much. But his eyes were sparkling and for the first time he looked animated. "It was the best idea they ever had, to bring me over for the Cultural Division. The Brazilians want to know America; let them know base-

13

ball. Baseball is *really* America. I don't care about books, music, theater, art, all that junk. I'm going to give 'em baseball, and they're going to love me."

"I hope so," Helen said.

Trainer Wilkes took a clean handkerchief out of his pocket and wiped his face and neck thoroughly, as if it were a hand towel. He looked at it and put it back into his pocket. "You bring your boy over when we get started, and we'll let him join a team," he said. "How old is he?"

"Six. That's a little too young, I think."

"All right. We're going to have a team for five-year-olds. Can't start too young. It must be pretty tough for the American parents here, so far away, trying to keep all the things we have at home."

"But there are certain compensations to travel," Helen said mildly.

Trainer Wilkes looked down into her face seriously. "You be careful," he said. "Just don't get into trouble. You don't know these people."

"What do you mean?"

"You'll know when you get into trouble," Trainer said. "You'll remember I told you."

Someone had put a record of American Christmas carols on the phonograph, and it sounded strange to hear them, almost as if it were really summer and someone were trying to be Bohemian. It was terribly hot. The men were beginning to wipe their foreheads and move closer to the opened windows, and the waiter walked about quickly with ice-filled drinks. The alcohol was only making everyone hotter. "God rest ye merry, gentlemen," the chorus sang in wondrously muted harmony. "Let nothing ye dismay." It brought memories of Westport in winter, of wreaths hung at windows with sloppily tied red bows attached by Julie, and of the smell of a fir tree and the crackle and heat of a hot fire when you sat too close to it in order to roast apples on long pointed sticks. Lately, more and more often, Helen had been dreaming at night of snow, of wide white fields turning blue at twilight, of window sills piled high with the powdery fresh snowfall and herself safe inside the room looking out at the white stillness and beauty. All

14

the inconvenience of a Connecticut winter—the icy roads that made driving the children to nursery school a hazard, the biting wind that made you feel you never would get warm again, the ache of wet feet and the beautiful white snow that turned so quickly into brown mud and gray slush—all these things seemed to recede. She remembered winter in Connecticut as if it were a Christmas card.

In the corner of the room on a table was a small Christmas tree, with gold balls and tinsel, and packages underneath it for the Burns's children. Somehow Mil Burns had managed to get real American gift-wrapping paper. Helen recognized it immediately. She had probably sent to the States for the presents, too. There were no other Christmas decorations in the room. Trainer Wilkes had been taken elsewhere by one of the guests, and Helen found herself standing alone. She was relieved. She looked at the other guests idly, noticing their clothes, listening to the Christmas carols with an ache in her throat. She wondered what her friends were doing right now in Westport. It was two hours earlier in the States. They were probably having dinner, or perhaps they were through with dinner and were wrapping last-minute presents furtively, trying to hide them from the excited children. I won't be home again for six Christmases, she thought. Julie will be a teen-ager. She'll be going to Christmas dances with boys and hanging mistletoe from the top door sill. And I'll be so much older, so much darker skinned, so much blonder, so much a stranger, that all my friends will have to learn to know me all over again, and I them.

She caught sight of Margie standing in a corner talking with two of the American women whom she herself did not know. Margie in her brown and white checked mousseline shirtwaist dress, the skirt propped out by a huge crinoline, looked like a Brazilian wife next to them—chic, pampered, wearing the latest Dior style. The other two women were wearing sunback cotton dresses, the kind Margie wore when she went to the grocery store. They were tanned and contented looking, and they wore a great deal of real gold jewelry set with Brazilian stones. Helen wandered over to them.

"I'll tell you one thing," one was saying in a midwestern accent. "I'm buying a lot of jewelry here. Diamonds especially. Real jewelry is so cheap in Brazil, and it's an investment. Believe me, people treat you better when you have real jewelry. You attract a nicer class of people back home when you have nice jewelry." She held out her hand and looked at her two glittering rings.

Helen tried not to laugh. "That's a lovely aquamarine," she said.

"Isn't it!"

"I'd like you to meet Helen Sinclair," Margie said. "This is—"

"First names," said the woman with the rings. "Ernestine. And this is Linda."

"How do you do," said Linda. She was in her late forties, a small woman, very thin, and she looked shy. Her hair was cut short and curled against her head in tight little snails, as if it had been over-permanented, over-set, and dried too much by the tropical sun. She wore rimless glasses and she had a huge red rubylite hanging around her neck on a gold chain.

"That's a lovely rubylite," Helen said.

"How did you know?" Linda said, smiling happily. "I love it, too; it's my birthstone. My husband gave it to me for my birthday."

"Helen's husband is a gemologist," Margie said. "She knows so much about stones it's terrifying."

"I told her not to stop there," Ernestine said sternly. She gestured at Linda's rubylite pendant. "That's all right, but she should buy *real* stones. Expensive ones. Diamonds."

"I like this one," Linda said.

"You listen to me," said Ernestine. "When you go back to the States you'll be sorry if you haven't bought a few really *good* pieces." She was a big woman, mostly bosom, and she had naturally blond hair which she wore in a pony tail. She looked about thirty-five.

"I'm sure Linda would rather have something her husband gave her for her birthday," Helen said. "I know I would. And this rubylite is a beauty." She smiled at the older woman, feeling

16

sorry for her, and wondering which one of these men was married to Ernestine.

"My birthstone is really garnet," Linda said, in a breathy, rather apologetic voice. "But this is red, so we thought it would count for the same thing."

"Why not?" Margie said.

"Where are you from?" Ernestine asked Helen.

"We lived in Westport, Connecticut, before we came here."

"We've lived all over," Ernestine said. "We lived in California for a while, and in Kansas, and we even lived in Seattle, Washington. Have you ever been there?"

"No, I haven't."

"I like Brazil," Ernestine said. She tossed her head, and the heavy blond pony tail flicked back and forth, rather like the tail of a percheron. When she spoke she showed large, white, even teeth, and she looked like the kind of person who would bite into something to see if it were real. "My husband's going to go into business here. He's thinking of buying land in the jungle and then selling it back in a couple of years when values go up. There's going to be a land boom in the Interior when they finish the new capital. It's going to be like the American West, only bigger. Bigger! When they finish the Belem-Brazilia Road, land values out there in the jungle are going to double and redouble."

The butler came by with his tray of highballs and they each took one. "How long have you lived in Brazil?" Helen asked.

"Seven years," Ernestine said. "Let's sit down; my feet hurt." She took hold of Helen's arm and led her to two unoccupied chairs against the wall. "Ahh . . . what a relief. You can't get a decent pair of shoes here, especially if you wear an eight and a half triple A. All the Brazilians have little square feet. Did you ever notice?"

"I'd never noticed," Helen said.

"Well, they do. Which one is your husband?"

"That tall man over there," Helen said. "Speaking to the Brazilian."

"Ah, how attractive he is! I love dark men. You're very lucky."

"I think so too," Helen said.

17

"That handsome one over there on the couch is *my* little boy." Ernestine pointed at a small, balding, rotund man in his early fifties. "He's cute, isn't he?"

Helen would hardly have thought of the word *cute* to describe Ernestine's husband, but she nodded and smiled. "Yes, he is."

Ernestine put her empty highball glass on the floor beside her chair and turned to Helen intimately, her face set in a determined expression of loyalty. She looked like someone about to pledge allegiance to the flag. She twined her fingers around Helen's arm. "Don't sell these people short," Ernestine said. "These are all wonderful people in this room. Of course, there are a few that are corny—two couples here whose names I won't mention because they won't be here very long. One or two parties and then they'll never be asked back."

"What's *corny?*"

"Wives who flirt too much with other women's husbands. Too much drinking. Acting unrefined. You'll see. Watch any one of the women at this party for half an hour and you'll see that she never does anything out of line. Oh, five, six years ago it was another story. There was lots of carrying on, lots of divorces. But now everyone who comes to Brazil to live has to be screened first by the State Department and they've gotten rid of all that. All these people here always tread the straight and narrow."

Helen had never actually heard anyone use the expression *straight and narrow* before. She looked at Ernestine, but Ernestine wore a look of staunch, almost sentimental virtue and not a trace of a smile.

"Let's go over and talk to the men," Ernestine said. She stood up and went over to Bert and the Brazilian, who had been joined by Trainer Wilkes and a tall, thin man Helen did not know.

The men were involved in an excited discussion, and Helen and Ernestine drifted over to the edge of their group without a word, listening politely as people do who are group-hopping at a cocktail party, not sure whether they want to stay or whether they are going to interrupt something highly emotional for the formality of introductions. Helen wanted to reach out and take Bert's hand, or put her arm around his waist. It would make too

18

much of an interruption; she would look like a possessive wife, she was afraid. She always tried to leave him alone at cocktail parties so he would feel free to talk with other people and would not feel that she was his Siamese twin just because she was his wife. After all, they were chained together for good, so they might as well pretend they were free. But she was longing to touch him. She looked at his face, at his lips as he spoke, and she remembered the moment they had had together that evening before all the household things had interrupted. "I'm thinking of something I'm going to do to you tonight." She could hear his voice inside her head now, saying that again, and she repeated it to herself. The conversation of the men rose and receded around her and she hardly heard it. She was watching her husband, pretending to be interested in the discussion, and she was thinking of the smoothness of his skin under that blue shirt. I can't help it, Helen thought; I want to go home and make love to my husband. I'm bored here and I can't think about anything else except that I want him to make love to me. She wondered if it were the time of the month when she could get pregnant, and if that was why she felt so alive and full of desire. But she felt that way more and more all the time living in Brazil. Perhaps it was the climate. Or perhaps the leisure, or perhaps because the sun and air on the beach made her healthy. I wish it were late and we could go home.

She loved the look Bert had when he was listening to something that interested him. His face came alight as if he had made a discovery in his relationship with the other person. All his relationships with other people were discoveries for him; she had never seen anyone so interested in talking with other people. And the others always seemed to respond to it, so that a person who was usually quite ordinary became a conversationalist with Bert, became self-revelatory, even if what the person had to show was, after all, something quite dreadful. People, even at their worst, were always amusing to Bert, and usually much more than amusing.

Helen reached out and took his hand. He returned the pressure, but absently. He doesn't know what I'm thinking, she thought.

He's not thinking about making love, and he isn't even dreaming that I'm thinking of it. He's put me on a shelf somewhere for a few hours and he hardly even knows I'm alive. Oh, I wish it were time to go home! Maybe I'm frivolous and silly not to be listening to all this cocktail-party talk where I could be learning something, too, but I need, I need, I need to be made love to. . . .

Reluctantly Helen forced herself to listen to the conversation around her. She let go of Bert's hand and fixed an expression of alertness on her face, and concentrated. The tall, thin man, whose name she did not know, was speaking.

"I haven't been here long," he said, "but I've been watching the Brazilians and I *know*. The same kind of hate that was shown to Nixon on his Pan-American tour is here too. They hate Americans because we have money and we drive our children to school every day in cars." He had a pinched face, lean and long and dark, and when he spoke he moved his hands nervously. He was wearing a Balinese printed sport shirt with short sleeves, open at the neck, but instead of making him look relaxed and festive it somehow only made him look more foreign and ill at ease. "You don't believe they hate us?" he asked. "You want to know something? The other day someone came by and spit on my front lawn, just because my car was parked in front and he knew it had American diplomatic license plates."

The Brazilian named Nestor held his hand up in a gesture of peace. He was small and neat, with silky dark skin, and he wore a seersucker suit. "But all diplomatic license plates are the same," he said, in almost unaccented English. "They all have a red background, and none of them indicate what country they're from."

"Someone spit on my front lawn," said the man in the Balinese shirt. "My wife saw him."

Nestor smiled. "That's because Rio is full of Portuguese," he said. "Portuguese love to spit. They spit anywhere. You might say it's a national habit. They just go along the street and spit. Do you know, they keep chamber pots under their beds, and when the chamber pots are full they just toss the contents out the window. Whoosh—out it goes on the street, on someone's head. Why, spitting is nothing. Sometimes people spit on *my* lawn too.

It must have been a Portuguese. It doesn't mean anything."

Trainer Wilkes leaned over and whispered in Helen's ear. "Never mind." He gestured at the man in the Balinese printed shirt. "You listen to him. He's one of the brightest minds here."

Helen looked at the man whose lawn had been spat upon. He was evidently a diplomat of some kind, a member of the Embassy. She realized how little she knew about politics and like or dislike, or even that frightening word *Hate*. She had been here for almost a year and she had never seen any sign that anyone hated her because she was an American. Am I dense? she thought. There must be all sorts of dangerous undercurrents that I've never even dreamed of, and that even now I can't bring myself to believe exist. Somehow, she didn't like the man in the gay shirt. He frightened her a little; he was so intense, so sure that other people's motives had to be bad. It was the exact opposite of the way she had always greeted life, and whenever she met someone who felt the way he did she was torn with a combination of resentment and inferiority feelings. He might be right after all, and she didn't want him to be. I must be an ostrich, Helen thought; and yet, he's so—what is the Brazilian word?—so *antipatico*.

"I spent ten years in the States, off and on," Nestor was saying to Bert. "There's a restaurant in New York I used to love, El Morocco. And the Stork Club. Do you know the St. Regis Hotel?"

"Of course," Bert said.

"I always used to stay there when I was in New York. Except one year when I stayed at the Plaza. I love your hansom cabs that go around the park."

"Oh, yes," Bert said.

"You know, it's a funny thing," Nestor said, smiling ingratiatingly. "The Plaza Hotel is the only one I ever found in New York that had adopted the civilized custom of bidets, and they don't work!"

"They don't work?"

"Never. They've been turned off, deliberately." Nestor smiled again, and made a little gesture of depreciation. "I'm sure they had good reasons. Here in Brazil *everyone* has a bidet, but unfortunately we often don't have enough water for even the simpler pieces of plumbing to function!" He laughed, and Bert laughed too. "It's true, isn't it? This is a country of paradoxes."

"Dinner," Mil Burns said, interrupting with a hand on Bert's shoulder. "Come on, don't you all be polite and let it get cold. Come on, everybody."

Helen turned to take Bert's arm, but Ernestine had already fastened on to him, smiling a great white smile. "I've been dying to talk to you," she heard Ernestine say.

Nestor turned to her. "May I help you get a plate?" he asked. "It's buffet."

"Thank you."

He was a nice little man, scarcely an inch taller than she was in her high heels, and he had a charming way of looking at her, as if he appreciated her but would not dream of making a pass unless she hinted at it first. It was that verge-of-a-pass look she had seen on other Brazilian men at American parties. They kissed your hand when they were introduced and when they said goodbye. They actually kissed your hand; they didn't just lift it a bare two inches and make a token gesture. But they never held your hand too long at their lips, and if they squeezed it before they released it, it was such a slight squeeze that it was more flattering than forward.

They found seats next to Margie and Neil on the sofa. "Are you having a good time?" Margie murmured.

"Sort of," she murmured back.

"Let's not stay too late," Margie said.

It was obvious that Mil had planned the menu with a great deal more nostalgia than practicality. There was ham and potato salad and Boston baked beans and brown bread and cold fried chicken and great buttermilk biscuits dripping with salt butter. The dessert sat on the sideboard: a large sticky-looking lemon pie, a chocolate pie covered with whipped cream, and a platter of brownies. The white-coated butler came around with a tray full of glasses of cold beer. It must have been a hundred degrees in the room, and the first bite of biscuit stuck in Helen's throat. She put her piled-up plate on the coffee table in front of her and took a cigarette.

22

Nestor leaned forward to light it for her. "You don't eat?"

"It's very hot tonight."

"This is a terrible summer," he said. "It isn't usually so hot in Rio."

She smiled. "Is that true?"

"I swear it. I hate the heat too. In the summer here I nearly die of it."

"My lord," Margie said, "look at my husband eat, God bless him."

Neil had devoured everything on his plate; he seemed oblivious to the heat. "What's the matter?" he asked.

Margie laughed. "Nothing, darling."

Neil stood up. "I'm going to get more. This is very good. Real kosher ham." He grinned at his wife. "Does anyone want anything? More beer? Nestor?"

"No, no thank you," Nestor said, looking slightly queasy. "I always eat a large lunch and then I eat very lightly at night. It's much better in hot weather."

Bert came over, with Ernestine following him. "Hi," he said. "Is there room?"

Helen and Margie moved over on the sofa, and Ernestine sat down. Bert sat on the arm of the sofa next to Helen, even though there was still room where Neil had been. "Your husband certainly worries about you," Ernestine exclaimed. "He insisted we come over to see if everything was all right."

Nestor stood up. "I think I had better look for *my* wife," he said. "I want to see if she's all right." He bowed slightly and left.

Ernestine got up from the couch and took Nestor's empty chair, next to Bert. "You can just *tell* he's a mining engineer," she said, taking hold of Bert's hand. "Just feel his hands! They're wonderful. So hard! You can tell he's been digging in those mines for jewels." She rubbed her fingers against Bert's palm. "Isn't it exciting to be married to a mineralogist?"

"He's a gemologist," Helen said.

Bert extracted his hand from Ernestine's grip. "That's slightly different," he said. "And my hand is this way from years of playing tennis. I'm sorry to disappoint you."

"Oh, you'd never disappoint me!" Ernestine cried. Her face was flushed from the heat and the highballs, and her nose and cheeks were shiny.

Helen felt Margie kick her lightly on the ankle. She turned to smile at her friend, and Margie winked at her almost imperceptibly. She could see that Margie was trying not to giggle, and looking at Margie's elaborately restrained face almost made Helen laugh with her. They looked away from each other then. But the moment she was not in contact with the contagion of Margie's amusement Helen began to wonder what was so funny after all. When Ernestine had said, "Your husband certainly worries about you. He insisted we come over," Helen had felt a soft happiness—the reassurance of love. No matter how many years she lived with Bert she knew she would never stop needing to have him show her he loved her. But, of course, he had not come over to see if she were all right; he had come here to escape Ernestine. It was a completely different thing. For a moment Helen almost felt like getting up with some excuse and leaving him here to suffer Ernestine's coy passes and tentaclelike fingers.

There is always the moment at a not quite successful party when you feel as though you have been dropped from a height of gaiety and suddenly everyone is unpleasantly revealed; and you are totally alone watching them, wondering what you are doing there anyway. These are the same people who were so entertaining a few minutes ago, you think, but now they just look tired, their chatter is forced and endless, and your face is weary from smiling at them. It is the moment to leave, but of course you never can leave just then, so the rest of the evening turns into a black abyss in which you wait and wait and wait, despising yourself for being so conventional and polite instead of inventing a headache or an urgent late appointment. It was that moment now for Helen. She looked at the large blonde flirting with Bert, at Mil Burns, at Linda in her tight little curls, and at all the other expatriate wives who were huddled together for protection and warmth in a strange land, guarding their old customs and keeping away the intruders. Mil and Phil had invited a Brazilian, it was true, but he was a tame Brazilian. He spoke perfect English, he

24

had spent years in the States, he had money, he acted chivalrous but not wolfish, he never expressed violent or controversial ideas. He was almost wearing a Brooks Brothers' suit. It seemed, Helen thought, as if they had invited the tame Brazilian as a sort of inoculation. They figured if they could survive him they would be immune, and eventually when they *had to* go out into the city and meet *real* Brazilians, then they would be safe.

What do they think they're going to catch, Helen wondered, mumps? And there are Embassy people here too, and Phil Burns the Brazilophile is so happy that he's snared a tame Brazilian and all these other international types. But except for a few topazes and amethysts and aquamarines and one or two foreign clichés in their conversation, these people might as well still be at home. Maybe I'm exactly the same; who is to tell? How *can* I be different, when this is all I know?

Margie tapped her arm. "We're leaving. It's twelve o'clock. Do you want to go?"

"Oh, yes!"

There was a confusion of goodbyes at the door; Mil telling them not to go, Phil arranging a luncheon date with Neil, a woman Helen had never seen before who happened to be standing near the doorway and who smiled at her slightly and said, "Goodbye. It was very nice meeting you." Ernestine trailed Helen and Bert to the door.

"This is the way the Brazilians say goodbye," Ernestine said, and flung her arms around Bert's neck, kissing him soundly on first one cheek and then the other. It was her own variation on the formal, airy little kisses Brazilian women always exchanged, and when she headed for Helen, Helen tried to avoid her, but it was too late.

Ernestine put her arm around Helen's neck and kissed her cheek, and drew her slightly away from the others who were congregated at the doorway. "Watch out for your Bert," Ernestine whispered intensely. She looked almost tearful. "Keep him on the straight and narrow!"

"Good night," Helen said. "Good night. Thank you. Good night, Mil dear. Thank you again. Good night." And they had escaped.

When she and Bert were safely inside their apartment, where the maids had left lamps lighted softly in the living room and the night breeze blew the curtains inward like children playing ghosts, Helen sighed happily. She dropped her shoes and purse on the floor and sank into an armchair. "Ah, how wonderful. Merry Christmas, darling."

Bert smiled. "Merry Christmas. Let's have a brandy."

"All right."

He brought two glasses of brandy and gave her one, and then sat in the other armchair. "Do you know what that woman was doing to me?" he said in a tone of delighted amusement. "I was watching to see if you noticed. She had me against the wall and she kept punctuating her conversation by bumping me with her pelvis. I swear it! 'Tell me all about mining,' *bump, bump.* 'It must be so interesting,' *bump, bump.*" He laughed.

"Oh, no!" Helen said. "And she kept telling me about these nice virtuous people and how no one was so *corny* as to have affairs any more!"

"She had hands like an octopus," Bert said. "I had to remove each finger separately when she was talking to me."

"I'm delighted you're so irresistible, dear."

"Oh, so am I." They both laughed.

"After we put out the presents, let's open ours *now*," Helen said. "I want you to see what I found for you."

They went to the closet and took out the gifts for the children, all wrapped, and piled them under the tree until they reached the lowest branches. Then they found the ones each had bought for the other. "You first," Helen said.

She watched his face as he unwrapped the small, heavy parcel. She wanted him to like it, to feel the way she had when she found it for him; and as always when she gave a present, she was a little afraid that it would not mean what she had meant it to, that it would be only another gift.

"It's beautiful," he said. He held it on his palm—a round crystal paperweight, glittering with colors from the lamplight, smooth and solid and heavy, with an inscription engraved on it.

"Read it," Helen whispered.

"*'Chance cannot change my love nor time impair . . .'*"

"I mean it."

"I know. Thank you, darling." He handed her a narrow, small box wrapped in white paper. "This is for you."

She could tell by the feel of the box that it was a piece of jewelry, and when she lifted the lid she saw that it was a gold bracelet. "Oh, it's marvelous! Thank you." She held out her wrist for him to attach the clasp.

"It looks very nice on you," he said. "I was afraid it might be too heavy."

"No, I love it."

He looked at the bracelet with his head cocked slightly, appraising the look of it. "Yes. I like it."

The living-room clock chimed softly. "I don't want to look," Bert said. "What time is it? No, don't tell me."

"It's only one-thirty."

"And the kids will come thundering in at six."

"It's not so late," Helen said softly.

He put his arms around her and kissed the top of her head. "Let's go to bed," he murmured.

He always went into the bathroom ahead of her because she took so much longer than he did, and Helen walked out onto the balcony that led off their bedroom overlooking the sea. The stars seemed very low and big in the cloudless black sky, and the beach was white with moonlight. Here and there on the sand she could see a tiny figure that sometimes briefly moved apart so she could see it was really two. None of the lovers below on the beach seemed ashamed that they were loving each other in public. Even if the night had been a disguise, fifty feet away on the sand there was always another couple as oblivious and occupied as the first. They were the poor from the crowded mountaintop *favellas,* and the not quite so poor from the Copacabana slums, taking the only real pleasure they had; and they were the young romantics who liked to make love on a moonlit beach, and some of them were wealthy drunks who had wandered from a party and were not quite sure how they had arrived on the beach at all.

It was a night for love. But every night in Rio was a night for love.

Behind her, she heard Bert walking barefoot out of the bathroom and pausing to turn down the sheets of the bed. She went back into the room and smiled at him, full of love and secret excitement, and went quickly into the bathroom. She had taken a bath before they went to the party, but she wanted to take another one, quickly, quickly. She turned the cold water tap on full and poured in a handful of lemon-scented bath salts, because she knew it was a fragrance he liked. Waiting for the tub to fill, Helen brushed her hair, looking into the mirror at her eyes, which seemed to have become all pupil, great and dark. She would not take off any of her make-up. She loathed the idea of being one of those wives who come to their husband's arms bristling with curlers and shiny and pale with cold cream. How could anyone bear that?

The bath water was slightly tan from the rusty pipes, but she had learned to ignore that, and when she had dried herself she dusted her body with powder, quickly, quickly, and once dropped the puff into the sink by accident because her hands seemed unable to hold on to anything in this moment. She kept a bottle of the lemon-scented cologne in the medicine cabinet and splashed it on her shoulders, her breasts, the insides of her thighs, and left it standing uncapped on the sink.

The bedroom was dark, but moonlight made objects stand out in gleaming silhouette. He was lying on his back, covered only by the sheet, lying very still. Helen walked quietly to the bed on bare feet and slid under the sheet beside him. He did not move. She raised herself on one elbow and looked down at his face, illuminated by the whiteness of the moonlight. His eyes were shut, shadowed, and the dark semicircles his joined eyelashes made did not even quiver under her cool breath. He was breathing deeply and softly, the otherworldly breathing of the dreamer in his first secret hours of sleep.

Oh, no, darling, Helen thought, no; wake up, wake for me. She tried to will him awake by looking into his face, remembering that somewhere she had heard it was possible to awaken children and lovers by watching them as they slept. He only sighed and slipped deeper into his dream. On the table next to his side of the bed Helen saw that he had turned his little clock so he could see the face when he awoke. She looked at the illuminated hands with loathing, changing them in her mind into time itself, all the hours of her days and nights, marked off and rigid and ritual.

She moved away from him then and lay on her side of the bed, listening to the tiny ticking of the clock and the sound of Bert's even breathing. Why is a man always able to fall asleep so much more quickly than a woman? she wondered. She turned on her side, trying not to waken him. Her eyes were becoming accustomed to the dark so that she could see everything in the room clearly. She did not like to sleep naked, so after a while she got up and took her nightgown out of the closet and put it on, and then lay down again, and waited for sleep.

Lying tensely in the dark, she was suddenly overwhelmed by a wave of loneliness and futility. She remembered what she had thought earlier that evening watching Margie and Neil: I'm glad I have a happy marriage. It's always going to be there . . . always going to be the same. The same? If sameness meant tolerance, indifference, habit, then their marriage would always be the same. But it had not always been this way. A long time ago, just nine years, she and Bert had been loving strangers, excited and wondering with the freshness of their love, reaching out to touch each other a hundred times a day, making mistakes together, alone together, lucky—no, charmed. . . . And now they were strangers again, alone together again in a new world, and there was loneliness. Perhaps if they had stayed at home among the reassuring, familiar things she never would have noticed the change, accepting it only as a sign of the passage of time, but here, halfway around the world, alone with Bert, she was afraid.

She could reach out to him now, touch him, make him awaken from sleep, but she would only awaken the stranger. He might murmur, groan with weariness and protest, open his eyes in startled question: Is everything all right? The children? But never with the smile of sleepy love that knows the answer—everything is all right, I just wanted to be sure you were still there, I wanted

29

to tell you I am here. There was no magic kiss to awaken the dreamer to the beautiful image of the past.

Merry Christmas, Helen said to herself, and felt her own smile like a grimace in the dark. Merry Christmas. But, after all, Christmas morning too was for children, like everything else that was filled with mystery and excitement. The grownups, as Bert would say, had to pay for the presents.

CHAPTER *2*

A half hour after midnight on Christmas Eve, or more accurately, Christmas Day, Margie Davidow followed her husband into their apartment and turned on all the lights in the living room. The martinis she had drunk in the kitchen before dinner and the gin-tonics she had consumed during the party later had worn off, and she felt sober, tired, and slightly apprehensive. She didn't like this feeling of complete sobriety at night, especially after she had been high, because she was still too close to the feeling of wonderful fuzziness that had vanished.

"Why are you putting on the lights?" Neil asked, behind her. "I want to go to bed. Aren't you tired?"

"I . . . thought I'd stay up a little while. You go to sleep, darling. You worked today; you must be exhausted."

He put his hand on her shoulder. "I'll stay up a little with you. Let's have a drink."

She felt the churning begin then, in her stomach, and her heart began to beat so heavily she wondered if some night she would end up having a heart attack. But it was impossible; young women of twenty-five with healthy constitutions never had heart attacks just because of panic. "All right," she breathed, and the sound came out as if someone were holding her very tightly around the waist.

"Scotch? No, you'd better stick to gin."

She watched Neil measuring out the drinks and saw that he

was making hers a good deal stronger than his. The docility of the gesture, the resignation it implied, filled her with guilt, and she wanted to go to him and put her arms around him. She almost did, and then she stopped, knowing he would misunderstand. She shut her eyes and wondered if she were going to cry.

"It was a good party," Neil said. "Didn't you think so?"

"I had fun." She took several swallows of her gin-tonic, waiting for it to warm her and knowing in despair it would not. She never could get drunk after she had eaten a large supper; she simply was not made for it. She would be sick first, and that would only make matters worse.

"If you want to," Neil said quietly, "we can play chess for half an hour or so." He was standing by the little marble-topped table that held the chess board, with the chessmen already standing on it ready for the war. He touched the Queen with his long, clean fingers, and the touch seemed almost sensual. Margie shook her head. "You shouldn't smoke so much," he said abruptly.

"I'm sorry." She put her cigarette out quickly and folded her hands in her lap, feeling her nails cutting into her own knuckles and powerless to stop.

There were so many things they loved to do together: play chess, listen to music, talk, talk, talk. Sometimes, when they just wanted to talk together, she and Neil could stay up all night, each of them glancing at each other in delighted surprise when they saw the sky beginning to lighten with dawn. Sometimes then they would go out and walk on the beach, hand in hand, like friends, and perhaps they would swim when the beach was fully light. There would be no one there at seven o'clock, except for a few maids who went swimming before they returned to cook breakfast for their awakening employers. And then Margie and Neil would go back to their apartment and have coffee and toast and eggs, ravenously, and he would slap his forehead with the palm of his hand and laugh and say, "It's all right for *you;* you can sleep all day!" He would kiss her goodbye and go to the office, and she would pull the heavy curtains across the bedroom windows and curl into bed, the sheets still cool from the night breeze, and she would sleep, thinking how much she loved him. But on a night like tonight, when he did not want to talk, there seemed to be nothing for either of them to say; except for the one thing that neither of them dared say.

"Come on," Neil said. "It's late."

It was hopeless even to try to finish her drink; the taste of it was making her feel ill. She put the glass on the coffee table and stood up.

When they walked down the hall to their bedroom Neil put his hand on the back of her neck, and then she knew. She knew, as if there were a sign language for people who have been married for several years and know each other's habits so well they imagine what they know is the other's thoughts. But it's never the thoughts, Margie thought; it's only the habits. She looked at their shadows joined ahead of them on the white carpet and she felt very lonely.

"Look," Neil said, pointing. "There's a saying in Bali that when two people walk together and their shadows join, they'll be together for the rest of their lives."

"I hope so," Margie said softly.

"What do you mean, you *hope* so?"

"I love you."

"I love you too, Monkey. You know that."

"I wish you wouldn't call me Monkey."

He looked at her, astonished and almost hurt. "Then I never will again. If you didn't like it, why didn't you say so?"

She shrugged. "It didn't seem . . . to matter."

He put his hand on the back of her neck again and began to stroke her, very lightly. "It does matter."

She went into her bathroom and shut the door, and a moment later she heard the groan of plumbing and the splash of water as Neil turned on the taps in the sink. He's brushing his teeth now, she thought, and felt like an idiot who had to catalogue the everyday occurrences of life in order to make them seem real. She sank down on the edge of the tub, consumed with inertia, and watched a *barrata* scuttle behind the sink and disappear. That was a small one, she thought—clinging to things, to objects. There are clean towels on the rack tonight. I like these pink ones. I must write to Mother and ask her to send me more just like them, and some beige ones for Neil. He likes beige towels. She felt her heart beating so hard it seemed to be pulsing in her eye sockets. How long can you keep on bribing him? she screamed at herself silently. He wouldn't care if his towels were beige or Hell's own color if you gave him what he really needed. She stood up then, moving as carefully as an invalid arising from bed after a long illness, and went to the sink to prepare for bed.

Neil had turned out all the lights but one of the small lamps on their double dresser, and he had pulled the curtains closed and taken off the spread. They kept a small portable radio in their bedroom, and when she walked into the room he was still fiddling with it, trying to find a station that still played music after midnight. He looked up at her almost guiltily, as if he had been trying to arrange everything nicely before she arrived and she had caught him too soon. His look filled her with compassion and reminded her how deeply and protectively she cared for him, so that the first moment after he stepped toward her and took her in his arms she felt calm. She put her arms around his neck.

"Your hair smells nice," Neil murmured.

Her thought swirled to perfume then. What kind was it? Oh, yes, Fleurs de Rocaille. It was nice perfume, she liked it too, it was nice, it was nice. . . . She tried to direct her thoughts away from his hand where it was stroking her breast, and she closed her eyes. I love him, she told herself; he's the only man I ever loved. She felt his fingers inside her brassière then and she took a deep breath, trying to will the physical reaction of desire, concentrating, praying that she could force herself to rise to his caress, so that he would not know, when what she really wanted was to scream.

"Why don't you get undressed?" he whispered.

Margie removed her clothes slowly, knowing that Neil was watching and hating herself for the numbness that did not permit her to hurry for him. Some compulsion made her hang her dress in the closet instead of dropping it over the back of a chair, and she could not stop herself from hanging up her crinoline too and folding her bra and underpants neatly on the chair even though she would only toss them into the laundry hamper tomorrow. She had never been a compulsively neat person, only tidy, but tonight somehow the folding of her clothes took on a monstrous importance, as if she could never think of another thing if it were not done properly. I should have gone to bed first, she thought desperately, and pretended to be asleep. But I did that three times this week, and he must know . . .

She knew he was nervous because his hand on her hip was trembling slightly. Perhaps it was the vibration of his nerves communicating itself to her, or perhaps it was something else, but suddenly Margie felt herself begin to tremble. For an instant her husband mistook her trembling for the beginning of passion and he rose on his elbows and covered her with his body, and only then he realized that it had not been excitement but revulsion. For one moment their eyes met, unguarded, and Margie saw in his face such a look of open misery and bewilderment that it almost made her heart stop. He rolled away from her and lay on his stomach, his face in his arms.

"This is the last time," Neil said. "The last time." His voice was muffled.

"What? I can't hear you. I can't hear you," Margie said, and as soon as the words were out she cringed from them because they sounded so heartless and stupid. She wondered for a terrified instant if he were crying.

He shook his head and sat up, looking for a cigarette on the bedside table. He did not look at her until he had found one and lighted it. "Do you want a cigarette?"

"You must hate me," she whispered.

"It's funny, that's just what I was thinking about you."

"Hate you? Oh, my God! Oh, Neil, I love you! I do. You don't believe it, I know, but I do, I *do!*"

He smiled at her bitterly for a moment and then his face softened. He reached his hand out to touch her and then suddenly drew it back as if he had remembered how repellent his touch seemed to her. Margie reached for his hand and took it in both her own. "Please," she said.

"Do you mind if I ask you not to touch me? I'm human."

35

"Please," she said, and then her throat closed and she could not speak.

"It wasn't like this in the beginning," Neil said. His voice was preoccupied, while he remembered. "I think for a while you almost liked it. In the beginning I thought you were this way because you were nervous, because you were a virgin. It even pleased me, in a way, your being so stiff and held back. I thought I could teach you so many things. I wanted you to learn to like making love. I wanted to be the one who gave you the gift of love. I would have given you anything, Margie. I think today I still would—anything—in spite of this. I'd give you anything."

"You do!" Margie cried. "You've given me my whole life."

"Except I come with it, don't I." He looked at her stricken face. "I'm sorry I said that, darling." He reached over and stroked her hair with a gesture that was tenderness completely without passion. "I know it's not your fault," Neil said. "The only thing I have to keep telling myself is that it's not my fault either."

She realized then the extent of what she had done to him, and she closed her eyes, wishing she could die, disappear, vanish from this bed and this room and this life they had made for each other.

"Sometimes," Neil said, "two people just aren't right for each other in bed. Everything else is all right, but when they make love it's a nightmare. I don't know what it is. Maybe it's chemistry."

"I love you," Margie said. "I *love* you. Please believe me."

"I believe you."

"Maybe . . . there's something wrong with me. I've thought about that a lot. Maybe I'm . . . a Lesbian."

"Oh, don't be stupid!" There was genuine anger in his tone. "Don't ever say that again or I'll hit you."

"Maybe I am," she repeated, and then she began to cry. The image rose up before her of a weird sexless woman, an outcast, dressed in mannish clothes, with hair cropped short and a belligerent, lost, sexless face. She had seen Lesbians dressed as men in the Greenwich Village queer bars where she had occasionally gone as a lark when she was an N.Y.U. freshman, when she and a date and another couple had made a rather supercilious tour of the smoky dens where the third sex gathered. Her feeling toward those women then had been revulsion, and when once she had seen a Lesbian fondling the shoulder of a girl who couldn't have been older than Margie herself, she had been more disgusted than pitying. True, she had never had any wild feelings toward a man, but she had never had any feelings at all for a woman except fondness.

"Have you ever wanted to make love to a woman?"

"Never!"

"And to a man? Tell me the truth; there must have been someone who aroused you before you met me."

"No . . ." Margie said slowly. "I always liked kissing if it was a boy I liked, but I was so young when I met you . . . I don't know. I never really thought about sex . . . I don't know."

They were lying side by side on the bed now, talking of the problem, with no more physical feeling between them than if they had been brother and sister or father and daughter. Neil touched Margie's cheek with his finger where it was wet with tears and gently wiped them away. "You're still young," he said. "You're twenty-five years old, but that doesn't mean anything in terms of love-making. We've been sleeping together for years, but in a way you're still physically untouched. It just isn't for us, that wonderful thing; not for you and me together anyway." He reached for her hand and held it tenderly, winding his fingers around hers without demand and with much love. "From now on we'll have separate rooms," Neil said quietly. He smiled at her. "Like very, very rich millionaires. Everything will be all right. I love you and everything will be all right."

"You don't want to leave me?"

He shook his head. "No. I don't want to leave you."

"You really love me, don't you," Margie said. She felt very tired, spent from crying and from emotion.

"Yes."

"Thank you."

"You don't thank someone for loving you," Neil said.

"I know. But I thank you anyway."

Margie Davidow, nee Haft, had been born in the thirties in New York City and had been brought up in a way that was so similar to hundreds of other upper-middle-class Jewish girls in New York that it was only a wonder she had not met Neil Davidow until she was nineteen years old. She lived with her parents and her younger brother Tommy in one of those enormous gingerbread-encrusted apartment buildings on Central Park West which bear names like Beresford and Majestic and San Remo and Century. The apartment house where the Hafts lived was called the Grosvenor. In the springtime they could look out of their windows and see the trees in the park beginning to bloom. They had been living in the same apartment for so long that by the time Margie was old enough to be called on by boys they could still afford the eight large, high-ceilinged rooms that looked so impressive to anyone living in a city as crowded as Manhattan. They had a colored cook and maid of all work who had been working for them ever since Tommy was born.

Lawrence, Margie's father, was in the electrical-equipment business. He had been born in New York, but his two older brothers and older sister had been born in Europe and brought here when they were very young. His wife Etta had been born and brought up in Brooklyn, in the old days when there were many fine houses on leafy, tree-lined streets and all the outlying districts of Brooklyn were farms. Lawrence and Etta were extremely devoted to and proud of their two children—of their son Tommy, who clearly had the brains in the family, and of Margie, whom they considered very pretty. They had always known that Margie would marry young. She had been sweet and shy as a child, and although she loved to read she was not particularly interested in school work. She went to public school, and they planned to send her to a private high school. When she was twelve she went to a riding camp in Massachusetts called Oka-noka-wokee, where she had the usual crush on the riding counselor, an athletic young woman, who was the beloved of most of the young girl campers for no particular reason except that she was attractive, rode well, and there were no boys. When, a month after camp closed, Margie received a post card from the riding counselor, she put it into her diary and saved it, sentimentally, until years later she happened to find it again when she was cleaning her room prior to her marriage to Neil. She had looked at the post card, an innocuous thing bearing a pleasant, trite, and meaningless message, and she had wondered how even the over-sized handwriting could possibly have seemed so romantic and unique to her years before.

Margie had attended the riding camp for three years and had stopped going because it bored her. Her parents had a summer home in Mount Kisco, an hour away from Manhattan, with a working fireplace in the living room, a barbecue pit and a wooden glider in the back yard, and a marble pedestal bearing a large silver ball on the front lawn near the driveway. Saturdays and Sundays they went to the Sunny Hills Country Club, where Mrs. Haft hoped Margie would meet nice young people, particularly boys. Until she was fourteen, Margie was rather afraid of boys. Then she decided she liked them. She went to the swimming pool at the club, and to the dances, and allowed herself to be kissed good night at her front door, and occasionally kissed a good deal more in a parked convertible when she was much older; and until her marriage she always associated passionate kissing with the sound of a car radio and breath that had the scent of gin. She had never really been in love with anyone until she began dating Neil. As a matter of fact, most of the time during those summer nights in her late teens, she paid more attention to the popular songs being played on the radio than to the mouth against her own, and just when she was beginning to forget the music and pay attention to the lips she always found herself obliged to wrench a hand away from the hem of her skirt.

She did not consider her virginity—and more, her almost abso-lute innocence—something either to be proud of or to do violent battle to preserve; rather, it was a fact of her existence, like the fact that she had dark brown hair and was five feet three. She was also a virgin. It was not even a question of character.

Margie attended Sunday school at Temple Emanu-El on Fifth Avenue, where her mother hoped she would meet other nice young people. When she was thirteen she was confirmed, and attended seven confirmation parties in one afternoon, at which lemonade and cookies and small sandwiches were served, and at which one girl received twelve almost identical sterling silver brooches from various classmates. The Hafts were not particularly religious. They went to Temple on the High Holidays, and sometimes Margie's father went on Saturday mornings as well. Margie's grandparents on both sides had kept kosher. Her parents never ate a pork chop or a roast suckling pig, but they ate bacon if it was served at someone else's home. Somehow it seemed as if there was something not quite so porklike, so alien, about bacon. A religious holiday, to Margie, was more of a gathering of all the relatives than an actual spiritual event, and she liked her relatives very much, especially all the young cousins. Once, in college, she was invited to go to the theater on Passover Eve by an agnostic boy she had been dating, and she had instantly refused, feeling for the first time a little as though she might be struck dead if she sat at a musical comedy instead of at the traditional family table. But religion was never something she turned to in times of stress, and secretly she believed that although God was good and infinite, He really was much too busy with things like people dying of cancer and automobile accidents to look down and pay attention to her own tiny crises. She hesitated to ask Him.

When Margie was sixteen her parents gave her a Sweet Sixteen party at the Cottage of the Hampshire House hotel. Her entire class at the Birch Wathen School was invited, and since there were more girls in the class than boys, several of her young male cousins were recruited, as were the older brothers of her girl friends. The party was expensive and a great success. The guests drank champagne punch which was mainly made of ginger ale, and considered themselves very sophisticated, and Margie, combing her long hair in front of the mirror in the ladies' room, decided that when she was graduated from college she might try to be a movie actress, playing character parts. She did not confide this ambition to anyone, afraid someone might laugh.

At that time Margie was attending social dancing classes at Viola Wolff, as were most of her friends, and she liked to dance. She was very graceful and light on her feet, and she always looked forward to the weekly evening dances under the watchful eye of a chaperone. She had her first real night-club date, a double date with another couple, at the Coq Rouge. The boy she was dancing with was seventeen, the son of one of her mother's associates at Hadassah, and he was very handsome, rather like Van Johnson. But when they were dancing closely together the boy had a physical reaction to the touch of Margie's taffeta-covered thighs, a reaction which must have been much more embarrassing to him than it was to her. Margie's first reaction was one of fright. She was thoroughly educated in sexual matters via several graphic and pompous books her mother had given her four years before. But the books had been mainly occupied with procreation rather than pleasure, and Margie's first thought when this unexpected *thing* prodded her leg was, But I don't want this responsibility. It's too much! Her mind was filled with pictures of marriage and motherhood, not seduction, and when she suggested they sit out the rest of the dance the boy was as relieved as she was. Girls like Margie frightened him; they seemed so cold.

When she grew older she went to more dances, and to more night clubs. Her grades at high school were not particularly distinguished, and it was decided she should go to N.Y.U. for one year and then try to transfer to one of the seven women's colleges. At the end of her freshman year at N.Y.U. she met Neil Davidow, at the annual Thanksgiving dance given for the Guild for the Jewish Blind, commonly known more familiarly as "The Blind Dance," and then she decided that she did not want to go to college out of town after all.

Margie's parents did not object to her decision. They liked having Margie at home, and they suspected even before Margie did that Neil Davidow might be a prospect for marriage. Margie's brother Tommy was studying to go to medical school. Margie often said, with great pride and no envy whatsoever, that God had given all the brains to Tommy and had none left for her, even though Tommy was two years younger. After she met Neil Davidow at the Blind Dance he invited her out for the following Saturday night. They went to dinner and to the theater. He asked her again for the following Saturday and she accepted. Neil was twenty-five at the time, and a stockbroker, and he seemed to Margie to be very old, sophisticated, and rich. He took her to dine at places where her college friends never could afford to go. He took her to see all the good plays, and to the opera. When he began to come over on Sunday afternoons to do the crossword puzzle in *The New York Times* with her he already seemed like a member of the family. Neil had been living with his parents on Park Avenue, waiting until he could save enough money to have an apartment of his own. The year he met Margie he took his own apartment, a large room with a dressing room and kitchenette in the East Seventies, and Margie's mother fell into the habit of inviting him to the Haft apartment for dinner once a week because "the poor boy must be starving having to eat his own cooking." After an evening of an enormous dinner and then two hours of Neil's being left discreetly alone in the living room with Margie while her parents went to watch television in their bedroom, Mrs. Haft would always pack up a large box of leftovers for him to take home "so at least you won't have to eat your own cooking tomorrow."

After he had been dating Margie for six weeks Neil invited her to his apartment for dinner. She arrived, dressed in a black velvet dress, nervous and shy and domestic.

For several weeks now she had been thinking of what it might be like to be married to Neil. He had not yet said he loved her, and actually Margie could not decide whether or not he did. She did not know whether or not she loved him. But she could not help thinking of marriage, partly because she knew by her mother's elaborately casual remarks that her parents were thinking of it, and partly because Margie at nineteen and a half could not think of any realistic way to spend her life except as someone's wife. She already knew that Neil was kind; he was kind to her and he seemed to be a kind person by nature. He had money which he had made on his own, he had a wonderful future, he was intelligent, and he was nice looking. She could not think of any other qualities she could want in a husband—except for a wildly romantic passionate love. Love of that sort, that would burn forever but never consume, seemed so far to be something depicted only in movies and girlish novels. She had never known any married people who were madly in love. Certainly her parents were not. They were more like two halves of one person existing together very calmly. They fought sometimes, but it never meant that there was a rift. The attitude Margie's mother and father had always shown to their two children was that they were Parents, with a capital *P,* and the idea of them as lovers in some faraway past seemed incredible. It was almost easier to think of them as blood relatives than as lovers, because, as many old married people do, they actually looked alike.

A month before, one of Margie's older girl cousins had become engaged, and there had been a large engagement party. The cousin, Joan, and her fiancé had spent most of the party nuzzling each other and gazing with big soulful eyes, as if they could not wait to fling themselves into each other's arms. But to Margie, watching and feeling rather embarrassed, it almost seemed as if the engaged couple were playing an expected role. Something about it did not ring true to her, though if anyone had asked her to explain why she felt so, she would not have known how to reply.

Thinking thus of marriage and love, she entered Neil's apartment, and for an instant she was so afraid he might be able to read her thoughts that she could not meet his eyes. Neil mistook this for shyness because she was alone with him in his bachelor apartment, and when Margie seated herself gingerly at one end of his black tweed-covered sofa bed he carefully sat several feet away from her and offered her a cigarette. The gesture, at arm's length, was awkward, and Margie, who seldom smoked, was unable for a few moments to make the cigarette light. This embarrassed her further, and she dropped the lighted cigarette into her lap.

Neil was up in an instant, trying to brush off the sparks, which really had done no harm. "You're all right, aren't you?" he asked worriedly.

"Oh, yes."

"Have a drink. Would you like a martini?"

"Rye and ginger, please. Very, very weak."

He occupied himself for a few minutes making the drinks, and Margie strolled about the large room looking at his paintings and books. She had never been in his apartment before, mainly because it had taken him a long time to acquire furniture. It was a typical bachelor apartment, with a television set facing the sofa bed, a desk serving as a room divider, and a coffee table in front of the sofa bed which doubled as a dining table. The bar was actually a collection of liquor bottles on the drainboard in the kitchenette. Everything in the room was expensive, modern, dark, and extremely stark. The walls were beige, and the rug was banker's gray, and the tweed covering the chairs and the sofa bed all was black. To Margie it seemed very masculine and sophisticated, and somehow mysterious. She realized for the first time that men had secret lives of their own, as distinguished from fathers (who lived in frilly bedrooms with mothers) and little brothers (who lived in childlike rooms decorated by mothers and kept neat by maids). She wondered if Neil ever made love to girls on that sofa that could be transformed into a bed at a moment's notice.

"How do you like the apartment?"

"It's beautiful," Margie said.

The very, very weak rye and ginger ale was not so weak as all that. Margie felt herself becoming less shy.

"Do you know how to cook?" Neil asked.

She shook her head. "Do you?"

"Very well. Despite what your mother thinks." They both laughed. "At least, I can make good steak and salad, which is what I like best anyway."

She thought of him living alone here and eating steak and salad every day in a Spartan way, in contrast to her mother's overrich, well-balanced meals, and it made him seem very masculine. He went to the phonograph and put on a stack of classical records. Next to the phonograph there was a small table holding a chess set with the pieces arranged on the board to begin a game.

"I like Bach," Margie said. "He's my favorite."

"Mine too."

This time he sat down next to her on the sofa and a moment later he took her hand. "You have pretty hands," he said. "So small."

"The boy I'll get engaged to is lucky," Margie said. "He'll only have to buy me a little diamond and it will look much bigger on me." She smiled at him to show it was really a joke; and yet, was it so much of a joke? She looked down at her hand again, unable to speak.

"We've never been alone together like this," Neil said. "Do you realize that?"

"We've been alone lots of times!"

"Oh, yes, in your apartment, with your parents breathing heavily in the next room. And in the theater, with people all around us. And in very dark restaurants, with waiters who have X-ray eyes. Six weeks, do you realize? We've never been alone."

"I like it," Margie said softly.

"I do too."

Neither of them said anything for a moment. They were alone, and they had nothing to say. All the talking they had done had come easily, as if in the public places where they had talked to each other, conversation had been their only form of personal contact. Otherwise they would have been quite apart from each other. The curtain rises, the play begins, and each spectator is alone. Neil was not the kind of person who likes to hold hands in the theater; he had too much interest in the play. In restaurants he ate, he talked, he did not bump knees or clutch hands beneath the tablecloth so she would have to cut her meat with the side of her fork. In the bars where they had gone he always knew the bartender and usually had an extended conversation with him. At home there were always her parents. But now they were alone and intensely aware of it.

"I never went out with a girl as young as you before," Neil said. "Except, of course, when *I* was nineteen. I usually go out with girls of twenty-five."

"I guess you think I'm a baby."

"No. No."

"Well . . . I don't mind telling you . . . sometimes you seem so much more grown up than I am that I'm actually afraid of you. You know so much."

He seemed amused, and pleased. "The better to teach you, said the big bad wolf."

"You're not a wolf."

"No?"

She withdrew from his touch then, slightly nervous, and reached for her drink. She did not know why she was nervous; actually she was not the least bit afraid of him. They had kissed many times on the sofa in her parents' living room, but Neil had never tried to do anything farther. The drink was making her brave.

"Have you ever—no."

"Have I ever what?" he asked.

"No," she said. "I'm terrible. Strike it from the record. I'm drunk."

"You're not drunk, and I won't strike it from the record. Have I ever what? Wanted to make love to you?"

"Oh, no! I meant . . . have you ever made love to those twenty-five-year-old girls?"

Neil laughed. "Of course."

Of course, he was twenty-five, he was a man, she had not thought he would be celibate. And yet, when he actually admitted he had had affairs, the first picture that came to Margie's mind was not Neil naked in this bed with a girl but the face of the girl as it must have looked the next morning, saying goodbye.

"What are you thinking?" he asked.

She shook her head.

"What? You look as if you had appendicitis."

"I do? I do *not*."

46

"Yes you do," he said, smiling. He put his arm around her. "What are you thinking?"

"I'm wondering . . . what do these girls think? What do they say to you? Are they terribly in love with you? Do they suffer?"

Neil laughed. "I *hope* they don't suffer. They never look to me as if they're suffering."

"Oh, you think I'm an idiot!"

"No," he said, quite serious then. "No, I don't. I think you're a wonderful person."

It was the first time he had actually expressed any feeling for her, and Margie looked up at him, startled. *A wonderful person.* It made a glow start through her. What a beautiful thing to say.

"And I *have* wanted to make love to you," he went on. "In case you're wondering that too." He kissed her hand and the inside of her wrist and then her mouth. They kissed for a long time without breathing much. Margie began to feel lightheaded. She listened to her heart beating and she kept her eyes closed, recognizing the light waves of feeling she always had when she had kissed for several minutes. She waited for the waves of feeling as if her entire body were a landscape and she were the observer, in it and yet not of it. She sensed the feeling then and she kept herself very still, trying to keep it, grateful and wary at the same time.

She thought at first he was stroking the nape of her neck and then she realized that his hand was reaching for the zipper at the back of her dress. The movement distracted her. She opened her eyes and she saw, over his shoulder, that the brown and beige and gray lithograph on the wall was hanging slightly crooked. Suddenly that seemed much more important than anything else. The feeling had gone. She felt cool air on her back as Neil slid down the zipper of her dress, and she pulled away from him.

"No, really," she said, trying to reach her zipper with both hands.

"I'm not going to do anything," he whispered.

"Of course you are." But she said it distractedly, straining to reach the zipper, not upset at all. She was not afraid of her own passions with him, so why should she be afraid of his? This was

47

Neil Davidow, who liked her, whom she liked, and she was not afraid. She only felt, inexplicably, very lonely and sad.

"You're right," he said. "I was." He reached around and pulled up her zipper. "Would you like another drink?"

"No, thank you."

"All right, then I'll start the steaks. We might as well eat; it's seven-thirty. And after dinner I'll teach you how to play chess."

"Chess?" Margie said, rather stupidly. Her feeling of loneliness was vanishing under Neil's matter-of-fact warmth.

"Chess," he repeated. "If you're going to be my girl you're going to have to know how to play chess."

"Your . . . girl?"

"You know," he said. "Girl friend. Steady. Engaged to be engaged."

"Oh," she breathed. "Oh. Yes!"

When Margie and Neil became engaged after going out together for five months everyone said they made an ideal couple. They had everything in common. They had a similar family background, they both loved music and theater and chess, and his maturity would make a good balance for a girl who had just turned twenty. He was then twenty-six, but he looked and acted older. He was a college graduate, employed by an excellent brokerage firm, and they could even live in his apartment for a while until they needed something bigger. Margie's parents gave a large engagement party to announce the happy news. Her mother confided to Margie afterward that she was secretly very proud that she and Neil had enough dignity to refrain from nuzzling each other in public the way cousin Joan and *her* fiancé had. Margie's mother also thought that there should be a very short engagement. She did not believe in long-drawn-out engagement periods. The young couple would be too apt to give way to their animal instincts if they were kept waiting so long. After all, they were both young and healthy and in love. No, a short engagement was the best idea for young people. So four weeks after her engagement party Margie and Neil were married. She had been so busy rushing around to shop for her trousseau and planning for their formal wedding that in the whole four weeks she saw Neil only ten times, and on those evenings she was so tired that all she could do was go to a movie with him and say good night very tenderly at the door at eleven o'clock.

The wedding was held in the Plaza Hotel in New York City. For years the Plaza had seemed to Margie to be the epitome of East Side Gentile elegance. The chauffeured Rolls Royces waiting outside for old ladies who were rich enough not to care that they were wearing styles that might be forty years old, the chic women in flowered hats who sipped cocktails among the potted palms and chirped like tame birds, the people who had been living there in the same suite for twenty years and went every summer to Europe with their own maids—all of this had seemed a part of a glamorous adult world that had nothing to do with her wholesome and boring life on Central Park West. But now her wedding was to be held there, and this suite had been reserved for her and her bridesmaids to use as a dressing room. When Margie looked around the luxurious suite it seemed to have a sterile, disappointing look, because no one was going to sleep there that night and there were no personal articles laid out on the dresser, nor books, nor flowers, nor any of the clutter that people leave wherever they live. Her new, monogrammed suitcases were lined up in the corner. Only the overnight case was still open, for last-minute make-up. There was a large straw hat to wear on the beach in St. Thomas. It was too big to fit into any of the suitcases so she would have to carry it in her hand on the plane. Her mother had taken Margie's new going-away suit out of its tissue-paper nest and box and hung it in the closet. It was the only thing in the closet except for her mother's mink stole (which her mother would later wear) and a dozen empty hangers that swayed together, emitting a ghostly sound, like little skeletons, when you touched them.

For bridesmaids Margie had her two closest friends from the Birch Wathen School, who were both pretty and the same height, which had made choosing dresses for them easy, and a rather

49

unattractive young cousin of Neil's, whom Margie had invited to be polite. Since Neil had no sisters it seemed a nice gesture to ask one of his relatives to be in the wedding procession. Neil's cousin had red hair and a pinkish complexion, which was even pinker now with excitement. Because of her they couldn't have pink bridesmaid's dresses, which Margie would have preferred, so they had pale blue. The matron of honor was Margie's married friend Sue. The bridesmaids were milling about, trying to tilt their flowered tiaras to the most becoming angle, squealing over Margie's hand-embroidered French underwear, and her shoes, which were appliquéd with the same lace as the dress, and finally the dress itself. The crinoline for the wedding dress was so stiff and enormous that it had to be stood up in the bathtub until she was ready to put it on. It was the only thing in the bathroom that seemed to have any relationship to her and her life; the rest was immaculate, white, and cold. Here she was, in the place she had always thought about with stars in her eyes, and it was nothing but a hotel room that she would be in and out of in a minute, leaving not a trace of herself behind, nor of this most important day of her life.

The affectionate noise of the girls disturbed her, and her mother trying to be helpful made her nervous. Her father had been banished to the living room of the suite, where he smoked a cigarette. Margie stood as stiff as a doll with her arms above her head while her heavy wedding dress was slipped carefully over her head, carefully so as not to disarrange her hair or her make-up. Her matron of honor did up the hooks in the back, and her mother delicately smoothed Margie's hair, which had been coiffeured that morning and had luckily not been disarranged by the dress at all. Margie put on her veil, attached to a Juliet cap of real orange blossoms that gave off a faint sweet smell that belonged to a warm, faraway land. She looked at her reflection in the full-length mirror, and through the veil she seemed to herself to be a beautiful stranger, a bride doll on a wedding cake, a model in a bridal magazine. Margie could not see the expression in her own eyes through the misty white veil, and so she seemed to herself for that instant to be all brides on their wedding day, one of an endless procession, reflected and re-reflected in that mirror on and on until eternity, a life force; girls on the threshold of womanhood going to be united with their loved mates, billions of tremulous important brides, each as tiny and unimportant in the eyes of the universe as the tiny stars that make up the bridal carpet of the Milky Way, and yet at the same instant more of an individual than she had ever been in her life.

For a moment Margie, standing before the mirror, was breathless with the realization of how important she was, and of how unimportant she was. It was as if she could see the whole meaning of life revealed. For that moment the chatter of the bridesmaids seemed as hushed as the whisper of their taffeta skirts. There was no one in the room for her except herself, and her reflected strange self, and those billions of brides with veiled eyes, taking measured steps into the heart of the measureless universe.

Her father was standing at the doorway of the room looking at her, and there were tears in his eyes. Margie ran to him and put her arms around his neck. "Look out for the veil!" her mother cried, and then it was all over; she was Margie preparing for her wedding and these were her parents and friends, and there were still many little things to be done before the ceremony, like being sure that the right person had the ring, and the plane tickets, and that Great-Aunt Fanny would be given a seat down front because her hearing was not what it used to be.

They went to the Virgin Islands for their honeymoon, for two weeks in a luxury hotel. It was the beginning of May and the weather in the Caribbean was bright and hot. Margie and Neil lay on the beach under the sun, putting suntan oil on each other, went skin diving with masks around the coral reefs under the transparent sapphire water, and strolled through the narrow old streets of the town, hand in hand. It was on her honeymoon that Margie Davidow fell in love with her husband for the first time. The feeling was so new and so unexpected (because she had thought she loved him all along) that it came to her as a shock. She had never felt this depth of tenderness and admiration for anybody. She had never before been alone with one person for

51

so long a time, and with Neil she was never bored. Being with him all day, every day, gave her a dependence on him she had never known before. She almost could not bear to have him out of her sight, and since they did not know anyone else in St. Thomas he never was out of her sight for more than half an hour. The only thing that was strange, the only moments when she was completely and frighteningly alone, were the nights when they were the most together.

She had expected the act of love to hurt her at first, and it did, but for longer than had ever been written in her pristine books. It was mainly because she was tense, and the more she tried to hide this from Neil the worse everything became. Many girls Margie's age come to their marriage technical virgins, but Margie was completely one, body and mind. She was pleased and embarrassed that everyone in the hotel knew they were a honeymoon couple. Her pretty new clothes, her self-concious pretense at casual worldliness, gave her away. The hotel manager even sent them a bottle of champagne the first night. Margie saved the cork, in her suitcase. On picture post cards, which she sent to her friends in New York, she wrote her married name with a flourish, and then looked at it, not quite believing all this was really her.

It was in St. Thomas that Margie discovered banana daiquiris, that they were sweet and deceptively mild, that they did not taste like liquor (which she detested), and that if she drank three before going upstairs to bed she could feel a pleasant numbness and the stirrings of desire. It was easy to fool Neil about the banana daiquiris because he could not drink more than one, claiming they were too sweet and a girl's drink. To him they seemed a minor vice, like chocolates. Fortified by the banana daiquiris, Margie lay in her husband's arms, stroked his face, and thought how wonderful it was to be cherished. She liked to be near him, and at those moments if she had known what reactions to pretend to be having she would have gladly done so. She would have given anything to be able to make him think he was giving her pleasure. But it was impossible to imitate a pleasure she had never known.

52

When they returned from their honeymoon and moved into Neil's apartment Margie purchased a blender to make the banana daiquiris and furtively bought a book about the art of married love. She bought the book on Forty-second Street and Broadway, terrified that someone she knew might come upon her and discover the shameful purchase which as much as admitted that things were not going as they should. The book, a modern one, told her that woman's delight was overrated in other books and that it was not necessary to enjoy love-making every time. *Every* time! Margie thought. There were no stage directions for imitation. It was about this time that she began to look carefully into the eyes of her married girlfriends when they lunched at Schraffts, trying to find out their secret, certain that she was alone with hers. Sometimes, ripping at the paper doily delicately with her fingertips, she almost asked a question that might give her away, and then stopped in time.

One day she had lunch with her matron of honor, Sue, who had been married for a year. Sue had accomplished what they call "marrying well," and she looked it in her new, expensive dress and alligator handbag. It was also a love match, and Sue was much envied among her friends.

"We're trying to have a baby," Sue said. "You know, I've been making up names for imaginary children for years. I'm dying to have one."

"You'll probably be a wonderful mother," Margie said.

Sue sighed and stirred her soda with the straws. "I'm getting so *tired* of trying," she said quietly.

For a moment the significance of what her friend was saying did not quite get through to Margie, and then suddenly it hit her with the force of a physical blow. *Tired of trying!* But what you did when you were "trying" was supposed to be that wonderful lost trip away from the world. Margie opened her lips, almost ready to confide, to pour out all the bewilderment and fear of loneliness, and then she closed her mouth so tightly that she gritted her teeth. She would die rather than confess a failure that would point disgrace to Neil, imply disloyalty to him and their bond together. She scooped up the bits of paper doily she had torn and deposited them in the ashtray. "I *hate* doilies," she said vehemently. "They're so *messy.*"

It was at the beginning of her second year of marriage that Margie began to have strange, disturbing sensations, a burning and fluttering, a shortness of breath. She first noticed it in the spring, when she and Neil went to the Memorial Day dance at the country club. She was dancing with the husband of one of her friends, a young doctor who had been away in Ohio doing his internship in a hospital there, and had just returned with his wife and child to set up his practice in New York. He was a little older than Neil, but he looked younger, almost collegiate. Margie had seen him only once before, at her friend's wedding, and now she realized for the first time that he was a very attractive man. There was a kind of intimacy and joy in the way he danced with her, nothing actually forward and yet there was a complete awareness of her as a pretty woman. A few brave couples were dancing on the terrace, although the late May night was chilly, and Margie and her partner were among them. It was dark, and she could hear the sound of the wind in the trees and the soft shuffling of feet on cement above the music that came out through the opened French doors.

"Cold?" he whispered, smiling down at her.

"No."

Suddenly Margie felt a weird fluttering constricting her heart. Her lips seemed to swell, to burn, to fill with the pulsing of her warm blood. For a moment she had the wild impulse to reach up and kiss this man full on the mouth. She pulled away from him with a violent physical effort and shivered.

"You *are* cold," he said. "Come on, we'll go inside. Some doctor I am, making you catch pneumonia."

That night when Neil wanted to leave the dance early Margie immediately agreed, although usually she tried to linger. All the way home beside Neil in the car she held on to the feeling she had struggled with on the terrace, ecstatically and guiltily; nursing it, holding it inside her like a great, stirring, growing flower. At home, he made love to her. And in the middle of it she looked up at his face in the semidarkness, the face of the man she respected and loved, and she thought how ridiculous and grotesque their posture was, like two people in battle trying to kill each other. She wished that he would hurry, get it over with, finish. And waiting for the telltale sigh that showed he was through, Margie for the first time hated herself and wondered in terror and guilt why the feeling of being a woman never arose to the touch of this man who deserved it more than any man in the world.

After they had been married for two years Neil had the opportunity to go to Brazil to represent the South American branch of his firm. He discussed it with Margie and she agreed quickly. She wanted to get away. Perhaps in a strange and tropical place, away from all the memories of her childhood, she might find her real self. Perhaps she could have a new life. At any rate, it was what Neil wanted, and she wanted whatever might make him happy, for she knew that this new restlessness in him was mainly the fault of something in her which he was only now dimly beginning to perceive.

CHAPTER 3

"You look like a little boy playing cowboys," Helen Sinclair said. Her tone was light but she felt hurt, and under the lightness there was a note of cruelty. "You pack those dirty old clothes and those leather boots and your eyes light up."

"It's great," Bert said.

"I wish you'd take me."

"You wouldn't like it. The Interior's no place for a woman. It's primitive, the hotel—and it's always *the* hotel—is unimaginable, and there are only men at the mine."

"Well, at least there aren't any women."

"You think I'd go five hours by plane and nine hours by jeep just to find myself a girl?"

"That would have to be quite a girl."

"Women can never understand how men like to go off just with men sometimes," Bert said. "You complain to me how it gets on your nerves to have to sit with the girls and jabber at the golf club for an afternoon; can you imagine what that does to us?" He was smiling, so she knew he was half teasing. Still, it annoyed her.

"What could be so terrible about the hotel? It has screens, doesn't it?"

"Screens? What are those?"

"Then I'd take citronella. What else do they have—cockroaches?"

"As big as canaries."

"I'm used to them. In fact, I'm getting to like them. It doesn't have bedbugs?"

"Bedbug City."

"You're teasing me. Aren't you?"

"A little."

"Well, why do you have to be so nasty?"

"Because I don't want you to go, that's why," Bert answered cheerfully.

"*Why?*"

"You don't come to the office with me."

"The office is different," Helen said. "It would be rather boring for me if I didn't know what was going on. I wouldn't be bored in the jungle."

"You would, after you'd used up your whole roll of color film. This is what the men do: work, drink, gamble, fight. That's all. What would you do?"

Be with you, Helen wanted to say. But it sounded stupid. She could be with him at home, in a lovely apartment on the beach, so why did she have to go for five hours in a rocky plane and nine hours in a spine-punishing jeep over jungle roads to be with him in the company of mud, dust, flies, mosquitoes, cockroaches, and quite possibly bedbugs? Because that side of her husband was a mystery, she thought; and even when she tried to imagine sleek, civilized Bert in a place like that, even when she watched him pack the rough clothes and boots, she could not quite imagine what he would be like. It was a side of his nature that was forever forbidden to her, by his choice, and although she was sure it would reveal no mystery that was not partly evident in the whole man himself, yet it was a tantalizing mystery because Bert forbid it to her. My husband, Helen thought, and yet, a week out of the month he has a secret life.

"When do you have to go again?" she asked, in a voice this time washed free of cruelty, this time only wistful.

"After the New Year. You have me for two whole weeks."

"Oh, Bert. I wish . . ."

"What?"

"Nothing. I wish a lot of things."

He looked exasperated, and she could tell he was deciding whether to humor her or try to change the subject. This look of his was new, but already she had seen it often enough so that it was familiar to her. Somehow it hurt her more than any remark of his could have; whatever he did or said she couldn't bear him to be condescending. "We're going to a party tomorrow night," he said finally. "A real Brazilian party, given by a Brazilian for Brazilians. I thought you might like that."

"I'll love it," Helen said. But she hardly heard him. She smiled at him, and he seemed satisfied—no, relieved—and he went quickly into the part of their apartment that was reserved for his work. The library. We even have a library now, Helen thought ironically. We're rich.

This curiosity to enter the intimate places of her husband's mind was a new thing with her, brought on by the loneliness and strangeness of life in Brazil. A year before, in Westport, she had driven Bert to the station in the mornings to catch the seven-fifty-two, kissed him lightly goodbye, and turned her head toward her own new day. His absence from her was a kind of vacation in the old days, a time to catch up on all the womanly things she never seemed to have time for. But now, in Brazil, a land where a married woman's only occupation was being a woman, she was tanned, coiffeured, massaged, neat, rested; and nervous. She knew that she looked more like a woman than ever before in her life, and an attractive one, but she felt less like a woman than she ever had in Westport and she did not know why.

More and more, she noticed, she was beginning to relive the past, and she knew this was neurotic but she could not stop. It worried her; middle-aged women like her mother hashed over the past all the time—it was almost a sign of aging—but a *young* woman of twenty-eight . . . I *am* young, she told herself without conviction. I am! But why did the early and cherished recollection return of Sunday mornings in their first apartment in Riverdale before the children were born; when she had a life here, when she was still young, when she was loved?

In those first months of their marriage Bert had liked to sleep late on Sundays, and Helen, who had never liked to sleep late, had found herself filled with a pleasant drowsiness as she lay beside him, feeling completely secure. She would doze and wake, and turn to look at this newness and wonder of a man who wanted to live with her forever and lie beside her for Sunday mornings for ever and ever too; and then she would doze again, content, until he awoke and they would make love. That winter, before she conceived Julie, was a period completely separated from any other time in Helen's life. It was the first time she had really felt herself to be a woman; not a girl, not a mother, not a hostess-partner-helpmeet, but a *woman*. Under the sheet and blanket, closed in with the man she loved, surrounded by nothing but the fabric that sheltered them together and isolated them from alarm clocks, telephones, voices, all the demands of the world, Helen was happier than she had ever been before or since.

When Julie began to move and show life inside Helen's body, Helen began to feel as if her mind had separated into two minds, her own and the one that had to think for the child's future. She always thought of her babies as people, even before they themselves knew they were babies. When Julie, a few weeks old, lay helpless in her crib in Helen's and Bert's bedroom, Helen felt there was a person in the room. Julie had colic when she was very young and cried at night for hours. When she was older and no longer had colic she had become even more of a person, a person who could wake to the sound of stifled noises from a nearby bed, who might wake silently and not cry but only listen and not understand. Helen adored the baby, but there were moments when she resented her presence, because she herself was still very young and so was Bert and they had been alone together for so short a time.

As the years went by, Bert's morning habits changed; he no longer stayed in bed until noon on Sundays. Often he would wake up and go into the living room, still in his pajamas and bathrobe, to do work he had brought home from the office. Helen had to get up too and attend to Julie, and then later both Julie and Roger.

Now in Rio she could sleep as long as she liked, but it was too late. The children would be off to school or now in summer to the beach or the club with Mrs. Graham. Bert would be at the office if it were a weekday. Helen would awaken alone in the double bed and she would stretch out her hand to touch the wrinkled sheet where Bert had lain. She would close her eyes for a moment and pretend he was still there, that they were still very young and alone together on a Sunday morning. Those mornings were very far away now and idyllic, totally out of reach again for the rest of their lives until they were old, and the children were grown, and Bert was retired. *What was the use?* Bert had changed, she had changed, so that even in Rio, living like millionaires on the American dollar, their private hours were different anyway and their idyllic mornings lost forever.

Bert went away to a mine somewhere at least once a month, to Rio Grande do Sul, to Minas Gerais, to the State of Bahia. They were all only names to her. She thought how funny it was that all she knew about the Interior was learned from travel books of photographs, while her husband went there all the time. She had two maids and a governess for the children. One of the maids did all the shopping and the cooking, the other cleaned, sewed, polished the silver and waxed the furniture. Helen took care of her appearance, took naps, read. She wrote many letters home to friends, not because she had any news but because she was homesick. They wrote back that they were envious. She bought material, she went to the dressmaker, she lay on the beach on a straw mat with her eyes shut behind dark glasses and she imagined her brains turning into white bleached fluff and blowing away. If she sat up and looked around she could always see the same women —and men—whom she had seen on that same beach for ten months. She often wondered who supported those men who lay so bronzed and casual under the sun every day from ten until two and then repaired to the swimming pool at the Copacabana Palace for lunch.

Margie Davidow dropped in to see her nearly every day, or she would go to see Margie. An unimportant thing like going to the dressmaker they would do together, making an appointment for it, because that would make it seem important. She knew there had been one time, a few years ago, when Margie had gone to the movies every afternoon for three months, sometimes even seeing the same picture two and three times rather than see nothing.

Sometimes Helen felt panic, as if she had actually lost something tangible, or as if some harm had come to someone she loved. Was it to the children? She was losing them, she was losing their childhood to a kindly employee. But it wasn't only the children, because they loved her; they ran to her and she to them with joy; they got along with her much better than they had when she took care of them all the time. They seemed to have grown up, become independent, although she knew they were still almost babies. It was such a quiet, well-ordered household, filled with people, filled with living, never empty. Why, then, this feeling of loss . . . for what?

She remembered, at times, the way Bert had looked when she had first seen him, and the way she had looked and thought; both of them so young they would be strangers to themselves now. She was nineteen and a sophomore at Pembroke, and she had gone to New York for a football weekend with a dull boy whose name she only remembered later because it had been that weekend she had met Bert. She had gone to a cocktail party at the Biltmore Hotel after the game, a party held in one of those small rooms five college boys crowd themselves into even though it was rented only for two. Her date was already half drunk, from a pocket flask he had carried in his overcoat pocket. It was cold out and beginning to snow. When she walked into the crowded hotel room full of post-game revelers the first thing she had thought was that every boy there was six feet tall, with a blond crewcut and a thick neck and big shoulders and no face. Every one of them wore a dark gray flannel suit, and she couldn't even decide which one she wanted to talk to first because they all looked alike. On a littered table in the corner of the room there was a punch bowl filled with Purple Passion. Standing alone next to the punch bowl was a boy who looked so extraordinarily different from all the others that she couldn't take her eyes off him. He was tall and thin, and he didn't have a blond crewcut or a thick football neck, but black hair, slightly wavy, worn rather long for a college boy. His face had a look of miserable intensity, all the thoughts inward, and he wasn't drinking anything, nor was he talking to a girl.

"Who's that?" she had asked. "Who's that?"

"Bert Sinclair. He goes to Columbia. A member of the enemy. Why? You like him?"

"He looks . . . so sad."

"I don't know why he should. The bastards won today."

"Introduce me. Please."

"Ah, wait. Have a drink. Kiss me. I love you. Do you know that? I think I love you."

"Today you do," she had answered, laughing and escaping his encircling arm. At nineteen she had already learned that a nineteen-year-old boy can love a girl very much on Friday and be just as surprised as she is on Monday when somehow the love just isn't there any more. Knowing that, and having been the recipient of several bewildered apologies ("I just wanted to tell you that I don't love you any more. . . . I'm terribly sorry"), Helen was more surprised than ever when a year later she found herself married to Bert Sinclair.

And here they were in Rio. What had she lost—the past? But you always lost the past. Herself? Bert? *What?*

In the morning at the Gavea Golf Club the air buzzed with heat, as if it were a living thing. The pool was full of children, shrieking, splashing, jumping in and clambering out to jump in again, holding their noses, holding hands, showing off for one another. They were thin and shapeless, sleek with water, their wet bathing suits plastered to their bodies and showing only that they were children. On the faces of the very young ones was the sign of beauty that is evident in all the very young. The older ones, preadolescents, were in the awkward and ugly stage, with features growing out of proportion to one another, but some of them were already showing promise of a much greater and dangerous beauty. All of them seemed to have an inexhaustible, terrifying energy to repeat and repeat the monotonous acts of leaping, climbing, leaping, and climbing again. Helen arrived with Julie and Roger at ten-thirty.

It was already too late to find any more of the adult-size canvas chairs, so she took three of the children's chairs, the miniatures that everyone left for the unfortunate latecomers, and she put them side by side beside the pool.

"Julie, *please* wear your glasses."

"I don't like them."

"If you wear them now, you won't have to wear them when you're grown up. And besides, you look cute in them."

Julie looked exactly as Helen had when she was young, with honey-colored sun-streaked hair cropped short for the heat. She really looked sweet in the glasses, little pink harlequin spectacles, and she needed them. It was strange, Helen thought, how you always felt more tender toward a small child who wore glasses; she looked so much like a tiny adult, and yet you knew she could be hurt like a child.

"Look how cute you look in them."

"She looks beautiful," Roger said loyally.

"You think so?" Julie asked, wrinkling up her nose.

"Not making that face. You look like a monkey. Your face will freeze that way."

"It will not," Julie said calmly. She crossed her eyes and jumped up and down like a monkey, making chattering noises.

"*Please* don't do that!" Helen begged, but she couldn't help laughing. Even imitating a monkey, Julie couldn't look unpretty; she had a delicacy and sweetness of features that Helen couldn't imagine she herself had ever had to that extent. Her skin was deep golden tan and silky, her large-pupiled myopic eyes could change from a mischievous glitter to sympathy in an instant. She was only eight, but so reasonable it sometimes hurt to think that Julie already understood much of the private sensitivity of other people that children usually ignored.

Her two children: they seemed at that moment, laughing beside the pool, so alive and precious and beautiful that she reached out for both of them. She kissed Roger first because he was closer, feeling the delicacy of his cheekbone beneath the taut, elastic

63

skin. He was all energy and tiny bones, throbbing in her arms like a captive. She wanted to protect him from everything, never let anything bad happen to him, not even a cut or a bruise. . . . She opened her arms reluctantly and let him go.

Julie took off her glasses and folded them almost prissily, holding them out to Helen. "I can't wear them in the water. Please hold them."

"And please hold my candy." Roger gave her a paper roll of sticky Drops.

"And my pack of gum, please."

"And *my* gum!"

"That's my towel."

"That one's mine."

They were off into the water, leaving Helen surrounded by towels and beach things, all the minutiae of their travels. The cement around her feet was wet from splashed pool water, and the back of her child's chair was so low that she had to sit bolt upright. She had brought a book to read, but she was too nervous to take her eyes off her children for long, even though she knew they were both good swimmers. Julie had pulled on a bathing cap with great care, as if she were preserving an elaborate beauty-salon set instead of hair chopped off almost like a boy's. She already knew how to dive off the diving board and did it well. Roger swam with his face in the water for so long Helen wondered if his swimming instructor had mentioned to him you had to breathe. He was as fast as a newt.

She had not come to the club for a long time and she did not know many people. No one spoke to her. To the left were the golf links, permanently green, dotted with bright-shirted players, mostly women because today was a weekday. There were also some teen-aged boys who were on vacation from school. Beyond the golf course were the mountains, encircling everything, green and purple and blue in the heat, and above them the bright blue sky. The view was so beautiful Helen never tired of looking at it. She could not understand how people could look down at a golf ball when they could look up at such mountains; but perhaps they could do both.

She had sent Mrs. Graham to town for the day with an excuse so she could take care of the children herself. This would be the new regime: the pool and beach alternately, governess only at night; Helen would set the rules. She would spend all her time with Roger and Julie. Things would be different from now on, she would have the children, and eventually she would make friends with other women who had children, and her life would be quieter perhaps, different, but filled with love. . . .

A young mother with dark hair and a striped bathing suit with a longish skirt was lying in a beach chair beside one of Helen's empty ones. Helen moved the towels and moved over beside her. "The pool is crowded, isn't it!"

"Yes. *Look out, Timmy! Don't you go in there!* Just your feet, Mother told you."

"Is that your little boy?" Helen asked. She gestured at the fat, petulant-faced little boy perched on the edge of the pool, wearing blue bathing trunks and a rubber tube shaped like a swan.

"Yes. That's Timmy."

"He's sweet. How old is he?"

"Going on four. Even with his tube on I worry about him."

"Those two are mine." Helen noticed that Julie had found two little girls her age whom she seemed to know, and that Roger was playing with a boy who seemed at least a year older than he was and who didn't seem to notice the age and size difference at all. "I should introduce myself. My name is Helen Sinclair."

"I'm Ann. You have two children?"

"Yes." There was a silence. Ann waved and blew a kiss at Timmy. "How many do you have?" Helen asked finally.

"Just this one so far. I'm expecting another one in six months."

"How nice."

"I think it's nice."

"Have you lived in Brazil long?"

"A year."

"So have we! Isn't that a coincidence. Do you like it?"

"Oh, yes. Don't you?"

"Yes."

The child named Timmy had noticed that his mother was talking with someone and he came over and buried his head in his mother's skirt. "I want gum," he whined.

"All right," Ann said, searching in her beach bag. "Say hello to Mother's friend."

Timmy's head gave an imitation of a pile driver and he seemed to be trying to disappear back into his mother. "Oh, he's impossible," Ann said.

"It's all right."

"Here's the gum, Timmy." The child looked up, his sunburned little face redder than usual. "Here, sugar-plum." He snatched the gum and retreated behind his mother's beach chair, still holding on to her with one hand, the other hand grasping the stick of gum. He put the end of the stick of gum into his mouth with the silver foil still on it and looked at Helen with round, resentful eyes.

"Don't eat the paper, Timmy," Helen said.

"Oh, he won't," said Ann.

"Do you come here often?"

"Nearly every day. My child likes it."

"It's nice for children."

Long silence. Now, Helen thought in sudden irritation, we've discussed the children, so it's time to begin talking about our maids. Isn't that always next?

"This is a very good book," Helen said, holding up the book she had brought to the pool. "Have you read it?"

"I think my husband has," Ann said vaguely. "Timmy, don't you want to wear your sun hat?"

"Mmmm!" Timmy squealed, in an unidentifiable monosyllabic sound that seemed to be one of protest. His sunburned face became more petulant than ever and he tugged wordlessly at his mother's arm.

"He wants to go into the water," Ann said. She stood up. "Excuse me, I have to attend to my child." She sounded much more righteous and proud than apologetic, and she leaned down to take Timmy's hand in her own and took him over to the pool without a backward glance. Helen watched her climb into the pool and hold her arms out for the little boy to jump into them. "Come on, Timmy! Jump, darling!"

Well, Helen thought, that's that. She looked again for Roger and Julie and saw that they were perfectly happy with their friends in the water and did not look cold. She looked at her watch. Nearly twelve. It was too early for lunch, but at least eating lunch would give them something to do. What's happened to me, have I lost touch? She thought guiltily. I couldn't even talk to that woman. Or *she* couldn't talk to *me*. Why can't *I* be so involved in my children that I don't care about anything else? But she thought she knew the answer. Roger had never, even when he was a baby, hidden his face in her skirt and clung and scowled at the world, and she was grateful for it. Perhaps it was more difficult to keep an affectionate distance and feel lonely than to have a child who was so jealous that he could not even allow you to converse with a stranger.

She had some difficulty persuading Roger and Julie to come out of the water, but at last they were dried and dressed and she took them to the clubhouse. They found a table on the gallery that bordered the second floor and had a view of the green golf course and the mountains. Helen liked having lunch with her children. Their conversation always amused and surprised her. So when she saw Mil Burns coming toward her with her own two younger children in tow, Helen was not altogether glad.

"Hi," Mil called. She always sounded a little wry, even when she was saying hello. "Have you got room there for me and my brood?"

"Of course," Helen said. "We'll get another chair. Here." She moved a chair from a neighboring empty table.

"Whew!" Mil exclaimed, sinking into a chair and fanning her face with a paper fan printed with the advertisement of a local jewelry store. "Governess's day off. You too?"

"Not exactly," Helen said. "I needed her to do some things in town."

Mil's two younger children were boys, one the same age as Julie, the other a little older. Confronted by two boys, besides her brother, Julie immediately became very quiet and ladylike and self-conscious, folding her hands on the table in front of her and staring at her water glass. "Why don't you children go to the buffet and find something you like?" Helen said.

"Go on," Mil said, not unaffectionately. "Beat it."

The boys were up immediately, and Julie followed behind, looking rather like a terrified girl going to her first dance. "Aren't you coming, Mom?"

"In a very short while," Helen said. "We're going to have a drink first. Please see that you little brother doesn't take *only* dessert."

Mil waved for the waiter. "Last night the lights went out," she said. "As usual. They were out for forty minutes. Naturally, everything in the freezer started to thaw. Those stupid girls didn't know what to do with the food. They started to put it back. I had to tell them to cook it. Now we have enough roast beef for a siege."

"You could always give another dinner party," Helen said. "I'm sure your friends would be delighted."

Mil fanned her face and neck. "No, thank you. I nearly had a nervous breakdown from that one. You know why everyone has two maids in Brazil? Because one is too stupid to do the work of one, that's why. It takes *two* to do the work of one, and then only if you're lucky."

"Mine are wonderful," Helen said mildly.

"Oh, sure. Like laundry. I told Phil if he didn't get me a washing machine from somewhere I was going to leave this stinking place. You think I'm joking? But you can't *get* them. Did you ever hear of anything so primitive as doing all the wash for a family of five by *hand?*"

"The maids do it," Helen said. "You don't. Back home hand laundry is considered very fancy." She didn't mean to enter into an argument, but somehow today she felt as though the world was full of stupid, limited people, leading their own little lives oblivious of anyone else. She didn't know why she was so irritable. Perhaps it was the heat.

"I tried sending Phil's shirts out to a washerwoman," Mil said. "My next-door neighbor had one she said was wonderful. So this Negro woman arrives, and she takes the laundry up to her house

68

in the *favellas* somewhere, and four days later it comes back all nice and clean. I keep sending it, and pretty soon I notice the things are beginning to wear out. You know, these people wash your clothes on rocks, just like the Dark Ages. So then I find out that this washerwoman is washing Phil's shirts and then giving them to her husband to wear for one day, and then washing them again to bring them back to me! These people don't even own any clothes. That's how they save money. They wear your clothes, and sleep in your sheets too, and then they wash them and you never know it."

"How awful! How did you ever find out?"

"My neighbor told me," Mil said.

"But how did she find out?"

"Somebody else told her. You discover these things. I tell you," Mil said, "Brazil isn't as pretty as it looks."

"I guess I'd be furious if it happened to me," Helen said thoughtfully. "But I can't help thinking it's amusing, too. Imagine having so much initiative to think up a scheme like that."

"Ha!" said Mil. "Initiative? Initiative is one thing these people do *not* have. Initiative, my foot. This is *mañana* land, in case you didn't know. Did you ever try to have something fixed?"

The waiter came over with gin and tonic. Mil lifted an ice cube from her glass with her spoon and looked at it closely. Then she waved the waiter away. "It's all right," she said, as if conferring an important scientific verdict. "The ice is all right. You can eat and drink practically anything in this place. That's why I come here. But still, you can't be too careful anywhere."

"You don't like it here, do you?" Helen said.

"Don't like it? I *loathe* it!"

"If you hate it so much, you don't have to stay forever, do you?"

Mil's lips formed a thin line of distaste. "My husband adores it here. He wouldn't leave if you paid him. Oh, I've argued with him plenty. He tells me that I have a nice big apartment on the beach and two maids and a *baba* for the kids, and how happy that should make me. He's like all the American wives here; they just love it because they can afford a maid. Well, I wasn't poor as a girl, you know. Back home in Chicago my parents had a maid."

"So did mine," Helen said. "But that isn't why I like Rio."

Mil looked surprised and slightly aggressive. "What could you possibly like? The sticky heat? The bugs? The stupid people?"

"I don't know many Brazilians," Helen said, "but the ones I've met aren't stupid. I liked them."

"You *liked* them?"

"Yes."

"Why?" Mil said. But it was not a question, it was a statement, and Helen knew that to answer it would mean a meaningless battle. She wondered why she had entered this discussion at all. She knew how Mil felt about Brazil; Mil let you know often enough. It was almost, Helen thought, as if she were talking with Mil to sharpen the razor edge of irritation and anger she felt in herself today. It was painful, but it was a feeling, and it made her feel alive.

"You know," Helen said, "tonight I'd like to do something that would be fun. If you and Phil have nothing to do we could all go out to dinner and then see an American movie."

"I haven't been to a movie in six months," Mil said unpleasantly.

"You haven't?"

"The last time I went I was bitten by fleas. You can go to the movies and be eaten alive if you want, but I have no intention of putting on hip boots and heavy slacks just to see some old picture that was Grade B back home last year."

"We'll go to a theater that doesn't have fleas."

"No, thank you."

"You're never going to go to a movie again?" Helen asked.

"Never as long as I'm in Rio."

The children came back, their plates piled with an oddly indigestible combination of items from the buffet. Helen was glad to see them. They were so fresh and enthusiastic, they loved whatever happened to then because it was new, and even if it was not new they brought a freshness to it. They loved the beach, the sun, the air, the freedom of wearing almost no clothing; they were learning to speak Portuguese with a facility that amazed her. Al-

70

ready, Julie had become friendly again with Mil's boys, and both of them wanted to sit next to her.

"What in God's name are you eating?" Mil said to Roger. "*Feijoada?*" She turned to Helen. "You're going to let him poison himself?"

"I like it," Roger said, looking at Mil sympathetically, as if she were depraved and ignorant.

"It isn't going to hurt him," Helen said.

"All right," said Mil. "They put pigs' ears in it."

"You eat scrapple, don't you?" Helen said.

"Go ahead and eat pigs' ears," Mil said disdainfully.

"Haw!" Mil's elder son shouted. "You can't make a silk purse out of a pig's ear!"

"But you can make *feijoada!*" Julie shrieked. They both began to laugh and push each other, and Mil's younger son, not to be left out, began to laugh too, wildly, although he was not quite sure what was so funny, and he gave Roger a shove.

"Pig's ear!" the little boy shouted. "Pig's ear!"

Roger turned to him calmly. "You're a pig's ear," he said.

"And you're a pig."

Helen felt fury rising in her like new, warm blood. "*Stop it!* All of you. I don't want to hear any more screaming. If anyone here doesn't care for what anyone else is eating, he can just shut up."

"Well, who do you think you are?" Mil asked. "Your Julie started it."

"*You* started it, if you want to know," Helen said coldly. For no reason at all she felt as if she were going to cry, and she shut her eyes and turned her head, pretending to be looking out at the vista beyond the gallery railing. There was silence, punctuated by a nervous giggle from Julie. With an effort, Helen composed herself. "It's nobody's fault," she said, trying to smile. "Let's all try and be quiet, children. There are other people eating here too, and they don't want to have to listen to children guffawing."

"What's guffawing?" Roger asked.

"Laughing," Helen said. She ruffled his hair, smiling down at him, and she wanted to kiss him. My strength, she thought, is the people I love. That's the only thing that keeps me alive. And then she was surprised at herself for this entire outburst out here on the harmless gallery in the bright sunshine, and she wondered what was happening to her.

Although the children continued to eat as though nothing had happened, there was a noticeable coldness from Mil. Helen tried not to care. Mil was a bigot, and if she had not come here and plunked herself down with her children nothing would have happened. And yet, what *had* happened? Nothing, really; a children's scuffle, that was all. Something that could, and did, happen every day. But Helen suddenly could not finish her drink, and she did not want anything to eat. When the waiter came over to their table with menus she ordered only coffee. Mil glanced at her with upraised eyebrows, as if to say, Well, look who's sulking! The meal seemed endless. She heard the children's chatter, like the chirping of tame birds, and after a while she listened to it, and it soothed her. Their faces, even Roger's, partly smeared with the brown sauce of the *feijoada,* seemed beautifuly formed and clean.

The woman called Ann, whom Helen had spoken to at the pool, passed by their table, holding her child by the hand. She waved distractedly. "How's your sewing coming?" she called to Mil, not waiting for an answer.

"Pretty good," Mil called.

"Are you still sewing for the hospital bazaar?" Helen asked Mil.

"Yes. Might as well do something. You ought to try it."

"I never could sew anything well," Helen said apologetically. "I'm just about at the putting-on-a-button stage."

"It's just something to do," Mil said. Now that she could criticize someone else she seemed warmer and friendlier. "Most of those women have nothing else to do," she said. "This is a big deal in their lives."

"I know," Helen said. She sipped at her coffee. She wondered what Bert was doing at the office, and thinking of him she felt a stab of longing that hit her with an actual physical pain. The sunshine seemed very hot. She imagined him in the city, having lunch with some men in a crowded restaurant, the Jockey Club perhaps, or the American Club. Maybe he would let me come into town and have lunch with him one day, she thought. He probably wouldn't like it; he's so busy. . . .

But she knew, even as she wondered, that Bert would not like it at all; he would consider her presence an inconvenience, even a nuisance. Perhaps it was. She didn't know any more; she didn't know anything. She realized suddenly that whatever had happened between her and Bert this past year had made her lose the ability to judge.

CHAPTER *4*

A few minutes after noon, which was too early for Brazilians to think of lunch, Leila Silva e Costa drove through the mountain resort town of Cidade d'Ouro on her ascent from Rio to the town of Cidade d'Azul high above. It was a four-hour drive from Rio to Cidade d'Azul, and because she knew she would have to return that same afternoon she was already nervous with anticipated fatigue. She was driving an American car, a four-year-old Pontiac that had cost her five thousand dollars this year. By the standards of the ancient and disintegrating automobiles that crept down Avenida Atlantica every evening from five to seven in the daily traffic jam, Leila's car was a good one. At least it worked.

She had opened all the windows to the cool mountain air, and as she passed through Cidade d'Ouro she looked at the yellow stucco, sun-splashed homes that had given the town its name— City of Gold—and seemed never to have changed. She had spent all her summers in Cidade d'Ouro when she was a child, when the family was all together—her father, her mother, her three older sisters, her older brother. She had been the youngest, the baby. Now her father was dead, her brother was dead, her oldest sister lived in São Paulo and never invited Leila to visit her, and her two other sisters lived in Rio but hardly spoke to her at all. The sight of the narrow, winding cobblestoned streets, the little river trickling under the bridge, the yellow houses, the splashes of red geraniums, the old-fashioned pastry shops, filled Leila with *saudade.* It seemed so long ago that she had been the prim, fat little girl walking along those streets with her French governess; it seemed a hundred years ago. And yet she was only twenty-nine, and she looked younger. When people saw her with her enormous twin sons of eleven, nearly as tall as she was, and her two beautiful daughters of ten and eight, they could not believe it. Or at least they said they could not believe it. Women married and bore children very early in Brazil.

It had been hot and cloudless when she left Rio in the morning, but the mountains here were like a cup for the sky, so as she drove up the winding mountain road she could see fog ahead. Below her, as if she were in an airplane, were clouds. It was a private world. On one side of her was the mountain, green with vegetation and red with the fertile soil where the mountain had been cut to make the road. On the other side was a low white metal fence, bent and twisted in many places where cars and trucks had careened into the abyss during nights of rain and fog. And below that was the vast green valley, beginning to disappear into mist, and the wide, fecund, rolling land. Brazil was so big you could never get to the end of it. Even driving eight hours in one day, as she was going to do, was not so unusual. People drove to Cidade d'Ouro to visit friends for lunch, and that was a three-hour drive if you went fast. You could drive for five days and nights across the country and still be in Brazil. You set your mind for distance when you lived in Brazil, as if it were a slow-moving clock, and you thought in terms of great spaces and great mysteries of closed jungle.

As her car climbed the mountain Leila knew it was going to rain. It had been raining steadily since the beginning of December in Cidade d'Azul, the blue city at the top of the sky. Already the air was cool and moist. Along the side of the narrow road were wild hydrangeas, blue and purple, rain flowers, some as pale as water, some azure and rich with the color of the sky itself. All the years that she had been coming up this road to Cidade d'Azul, Leila had been looking at those hydrangeas, and to her they were the color of tears.

Her fingers reached for the dials of the car radio, and she tapped the dashboard nervously waiting for the music. She wanted jazz, American jazz, or perhaps Carnival music. Carnival music always made her happy. She was humming between her teeth, her face set, her long black hair blowing around her face in the wind from the open windows. The first drops of rain appeared on the windshield, and rain blew in on the wind, dampening her face and sleeve, but Leila did not close the window. She sang with the jazz, her eyes wide open and fixed now on the difficult road that was a demon even though she knew it so well by now, her foot on the accelerator making speed.

Leila Silva e Costa was a beautiful woman, or perhaps it might better be said, a beautiful girl. There was something in her face that was the look of an adolescent girl—not the features, or even the expression, but something reaching from inside, a confusion and restlessness and innocence. She had black hair and, like many Brazilian women, large blue-green eyes with long black lashes, like the eyes of a cat. Her eyes were her best feature, very striking in her tanned face. The rest of her face was delicately molded, and, unlike many Brazilians, she had good teeth, white and small and her own. When she had been a child fighting with her older brother she had often resorted to biting him, and sometimes scratching, so he had given her the nickname of *Gatinha*. Her brother was gone, they were all gone, and no one had called her Little Cat in years.

She reached Cidade d'Azul in pouring rain. It was gray and cold, the kind of miserable grayness that seems to have set in for weeks and weeks. Leila parked her car across the street from a small German restaurant and ran through the ankle-deep puddles to the shelter of the warm room. There was a large Brazilian family eating at one table, the parents and the old grandparents and the many children all together. At a small table against the wall was an English couple dressed in Bermuda shorts and raincoats. They had probably rented a house in Cidade d'Azul for the summer, not knowing about the rainy season—their pallor gave this away, and their look of bleak bewilderment. Leila sat at a table removed from the ones that were occupied and ordered broiled chicken with fried potatoes and palmitos and a bottle of beer.

She tried to keep her thoughts confined to this small, brightly lighted room with the painted biscuit tins lined up on shelves, and the huge wheels of cheeses, and bottles of wine beside them, but already in her mind these bright everyday things were melting away and she could see the gray, secret walls of the convent. Even on a sunny day the convent seemed gray, silent, with a hidden life somewhere within that even she could never know. She knew the nuns had a garden in which they raised all their own vegetables, and perhaps flowers too, but it was a secret garden. All Leila knew was the outside of the building, and the small visitor's room with the picture of Saint Peter on the wall and the double row of bars behind which, one afternoon a month, she was permitted to see the face of her mother.

She paid the waiter and ran out again into the rain. Imagine! she thought. To live here where it rains every day all summer and is so cold! She wondered if her mother minded—or even noticed —the rain. Strange that she had never thought to ask. She always had questions ready, but when she was face to face with her mother in that short time she always forgot everything she had planned to say.

She parked the car at the curb in front of the convent and ran up the steps, splashing water on the hem of her dress. The little custodian dressed in black who opened the door knew Leila well and gave her a reserved, timid smile. Only her eyes showed friendliness. You are fortunate, the eyes said. How proud you must be.

"You may enter."

Walking down the immaculately polished floor of the narrow corridor Leila felt her heart beginning to pound, as it always did when she came here. She was acutely conscious of her wet shoes and of the sound they were making in the great silence. She felt like a little girl again, a naughty child with wet feet, and she stiffened, trying to walk as quietly as possible. Not that it could offend anyone, really; the entire place seemed deserted, everyone hidden away. The custodian left her in the tiny visitor's room and shut the door.

The only furniture in the room was a hard wooden chair and a small table with a drawer in the front of it. Once Leila had opened the drawer and found it empty. The walls were painted a dull, indistinguishable color. The picture of Saint Peter on the wall was the only decoration. But none of this mattered. The focal point of all eyes, of everything in the room and its reason for existing at all, was a kind of great window in one wall, completely barred with metal bars set two inches apart and bearing short, sharp, metal spikes pointing outside at the visitor. Two or three feet inside this row of spiked bars was another row of bars, this time without spikes. Behind them was a thin black curtain blotting out all sight. Looking at this forbidding array you could not help feeling that whatever was on the other side being protected was somehow superhuman, unreal. You could not believe that the black-robed figures who might speak to you were really only women, pious women, who had said farewell to whatever you knew of life. And perhaps they no longer were.

The black curtain moved aside. Leila was a daughter, the closest blood relative, so she could speak without the curtain and she could see. Her hands were so cold they were almost numb. She was filled with resentment and love and loneliness and anguish, and she could hardly speak.

"Hello, Mother."

"Leila. How are you? You look well."

You don't care! Leila wanted to cry out, but she tried to smile. "I'm well. How are you?"

"I am well." How calm her mother looked, how detached, and how strange. On her pale, scrubbed face, the heavy black, unplucked eyebrows stood out as the main feature. Her eyes were quiet, calm, and said nothing. "How are the children?"

"I don't know what to do with them!" Leila burst out. "The boys miss their father terribly. They won't mind me; they won't do anything I tell them to. And Teresinha is so shy she has no friends at school. I can't do it myself."

78

"He will come back. You must take him back," her mother said evenly.

"He won't come back. He's married. You know he's married again."

"He is married to you. There is no other marriage."

"Mother, I need you," Leila whispered. She tried not to cry, holding her breath, feeling her heart struggle in her chest like a caught fish straining for life. "I can't do it myself. I have no one."

"You have God."

"I don't have anybody!"

"You must take your husband back," her mother said calmly. "Many women have suffered more than you have because of their husband's sin. He is your husband, and you are his only wife. You can suffer much for him. It has been done before."

Anger at her mother's calm, sure tone gave Leila strength. "He doesn't want to come back," she said, enunciating clearly. "*He* left *me*. He doesn't want me. He wants *her*. He doesn't want to be married to me. He told me so. You know that, Mother. You know that. Only you never will admit it."

"Your divorce caused me great pain," her mother said quietly. "It was a sin in the eyes of God. I pray for you, always."

"I need more than prayers."

There was silence between them then as they looked at each other, but it was not the kind of silence that makes a bond between two people who love each other. Leila stared at her mother's face, winged in black cloth like a pale, half-shrouded portrait, and she wondered what her mother was thinking. I don't know her any more, Leila thought. She's my mother and I don't even know how she feels about me any more.

"I can't bear to talk to you from behind these bars like an animal in a cage," Leila cried.

Her mother smiled distantly. "Your only cage is the prison of your own sin."

"If I were *dying*, Mother, if I were dying in the hospital of *cancer*, would you come out to see me? Would you come to me if I called you from my *deathbed?*"

Her mother's smile was less distant. "I would pray for you."

"But you wouldn't come out to me."

"God will take care of you."

"Sometimes I . . ." Leila began. Sometimes I hate you. But she could not say the words aloud, even though they were crying out inside her. Something prevented the utterance; perhaps awe, perhaps love.

"I pray for all of you," her mother said.

"All my life I was guarded," Leila said. "Don't do this, don't go there. You never let me think for myself. I had a governess until the day I was married. And then, for no reason, you disappeared into this convent. I have no one, Mother. I'm alone. I don't know how to be alone. I don't know how to take care of myself. What about me? Is my life over now; am I dead for you?"

"I had reasons."

"You couldn't face life."

"Can you?"

"I'm . . . sorry," Leila said with effort. "I didn't mean to come here and fight with you. We always have a fight, don't we?"

"I have learned how to forgive you."

"Maybe someday . . . I'll be able to understand you," Leila whispered.

"I must go now," her mother said gently.

"I'll come back next month."

"That will be good. Goodbye."

"Goodbye, Mother." The black curtain dropped, and her mother was gone. There was no sound. Leila wondered for one crazy moment if her mother were still sitting there behind that curtain, if an anguished cry could bring her back even for a minute, for one more goodbye, for all the things that should have been said or perhaps for more things that should never have been said at all. The room was very still. It was such a bare room, with almost nothing in it, but it was so filled with wild, mute thoughts that there was no room for furniture or decoration. No wonder it's bare, Leila thought bitterly. She stood, and walked around the small table to the bars. She took hold of one of the bars with her hand, between the sharp, neat spikes. The metal

80

was not as smooth to the touch as it was to the eye, and when she took her hand away it smelled metallic.

I can't even touch you, Leila thought. This metallic scent is all I have of your flesh and blood and bone.

She turned and opened the door, and walked quickly down the silent corridor, not caring now how much noise her shoes made. The custodian let her out.

"Would you like to go into the chapel for a while?"

"No, thank you," Leila said. "Goodbye. Until later."

"Happiness."

"Ah, yes," Leila said. "Happiness to you, too."

Driving back down the mountain, she was forced to go slowly because of the great patches of fog that made her feel as though she were in an enormous, cold, Turkish bath. In some places she could not see anything ahead, even with the lights of her car turned on. Perhaps this was what Heaven would be like—clouds and quiet, and a sense of limitless height. Perhaps this was the dream that sustained her mother's life. Leila believed in heaven implicitly, as she believed all the things she had been taught, but since her divorce she had begun to read books that told her of psychology and love and lust and earth. She had begun to read avidly out of frustration and loneliness, and a feeling that if she had not been such a limited person perhaps her marriage would not have failed. Somewhere in those books there must be an answer to the bitterness of life and to the questions faith could not answer. A few years before it had been chic among her friends to be intensely religious, to go to church and speak of God. It had been a fad, in a way, and Leila had not been able to join in it, although she of all people, with a mother in the convent . . . And now psychology was the rage. Women who had been given the most perfunctory of educations, aimed completely at a protected marriage, were trying to read and to talk about what they had read.

She had talked once of a book she liked with a friend who seemed extraordinarily intelligent. And later she had seen all her friend's comments, verbatim, in a magazine review. Leila had been so annoyed at this deception that she had not even realized until much later that at least the friend had had the intelligence to read and memorize the review. But it was a fad, like memorizing a new card game or a new dance step.

Emerging from the fog to lower ground, she pressed the accelerator down, driving faster, recklessly. She turned on the radio, finding jazz. There was no answer in her books, none at all, for loneliness and dependence and desertion. She had married when she was still an adolescent girl, and she had leaned on João Alberto, depended on him, expected he would be there forever. During the years of her marriage she had never changed at all, not even when she had begun to suspect that her husband was interested in someone else. She had suffered, she had wept, she had waited; but she had not changed. When he finally left her and married someone else, Leila had mourned for three years, as if she had been a widow instead of a divorcée. She did not have the slightest idea of what to do with her life. She had been a matron at seventeen and now she was a teen-ager at twenty-nine.

Life was easier for the young girls in Brazil marrying today, because they had more freedom than she had been given, and they at least had an idea of how to think for themselves. Some of them had gone to the university. Some of them had even taken jobs, even though they did not need the money. When they became engaged many of them were permitted to go out with their fiancés without a chaperone's coming along too. It was all different today. Often Leila felt she did not belong anywhere. The old, sheltered, governed order which had prepared her for its own kind of world still existed, but it was inhabited by married women with families, who led the life they had been trained to lead. For the modern young girls of Brazil, freedom was a gift. The ones who had it knew what to do with it. But Leila was right in between the old and the new, and freedom meant not adventure but peril, loneliness, and unwanted responsibilities which belonged better to men.

No matter what happened to her, it always made her think of her husband. Her friends teased her; they said no man could be as unforgettable as all that. She still spoke of him often: "My husband used to say . . ." or "When I was with my husband . . ."

82

Even while she was speaking about him and praising this or that which he used to do or say, Leila was aware that João Alberto was not really such a unique, superior, and marvelous person as she pretended; it was simply that he was her husband and she loved him. She looked back at the days of her marriage, even the unhappiest days, as a sanctuary. Now that she was separated from them by time and had read all those books, she could see certain events more objectively and she realized that she had not known João Alberto as well as she thought she had, even though they had known each other since childhood.

In the world in which she had been raised you grew up together and married each other; it was a simple, small world for all its formalities. João Alberto was three years older than she, and she had always adored him because he was handsome and intelligent and sensitive. During the summers in Cidade d'Ouro all the children played together; her older sisters and brother, João Alberto and his sisters and brothers, and the young cousins of the two families. She had always wanted to marry him, ever since she could remember, and then from the time she was fourteen on she had *known* she was going to marry him.

She remembered often the day he had written the poem for her. And she remembered too that he would read poetry to her from a book and it was so beautiful that she would cry. Looking back now, she remembered other things that were not so sentimental and lovely. She remembered that when the children had gotten into some sort of mischief together and had been caught it was always João Alberto who would be the first to confess and to tell on the others. She wondered now if it was that weak trait in him that had made him leave her years later, if perhaps their entire lives together from childhood were paved with clues that would explain the harm they had visited on each other as adults.

She remembered her eighteenth birthday, the first one she had ever spent away from home. João Alberto had taken her to Montivideo, in Uruguay, for a vacation just after the twins were born. It was not far from home, but she was homesick, and awakening in that strange bed in the strange hotel on the morning of her eighteenth birthday Leila realized that only a year before she had been a virgin and a child, and now she was a wife and the mother of two infants. The entire situation seemed overwhelming, and recalling her parents' house where she had happily spent all previous birthdays Leila was so depressed she could not speak. The worst of it was that João Alberto was not in the room when she awakened, and she could not imagine where he was. She lay on her back and stared at the sunlight on the ceiling, inert under the weight of her homesickness.

Then the door to the bedroom was kicked open, and João Alberto came into the room carrying a huge white-frosted birthday cake on a plate in his two outstretched hands. He put the cake on the quilt beside her with a flourish, so happy with the pride of what he had done that he looked like a small boy again.

"Good morning! Happy birthday, my heart!" He kissed her so tenderly that all her homesickness and depression disappeared, evanesced, floated away like the smoke from a blown-out birthday candle. "I brought you a birthday cake for breakfast," he said.

"We'll eat it for breakfast, then!" she cried happily. "Bring a knife! No, no, I can't eat it; I'm too excited."

Who else could have found a birthday cake in the morning at a hotel, complete with her name written on it in chocolate and a pink, sugary heart? Who else would have crept out of bed while she was still sleeping, to bring it back? Who else would have suspected that even though she was on a vacation in a beautiful city she would be taken with homesickness and loneliness when she awoke on her birthday? On that birthday morning Leila felt there never was a man so sensitive or so kind as her husband, and now, years later, when she remembered it, she held the memory to her heart purely and emotionally, untouched by anything wrong and unhappy which had come afterward or even before.

Oh, what could she do now? All this love, all these beautiful things, were only memories, existing only in her own mind. Probably João Alberto had forgotten them. And if he had forgotten them, and if they had happened so long ago, perhaps they did not exist at all. Everyone was gone—her husband, her mother, her family, and there was no answer, not even from her mother, who loved her still. The only thing that was real was this road and this steering wheel, and later the hours of the night. Leila knew what she was going to do tonight. She would do what she always did when she returned from these terrible eight hours of treacherous driving, and from the more terrible ordeal of trying to see some answer in her mother's face. She would call up some man and go to a *boâte*, or to a party. She would dance the samba all night and she would drink champagne. She wanted to do the wildest things she could do, to tear apart the cord between her life up on that mountain and her life below. Her life below was the one she had to live, the one she had to bear. She would drink, and dance, and she would laugh. Perhaps some night she would even have the courage to forget João Alberto, who had forgotten her, and she would make love.

CHAPTER 5

When she came home from her day at the Gavea Golf Club
with the children Helen Sinclair remembered that she was going
with Bert to a Brazilian's home, to her first really Brazilian
party, and suddenly she was refreshed and delighted. The party
seemed to take on an importance beyond reason, as if it were
some kind of salvation. All through this long day she had not been
able to escape the feeling that she had failed, that soon Mrs.
Graham would be taking the children to the club again, sitting
beside the pool as custodian of the towels and clothes and chewing gum. Her mind told her this was not such a dreadful thing,
that, after all, to be like those placid women who wanted no conversation other than the limited chatter of tiny children would be
a hypocrisy and, even worse, an unnecessary one. But her heart
told her she had deserted her children and in so doing had herself
been cast loose, like a balloon without a hand for its string, left to
float purposelessly in the empty sky.

"I only met this Brazilian yesterday, at lunch," Bert said. "And
he invited us to his party. You'll like him, he's charming. His
name is—believe it or not—Baby Amaral."

"*Baby?* He's either young or a playboy."

"He's neither. He's about fifty years old. A lot of Brazilian men
are named Baby; their governesses named them and the name
stuck when they grew up. But that's a lot better than the ones
who had German governesses when they were young. *They're*
apt to be named Bubi."

"Booby? My lord, I wonder if anyone told them what it means in English." Helen smiled at Bert, thinking of the odd names, but she could not help feeling a little envious. How much he knew that she did not know, the places he was allowed to go, the people he met! He did not have to sit by a pool all day, with sewing for a hospital his only diversion. "I'm so glad we're going to this party tonight."

"To tell you the truth," Bert said, "I'd rather not go. I'm exhausted. I'm going only because I think it might amuse you."

"We don't . . . have to."

"No, we'll go."

"You'll enjoy it when you're there," Helen said, beginning to feel guilty. "You always love to meet new people."

"I know," he said resignedly and went off to the shower.

Why did he have to tell me that, Helen thought unhappily. Now I'll feel as if I'm driving him to an early grave, like those dreadful women you read articles about in magazines. Now I won't enjoy the party. This whole day has gone wrong, and I'm tired from doing nothing, and I've failed my children, and now I'm failing my husband. What I should really do is give him a quiet little dinner and go to bed early. What's the matter with me, anyway? I never used to be like this.

She went determinedly into the bedroom and began to choose accessories and jewelry for her dress. They were going to that party and she was going to enjoy it, that was all. It would certainly be a waste of time if *neither* of them had fun.

They had some difficulty finding the street address in the dark because it was a neighborhood neither of them knew. Great leafy trees lined the street, and behind a wrought-iron fence they could see a lush garden with lights strung among the trees. When they walked up the path through the grass to the house they could hear an orchestra playing on the other side of the house, and the sound of people talking. Bert seemed cheerful, and he looked very handsome in his white summer dinner jacket, and not tired at all. Helen felt happier. There was a kidney-shaped swimming pool in the garden in back of the house, with people gathered around it dressed in evening clothes. The orchestra was in an enclosed porch affair with one open side, which must have been the patio of the bathhouse. They were playing an American popular song with great spirit, and for a moment Helen almost thought they had made a mistake and gone to the wrong party. There were large palm trees in the garden, and white wrought-iron furniture, and stuck into the bark of the palm trees were red, blue, and green pointed glass Christmas balls, bristling with bright glassy colors all the way from the grass to the palm fronds above, like some kind of strange tropical growth.

Baby Amaral came bounding out of the patio to greet them. He was short and plump and easily fifty, with a kind, eager face. "Ah," he said, "How are you? Well?" holding out his hands. "How are you?" He shook hands with Bert with one hand and put the other arm about Bert's shoulders, rocking back and forth in that embrace as if they were a pair of tango dancers. Bert patted Baby Amaral on the back too, and rocked and smiled and laughed, and the two of them looked more like long-lost brothers who had finally been reunited than two people who had only met for the first time the day before at lunch.

"How are you?" Bert said. "Ah, fine, fine." He turned to introduce Helen. "This is my wife, Helen."

Baby Amaral lifted her hand to his lips briskly, all respectful formality. "A very great pleasure. I'm glad you came."

"So are we," Helen said. "Thank you."

"Listen to the orchestra," Baby said. "They're going to play all American tunes tonight. I bought the sheet music for them. And we're having American food later. I love America."

"We love Brazil," Bert said.

"You do?" he asked happily. "You too, Helen? Do you like Brazil?"

"I love it."

"You love it! It's a wonderful country. I'm glad you love it." Baby beamed at her. "Everyone at this party is Brazilian, but most of them speak English very well. You won't have any trouble."

"I speak Portuguese," Helen said.

"You speak Portuguese! How wonderful! It's a very difficult language for Americans."

"Yes," Helen said. "It is hard, at first."

"Very difficult," Baby said. "You must be a very intelligent woman. Come, I'll introduce you to some of my friends. You must speak to them in Portuguese."

Helen glanced at Bert as they followed Baby to the first knot of people. Bert already had that avid expression on his face, like a cub reporter at his first fire, and she knew he was going to have a good time. She smiled at him lovingly and he winked at her.

"This is Leila Silva e Costa, Helen and Bert Sinclair." Baby went on, introducing members of the group, but Helen was lost in the maze of Brazilian names. Everyone seemed to have at least three names, many of them combinations of the same names and most of them unpronounceable. She looked at the first woman she had met. How extraordinarily beautiful she was! There was something more Parisian than Latin about upper-class Brazilian women—their hair styles, their clothes, even their finely cut profiles. And something about the light eyes many of them had seemed almost Egyptian.

"Excuse me," Helen said in Portuguese. "Please tell me your name again."

"Leila, And you?"

"Helen."

"You are American."

Helen laughed. "You can tell immediately, of course."

"Oh, please speak English," Leila said, in English. "I want to learn to improve my English. My English is too bad."

"No, it isn't bad at all."

"No? You don't think it's funny? I am taking lessons now."

A waiter came by with glasses of champagne. They each took one. "Do you want to sit down?" Leila asked. "It's very hot in this patio. Let's sit in the garden."

"Wonderful idea."

They sat in small white wrought-iron chairs beside the lighted pool. Helen looked down at the water longingly. "I'd like to jump in."

"We will, later. Do you have your bikini?"

"No. I never thought—"

"They will find one for you," Leila said. "Don't worry." When she smiled, her remarkable cat's eyes did not crinkle half shut the way most people's did but, rather, they opened wider, glittering, giving her an expression that was mischievous and young. Helen guessed Leila was about the same age as she was, perhaps younger. "Later we'll dance in the pool."

"My lord," Helen said. "It's like Hollywood."

"Have you been to Hollywood?"

"No. I've only read about it."

"I would like to go to New York," Leila said. "I know I would love New York. I want to go there to go to college. Perhaps I will someday." She lowered her voice and looked at Helen with concern. "Tell me—am I too old to go to college in the United States?"

"Too old?" Helen said. "Of course not. Grandmothers go to college in America, after their children are grown. Anybody can go."

"They won't laugh at me?"

"Not at all."

Leila looked pained, but she did not try to drop her gaze from Helen's face. "I never had any education," she said. "I was married at seventeen and I was so ignorant. The women here marry too young, I think. It's not good. I think that's why my marriage failed. I didn't know you have to work for a good marriage, and even if I had known, I wouldn't have known what to do."

"You're very honest," Helen said.

"Maybe too much?"

"No. Could we see each other sometime? Have lunch together one day?"

"Of course!" Leila said. "Tomorrow I can't, because I go up to the *favellas*. But after tomorrow. You come to my house for lunch."

"You go up to the *favellas?*" Helen asked. "To those shacks on the mountain?"

"It's a kind of social work," Leila said. "Some of the women do it. The people who live there are so poor, it's something terrible.

90

The police won't let them build any more houses because there are too many already. So during the night when it's very dark the people put up a house, very quickly, all in one night. And in the morning if the police come, they just say, What house? This house was here always."

"How can anyone put up a house overnight?"

Leila opened her eyes wide. "They're something terrible, those houses. Old pieces of wood, old gasoline tins, cardboard. When there is a big rain they disappear and the people drown, their chickens drown and float in the rain water, the—how you say—big black birds come—"

"Buzzards?"

"Yes. The black birds that eat people. So I go up there one day every week and bring clothes and food and sometimes medicine if the people need it."

"You're not afraid?" Helen said.

"Afraid? In the daylight? *No!* Not so many people can do this," Leila added rather proudly, "because you have to be a very good driver to go up those roads. Most of the time there aren't even any roads."

"Could I go with you tomorrow?" Helen asked. "Please."

"You want to go?"

"Yes. I do."

"With pleasure," Leila said. "I'll come for you in the morning. Around eleven o'clock." She began to search through her small purse. "Give me your address and telephone number. And if you have some old things, some clothing, maybe clothes for children, you could bring them."

"I'm sure I do." She thought of the clothes the children had outgrown, put away in a box on top of a closet, and of all the things she had which, although she never seemed able to wear them out, seemed old to her and worn and tiresome. In her mind she was already categorizing all this booty and was filled with a rising excitement. Perhaps we'll become friends, she thought. I'd like to have a Brazilian friend in Brazil. And then it struck her for an instant how somehow ridiculous it was that although she had been living in this country for almost a year now the only

Brazilians she knew well were maids and shopkeepers and her *massagista* and her hairdresser. And she only knew them as well as one knows people with whom one has lengthy discussions about the weather.

"I'm glad we met," Helen said.

"I too," Leila said warmly. "In Rio you always see the same people, every day, all the time, all your life from the time you are children. You go to parties and it's always the same people. Whatever you do, they know it before you know it yourself! And they are always gossiping. They call you on the telephone: 'Ah, I saw your husband on the street talking to a woman!' It's something terrible, this gossip. I'm glad I met you, too."

Although it was late it was still too hot for anyone but the most energetic to try to dance. The orchestra played, and people strolled by the pool, looking longingly at the electrically lighted blue water. Helen and Leila walked through the crowd, all of whom Leila knew and none of whom Helen had ever seen before. "That girl over there was Miss Brazil a few years ago," Leila said. "And that girl is engaged. To the man next to her. And that woman—isn't she beautiful?—is married to the tall man next to her. She's very intelligent too."

"It's funny," Helen said, "people actually standing with the people they're married to. At our parties, the first thing you do is get away from your husband or wife."

"Really?"

"In fact, when there's a dinner party with place cards you never sit next to the person you're married to."

Leila laughed mischievously. "The husbands and wives in Brazil are very polite to each other," she said. "When they are in public they never look at anyone else. But most of the men here have mistresses, and most of the women have had lovers."

Helen looked around her, not able to restrain herself from feeling shocked. How carefree all these women looked, and how poised. She had been friendly with a married woman in Westport who had been having an affair, but this woman had always looked harried, as if the strain of furtive meetings and a grand passion of the heart were too much for her to handle along with the running of a home and the care of a husband and two children. And she had another neighbor who suspected her husband was having an affair with someone in the city, and Helen remembered a horrible evening when she and Bert had sat with this wife waiting for her husband to come home for a dinner to which she and Bert had been invited. The husband had missed a train, and then telephoned, and then missed another; harmless enough; but Helen had watched the wife get herself systematically drunk on five martinis, and then she had known. Finally the three of them had sat down to the table in order that the roast not dry to a crisp. The conversation had been strained, full of forced gaiety and pointedly innocuous anecdotes. At moments like that everything you say seems to take on a terrifying unintended double meaning. Finally the husband had appeared, all humble thirty-five-year-old boyish charm. Helen remembered thinking at the time, Who would want to go to bed with *him?* But evidently at least two women did.

"The wives know about the husbands' mistresses?" Helen said.

"In time the wife always knows," Leila said. "You can't help finding out."

"But what do they do then?"

Leila shrugged. "Nothing. Sometimes take a lover and say nothing. Sometimes accuse the husband; and then he buys her a new bracelet or something she has been wanting and she forgives him. They fight and make up. A married woman has no rights in Brazil. We have no legal divorce. If a husband leaves his wife he doesn't have to give her any money, even for the children. So what can a wife do? It's better to be married than to be alone."

"How awful!"

"Yes," Leila said grimly. "It is."

Helen saw Bert standing against the bar in the patio talking to some men, and she went to him and took hold of his hand, feeling gratitude and tenderness toward him. He turned for an instant and gave her a brief smile. She felt Leila's fingers lightly on her arm.

"I must go and speak to that man over there," Leila whispered. "I like him *very* much." She smiled, this time a smile full of radiance that altered her entire appearance. She seemed like a child bursting with the secret of some forbidden trick she is going to play. She disappeared into the crowd.

Helen looked after her, wondering which one was the man, but he was evidently at the other side of the crowd, over by the shrubbery, and she could not see either him or Leila. She wondered if the man was Leila's lover, and if he was married. Now she looked at all these people with a new interest, realizing how little she knew about any of them. At home, on the few occasions when she and Bert went to a night club or to a bar in New York, she had been able to look at all the people and imagine she knew exactly what they were like. You could see a lovely young girl dancing with a wealthy-looking older man and you could say to yourself, feeling like an analyzer of life, He's married. She isn't. Or you could look at a young couple and think, He's in love with her and thinks she's in love with him, but she really doesn't like him very much. But here, in this strange place, Helen looked at the engaged girl with her fiancé and she had no idea whether or not they were in love with each other, or whether the girl was marrying only for security or escape from her governess. Or perhaps the man thought she would make a good mother for his future children. Would he have a mistress, or even several? Would she take a lover? In the early days of their marriage, when Helen and Bert still had unmarried friends, they could go to a party and Helen could tell which girl was working in an office and now wearing her only good black dress, and if she had come to the party only because she knew it would be a free meal. She could tell which girls had come because they were desperately looking for new men to give them love, or even friendship. Their searching chatter and round eyes that looked as if they could draw someone in to their depths by physical force alone gave them away. She had been able to look at a girl sitting with her elbow on a bar, leaning her chin on her palm and listening to a man talk, and Helen had imagined she even knew how many perfume bottles that girl had at home on her dressing table. But here—she didn't know anything. She had never even been inside the bedroom of a Brazilian woman like herself, and she had never seen the inside of the homes in which they had grown up and become what they were at this moment.

"I feel like a stranger," she said to Bert.

"Why?" he asked, surprised. "Aren't you having fun? Haven't you met people?"

"I don't mean at this party; I mean in Brazil."

"Well," he answered, as if it were the most natural thing in the world, "we *are* strangers."

But somehow, for some reason, the words hurt her.

A young woman with a beautiful body, dressed in a tiny bikini, ran out of the bathhouse and jumped into the pool. Another woman followed her, and then two men, all in bathing suits. The women swam and dived like porpoises, their wet hair streaming about their faces, although Helen was sure they had gone to the beauty parlor that very day to prepare for the party. The four of them lined up at the edge of the pool, kicking to stay afloat, smiling and calling out to their friends to jump in too. Their upturned faces glittered in the electric lights under the water, like masks.

"Helen," Baby Amaral said, "do you want a bikini? There are several in the dressing room that might fit you."

"I don't know . . ." she said. To tell the truth, she had not yet gotten the courage to wear the two narrow strips of cloth some of the Brazilian women called a bathing suit, although she had two brief maillots at home.

"Come!" Baby insisted. "It's so hot, don't you think so? Aren't you too hot? I don't want you to be too hot; you won't be able to enjoy your dinner."

Helen looked at her watch and smiled at him. It was nearly midnight. She wondered if Bert was suffering from hunger. He disliked waiting until so late to eat. As for herself, she had not realized how late it was. She trotted obediently into the bathhouse and found a bikini lying on a white wooden bench. When she had undressed and put it on she looked at herself in the mirror. Her tan ended at her waist and began again at the top of her thighs, but the bikini revealed a three-inch-wide strip of white skin below the waist that made her look, she thought, like a chorus girl dancing in a night-club line at a southern resort. Oh, well, she thought, what the hell. She ran out and jumped into the shallow end of the pool.

The water was cool and refreshing, but not too cold. It felt very sensual on her skin. She wanted, crazily, to swim with no bathing suit on at all. She had never felt this freedom. She smiled at a stranger and he smiled back, floating on his back and kicking his feet. Most of the people were swimming or floating, but a few couples were trying to dance in the water to the lively music of the orchestra.

"Dancing in the water is like a dream," she said. "When you try to walk fast and something holds you back."

"*O que?*" he said apologetically.

She translated, and noticed from the corner of her eye an attractive woman who could only be the wife of this stranger looking at her with a steely glance. For a moment Helen wondered what she had done, and then she realized that it was not what she had done, or was doing, but what she might do. Of course! she thought. This man and I might become lovers! The thought was so outlandish and amusing that she began to laugh out of sheer high spirits, and the stranger, after a momentary look of bewilderment, began to laugh too. If he knew what I was just thinking *he* wouldn't think it was so silly, Helen thought. She looked at him really, now, for the first time. He was an attractive man, lean, brown haired, perhaps thirty-two or -three. He had a kind of wolfine look to his face, partly shyness and reserve, partly a natural sex appeal, and partly the aloofness that comes from a certain kind of breeding. She tried to look at his wife more closely, but his wife had turned half away, momentarily in conversation with a friend.

He swam a little closer to Helen then and said in a low voice in almost unaccented English, "I apologize for playing a trick on you."

"You *do* speak English!"

He nodded, a barely perceptible nod, with a very small, careful smile. "I wanted to hear you translate," he said very quietly. "I love your American accent; it's so amusing. Forgive me."

"Of course."

He glanced at her, and she realized that standing this way in the shallow part of the pool it would appear to anyone looking at her as if she were not wearing the bottom part of a bathing suit at all. The water lapped just above the cloth. He glanced at her only for an instant, and then he smiled very slightly again and turned and swam away.

Helen felt strange then, as if she had been discreetly and very personally complimented, although what he had said to her had been impersonal enough. For no reason she suddenly felt rather frightened to be in the water so close to his wife, and she smiled at the woman and then climbed out of the pool. She went into the bathhouse to find a towel.

When she had dressed she paused in front of the mirror, repairing her make-up. She always carried a little vial of perfume in her purse, which she seldom bothered to use at parties, but now she searched for it and, finding it, put some on her neck and hair. It wasn't that there was any reason why she wanted to be particularly attractive tonight. Everybody had already seen her. It was just that . . . she felt like wearing perfume tonight. It made her feel that she was all of a piece—the look and the smell and the sensation inside, all one, all whole together.

CHAPTER *6*

"I wouldn't be so sure she'd show up," Bert said. "Brazilians have a habit of saying yes and then forgetting all about it. Or something important comes up, like their car breaks down." He looked more amused than regretful for her, and even a little smug, Helen thought with annoyance.

They were finishing breakfast, and the room was filled with yellow sunshine. Their living room was so huge that Helen had made one end of it into the dining room. She remembered often that their entire apartment in Riverdale, when she and Bert were first married, was the size of just this Rio living room alone.

"I'm sure she'll come," Helen said. She had had difficulty falling asleep after the party, but this morning instead of being tired she felt refreshed. She tried not to think of what would happen if Leila did not appear to take her to the *favellas*. The day stretched ahead of her, unbearably hot and dull.

"They have a word for it here," Bert said. "*Sumiu*. It means 'disappear.' It was the first word I learned in Brazil. You should learn it too." He stood up and dropped his napkin on the table. "It's an especially useful word in business," he added wryly. "See you tonight." He kissed Helen coolly on the lips, a gesture as casual as a handshake, and went to the door. She trailed after him.

"Goodbye . . ." Somehow she felt for the first time in Brazil as if she were not being left behind but as if her day were just beginning, as it had all those mornings in Westport. She felt like a child who has been driven in an automobile past a tantalizing locked gate every morning for years on his way to a dull day in school, and suddenly has been let out, the car has driven away, the locked gate has opened, and beyond it is revealed a vast, marvelous playground full of other children.

She gathered up all the clothes that Julie and Roger had outgrown, some of her own things, and a few shirts of Bert's that could no longer be mended, making a neat package. When the telephone rang she ran to it before waiting for the maid to answer it and then was almost afraid to lift the receiver.

"Helen?" Leila's voice said. "Do you still want to go with me today?"

"Yes, of course!"

Leila went on, arranging the few details of their meeting, and Helen noticed how differently she spoke on the telephone, as if the telephone intimidated her. She seemed to have more difficulty with her English, and the words came slower.

When Leila arrived, Helen was standing outside on the curb with her bundle. I look like an immigrant, she thought, amused. And I am one. Leila was dressed beautifully, in slacks and a shirt that looked as if her dressmaker had created them for her, her black hair loose, her face perfectly made up. She wore no jewelry, not even a wedding ring. She gave the impression not of a local Lady Bountiful going to gloat over her generosity among the poor but rather of a young girl ready for an adventure. Helen could not help liking her; and the feeling surprised her because usually she was not conscious of actively liking or disliking a new friend until she had known the person for some time. And another strange feeling—she was self-conscious. For a while she sat in the car and listened to Leila talking and could not think of anything to say.

"Have you been anywhere but Rio?" Leila asked. "Have you been to Petropolis? Have you been to Bahia?"

"No. My husband has been to Bahia, or at least to the State of Bahia, not the city. He travels a lot for business."

"You must go to Bahia," Leila said. "It's different, very old. Rio isn't Brazil. I like Rio the best, but it isn't Brazil."

"I feel as though I'll never know anything about this place," Helen said.

"I'll show you," Leila said. She sounded delighted. "I'll introduce you to my friends. Some of them are very intelligent; they know about books, they like to talk about Plato. Do you like Plato?"

"I . . . read him a long time ago," Helen said. "In high school."

"I have just discovered it," Leila said. "I have a very good friend, Carlos Monteiro. Do you remember him? He was at the party last night."

"No . . ."

"He is *very* intelligent. The first time I met him he said to me, 'What do you think of Plato?' I was so happy."

Helen looked at her. Leila was smiling admiringly, as if this Carlos had said to her, "How unique you are!" And perhaps in a way he had.

"I like very much to talk to him," Leila went on. "He's like a philosopher. He says . . ." She went on, elaborately trying to speak only of Carlos' brilliant mind, as if he were merely a friend one shows off, and Helen realized Leila must be in love with him. He was probably the man Leila had run to speak to near the hedge at the party. She was so elaborately intellectual about him, and yet she kept talking about him, as though merely to keep the discussion on him gave her the pleasure she missed when he was not actually with her. Helen wondered if he were Leila's lover. It was odd; a day ago she had not thought about anyone in this way, as lovers or not lovers, but today it was the first thing that came to mind.

"Do the women really have as many affairs as you said last night?" Helen interrupted.

"It's very different here than in America," Leila said. "My friend I spoke to you about—Carlos Monteiro—has been to America many times. He told me that American women have lovers before they are married, and then when they marry they remain faithful, as if marriage were the end. With us, marriage is

100

the beginning of our lives. A woman is never free in Brazil until she leaves her parents and governess and goes to live with her husband."

"How strange," Helen said. "It seems so cynical."

"Cynical? Why?"

"So unemotional. Unsentimental. I suppose our ways seem strange to you."

"But your wives can talk to their husbands about business," Leila said. "A girl never works in Brazil unless she needs the money badly to live, and even then, she always lives at home with her parents. Some of them take lovers before they marry, but those are very poor girls who find a rich man. It's a different kind of love affair. My husband used to come home and speak to me of the office sometimes, but he really thought I was much too ignorant to know anything. I used to tell him what I thought he should do, and he hardly paid attention. But then he would do it, and I always turned out to be a help to him. I think he really never knew that it was I who told him, after all."

They were speeding down the highway now, away from the suburb of Copacabana and toward the city of Rio itself. They passed through a tunnel, and ahead of them Helen could see a mountain covered with so many flimsy little shacks that the grass between them was hardly visible. They turned off the road and began to leave this civilized, asphalt-paved place, and climbed into a world that was leafy, damp, hot, and filled with strange smells and sounds. Below them there were the homes of the rich, and the bay, bright blue in the sun, and the mountains across it; the Sugar Loaf, black and humped like the back of a buffalo, with the thin thread stretching between it and the next mountain, the thread that was the cable that held the traveling car of sightseers who went daily to the top of the Sugar Loaf to gape at the view below. There was the Corcovado: the great white statue of Christ standing on top of the highest mountain with arms outstretched to bless and protect the harbor and the city. The sky was sapphire blue, but today because of the humidity there were clouds ringing the top of the mountain where the Corcovado stood, so it seemed as if the Christ were supernaturally perched on top of the clouds instead of on earth. It looked like a great white peaceful bird in the sky, motionless, wings outspread, hovering and yet permanent.

A black sow walked across the road in front of their car, udders swaying from side to side, her hide caked with mud. She was followed by what seemed like a herd of little shoats, plump and hairy and lively, and the one tiny runt, the extra baby for whom there was no teat to feed, so skinny it did not look like a pig at all, but rather like a large tailless rat. The mother sow was ugliness itself: obese, wrinkled, waddling, worn out, grunting; an elephant of a sow, a monster. The little shoats were rather cute; you could almost imagine one as some child's pet. It was hard to believe that they would soon grow to be as gross and ugly as their mother, and sad to believe that she had once been as pleasant to look at as they. Leila stopped the car to let them pass.

"Look at them," Helen said. "She produces, and feeds, and produces, and feeds, and then she dies. You're supposed to think it's noble, but it makes you think life's grotesque to see something grown that ugly."

"Wait until you see some of the people here," Leila said.

The shacks were hidden behind the trees and foliage, so that traveling along the rutted path in Leila's big American car Helen had the feeling someone might jump out of nowhere and menace them. Despite Leila's casual look, Helen was afraid. Her throat was dry. She did not trust people who were as desperately poor as these; not because they were any worse than anyone else, but because they lived with feelings she could only imagine: hunger, hopelessness, bitterness, envy, desperation. Knowing someone has basic feelings much stronger than your own always makes you fear him, especially if he is a stranger.

Leila drove through an opening between the trees. Now shacks could be seen, made of rough gray boards and corrugated metal and sheets of heavy paper. Leila stopped the car. "We have to walk from now on."

Helen's first instinct was to protest: But won't someone steal the car? But she said nothing, and got out of the car carrying her package, thinking, What a way to do charity, not with an open

102

heart but with the suspicion you're going to be murdered for coming here at all!

"There is one girl I always visit here," Leila said. "I like her."

There was a small clearing with shacks all around it. In the center of the clearing there was a sort of barbecue erection made of stones, with a flat piece of tin laid across the top of it. Smoke was coming out and there were two pots on this makeshift stove with food cooking in them. A middle-aged colored woman dressed in a shapeless white cotton shift that showed traces of once having been blue was standing over the pots, stirring first one and then the other. Several brown chickens scratched and pecked in the dirt around where she stood, and nearby on the ground there was a baby about five months old lying on a soiled towel, kicking its feet in the sunshine. The baby had a dirty pacifier in its mouth. In front of the *favellas* were ropes of clothesline attached to trees, holding a vast amount of clean washing—white sheets and shirts and rich-looking Turkish towels. There were some children's dresses that looked nearly new. Helen remembered the story Mil Burns had told her about what the washerwoman did with the rich people's clothing here in the *favellas* and she wondered if it were true.

"Good morning," Leila called in Portuguese. "Where is Maria?"

"Maria," the woman called out hoarsely. "Maria! Your friend is here." When she opened her mouth Helen saw that she had only four teeth, and these did not meet.

The door of the *favella* nearest them did not open, because there was no door. Maria simply came out of the dark hole. She was a light-skinned mulatto girl of about seventeen, with the full-breasted figure of a woman in her mid-twenties. She was carrying a Negro baby with very dark skin who looked as if he were still too young to be weaned. Her breasts looked it, Helen thought; they were still full of milk. Behind Maria trailed a little girl who was barely old enough to walk; she held on to her mother's skirt tenaciously, and Maria took small, slow steps because she knew that otherwise the child would fall. The little girl was even lighter skinned than Maria, and she had large blue eyes. A few steps behind her came a scrawny little boy of about three, who looked, oddly enough, like an Indian.

"Good morning, Dona Leila," Maria said shyly. She would be a more than pretty girl, Helen thought, if she would ever comb her hair.

"Good morning. This is my friend Dona Helen," Leila said.

"Good morning. How are you?"

"I'm well, thank you," Helen replied in Portuguese. "How are you?"

"Well, thank you. Come into my house," Maria said.

Leila cast Helen a warning look, as if to say, Don't act surprised.

She must think I'm an idiot, Helen thought, a little resentfully and a little ashamed that anything about herself might evoke such an opinion. But as soon as they stepped into the shack Helen realized why Leila had given her the look.

At first the odor almost made her gag. It was the smell of no plumbing, of no ventilation, sour, old, stale, greasy. Most of all, though, it was the smell of a hopeless life that was not even a life at all but an existence. There was one metal table, painted pea green, with a wooden chair that had once been painted white but now was flaking, and a silvery metal chair with a torn red leatherette seat. The beds were mattresses on the floor, soiled and stained, with neither sheets nor blankets. In one corner there was a large, stained, white enamel pot with a handle, the kind used for cooking, but this one was clearly being used for something quite different.

Leila did not seem disgusted. "You have a floor!" she said delightedly. "When did you make it?"

"A friend made it for me," Maria said. She tugged at her earlobe with her thumb and forefinger in the national gesture Brazilians use when they wish to show that something is the ultimate, and she smiled proudly.

"How beautiful!" Leila said. "I brought you some soap and some rags, so now you can keep the floor clean, and the table too." She opened the large canvas shopping bag she was carrying and began to put things on the metal table. "Here is canned milk for the children. You must put water in it to make it more, but you must boil the water first. One can of milk and also one and a half cans of water. Can you remember?"

"One can of milk," Maria repeated, "and also one and a half cans of water."

"She can't read," Leila said to Helen in English.

"Thank you, for the children," Maria said.

"It's nothing. I brought food too. Beef, palmitos, cheese, oranges. And a bag of rice."

"Here are clothes for the children," Helen said. She put her package, unopened, on the table. "Are those three all your children?"

"Yes," Maria said, looking down at the children affectionately. She touched the little boy on the head, lightly and with pride. "Riccardo." Then she touched the older girl, who let go of her mother's skirt and tumbled to the floor, sucking her thumb and staring at Helen. "Maria Lucia." Maria touched the baby's cheek gently. "And Pedro José."

"You are very young," Helen said.

"Seventeen."

She didn't like to ask the prying questions people often felt they deserved answers to in return for giving charity, but curiosity and surprise nudged her on. "How old is your husband?"

"I have never had a husband," Maria said simply.

"I mean . . ." Helen said quickly, "the father of the children. The one who takes care of them." She could see that she was the only one who was in the least embarrassed by all this.

"I take care of them," Maria said. She kissed the baby she held in her arms.

Leila smiled at Maria. "Maria really loves her children," she said to Helen, in Portuguese so Maria would understand too. "Many of the mothers here don't. Some of them even sell their children, to people who have no children. But Maria says she will never give any of hers away."

"Oh, never!" Maria cried. She hugged the baby even tighter and looked down at the other two: the ragged little boy, the girl who had finally struggled to her feet again and was once more holding on to her mother's skirt. Maria smiled then, thinking of something wonderful. "Sometimes," she said, "I dream of going far away. I would like to live on an island, or on a beach where it is very beautiful. Someday I will go away from this place. But if I go, I will always take the children. I dream of my island for the children, too, not only for me. I couldn't be happy if I didn't take my children with me. I like them."

"Before you have any more children you must get married," Leila said. "If you love the children. You cannot take care of more than these three unless you have a man to help you."

"Oh . . . I know," Maria said obediently. "I will try."

"You're beautiful," Leila said. "I'm sure many men would like to marry you."

Maria looked embarrassed. "No, not so beautiful."

"Yes you are," Leila said. "You are much more beautiful than any of the other women here. Really. I will tell you something important and you must think about it and you must listen to me. You must not go down to the beach at night with a man any more, until you marry. If you make love with a man you are going to have another child. You mustn't have another child until you marry; you're too young; it's too difficult for you to care for them alone. And besides," she added, almost as a useless afterthought, "it is immoral. It is a sin."

"I know," Maria said. She gave a little smile, wistful and almost hopeful. "Sometimes I work so hard trying to make clothes for the children, trying to wash, trying to find food. And I'm so tired. Riccardo cries for a banana, and I feel full of hate and sadness because I have no money to buy him a banana. Not even one banana. I had only this one dress to wear until you gave me more. I never had anything, and the children never had anything, and I was so unhappy I wanted to die. Often I still feel that way. But then I go to walk on the beach at night with a boy, and I look at the sea all shiny with moonlight. We walk in the little water on the sand and we look at the stars. The stars are so beautiful on the beach. When the moon is full and the sand is wet you can see your shadow on the sand. It makes me happy. Then I feel that I don't want to die. If I go to a beach with a boy and do those things that make more children it is only because those are the only beautiful things in my life."

Neither Leila nor Helen answered for a moment. Helen felt touched. It was true, what this girl said, and there was little they could do about it. Helen had seldom, if ever, heard a stranger speak so frankly and so simply to her, and as she had that first evening when Leila had told her of the failure of her marriage, Helen felt as if she had been given a gift. She had grown used to civilized hypocrisy in the name of manners, and evasion and self-deception in the name of dignity. Even now, when it had become fashionable to pretend to a brash self-analysis and public declaration of one's neuroses, these were only another form of charm, charmless though they often turned out to be.

"It's true," Helen said in English. "It's true."

"There is only one thing to do, then," Leila said to Maria. "Next week when we come here again I will bring you something. You will see."

Maria frowned, not quite sure whether she was being chastised or given another present. "What will you bring me?"

"Something to prevent children," Leila said. She shook hands with Maria. "Goodbye. Until later."

"Goodbye," Maria said. "Thank you very much."

"It's nothing."

"Goodbye," Helen said. Maria held out her hand, and Helen took it, feeling with surprise how rough it was for a girl of that age.

"Thank you very much," Maria said.

"It's nothing."

When they reached the open air again Helen felt as if she had been trying to hold her breath for ten minutes. She gulped in the questionably fresh air. Even the hot sunshine seemed refreshing after the closeness of Maria's shack. Maria trailed them halfway to the car. "Goodbye," she called, waving, still holding the baby in one arm. "Come back soon."

"If we want to prevent more children," Leila said to Helen in English, "we had better come back *very* soon." She laughed and put the car into gear.

"I never realized these people live this way," Helen said. "What did you mean when you said some of them actually sell their children?"

"They sell them," Leila said.

"But that's barbaric!"

"It is what they do."

"I don't even want to think about it."

"She is a good girl, Maria," Leila said. "And I think she's intelligent, too. Did you hear the way she spoke? It was like a kind of poetry."

"I'm glad we came," Helen said.

"How many children do you have?"

"Two. A boy and a girl."

"I have four. Your parents are living?"

"Yes."

"And they live in the United States?"

"Yes. In New York."

"My mother is a noon," Leila said.

"A what?"

"A noon. In the most cloistered convent in the world."

"You mean a nun!"

"Ah, yes. A nun? You must tell me when I pronounce these words wrong."

"I don't understand . . ." Helen said. "How can a woman with children become a nun?"

Leila looked straight ahead, through the windshield. "Her children were all grown," she said evenly. "They did not need her any more."

Helen thought back and remembered that once in the newspaper she had read about an American woman who had entered a convent after her husband had died, after obtaining some sort of special dispensation. She did not remember whether or not this woman had had children. "Your father is dead?"

"A long time ago."

They had nearly descended the mountain now and were able to drive faster. Helen looked out the window and saw in the distance the blue of Guanabara Bay and the small bright specks on

108

it that were the yachts of the rich. From their *favellas* the people who were the poorest in all Brazil could look down and see the yachts too, and the bay, and the view that was the best in all of Rio. How much in Brazil was a paradox! Even this girl beside her, driving surely down the rough mountain road; the girl whose mother was a nun, and who did not seem to think it was particularly strange that the daughter of a nun was going to teach birth control to a girl in the *favellas*.

"If you like," Leila said, "We can go to the Iate Clube for lunch."

"I'd like that very much." How strange it all is, Helen thought, how strange.

At the Iate Clube Leila parked her car under the trees in the parking lot and they walked to the terrace in front of the clubhouse that overlooked the water. There were palm trees set in the cement of the terrace, and white wooden tables, most of them empty. At the landing there were several speed boats of various sizes, and many larger yachts, and farther out in the bay were some huge yachts requiring smaller craft to get to them, and one enormous four-masted schooner. There were mountains around the harbor, and then the open water beyond, with islands just visible in the distance, grayish in the heat haze. Leila chose a table under a palm tree, a table that would have comfortably seated eight, and the two of them sat at it.

"This is one of the places where you come if you don't want to be seen by anyone," Leila said with a great smile. "If you are having a flirt with someone else's husband. . . . You see, no one will tell his wife because they will also be afraid that someone will tell *their* wives. How discreet people can be when they also have something to hide!"

"My lord," Helen said, "A married man's restaurant. But I don't see why the wives don't come down here en masse to find out if their husbands are 'flirting' with someone."

"The wives like very much to play cards in the afternoon," Leila said. "And they go to the hairdresser, and the dressmaker. On the weekends the families come here. It is very nice. The husbands and wives and all the children, all together very sweetly."

"I guess American wives are more aggressive when they think they're being deceived."

"Brazilian women are very jealous," said Leila. She saw a waiter nearby and hissed for him, between her teeth, like someone calling a cat. He seemed to take this form of appeal completely for granted and sauntered over smiling, bringing two menus. "But then," Leila added seriously, "I suppose every person has his own way of making trouble when he has been hurt."

It was nearly four o'clock when they finished lunch and drove slowly back to Copacabana. Leila let Helen off in front of her apartment building, after they had arranged to telephone each other in a few days and meet again for lunch. Helen watched Leila drive off alone, sitting up very straight behind the wheel, her black hair streaming down to her shoulders, completely contrary to the style of the other Brazilian wives but somehow very chic, and Helen felt sorry for her. She could not decide yet whether the main facet of Leila's character was the lusty good humor that seemed to bubble up over all the problems life had given her, or whether the smiles and glittering eyes were only a well-put-on veneer and the deep part of her was the sadness. Leila too was a paradox to her, and whether it was because she was a foreigner or a confused and complicated person, Helen could not decide. She knew, of course, that even though Leila spoke in English her thoughts were in Portuguese, but it was easy for a sheltered person like herself who had never before left home to assume through some strange mis-logic that Leila's thoughts would be American thoughts translated into Portuguese, instead of something vastly different.

That evening when the sun had gone down and the sky was black and filled with the starry outlines of constellations, Helen looked out of their living-room window at the beach. They had finished supper and the children were in bed. Perhaps that night not long ago when she had seen the couples making love on the beach, perhaps one of the girls might have been Maria. Tonight on the beach Helen saw a lighted candle propped up in the sand, and farther on the beach another, and another, until they made a long wavering line of lighted candles flickering all along the crescent of the beach in the dark. They were Macumba candles, she knew, the signals that somewhere up in the hills there would be strange religious rites tonight. Blood would be shed, even if it was only the blood of a living rooster, and the native believers would be gripped by strange powers and babble in a strange tongue. Some people said Macumba was only for tourists, suckers. And some believed in the black magic so strongly that they would not even whisper the dread word *Macumba*. But most people said there were two kinds of rites: the special flamboyant ones to impress gullible tourists, and the other ones, the secret ones, held in places that few people knew and wilder by far than the ones that were staged for show. The place on the mountain where Helen had been that morning was near one of the places where Macumbas were held, that she knew, and she was sure that many of the people in the *favellas* where she had been were believers and participants. Perhaps that middle-aged woman who had been stirring the pots of food. Perhaps even Maria, whose children would be wearing Roger's and Julie's clothes. Her own children's little clothes . . . That thought somehow made her feel closer than she wanted to be to the weird world of those people on the dark mountain, and Helen drew away from the window into her lighted family room, still seeing the candle lights flickering down there on the beach, and even after she no longer looked at them still knowing they were there.

Tonight she would be in her apartment, safe with her husband and children, the curtains drawn. Those worshipers on the mountain should only seem like a stage setting to her, for she was an outsider, almost a tourist. But already she had made a friend and seen a world she had never seen before. And in two weeks, after New Year's Day, Bert would fly to the jungle, to a world that was as remote and different from Rio as it was from those pagans on the mountainside. She knew there was absolutely no reason to feel he had deserted her, and yet this time, unreasonably and almost fearfully, she did not want to be alone with herself in Rio.

CHAPTER 7

On New Year's Eve, the *Revillon,* Mil and Phil Burns went to
an open house at the apartment of some American friends, where
everyone crowded onto the small balcony, drank champagne, consumed a cold ham and a cold turkey, and stayed up until three
o'clock in the morning. Margie and Neil Davidow and Helen and
Bert Sinclair also went to this open house, but they left shortly
after midnight for another party to which they had been invited,
half an hour's drive away, where everyone crowded onto the
small balcony, drank champagne, consumed a cold ham and a
cold turkey, and stayed up until three o'clock in the morning.
Leila Silva e Costa spent the *Revillon* at a night club with a married couple who were close friends of hers and who invited her
to come along with them because they thought she might be
lonely. She knew nearly everyone in the night club and she danced
with the husbands of various friends until seven o'clock in the
morning. On New Year's Day everyone slept until afternoon, and
then Helen and Bert took their children to an outdoor *chur-
rascaria* for lunch. Margie and Neil went to the beach. Leila slept
until six o'clock in the evening, being slightly hung-over from
drinking champagne, although she had not had very much.
Alcohol does not agree with Brazilian women, because of a national weakness of the liver. Altogether, everyone was relieved that
New Year's Eve was over and done with for another year, and
by the following day it was altogether forgotten. Work went on

as usual, and Bert Sinclair went off to a topaz mine in Rio Grande do Sul, where the darkest, hardest, most valuable gem topazes are found.

It was very hot in Rio. In their stifling little apartments dressmakers were busy stitching sequins and feathers and beads and pieces of fur onto elaborate costumes which would be worn at Carnival a month and a half later, their windows wide open to admit whatever slight breeze there was during the day. Great false birds' heads with varicolored plumage, empty bodies of golden dragons, limp black cloth faces of Blackamoors, lay on the wooden floor at their feet, like the aftermath of some monstrous carnage. Later these costumes and masks would come to life and parade across a floodlighted ramp high above the street to the applause and cries of street crowds who had waited for hours to see them.

Meanwhile it was hot, and every day the beaches were crowded from early morning until evening. In Copacabana someone drowned in the undertow nearly every day, and rich tourists emerging onto their balconies for breakfast these hot mornings might turn away squeamishly from the sight of a crowd gathered below on the beach—around something, and you always knew what—and decide to have breakfast inside the room after all.

The children were on summer vacation from school. Wives, if they could afford it, went up into the mountains with their children for the months of most intense heat, to Petropolis, Itiapava, Cidade d'Ouro, Terezopolis; or to the windy peninsula of Cabo Frio and Buzios. The husbands were summer bachelors, working in the city during the week and joining their families on weekends. In Portuguese summer bachelors are called *cigarras* if they enjoy themselves, because the *cigarra* is the locust who sings all summer. On weekday nights during the hot summer the nightclubs were filled with these *cigarras*, some of them dancing with girls, others alone table-hopping, enjoying their temporary freedom discreetly—in public at least.

Helen Sinclair wondered if there was a female version of *cigarra*, for a wife whose husband had gone off and left her in Copacabana. She was a poor sort of *cigarra*, she thought, because

113

she did not have the least inclination to go out and enjoy herself and sing, even if she had known how to go about doing it. She telephoned Mil Burns.

"Bert's away for five days. Last night there were Macumba candles on the beach again. They make me so nervous. I want to go to a Macumba once and for all and satisfy my curiosity. Do you think Phil would take us?"

"Ha," Mil said dryly. "You want to go to a Macumba? Good luck."

"Won't you come?"

"For what?" Mil said. "They're a lot of hokum. Candles and old Lindoya bottles. I can look into my garbage pail and see old Lindoya bottles, I don't have to drag myself to God knows where."

Margie had seen several Macumbas, one of which she was sure had been the real thing. "They made a circle of gunpowder," she told Helen. "Then they lighted it and the whole thing exploded into the most beautiful colors. Neil took pictures."

"Let's go," Helen said. "If I wait for my husband I'll never see one."

"Oh, I really don't want to see *another*," Margie said.

"Why? Is it boring?"

"Oh, no. You'll see why . . ."

"I'll never see why at this rate. It's so frustrating to be in a fascinating place like Rio and then never go anywhere or see anything."

In desperation Helen called Leila, although she knew Leila would be the last person to want to go somewhere like that.

"Of course I'll take you to a Macumba," Leila said. "I will bring some of my friends. I have spoken to them very much about you. I want you to meet them. We can go this week. There are two kinds of Macumba, the one for good spirits and the one for bad. I would rather go to the good one. But if you are in a hurry we can go to the one for Black Magic, because it is the one coming next. It doesn't really matter."

"Black Magic? They call up evil spirits?"

"People go there to wish bad things to people they do not like.

114

In a White Magic Macumba they pray for health and cures and good things. But we can go to the bad one. You don't have to be afraid."

"I'm not afraid," Helen said. "I mean, why should I be?"

But when she found herself at the foot of a steep flight of temporary steps that had been cut into the side of the mountain, she was afraid. It was a very dark night, two days after her telephone conversation with Leila. The Macumba candles had been lighted on the beach, and at ten o'clock she and Leila and a Brazilian couple who were old friends of Leila's drove in Leila's car up into the hills. At a crossroad there was a square of lighted candles set into empty bottles in the roadway. They turned there, and continued to climb, until they saw another lighted signal flickering in the dark. The trees were so leafy and thick above them that Helen could not see the stars. She told herself this was where the *favellas* were, that Maria probably lived here, but she could not help feeling it was all new and frightening, a place that would vanish tomorrow. From somewhere on top of the mountain they began to hear, then, the sound of voices in a singsong chant, very softly at first because they were far away, and then louder. Leila parked the car beside the mountain and they got out.

A crude wooden hand railing had been put up beside the flight of steps. It was almost impossible to see anything in the light of the flares that were set at the foot of the steps and then high at the top. No one spoke. The sound of chanting rose and fell, hypnotically, and somewhere a woman screamed as if she were carried away by religious ecstasy. In the darkness Helen could just make out the outline of another parked car, and somehow its ordinariness reassured her. It didn't seem as if any of the participants up there on the mountain drove a car; she was sure the car belonged to tourists, curious, ordinary people, perhaps even with cameras and flashbulbs.

"They are here," Leila said to her friends.

They walked to the other parked car, and standing beside it were the dark silhouettes of two men. "How are you? How are you?" came the whispers in the darkness, subdued. "This is my friend Helen Sinclair," Leila said in English. She introduced the two men in whispers; Sergio something and José something-else, and then the six of them filed up the steps.

Helen tried not to tug Leila's skirt as she followed her up the treacherous path, but she knew she was afraid. She was sorry they had come at all. It was a premonition, perhaps, or simply foolish nervousness; but she wished they had not come. There was something ominous in the air tonight, a feeling of change, a feeling of spirits released, that she had never known before, and it frightened her. She did not even know if the Brazilian friends of Leila's who filed ahead and behind her up these primitive steps were frightened too, or believing, or unbelieving and amused, or even prepared to be bored. Helen hoped they were bored; it would reassure her.

"I'm afraid," she whispered to Leila.

"So am I," Leila whispered back. She laughed, a low, throaty sound in the black night. "I am always afraid when I come to one of these."

At the top of the steps there was a wire gate, locked, and a flare set on top of a pole. In the distance Helen could see white-robed figures gathered in a huge circle, chanting and singing in unison. They waited for someone within to come to open the gate. "Psst!" one of Leila's friends called. Within the enclosure a very dark-skinned, thin man dressed in a pair of summer trousers and shirt walked over to open the gate.

In the light of the flare Helen turned for an instant to glance at the faces of the two other men who had met them beside the car. One of them was a pleasant-looking middle-aged man with a mustache. The other she had seen before—he was the man who had spoken to her in the swimming pool that other night at the Brazilian party. When she looked at him he recognized her in the flickering light and smiled at her. She remembered that wolfine face very clearly then, and she smiled back. Suddenly she was annoyed at herself for never being able to remember Brazilian names, and she resolved to learn and remember his if she had to repeat it to herself all night.

"What's your name?" she whispered to him.

"Sergio." He smiled at her again then, very slightly, and whispered very slowly and very clearly, "Sergio Leite Braga."

"Sergio Leite Braga," Helen repeated in a whisper, and she wondered if he were laughing at her. In the flickering half-light of the flares he seemed much more handsome than she would have remembered, his features finely chiseled in the light and darkness, not altogether human, like a satyr that had sprung out of this hillside.

"You must have been to many Macumbas before," she whispered.

"Never," he said.

She walked through the opened gate ahead of him, and the man who seemed to be the guide and gatekeeper motioned that all the men had to stand on one side of a partition and all the women on the other. Helen wondered whether this was because of religious reasons, or whether it might be to avert some kind of orgy. She followed Leila and the other woman and stationed herself with them on the women's side, next to the partition, slightly separated from the other women who were already there. There was a crude bleacher set up, with all the space on the wooden planks already taken by women who had arrived much earlier than they had. Some of them had spread newspapers on the boards before they sat, and most of them were dressed up as for a party or for church. Most of them were Negroes. A woman stood beside the fence with a sleeping baby in her arms, and nearby was another woman with a little girl about three years old who was already whimpering from tiredness. There was a huge, oblong clearing ahead of them, surrounded by a low wooden and wire fence. The clearing was lighted by hundreds of small candles set at intervals along the ground. There was no grass, only smooth, trodden earth. At the far end of this clearing there was a sort of large shrine containing brightly colored plaster figures of saints, and illuminated by so many candles that it was as bright as day. Helen recognized Saint George, in armor and a cape, carrying a long sword and riding a plaster horse. There were several smaller figures of Saint George too, and other saints whom she did not recognize. The entire gaudy display, with its pagan

117

art set upon shelves, reminded her incongruously of a booth of prizes at a country fair.

"Saint George," Leila whispered in her ear. "Patron saint of this cult."

"Of Macumba?"

"Shh!" Leila looked around to be sure no one had overheard. "Never say that word here. It frightens them. And whatever happens, do not laugh. If you laugh, they might kill you."

Helen had had no previous inclination to laugh, but now, knowing it was not only forbidden but dangerous, she had to try not to giggle nervously as if the laughter were some horrible compulsion that was going to burst free from her throat and doom her. There was really nothing even slightly funny here at all. Gathered at the side of the clearing was a group of about fifty colored women, most of them young, all of them dressed in flowing white robes, like a choir, and singing the sweet, hypnotic chant whose words were so old and changed by usage that Helen could not make them out. The women sang the same lines over and over, in a melody both savage and tenderly sweet, their voices high and innocent, like the voices of children. The song seemed to draw the listener to them, so that the longer you listened the more you wanted to sing it too although you did not know the words. Helen opened her lips and felt herself trying to sing, slightly self-conscious and not really caring, swaying a little to the rhythm and straining to catch any words that would be familiar to her so she could repeat them.

She could sense restlessness in the crowd. Something was about to happen, or should have already happened and had not. It was not the kind of restlessness you sense in a theater when the curtain is delayed, but rather a sensation of uneasiness, of concern. The choir of white-robed women continued to sing, louder now and even more persuasively.

A tall Negro man walked into the center of the clearing, wearing a costume that was a combination of that of a priest and a medicine man. His white robes and feathers flapped behind him. In his hand he held a stick which seemed to have been dipped in white paint or liquid chalk. An assistant walked behind him

118

carrying a bottle filled with this white fluid. The medicine man–priest began to draw a series of signs on the earth: circles, lines, a long cross. Every now and then he dipped the end of the stick into the white fluid. It reminded Helen of the stuff Bert used to use when he painted white lines on a freshly rolled tennis court on summer mornings. Those days seemed so foreign now that she felt as though she were the only person in this group who even knew such things existed. The choir of women kept on singing, more softly now.

The medicine man–priest lifted his head and howled out a line of some strange language. "Yes, yes," the women intoned. He stooped to draw more signs on the earth and then raised his head and spoke again, loudly, in a harsh voice. "Yes, yes," agreed the women. They continued to sing. In the distance, from a *favella* in the darkness, a rooster crowed. Everyone applauded. Evidently this was one of the signs they had been waiting for.

There was a sense of growing restlessness. Again the rooster crowed, a cry so loud and roosterlike that Helen wondered for a moment if it were artificial. The people applauded again. How could they make a rooster crow in the middle of the night? It made her skin feel cold. The women continued to sing, sweetly, monotonously, hypnotically. The rooster crowed again, but this time his cry was so loud and sharp that Helen realized how they had made him crow. She didn't want to think about it. She hoped they were only tweaking his feathers, not torturing him. She remembered then that in a Macumba blood had to be shed, and that often in these modern days it was only the blood of a living fowl, although sometimes it turned out to be human.

Whenever the breeze turned there was a stench from the open ditches which passed for plumbing here in the *favellas*. The ground was damp under her feet and she scarcely dared move in the dark. She glanced at the partition that separated the men from the women. She could see the raised heads of Brazilians with wide-open, glittering eyes watching intensely. No one turned to look at her. She realized that right now none of these people seemed to have any sex, male or female, but only the one common urge: to call up the spirits of Black Magic here on the dark mountaintop and hear the spirits speak through their own bodies.

The medicine man–priest walked around the periphery of the clearing now, looking at the bystanders. He stopped near to Helen and pointed with his hand to a man. The man came forward, through the opening in the fence, and walked into the clearing. He was wearing faded cotton clothes, like a worker, and he was barefoot.

Helen felt Leila's cold fingers on her arm. "Oh, I thought for a moment he was going to choose me!" Leila breathed, her eyes wide with fear.

"I wouldn't go," Helen whispered.

"You *have* to go."

The man who had been chosen hopped around the clearing in an awkward, stiff dance. Everyone watched him closely, in silence, except the white-robed singers, who continued their soft chanting. Suddenly he clutched his heart, his eyes rolled back in his head, his head fell back, and he emitted a guttural grunt as if he were choking. He stiffened, his hands at his sides, the fingers bent stiffly like the fingers of someone in an epileptic fit, and he crashed down to the ground, stiff and straight, not even putting out his arms to break his fall at the last second. There was a gasp from the crowd. For a few moments the fallen man did not move, and then he stirred weakly and began to writhe. Two men ran into the clearing from the crowd and helped him to stand and then almost carried him away. There was blood on his head and saliva coming out of his mouth.

The medicine man–priest looked displeased. He waved his stick and drew more signs on the earth. The assistant brought lighted candles and set them at various points on the white drawing. There was an obvious air of unease in the crowd now, and a stirring and whispering, as if something had gone wrong. A few feet behind where Helen and Leila were standing there was a wooden plank shack with an open front and a counter, like a sort of snack bar. The two men who had escorted the stricken man away reappeared and went to this shack, where a girl gave them tin cups of coffee. They whispered concernedly to the girl and she shook her head. Now several other people from the crowd were drifting up to the shack to refresh themselves, all of them whispering and looking worried. The girl who was giving out coffee and some liquid that looked like *cachaça* seemed so gentle and pretty that Helen took up courage to speak to her.

"What is it?" she asked softly. "What has happened?"

"It is bad," the girl whispered back. "That man was not supposed to fall that way. He disobeyed. The priest gave him a task which he did not do."

"What will happen now?"

The girl shook her head. She seemed reluctant, or frightened. "I don't know. They haven't decided. He will have to pay some kind of penance or else the spirits will not speak tonight. Perhaps he will be whipped." She shook her head again. "It is bad."

Oh, no, Helen thought. I don't want to stay here to see someone being beaten or tortured. I want to get out of here.

The medicine man–priest was in consultation with his assistant. More of the onlookers were walking about now, as calmly as if they were taking an intermission. Helen could not understand how they could be so calm; yet, it was not really calmness but resignation. They seemed to accept that something violent was going to have to happen before the spirits of Black Magic would be appeased, and until that form of violence was decided upon or showed itself spontaneously they were going to drink sugarcane alcohol and wait.

After a few minutes they began to go back to their seats. The singing began to grow louder. The man who had fallen went back into the clearing. He wore a small white bandage on the side of his head where he had been hurt by his fall. He began to hop, carefully and solemnly, around the outline of the white chalk drawing. Perhaps, Helen thought hopefully, they are giving him another chance. She shivered.

A large, stout old woman, dressed in a voluminous white sheet and puffing on a cigar, walked out of the crowd then and into the clearing. She hopped up and down with surprising energy despite her huge bulk, puffing intermittently on the cigar and letting forth a stream of unintelligible words. Everyone seemed pleased to see her doing this and watched her seriously and admiringly. The fat woman began to whirl. She whirled around and around, digging up the dirt with her bare toes like a pile driver, the bits of earth spraying out around her feet, her arms held stiffly at her sides, her fingers crooked like the claws of an arthritic. Then she fell to the ground and writhed there, babbling the unknown tongue, clawing at the earth with her stiffened fingers. Finally she lay still, her eyes rolled back so only their white showed. She was left to lie there where she had fallen.

A thin woman then followed her, and a very old man, both of them hopping and whirling independently, as if no one were watching them but the spirit that had overtaken their jerking bodies. *Ahhh* . . . came a sound from the crowd, a sound of awe and satisfaction. The spirits of Macumba had been called up; the spirits were here. The thin woman fell into a crouch, her head rubbing the dirt, her arms and legs curled together as if she were a sick animal. The old man tripped and sprawled awkwardly, and then tried weakly to get to his feet. A man entered the clearing from the crowd to help him, and when he was standing again the old man tried again to do this possessed dance, although he was so weak he could hardly move.

There was a young girl's frightened scream. From the bleachers a girl who could not have been more than sixteen tore herself away from the restraining hands of her friends and tried to crawl under the fence to get into the clearing. She hit her head on the wooden crossbar, so loudly that Helen could hear the crack, but she did not seem to feel it. Blood was pouring down her cheek from a cut above her eye, and the eye was beginning to close, but she did not seem to feel that either, and she danced and hopped until she fainted. The girl who had screamed began to sob.

"She is my sister!" the weeping girl cried out. "She is my sister! Someone help her!" She broke away from the others and jumped over the fence.

There were several people bending over the fallen girl, and two of them lifted her and carried her out of the clearing. Her sister followed, crying, holding on to the unconscious girl as

122

though her touch might save her. The blood she had left where she fell was beginning to seep into the bare earth.

People were beginning to come forward now as supplicants to the altar, to ask for favors. Kill my enemy, make my enemy sicken and die. My husband beats me; put a curse on him. Kill my wife, because I have found a better woman. Break my neighbor's legs; he has stolen from me. Requests in ominous whispers to the dark spirit, from hearts so full of superstition, resentment, and frustration that the force of these emotions alone filled the air like the power of a presence. It was not the black spirit of evil these people were calling upon, but the dark fears within themselves. Standing behind the fence, staring at the tiny winking candle flames, listening to the song that was as old and persuasive as the sound of the tides of the sea, Helen began to tremble.

I want, the people whispered to the dark spirit. I need, I need, I need. Take me away, into the sea, into the sky, into the heart of the candle flame. Give me a new life. Help me. . . . The night breeze wafted the ugly odors of poverty and filth, the rooster screamed from a dark shack, and the strange, sweetish cigar smoke hovered on the air, filled with fever dreams. Helen felt her body beginning to sway with the music.

Her feet moved, first only a tapping in time to the rhythm of the song, then forward. She felt herself inching toward the fence and she was powerless to stop. The clearing was almost filled now with people hopping and writhing, crying out in the sounds they had kept locked within their hearts, tortured, guttural sounds, the voice of the Macumba magic. A very old woman, bent over with arthritis, crept into the clearing and suddenly straightened up with a shrill cry of triumph. She fell to the ground then and crawled, her arms outstretched and fingers clawing ahead of her, oblivious of the dirt that covered her dress, her chin, even her mouth, as she strove to reach closer to the call of the spirit.

Oh, God, Helen thought, I don't want to be old like that and lost. I want . . . I want . . . She felt delirious. She wasn't sure what it was, but she knew that something had already been lost to her, and had been lost for a long, long time, stolen, unattainable. Loneliness filled her and she felt such an emptiness that it seemed as if there were no body inside her skin at all. She held out her arms and her empty hands, not knowing for what, moving forward and shivering in the warm night breeze.

She brushed by the partition as she moved forward and she felt a hand take hold of her shoulder, so lightly it might not have touched her at all. She stopped and turned her head. Sergio Leite Braga was standing against the men's side of the partition, reaching out with his hand, his face very white in the candlelight.

"Let's get out of here," he whispered in English. She realized then that his hand was cold, and he looked as if he were going to be sick.

"I . . . don't know," she whispered.

"I'm leaving for a while," Sergio said. His tone was forcedly casual, but he spoke so quickly she knew he would not give her time to decide. She suddenly felt that if he were to leave now he would melt back into the black, leafy mountainside and she would never meet him again.

She went quickly to Leila and touched her. "I'm going to wait in the car." She pushed past the others again, past the men's area, and out to the gate which led to the dark steps.

He was standing there waiting for her, and when he saw it was she he turned without a word and opened the gate. Two natives were standing there who had arrived too late to be allowed in. They were standing patiently and resignedly, leaning against the fence, and one of them carried a bottle of *cachaça*. They looked as though they would be willing to wait there all night.

Helen had to hold on to the railing and look carefully at the ground to keep her footing. When they had gone a few steps Sergio looked back to see if she were still there, like a man first coming back to consciousness, and then he slowed his pace so she could follow close behind him. They could hear the sounds of the singing and outcries all the way down the hill.

The air seemed very clear at the bottom of the hill, and the voices and lights were so far away that now they seemed only a bad dream which one could view with tolerance and no fear. But Helen could not stop trembling. She did not feel ill; she simply felt as if something within her had been exposed and was exposed still, throbbing and vulnerable. She did not know what to do to close it up and protect it again, so she waited and trembled.

Sergio took her hand, and his hand was no longer cold. "Do you feel all right now?" he asked.

She shook her head. "I feel so strange. I don't know what's the matter with me."

"I do too. I had to get out of there."

They began to walk slowly, hand in hand, toward his car. Although Helen had heard gruesome stories about what happened to people who ventured into the *favella* district alone at this hour of night, now she did not feel in the least afraid. She felt as though every evil thing which might happen was safely occupied in that orgy on the mountaintop. The plateau where they were was still high; through the trees she could see the far-away glitter of the city. She had a sense of height and isolation, but now not loneliness.

"I need a drink," Sergio said. "I think that would help."

"Do you feel strange?"

"Very. You know, my friends were smiling as if it were all a big joke. They didn't feel anything. But I felt something super-natural. I don't know what it was. I knew I had to get out of there, and when I looked at you I knew you did too."

"I felt as if I were going to join them in two minutes," Helen said. It didn't seem ridiculous to say that, even now; she was still too close to it. "I wonder why."

"Some people are more psychic than others," Sergio said. "It's a kind of extrasensory perception. How is it that one person can tell what another is thinking, when no one else senses a thing? We felt it, and our friends didn't."

"I was wondering if there was something in those cigars those people were smoking," Helen said.

"We weren't."

"No."

He opened the door of his car for her and helped her in. It was a small Brazilian-make car, something like a Volkswagen. "Can we leave?" he asked.

"We should tell them. . . ."

"They'll know we left. They have the other car."

"Yes," she said.

"Let's get a drink."

She nodded, and he started the car. As they drove slowly down the dark, bumpy road she felt herself beginning to relax. She thought of a gin and tonic and the warmth it would bring her. It occurred to her briefly to invite him to come home with her for a drink, but then she realized immediately that whoever saw them would think he was going to be her lover, and worse *he* would probably think so too. The thought of home was only an instinctive reflex; she did not really want to go home at all. The apartment seemed so foreign, so different and far away, it was as if by appearing in her own living room with her newly awakened emotions she would be making an entrance into someone's parlor covered with blood from an automobile accident.

They drove into Copacabana and he parked the car in front of a very small, air-conditioned *boâte*. There was only one other couple in the room, sitting in a dark corner, and on a tiny band-stand a man sat on a stool playing the guitar, with his eyes closed. There was a minuscule dance floor, and the walls behind the booths were made of illuminated glass with live fish swimming behind them.

Sergio ordered drinks, and Helen drank hers so quickly she scarcely had time to feel it sting as it went down. She felt the warmth then, and she also felt lightheaded. "I may live," she said.

"I hope so."

"Are you a Brazilian?" she asked abruptly.

"Of course. My father and grandfather and great-grandfather too. Why?"

"I don't know," she said, slightly embarrassed. She did know why she had asked, but she was ashamed to explain it. She had wondered because he seemed so familiar and like herself, so perceptive of whatever was in her, that she had the provincial inclination to reject anything that was foreign in him because that meant a mystery. "Because . . . you've never been to a Macumba before," she lied. "You said so."

"It's true."

"What made you come to this one, finally?"

"I don't think I'd better tell you," he said. "You won't believe me."

"Of course I'll believe you."

"I went there because I knew you were going to be there, and I wanted to see you again."

"You're right; I really don't believe you," Helen said. She laughed. "*Me?* After five seconds in a swimming pool?"

Sergio looked at her intently. It was not the way most people look at other people, because the other people are within their range of vision, but as if he were really looking at *her;* she almost saw herself reflected in his eyes. "Listen," he said slowly. For the first time she heard the very faint trace of a Portuguese accent. "After five seconds in the swimming pool, as you put it, would you have wanted to see me again? If some good friend had told you I was going to be some place tonight and you knew you would see me, would you have wanted to be there? Think," he said slowly. "I want you to tell me the truth."

"I never thought about it," Helen said.

"Think about it now," he said gently. His voice was soft but matter-of-fact, as if there was nothing preposterous in this question at all. "Sergio Leite Braga is going to be at the Macumba tonight. We are all going together. Would you like . . . do you want . . . to see him?"

She looked at her locked hands, remembering back to that moment when she had recognized him again; and then she looked at him and she felt that same small shock of recognition, but oddly intensified now. If someone were to ask her his question now she knew she would answer yes, or more likely she would not answer anything but she would be there. She shook her head. "It's too late to have an abstract discussion," she said. "I have to go home. I have some things to do, and my children—I want to be sure they're all right."

He smiled at her, but there was neither amusement nor taunt in it. He seemed vulnerable for a moment, and that surprised her, and then it did not surprise her. "And yourself?" he said softly. "Are *you* all right?"

"I? Of course."

"You're beautiful and charming and sweet. These are things that make other people happy. They aren't the things that make you happy."

"Is anybody really *that* happy?" Helen said. The vehemence of her own voice surprised her. Why, she sounded like Mil Burns, or even like Margie.

"What a sad and terrible question," Sergio Leite Braga said. He gestured for the waiter.

She did not speak to him until they were in the car. She felt again, as she had during the nightmarelike Macumba rites, like crying out, *Help me!* But this time she was really frightened, for she knew that if she ever said anything to hint at this she would be lost, and her family, and Bert, and everything she believed in. And yet, what exactly did she believe in? She remembered how many times in the past few years she had needed to ask Bert, Do you love me? Do you *really* love me still? And she had always felt abashed and even a little afraid when she asked him, for fear he would think she was childish, for fear he might laugh, for fear he might answer, I . . . don't know, Helen.

She had the obscure feeling that she had to test Sergio in some way, ask him some question that really did not mean what it said, some question he could answer in guarded words because he would know what she really meant. It would mean *Help me*, but it would be a harmless question, foolish perhaps but not dangerous, and she would never have to utter the dreadful words that would reveal herself to him and irrevocably, to herself. She glanced out the window at the streetcar tracks, and then turned her head swiftly to look at him, almost is if she expected to catch him looking at her with perfidy or lust or guile.

"You think I'm beautiful," she said.

"You *are* beautiful." He looked at her with that little smile. "I know it."

128

"Thank you," she said lightly. She turned away to look out the window again. She must have been drunk, she thought, because for no reason her eyes were full of tears.

"It's not midnight yet," Sergio said. "I want to show you something. Then I'll take you home."

She did not answer, and he turned the car and drove out toward the district of Laranjeiras, the place of orange groves. The streets were narrow and cobblestoned here and the houses were very large and old and ornate, the iron fences that surrounded them giving glimpses of palm trees and marble statues overgrown to their knees in tall grass. It was dark and still; everyone seemed to be sleeping within these dark mansions, or dead and gone into the past. He drove through a passageway at the end of an alley, and they were in a small courtyard, enclosed on three sides by silent houses—mansions, really—that seemed to be showing their backs. The courtyard was paved in old uneven cobblestones that gave a dull gleam in the light of the white moon. In the center was a dry fountain, fallen into decay, the dark mark of the water indelibly upon it like a frayed black ribbon. There were small orange trees set in front of the mansions, and a little curb, where horses had once stood, and carriages.

"This is a very, very old place," Sergio said quietly. He turned off the engine of his car, and they looked at the silent square and did not speak for a while.

"Who lived here?" she said finally.

"Wealthy families in the old days of Brazil. When the women married they never saw their husbands until the day of the wedding. Then they would come to live in a house like this, and they would stay inside it for the rest of their lives."

"And never come out?"

"Only to go to church," Sergio said. "And sometimes to visit relatives, but always in the carriage, and always with the chaperone. Their lives were inside their homes, with their children and servants."

"But if they didn't love their husbands?" Helen said. "How terrible!"

129

"It didn't matter whether they loved their husbands or not," he said.

"How terrible," Helen said again, more softly. She tried to imagine what it would be like, to be married to a man who didn't love her, who only cared about her as a mother for his children and a mistress of his great house. It was so easy to project herself into this cold image that she felt a wave of loneliness and longing that numbed her.

"But these women had their children," Sergio said. His voice was a whisper. "That was enough."

"It isn't enough!" Helen said.

He looked at her and smiled, and covered her hand lightly, touching the tips of each of her fingers separately with the tips of his own and lifting them one by one. "I want to make you happy," he said.

She was stricken with embarrassment by the way she had revealed herself to him. "You're so clever," she said bitterly. Then she realized she had only made everything worse.

"I am clever about you," Sergio said softly. "Are you offended?" She shook her head.

"I want to see you alone. Tomorrow. Will you see me?"

"We have nothing to say to each other," Helen said. "And you know it."

"I have a great deal to say to you. But it might bore you to hear me tell you what you do to me."

"Please don't," Helen said. She took her hand away from his, finally. "Look . . ." she said. "I . . . it isn't as if I were a single girl on a . . . a *vacation*, where I could meet an attractive man and say to myself, What harm would it do if I fall a little in love with him? Go and chase a tourist. Let her feel flattered. She probably has nothing to lose but her loneliness. She'd be going from nothing to something. I would have to go from something to something else to get involved with you, and I can't. I'm not that kind of person."

"You sound as if I'm taking something away from you," Sergio said. He looked amused, but not nastily so; his eyes were earnest.

130

"There isn't one thing I want you to give up—except, yes, one thing—what you blame on that poor tourist."

I'm not lonely, she wanted to say, but the words stayed in her throat as if she had been paralyzed. I'm not lonely. It seemed such an effort to say those words, such a tremendous lie, like inventing an entire life with one meager sentence; an impossible weight. She felt the words; they lay there in her throat, and they were too heavy to bring out. I'm not lonely, I'm not.

"Americans are always talking about love," Sergio said. "They say, 'I love you.' Then they say, 'I don't love you.' Or they ask, 'Did *I* say I loved you?' What nonsense that all is! Do you think love is something you give and later throw away, like a piece of cheap chewing gum? Wear it out and throw it away in the gutter and forget it? Use it, ashamed, with your hand over your face because it's a bad habit? You say if you were a lonely tourist you *might* allow yourself to fall a *little* in love with me. What is this 'little bit in love'? A not-so-good present for a distant relative who has to be invited to the Christmas party?"

"What do you want, then?" Helen asked.

"I want you to see me tomorrow."

"I can't."

"Your husband is not going to be back tomorrow," Sergio said. It was the first time either of them had actually said the word *husband*. The word seemed alien on his tongue, somehow, as if he had a completely distorted idea of what Bert was, and who Bert was, and how much Bert meant in her life. She felt a rush of loyalty to Bert and a feeling of shame and resentment.

"And your wife is away for the summer?" Helen asked coolly.

"My wife is on the farm," Sergio said. His tone was matter-of-fact, with some affection and loyalty in it too, strangely enough; as if there was nothing immoral or cruel in speaking of his wife and her husband at the same time that he was speaking about wanting to make love.

"You love her," Helen said.

"In many ways, yes. Of course I do. In time you grow to love a person who is kind and whom you respect." He smiled at her. "You're looking at me with those big eyes as if you're shocked that I didn't marry for love. Helen, darling, marriage was never invented to perpetuate love. It was invented by much wiser people than us, to perpetuate the good things, like the family and the home, and to raise good children. When two very young people love each other it is only a clever little wedge nature has for slipping them into the state of marriage. The first time a young boy falls in love with a young girl he's really only in love with the fact that she *is* a young girl. That's marvelous to him all by itself. But to make a whole marriage out of that would be a terrible thing."

"I can't believe that," Helen said.

"How old were you when you married?"

"That doesn't matter."

"And do you still love him the same way as you did when you were very young?" Sergio asked.

"That sounds like something Bert would say," Helen said. "But for different reasons." The name *Bert* just slipped out, and when she had said it she was shocked to find that she felt no disloyalty whatever this time.

"I do love my wife, in the same way she loves me," Sergio said calmly. "And I love my children so much I would die for them, I think, if I had to make the choice. I wouldn't think for an instant, Is this gesture wasted because this child might grow up to be a no-good and cruel to his mother? I love and respect my father. I love my mother, who died when I was very small. But none of this love is something you take and break off little pieces. You don't hand them out and say, 'Here, for you, and *here*, for you.' I don't love a little, the way you do, and be afraid all my life it is wasted. I love very much—very much—and it is never something lost."

"Oh, I do too," Helen breathed. Tears came to her eyes. "I do too. But I always feel as if . . ." She could not finish. She wondered if he knew what she meant.

"If you hold it to yourself it will hurt you," Sergio said. "I don't know anyone who hates the world who could not have used all that energy to make love instead." He laughed. "Do I sound like I make a sermon?"

"No," she said. She laughed too, then, and let him take her hand again. "I like you," she said.

"Thank you. I like that much better. If you like me very much I like it better than if you love only a little bit."

"Well, I won't love you a little," Helen said, gently and smiling at him. She leaned her head against the back of the seat and felt safe.

"No," Sergio said seriously. "You won't."

He started the car and drove slowly out of the courtyard, through the alley, and into the street. A streetcar rumbled by on the tracks, almost entirely empty, a few people sitting separately and sleepily in its lighted interior. Helen wondered where they were going. She wondered where Sergio would go after he left her. Home, perhaps, to an apartment that was empty now because his family was away at their *fazenda*. There might be sheets covering the living-room furniture, and on the small tables there might be photographs of him and his wife in the early days when they felt differently about each other. He might go home and sleep, or he might go to a night club to see his friends. Wherever he went, Helen had the certainty that she could ask him to take her with him and he would.

"What are you going to do tomorrow?" he asked casually.

"I have to take care of the children. The governess has the day off. I'll take them to the beach, I think."

"The beach in front of your apartment?"

"Yes." She wondered if he intended to risk being seen talking to her on the beach, if he would follow her there, or wait for her to come. She didn't know. She realized then that despite all the things they had said to each other, she really knew very little about him and the way he lived. "What will you do tomorrow?" she asked.

"Go to my office. Then I have a lunch with some very boring bankers, and a conference in the afternoon."

"Then you couldn't have met me anyway."

He turned to look at her quickly. "Then you *will* meet me?"

"No, no. I mentioned it only because you must have forgotten you had other things to do."

"Conferences can always be changed to an earlier time."

"What a casual attitude you have toward your work!" Helen said.

"You think it is strange?" Sergio asked. "Your American men are so busy working and buying big life-insurance policies. Then they leave their wives the life insurance. Life insurance is not a very good substitute for memories."

"*Your* wife must have lovely memories," she said nastily.

He did not answer for a while but he did not look angry. "All right," he said then, but he did not sound put down either. "Now we're even. I said a cruel thing to you and you said one to me."

"You turn at the next street," Helen said.

They turned on to Avenida Atlantica, the mosaic sidewalk showing patches of dark and light, some of the burned-down Macumba candles still flickering on the beach. The sea was tossing up white foam that lifted and separated in the moonlight.

"It's the next apartment house," she said.

Sergio stopped his car in front of her doorway. She let him get out and walk around to her side of the car and open the door for her, and then she stepped quickly past him. There was no one walking by; the street was deserted. On the beach in front of her apartment she could see two lovers sitting in embrace on the sand. "Good night," she said.

He lifted her hand to his lips and kissed it lightly. "Good night. Thank you."

"Goodbye," Helen said. "Let's not part with hard feelings between us. I'm sorry for anything I said that might have been rude or assumed too much in our very brief friendship." She stood there, smiling, waiting for him to make the formal apology in reply and have done with it. Manners would be the fence between them now, much higher and stronger than any antagonism or hard feelings could be. There was nothing so good as manners, she thought; nothing so useful, nothing so protective, nothing so firm and gentle. Her smile was frozen, polite, and she felt a hopeless sadness.

"We must never be rude to each other," Sergio said thoughtfully. "Never again."

134

Helen turned quickly and walked into the house, and while she waited for the self-service elevator she deliberately kept herself from turning around to look back until she heard the noise of his car motor starting up and the car driving away.

Upstairs, she went quickly to her bedroom and put away her purse and hung up her dress. She put on her silk bathrobe and walked past Roger's room, glancing in the partly opened door to where he slept very quietly, a tiny rise under the white sheet, a patch of darkness where his head was. How small he was, and how vulnerable. She was filled with love for him, and hope, and tender pride. In the next room Julie was sleeping surrounded by such an army of stuffed animals and dolls it seemed as if one night she would smother herself. They were all tucked in beside her under the sheet so that she had left herself only a small place, barely enough to turn in. She slept deeply, very still. On the studio couch at the far end of the room the governess slept, wheezing a bit in her sleep like an asthmatic old Scottie Helen had owned as a child. How can Julie stand it, listening to her snore? Helen thought. Children can take so much, it's amazing!

She stood there looking at Julie from the doorway and felt peaceful with love. Julie would be with her for years, and she would watch her grow, and give her things, all the silly and good and grown-up things that little girls wanted when they grew older. Could she die for her children, as Sergio had said he could? The thought made Helen shudder. She couldn't bear to think about such things; even reading in the newspapers back home about mothers who tried to rescue their children from burning houses had always made her ill with sympathy. Life was so filled with dreadful things: dangers and sorrows and lost years. It was better not to think about those things at all, if you could help it.

She walked into the dark living room and opened the heavy curtains, looking out at the beach and sky. In the distance she could see the outlines of the mountains in the clear night. How calm Sergio had been when he had spoken of dying to save his children! Perhaps I am a monster, Helen thought guiltily. I'd rather never think of anything so horrible at all. I couldn't say,

I'd die. He must feel as though he's lived a very happy, good life if he can speak of giving it up without shuddering. I couldn't. I'd feel that everything was wasted—everything—and that I'd vanished without very much ever having happened to me . . . as if I don't matter.

It was odd, she thought, that she could stand here in the home that belonged to Bert and her and think of Sergio so easily, without any guilt or fear. It was easier to be with him now when he was not here than it had been when he was right beside her. She almost missed him. Strangely enough, in her own home with all its personal identifications holding her as if they were hands, she allowed herself to like Sergio Leite Braga for the first time without judgments, and she missed him. In the home where even the thought of him should have seemed a treachery, the memory of him entered and was welcome. She held out her hand, the hand he had touched with his lips, and she noticed that it was shaking.

CHAPTER 8

In Rio nobody thinks it is very strange if an entire apartment building falls down. It is not usually a tragedy, because the tenants have at least a day's warning to evacuate all their belongings. Usually the building begins leaning well in advance. Often a large crack appears across the face of it. Large buildings in Brazil are made of poured concrete rather than with steel structures underneath. The concrete contains a smaller or greater amount of sand, depending on the reliability and honesty of the builder. In one apartment house in Rio the landlord wanted to get rid of his tenants so he could get new ones and raise the rents. So he announced that the building was about to fall, and the disgruntled tenants moved their things outside to the street and waited. Nothing happened by nightfall, so they went back into the building to sleep. A week later he warned again, and again they went outside with their possessions to wait. Everyone has a great loyalty and curiosity about his apartment house in Rio; it would never occur to anyone to go away to a hotel and allow the building to fall down all by itself. The tenants waited again, and when the building did not seem even shaky, they moved back in again. By this time many of them were so tired of this nonsense that when the landlord gave the warning for the third time they moved away for good. It wasn't that they thought their building was a death trap. It was simply that their landlord was getting to be too much of a pest. He happily raised the rents, and the building is standing to this day.

In America people like to watch buildings being constructed. They stand outside the fences which have been erected to guard the excavation and they peer through conveniently placed peepholes. In Rio they like to watch buildings fall down. So one night in the middle of January there was a large crowd gathered in front of a fairly new, modern, twelve-story apartment house waiting for it to fall. The building was made of beautiful clean white stone, with great glass windows overlooking the hills. The name of the building was written in gold letters on the plate glass of the lobby doors: EDIFICIO APOLLO. The apartment houses in Rio are named poetically—Edificio Chopin, with two wings named Sonata and Preludio, is one of the most famous. The Edificio Apollo was not nearly that elegant, but it was a nice building, and some of the crowd gathered outside on the sidewalk were heard to murmur that it was a shame it was going to fall.

Margie and Neil Davidow had come to watch because an American expatriate friend of Neil's named Mort Baker lived in Edificio Apollo or, rather, had lived there until that morning. Mort Baker was a sculptor, working mostly in marble and some cheaper Brazilian stones. He was twenty-nine years old, with a lean, cynical face, hairy wrists, very white teeth, black hair cut in a crewcut, and a very dark, carefully cultivated suntan. He had been born in Pennsylvania, had lived for a while in Greenwich Village in New York and on the last vestige of the Left Bank in Paris, and for the past four years had been living in Rio because it was inexpensive for Americans, and beautiful, and he liked the beach. Now he was sitting on one of his suitcases smoking a cigarette, surrounded by four other suitcases, two huge cartons of books, a dozen small stone statues of various sizes, and a wooden crate of stonecutter's tools. He wore a pair of Army suntan trousers that had been cut off a good deal above the knees, because it was a hot night, and a light gray sweatshirt of the kind that college boys wear after they have been rowing on crew. Margie was sitting on one of his suitcases, holding a small transistor radio on her lap. Mort had three other transistor

138

radios, the smallest of which he could keep in the pocket of his shirt. Neil Davidow was standing beside Margie and Mort, trying to adjust his camera to take a picture of the building at the exact moment when it would begin to fall.

A television station had brought cameras and lights, setting the lights up along the sidewalk so that everything was very brightly lighted. It gave the impression of being a movie première. Most of the people in the crowd seemed filled with excitement, as if they were waiting to see movie stars. A reporter walked from person to person in the crowd holding a little microphone and interviewing them for a local radio program. Two Kibon ice-cream men, in rivalry with each other, had set their small yellow wagons on the curb to service anyone who might be hungry. There was also a man with a glass-topped wagon that made popcorn, and a man who was selling Coca-Cola. Several of the onlookers who were of a practical nature had provided themselves with sandwiches from home, which they munched while they waited and washed down with Coca-Cola from the cart.

"I feel so bad for you, Mort," Margie said sympathetically. "I wish we could have brought the big statue down. I feel sick about it; I really do."

"It doesn't matter," Mort said. He did not seem particularly depressed. "All the time I was working on that statue I kept wondering how I was ever going to get it out the door. I finally realized it was impossible." He shrugged. "At least this way I'll get it out of the house."

"Oh, Mort."

"It's a great solution," he said. He laughed. "What I'm really worried about is where I'm going to live now until I find another apartment I can afford."

"You can live with us," Neil said. "Can't he, Margie?"

"Of course."

"No," Mort said. "It's too much trouble."

"Don't be silly," Margie said. "That's what friends are for." She smiled at him, the smile of a happily married housewife who mothers all her husband's bachelor friends. "We have lots of room. But only one thing—you can't make any ten-foot-high marble statues in *our* apartment."

"I'll make you one and you can keep it," Mort said. "It will be a house gift."

"That's really why we invited you," Neil said.

Mort took a handful of cruzeiros out of his pocket and waved at the ice-cream man. "What do you want, Margie?"

"Chocolate, please."

"Let me get it," Neil said. Mort waved him away.

They ate their chocolate ices sitting on the row of suitcases and watching the motionless building like people waiting for the main feature of a movie to begin. Now at last the building, which had been tilted slightly since the day before, seemed to move almost imperceptibly and settle lower to one side.

"It's moving!" Margie cried.

"It'll take another hour at least," Mort said calmly. "I've seen this before."

"What I can't figure out," Margie said, "is why nobody tries to save it. Can't they prop it up or anything?"

"Are we far enough away?" Neil asked worriedly. "Will we get hit with something when it falls?"

"Just a photographer's flashbulb," Mort said. "Modern living." He gestured. "You like that? They've got television here to record the crash, but no one's figured out how to keep the building up."

The roving reporter came by with his microphone and stopped beside them. "Did all of you live in this building?" he asked them in Portuguese.

Mort stood up. "Just me," he answered.

"American?"

"More or less."

"What is your name, Senhor?"

"Mort Baker. Do you mind if I ask *you* some questions?"

"Please, Senhor."

"Do you know why this apartment is going to fall?"

"It is the foundation," the reporter said. "The ground is too soft, too wet. You see, the two buildings on either side are standing very well. So the builder thought the ground would hold

140

this building also." He shrugged. "But for some reason, it did not."

"You would think they would know," Mort said.

The reporter opened wide, innocent eyes. "But how can anyone know?" he asked reproachfully. "Those two buildings stand, this one falls. The ground could not hold all three of them."

"Excuse me, Senhor," Mort said. "I hope you will not think I am impolite. But do you think that if the builder had used less sand in the concrete this building might not be now going to fall?"

The reporter looked scandalized. "Oh, no," he said. "The buildings in Rio are very well built! You must use concrete in a tropical country. It is the soft land underneath that makes the buildings fall, not sand in the concrete. You can look at most of the buildings that fall down lately. You will see how well built they are. The buildings always fall down in one piece."

"That's well built," Mort said. "I always feel safer in an apartment house that I know is going to fall down in one piece. Thank you, Senhor."

"Is nothing. Thank you, Senhor."

The reporter moved away into the crowd. Neil began to laugh. Mort gestured at the leaning building. "One piece," he said. "It's nice to have security, isn't it?"

"I think we need a drink," Neil said.

"We can lock all the suitcases in our car," said Margie. "We can still watch everything from the café on the corner."

They carried the suitcases and cartons and statues in shifts to Neil's car, which because of the crowds he had been forced to park two blocks away. By the time they got to the outdoor café all the tables were already taken by the curious, their chairs turned to face the leaning building. The waiters rushed in and out happily, doing a capacity business, offering advice and words of wisdom about other buildings which had fallen during the past year. The most famous fallen building was a new one, which had toppled shortly after it was completed, even before all the new tenants had had time to move in.

One waiter said six buildings had fallen in the past twelve months. Another said twelve buildings had fallen in the past six months. "Have you noticed that expensive new building down the

141

street?" someone asked. "It has a great crack in the front of it already. It will fall by next year." No one seemed either indignant or surprised that this would happen. They seemed to take the crashing of apartment buildings philosophically, as one accepts the crashing of airplanes, and as much less of a tragedy because you could not get out of a doomed plane in advance, suitcases and all, the way you could from an apartment house.

Neil ordered three glasses of *chopp* beer. He ruffled Margie's hair and smiled at her, and she smiled at him. He had taken to being very demonstrative in public since they were no longer sleeping together. At first it had puzzled Margie and filled her with pain and sympathy for him because as soon as they were alone together inside their apartment he left her scrupulously alone, and she thought he might be using these public moments to feel the touch of her he so desperately wanted. But then she realized that Neil was too restrained for that. He was all pride. He could never paw her and brush against her like a high-school boy with a shy date, pretending it was horseplay or an accident. Neil received no more pleasure from these public contacts than she. It was pride that prompted them, a public avowal that he and his wife were just like anybody else.

Mort Baker shook his head. "It's great to see two people who really *have* something together," he said. "Like you two. Some of the married people I know are like two enemies who find themselves sharing a cab. Like one of them is eating garlic and the other one has his feet on the first one's seat, but they can't stop the cab and get out because there aren't any other taxis. I always think you two have one of those crazy, lucky marriages."

"We do," Neil said.

Margie smiled weakly. "I guess we can stand each other," she said, trying to keep it light. "It's been five years."

"That long . . ." Mort said, sounding rather amazed.

"My parents have been married for forty years," Neil said.

"Oh, I didn't mean that," said Mort. "I meant, that long to be happy. I can't remember being really happy for more than three consecutive days."

"That's because you don't settle down," Margie said. She wasn't

142

quite sure whether what she was saying was a pose or whether she really felt so motherly and righteous. "You ought to find a girl you love and get married."

"Margie's always trying to marry everyone off," Neil said fondly. He stroked her forearm where it lay on the table.

"She could marry me off in one minute," Mort said. "If she were available."

"You mean me?" Margie said. She laughed. "Thank you. Do you hear that, Neil?"

"He has good taste," Neil said. "That's why we're friends."

They all drank their beer. There was an air of friendship among them, and Margie felt secure. Once in a while they would glance toward the spotlighted area where Edificio Apollo was about to crash down, and that gave their entire meeting an edge of danger, of excitement. Margie looked at Mort. He was nice, she thought; a really *nice* person, even though he went off on occasional "honeymoons" with girls. And he was funny. The girls never seemed to mind their honeymoons without marriage, and they always flirted with him afterward on the beach, as if hoping he would take them on another. "Honeymoon" was his own term, and he really made it that way. Neil had told her some of his stories, the ones she was not supposed to let on she knew. He always took the girl away from Rio, because if you lived in Rio all your life it wasn't that exciting. And he might starve for a week afterward, but every day the hotel room would be filled with flowers. She remembered before Edificio Apollo had been built, when Mort was living in a rooming house of sorts. Even his landlady had liked him. He wasn't just any lover; he was a real Brazilian-type lover, *muito sympatico*. "He is not here, the American," Mort's landlady would say to callers. "He is in Porto Allegre on his honeymoon."

Neil gestured at the waiter for more beer. Margie covered her half-empty glass with the palm of her hand and shook her head. She hardly drank anything any more; she hardly needed to. There were so many things to enjoy: the beach, the sun, the ocean, the sounds and sights of people in the street, books, her records, even her long evenings alone with Neil. At first she had felt the old panic when he walked near to her or touched her lightly, but then she realized that when Neil had said, "Never again," he had meant it. So with the vanishing of fear the need to dull her senses disappeared—for she realized now that alcohol had dulled them, not heightened them as she had pretended to herself. In a way, these summer days were the happiest Margie had known during her entire marriage, and although the thought often occurred to her that her life with Neil was abnormal and even portended disaster, yet she was happy. She loved him more now, when she was no longer afraid of him, than she had ever loved him before. Perhaps her parents had been right, perhaps love grew between married couples and transcended sex, until the couple was as one: blood relatives, identical twins, even Siamese twins, bound by a blood line of wordless communication.

She remembered feeling about her parents that they had never slept together as lovers—except for the appearance of herself and her brother Tommy, which at least proved irrefutably that they had twice. She wondered what her mother would think if she ever knew the relationship that existed between Margie and Neil. I can't give you any grandchildren, Mother, because Neil and I never do that. And her mother would look at the ground, or the wall, terribly embarrassed, terribly hurt, and ask, Are you fighting? Don't you love each other? Her mother would never think to ask, Are you in trouble? Or is he? Her mother never thought anyone was sick or troubled in the mysterious areas that linked the mind and body inseparably together; even the two young bachelors who shared a small apartment on the same floor as the Hafts, who dressed in trousers so tight they could hardly bend their knees and took turns walking their elaborately coiffeured French poodle. The bachelors would stare straight ahead when Margie and her mother were in the elevator, one pouting, the other with the iciest round blue eyes Margie had ever seen. Those eyes and the look they gave her made her shudder. And her mother would often say wistfully, "I wonder why those two good-looking boys never go out with girls. I guess they can't find one they think is good enough."

"What are you dreaming about, Margie?" Neil asked.

"I dreamed I went to a house-falling in my Maidenform bra," she said lightly. She smiled at him, and at Mort. "You two should be glad there's a woman here who's not trying to monopolize the conversation."

Neil and Mort pushed back their chairs. "Let's go back and get our ringside seats."

They walked back to the building and stationed themselves in front, at a safe distance, among the crowd. "Imagine," Neil said, "how many unhappily married men are going to be left without their *garçoniers* when this house falls."

"What's a *garçonier?*" Margie asked.

"It means 'little boy's apartment,' " Neil said.

"No, really!"

"It's a small apartment married men rent when they want to be lunch-hour bachelors," said Mort. "They keep it by the year and they take girls there. To play. Hence, 'little boy's apartment.' "

Margie smiled at him. "You sound the faintest bit disapproving. Or am I hearing noises in my head?"

"Hell," Mort said, "I am disapproving. What the hell do people have to get married for if they want to wreck it? We have to be a little bit better than the savages, not that there's much difference except the savages have more sense."

"I learn more about you every month," Margie said.

"That's a pretty big-time handicap," Mort said wryly. "I'm with me every day and I haven't got the scene figured out yet."

Neil put his arm about Mort's shoulders and the other arm around Margie's waist. "You'll have a lot of time to get to know each other when Mort is living with us," he said. He looked at both of them with pride—his friend and his wife. For some reason she could not understand Margie felt resentful. She was not even quite sure whom she felt resentful toward. Neil was being magnanimous, inviting an attractive bachelor with a lover's reputation to live with him and his wife, absolutely certain that nothing would happen between them. He smiled at Mort like the perfect husband and lover, confident and generous. And why not, Margie thought. He knows his wife doesn't care for *any* man. And then she realized why she felt resentful. She felt cheated somehow, short-changed. How much better it would be if Neil felt about her as if she were a real woman, whose fidelity he could feel confident of just because he was her man, not because she was a sexless child or a stick of wood!

She drew away from both of them and stood by herself. "Look," she said. "I think it's tilting! Look, look!"

A sigh of pleasure and excitement went up from the crowd. The newsreel cameras from the television station began to whirr. The roving reporter crouched over his hand microphone, holding it up to his mouth with both hands and speaking excitedly into it. A small, fat photographer, dressed in sweat-drenched whites, pivoted about snapping pictures, first of the building, then quickly of the faces of some of the watching mob, then quickly again to the building. He looked like a whirling dervish. A little boy had been eating a Kibon bar and stopped with his mouth wide open in awe, clenching the ice cream in his fist until it melted and ran down over his shoes.

Slowly at first, as it were a movie in slow motion, the building began to lean and to crack from its displaced weight at almost the same time. It seemed about to break in the middle. This is one that won't fall down in one piece, Margie thought excitedly. There was a rumbling sound, but you could hardly hear it because everyone in that huge crowd was jabbering and squealing and crying out at once, poking each other, pointing, jumping up to see. Two girls were holding each other's heads, their eyes closed, and screaming as if they actually knew what was going on. There seemed to be two definite groups: the people who had lived in the building and had never seen this phenomenon before, and the people who always came to watch buildings fall down and were enjoying every moment of it. There was even an ancient beggar woman, dressed in what looked like a bundle of dirty laundry, who looked as if the only thing keeping her alive this late in life was this show before her.

Up until the last moment you could see that it was an apartment house. You could see the windows, some with curtains or draperies visible through the glass. The lights had gone out. It was a living building, where people spent their lives, and then it was sick and toppling, and then it fell dead, still at that last second a building, with a thunderous crash and a cloud of dust, and lay flat, enormous, lying across trees and sidewalk alike, the dust still rising about it. A huge section of it, consisting of several stories, lay intact. Your thought was: Why is that building sideways instead of upright? And then you saw the white porcelain toilet lying on the rubble-strewn lawn in the bright grass, like a weird lawn ornament.

"Look, Mamai!" a little girl cried out. "There is my bedroom wallpaper!"

A few policemen, dressed in tan uniforms and helmets, were trying to keep the people from rushing forward to help themselves to articles of furniture which might belong to someone else. No one appeared bad-humored about this. Some were souvenir hunters, but they could come back another night. Without a word Mort darted through the straggling line of police and disappeared among the piles of concrete and wood.

"Oh, my God," Margie said. "What's the matter with him?"

She and Neil walked cautiously through the crowd, trying to find where he had gone. Now that the excitement was over the crowd was beginning to disperse. The corner café was again becoming crowded, and the little boy who had spilled his ice cream had begun to cry. Then they saw Mort sprinting over the fallen articles of plumbing, coming toward them, waving and looking very happy.

"Hey!" he cried. "Guess what? I found my statue! It's okay. Just a few chips I can fix up in the morning. You know, it looks great lying there in all that grass. I may donate it for a park monument after they clear this piece of land."

"If they know what it is," Neil said.

"Never mind," said Mort. "Culture. They'll learn to love it. Kids can play house on it. Dogs can stay cool lying in the shadow of it. And one thing you can be sure of—no matter how much graft there is, no one can ever steal *that* statue."

They all laughed and went off to find the car.

CHAPTER *9*

How many amnesia victims start their new lives doing exactly
the same thing they were doing before they lost their memory?
Do we remain in a pattern of life year after year because of enthusiasm or habit, happiness or convention? The ghosts of the
past rise up wherever we turn and pluck at our sleeves, blue-
coated street-corner monitors for schoolchildren, holding our
grown-up bodies to the white safety line. If we live in the town
or city where we grew up, how can we escape passing landmarks
of memory every day? The woman shopping for her child's clothing passes the bus stop where she waited every week for the bus
that took her downtown to the dentist to have her braces tightened when she was a child herself. She might smile to herself,
thinking that life goes on. Or she might be walking quickly to
meet her lover, and she might then stop, looking at the houses
that look so much shabbier now, and the bus stop where she
dreamed her adolescent dreams, and her step might become reluctant as she realizes how much she has changed. It is one thing
to emerge from the apartment of her lover at twilight and hurry
to her husband: she has already told herself that her husband is
unkind, does not love her, is a beast. Perhaps she is right. But
how can she pass all the places of memory and of habit, the little
restaurant where she used to go with her husband when they
loved each other and were delirious with love, the park where she

walked with her father on Sundays when she was a child and he had such hopes for her happiness? They are too much, these memories; they color her life; they spoil everything. Why can't anyone start out fresh? she thinks in desperation.

But for the uprooted expatriates, the homeless in new homes that they still feel ill at ease in, a twilight street is just a street. A tree with sun in its leaves is only a beautiful tree, more poignant now if looked at after an experience of love. A woman running to her lover thinks only of him. A woman emerging from an apartment that had been darkened against the afternoon sun stands for a moment on the sidewalk blinking, shading her eyes. She sees the street; it is any street, a little noisier, a little brighter perhaps, because she is emerging from a total, intense experience into a fragmented one. She adjusts to the light, to the sounds, and hurries on, looking back just once at the shaded window of her lover. How beautiful this afternoon is! she thinks. I will always remember this day, and this street, and that tree. But all her memories of this day will go forward, not back. It is a great eraser of guilt.

Helen Sinclair thought all this as she sat in the rooftop restaurant of a hotel on Copacabana Beach waiting for Sergio. She had waited for him on the beach that first day, sure he would not come, and he had come, late in the afternoon, with Carlos Monteiro for protective coloration. Carlos Monteiro looked like the perfect businessman; even in bathing shorts he seemed about to give dictation to an imaginary secretary or pick up an invisible telephone receiver to make a deal. The two men walked at the edge of the sea, talking with their heads together, like two partners who had decided to leave the office early because of the heat and continue their discussion on the beach.

The beach was always the most active place in Rio, strangely enough. People might be consumed by good-natured apathy everywhere else, but on the beach they suddenly came to life. There was always a soccer game, sometimes in uniform. There were always couples playing an animated game that looked like a cross between ping-pong and handball, with little paddles and no net, leaping about on the hard sand. Helen sat under a beach umbrella, her two children digging sand castles beside her, looking like a model American mother, trying to pretend behind her dark glasses that she had not seen Sergio Leite Braga approach, and that, in any case, he was nothing to her.

"Helen," he said gravely. He leaned down to take her hand. He introduced her to Carlos Monteiro, whom she remembered. He smiled at her children, who glanced at him curiously.

"Say how-do-you-do to Mr. Leite Braga and Mr. Monteiro," Helen said to Roger and Julie, feeling so strange as she did so. They were polite children; she was proud of them. Roger stood up and shook hands with Sergio. I wonder what his children look like, she thought suddenly.

Sergio crossed his legs and swooped down beside her like an Indian. He was lean, and golden tan from the sun, his shoulders and neck and upper arms hairless, the skin so smooth she wanted to touch it. She wondered what Sergio had told his friend. What could he have told him? There was nothing to tell.

That was the first day. When she was with Sergio she resented him—his sureness, his spirits, his air of knowing what happiness was and of being able to grasp it whenever he wanted to. What makes him think he's a good person? she thought resentfully. What makes him . . . And when she was away from him she felt somehow glowing, beautiful, because he thought being with her was happiness. With *her,* who no longer knew what happiness was!

The second day he telephoned her. Had she ever seen the Iate Clube? He would take her there.

Oh, yes, she said; she had been to the Iate Clube. Her feeling of resentment arose against him again. The yacht club was where married men met ladies for lunch, Leila had told her, and now Sergio thought he could go there with her. No, Helen said abruptly. She did not want to go to the Iate Clube.

Where would she like to go, then? He did not ask her *if,* he asked her *where.* He never gave her the choice of refusing. And Helen felt guiltily grateful for that, because if he had asked her, *Would* she have lunch with him, she would have been obliged to say no. Had she ever been to the Floresta de Tijuca? he asked. It was so beautiful. "Thank you," Helen said, more coldly. "I was there one Sunday with Bert and the children."

150

"I love it," Sergio said. "I take my children there very often. It's so cool there and peaceful."

By telling her so calmly that he had taken his children there too (and perhaps his wife as well?) Sergio made her feel so helpless in her conflict that she wanted to lash out and hurt him; and then suddenly for the first time she felt the first real tenderness toward him.

"I'd rather go . . . somewhere new," Helen said.

Then he told her about the restaurant on top of the hotel, with a view, with air conditioning, and they met. She had the feeling as they talked and picked at their food that he was waiting for something, that he knew her better than she knew herself. She felt herself falling into his control as one falls into weakness from too much wine, a feeling that is safe because it is imperceptible to the other person and easy to disguise. As long as Sergio did not know, she thought, she was safe; and so she smiled, and acted calm, and looked at his curved mouth instead of his eyes, feeling giddy with pleasure and smug with the secret of her deception. She had never been to this restaurant before, and from this height the view of the beach and tiny bathers seemed new. All the people dining in the room were Brazilians, and she had never seen any of them before. It was only a few hours out of her life, harmless, without past or future either if she wished. And because it was so unimportant it became very important.

After lunch she said she had to rush home to take Julie to a birthday party: it was a lie. Sergio accepted the lie and took her home in an ancient taxi, keeping the taxi to go on to his office. She was so pleased with herself at having deceived both Sergio and herself, at having ended this secret luncheon with no incident, that when he kissed her hand and told her he would meet her the next day she accepted before she realized what she had done.

I am a fool, she thought, a fool. But she lay on her bed and got up to close her door and lay there again in a semi-stupor, afraid that if she had left the door to her room open one of her children might wander in and see her secret happiness revealed upon her face.

So today Helen was waiting for Sergio again, and it was the

third day since the night they had really met at the Macumba. Bert was coming home that night. She did not feel guilty toward Bert, strangely; she only felt rather sad because she would have to tell Sergio that she could never see him again. She wouldn't say, *Never;* she would simply say that Bert was coming back. But she knew she would never telephone Sergio to tell him the next time Bert went away again, and she was sure Sergio would forget about her by then. She looked out at the sky and the beach below, white with heat haze. She was cool in the air-conditioned room and she shivered, clasping her hands together on the table-cloth. Because she was here the second day in a row she felt rather as if it were her special place, hers with Sergio, and she knew that she would never come here again with Bert or any of their friends. No, Helen thought then; she would come here eventually, and that was what was making her feel this wistful loneliness. She would come here some night in the not-so-distant future, for dinner with Bert and another couple or two, and they would all laugh and splurge on the fine French food and wine, and perhaps they would sit across from the small table where she was going to sit now with Sergio and where they had eaten yes-terday. There would hardly be any ghosts of herself and Sergio sitting at this small table, she told herself; it wouldn't mean any-thing at all. She might even look back at these three days and not be quite sure they had ever happened, like a date one had years ago in college. The thought made her sad.

Sergio slid on to the leather banquette beside her before she knew he was there. "You look sad," he said quietly. "Don't say anything; wait a moment." He was holding a fresh rose in his hand and he slipped the stem through the top buttonhole of her dress. She could smell the scent of the rose very faintly, fresh and sweet.

"Thank you," she said. "I never buy roses; they're so expensive."

"One?" he said. "*É nada.*"

"That's what a housewife I am," Helen said. "You give me a rose and instead of saying, 'Thank you, how romantic,' I say, 'Thank you, how expensive.' As if you should have given me butter or cheese instead. Now what in the world would I do with butter and cheese?"

"We have known each other for three days," he said unexpectedly. He seemed surprised.

"That's not very long."

"No."

"Bert is coming back tonight," Helen said.

Sergio nodded.

"Three days," he said again.

"I told you he would be back soon," she said. "He only went to see a mine. I . . ."

"Will you see me when he comes back?"

"I never thought of that."

"I thought of it," Sergio said. "I didn't know whether I ought to ask you. I thought, Perhaps she really loves him and can't be with anyone else. Or perhaps she doesn't love him enough to make it be everything, but perhaps she's afraid to be with me. I was thinking about it this morning. I want to see you if it will make you happy. If it will make you unhappy, then I'll go away. It's up to you."

"I don't know what to say," Helen said. "I don't know what to say. . . . I *do*, I do know what to say, but I . . . can't say it."

"That's why I never left anything up to you," Sergio said gently. He took her hand. "We had so little time. I couldn't wait for you to argue with yourself. But now it's more important because it involves more than three days. It means a long time. That's why I want you to make the choice."

"The choice?" she asked, frightened.

"I think everyone has a right to have good things happen to him," Sergio said. "I want things to happen to me and they do. I'm never bored or lonely. You are."

"Yes. I . . . was."

"I'm married too," he said. "I will always be married to this woman, and you will always be married to this man. You are married. Also you are an American, also you have blond hair. These are all simply facts about you."

Helen smiled. "When you say it, everything seems so simple."

153

"We have an old saying in Brazil," Sergio said. "According to the law of aerodynamics the bumblebee cannot fly. But the bumblebee does not know the law of aerodynamics and so he flies."

Helen reached out her hand and touched his lips very lightly and he kissed her fingers. He took hold of her wrist and kissed her palm. He had spoken of love, in terms of what loving someone meant in his life, but neither of them had actually said he loved the other. Even now, Helen could not really think of it. Love, in her terms, meant commitment, promises, responsibilities and serious things. She had loved only one man in her life and she was married to him. But even so, she could not bear to lose this other man who was here beside her. She had never really believed women thought this way until now. She and Sergio had never said they loved each other, even if it were a sort of lie. She could neither bring herself to lie to him about it nor even to ask him about it. There did not seem to be any need. The only need was not to lose him.

"Will you always keep everything simple for us?" she asked. "Will you?"

"Will you?"

"I can't even keep things simple for myself."

"You're very beautiful," Sergio said.

"Thank you."

"Don't ever say thank you when I tell you you're beautiful."

"All right."

The waiter came over and stood by their table holding a menu. Sergio ordered for both of them, and the waiter went away.

"How strange . . ." Helen said.

"What?"

"When I'm alone with my husband there are always the children there, or the servants, or our friends. And when I'm alone with you there's a waiter or a taxi driver or a room full of strangers. Do you know that I haven't been alone with anybody— really alone—for eight years?"

"And you think that's the way your life has to be?"

"When you grow up you try so hard to keep a little part of your life separate, just so it will belong to you. You don't think you'll ever have the luxury of being alone with someone you love until you're too old to care about it. And we're all so *proud* of ourselves for turning ourselves into public property."

"To be alone with the right person for a little while can be a lifetime," Sergio said.

"When I said thank you before," she said, "it wasn't only because you told me I was beautiful. It was for a lot more."

"I want to make love to you," he said.

For an instant Helen thought of how it would be, allowed herself to think of it, and then it seemed too far away, across a bridge she could not cross. She shook her head. "I don't know," she said very softly. "Please give me time. I don't know."

He was looking into her face and she could see his eyes move, like someone reading a page. She had never seen anyone look at her that way before. At first it startled her and she had a moment of resistance; then she was flattered and touched. She felt herself become weak and gentle under the movement of his gaze. She knew then that one person alone looking into a mirror is never beautiful; it is only when two people are together and know they are beautiful to each other that they really are. But she knew too that other forces are at work: the past, the demands and needs of other people, the whole framework of separate lives that meet and part again. She wondered if she would ever find enough courage in the knowledge that Sergio found her beautiful and desirable to make that beauty last when he was gone. Someday he would go away from her; that was inevitable and she was not alone. The tragedy would be that when he left, or when she left him, someone who thought she was a special woman, separate from all others, would be gone, and gone with him the proof that she was.

She gave a shaky laugh. "I'm thinking about the end already," she said, "and we haven't even begun."

"We have begun," Sergio said softly and intently. "Oh, yes, we have."

This time she lifted his hand to her face, as he had lifted her hand many times to his lips, and she laid her cheek against his fingers. It seemed a natural gesture, something she had a right to do. She remembered the thoughts she had had before he entered the restaurant, her resolution to end their meetings, and then she ignored that thought as quickly as she had put away the thought that they would become lovers. She knew they could not remain in this in-between state forever, that the in-between stage was perhaps the shortest of all. But she would not think about it. For the first time she would not think about anything at all; she would only let things happen. If the bumblebee, not knowing he was not able to fly, could therefore fly, then she would be that way too. She did not know yet whether she had changed since she had known Sergio or whether she was for the first time finding out what she really was like. But she knew she was no longer frightened.

"What are you thinking now?" Sergio asked.

"I'm wondering how I could have lied to myself for three days."

"We all do that. It seems safe."

"But no more."

"You're different, suddenly," he said. "You're gentler."

"I am?"

"Gentler . . . and lovelier. No more tenseness in your face. Your eyes are different. I can see into them."

"What do you see?" she asked, trying not to lower her gaze.

"What is the best thing you would want me to see?"

"This may sound odd to you," Helen said. "I . . . what I want you to see is . . . a woman."

He sounded almost awed. "You are that," he said. *"Oh, you are that."*

CHAPTER *10*

During the hot nights in the weeks preceding Carnival, people danced and dined outdoors at the *piscina* of the Copacabana Palace, ate broiled filet that was cooked on hot coals and skewered on long swords in the tiny back yards of outdoor *churras-curias,* sat at tables overlooking the mosaic sidewalk and the beach and the stream of cars on Avenida Atlantica and drank beer from heavy glass steins in cafés that looked more like cafés in France or Germany. Rio was filled with tourists, cheerfully paying high prices they thought were low, innocent of spiraling inflation that set angry passengers to overturning and burning buses during the daytime. There were tourists from everywhere, from Europe, from North America, from other parts of South America. There were also the usual Rio café habitués; the handsome, seemingly jobless young men, tanned to the color of a gentled, honeyed cordovan from months of lying on the beach, emerging clean-shaven and white-toothed from bachelor apartments of incredible disorder, of three-legged beds, empty beer cans under the bed, torn sheets with shoeprints on them, cigarette holes burned blackly into the mattress, a whole world of endless young orgy shut away behind locked doors.

Inside Sachas, open "from seven to seven," the wealthy danced to a lively orchestra in an air-conditioned room and drank real whisky from its original bottle set on the white tablecloth with a bucket of completely transparent ice cubes made of purified water. In the smaller, less expensive *boâtes* (Brazilian café society loves French words but spells them its own way) there was louder conversation, perhaps guitar music, perhaps air conditioning, and the lights were brighter. And then there were the tiny bars along the beach where an opened door emitted a blast of frigid air and the sound of a phonograph being played, and perhaps the sweet-flower smell of antiseptic. Outside these bars prostitutes sometimes barely into their teens loitered, called out, clutched at a passer-by's arm, waited all night until they found a customer or perhaps ended up alone, dozing hopelessly on the steps of an apartment house, their heads on their knees, their arms wrapped around their heads.

This was Copacabana, but in other parts of Rio it was quieter. People waited in line to pay twelve cents to see an air-conditioned film, or they sat with their families at late dinner in their apartments, or they put their children to bed. It was summer, which is always a crazy time, different from any other time of the year; but most of all it was before the Carnival, and anything could happen.

In her apartment at Ipanema, Leila Silva e Costa was entertaining Carlos Monteiro at dinner. She had entertained him before, with friends, and several times he had taken her to quiet, obscure restaurants to dine, but she had never before invited him to her apartment alone. He seemed even more nervous than she was. He arrived at eight, having been invited for eight; and this surprised her. Most Brazilians arrived up to an hour and a half late. Being excited, almost like a schoolgirl, Leila had been all ready by eight o'clock herself, so it was no tragedy.

He followed her into her library and stood there admiring her shelves of books, which he had seen before, a glass of whisky in his hand, blinking his eyes nervously. She had put a stack of classical records on the phonograph, but because her children were always getting at the phonograph and record collection trying to play with them, the records were terribly scratched and Leila was ashamed. She knew an intellectual like Carlos would think she was a careless woman who did not take care of beautiful things.

"My children . . ." she said.

158

"Yes?" He turned to her and took a quick gulp at his whisky.

"They have ruined the records, I'm afraid. I can't prevent them. I hope it isn't all spoiled for you."

"Oh, no," Carlos said. "No. Schubert's *Death and the Maiden*. Very lovely."

"It's very tragic," Leila said. "I sometimes feel when I listen to it that it was written for me."

"For you?" He seemed startled. "Why?"

"The violins seem to reach out for me when I listen to it. The way Death was reaching out for the Maiden. I don't know, really. I only know how I feel." She smiled at him, her eyes opened wide, and sat on the couch spreading her red chiffon skirt about her. She had had this dress made especially for him; it had been completed today. The color of fire. Perhaps he would think of her differently in it.

Carlos did not sit down. He turned again to look at the titles on the spines of her books. "You have read Voltaire!"

"In French," Leila said demurely.

"One must read *Candide* in French in order to get the true flavor of the style."

"Yes," she said, although she had never read it any other way. "Will you have some cashews with your whisky? A small sausage?"

He came over to where she was holding out a little silver plate and he took a sausage. He gave her a nervous smile but he did not sit down. She thought he looked like a man of the world, a scholar who knew how to make money as well. He wore a beautifully cut Italian silk suit. He was of medium height and thin, with graying hair that made him look older than forty, although she knew he was forty because in Rio you knew everything about everyone. He had a clear-cut, aquiline profile and vague, scholarly eyes. Leila thought he was very handsome. But he had never married. Forty years old and never married . . . She wondered if he would think he was too old for a woman of twenty-nine. No, men of forty usually thought *she* was too old for *them!*

She moved the corner of her red chiffon skirt aside to make room beside her on the couch. "Sit down, please."

159

Carlos sat next to her and drained his glass of whisky. He seemed less ill at ease. "I like you very much," he said.

"Do you!" She knew her smile was radiant, but she did not care. She had never been much good at hiding her emotions from anybody; whenever she felt happy it came bursting out.

"You are the only woman I can talk to," Carlos said.

"I hope we will talk together many, many times."

"I hope so too."

She put more ice into his glass and poured more whisky. For herself, soda water, with a drop of whisky to color it, like a child's drink. When she leaned forward to give Carlos his glass she hoped he could smell the perfume she had put all over her shoulders. It was real French perfume, not the *barato* they sold here and pretended was real.

The maid came in to announce dinner. "Please take your drink with you," Leila said. "She serves very slowly." She led the way into the dining room, walking with her back very straight, wondering if Carlos were noticing how tiny her waist looked in the full-skirted chiffon dress. She was none the worse for having had four children; she hoped he would realize that.

They sat opposite each other at the narrow end of the long, rectangular table. There were lighted candles in silver candelabra. It was a lengthy dinner with many courses, but all of them very light because of the heat, so that he would stay for a long time but not become so full that he would become unromantic. She wondered briefly, as they sipped at their delicate wine, if she really wanted Carlos to become romantic. This was the first time she had thought seriously of a man since João Alberto, and yet with Carlos it was entirely different. She admired his mind; he even awed her. He was handsome, in a distinguished way that awed her too. She did not feel a physical urge toward him as she had toward João Alberto, and yet, lately, she felt a stubborn, maddening urge for him to kiss her. At least he could kiss her. It was not kind of him never to try to kiss her, even when they were alone in a romantically darkened restaurant, or in his car, or at her doorway saying good night. It made her feel as if he did not want her or care for her at all; and yet tonight he had said that he *did* like her, that he liked her *very much.*

"You have such a look of concentration on your face," Carlos said. "What are you thinking?"

"I am thinking of Plato," Leila said with a little smile.

"Perhaps Plato the man, not Plato the writer."

"So I have that kind of look?"

"I think you do."

"To tell you the truth," Leila said, "I was thinking what a terrible thing it is that you have never kissed me."

"Now?" He did not seem startled or frightened; he seemed only amused. "Do you want me to kiss you now?"

"Why not?"

He rose, laying his napkin neatly beside his plate, and leaned across the table. Leila half rose too, and Carlos laid his hands very lightly on her bare shoulders and kissed her gently on the lips. "There," he said, smiling, and sat down again, and arranged his napkin across his lap.

Leila's head was swimming. She sat down again, slowly, like someone in a trance, her wide-open eyes fixed upon his face. She could hardly remember the kiss, it had been so light and brief, and yet he *had* kissed her, he had touched her bare skin with his hands, he and she were not apart. She sat there smiling tenderly at him and now it was she who was nervous.

"Do you know something?" Carlos said softly. He shook his head, smiling back at her. "You are only a child. A beautiful child. Someone should take care of you."

"Yes . . ." Leila breathed.

"Someone will," he said. He put his hand on hers and patted it. "How soft your skin . . . *Someone will.*"

The rest of their dinner passed as vaguely as a dream for her. She dimly heard herself whispering to the maid, offering Carlos more wine, suggesting he have a cigar with his *cafezenho.* She had been running a home since she was seventeen and presiding at dinners—twelve years—and it came automatically. But she had been dating men only one year, since she had recovered from mourning her lost marriage, and she felt confused and elated.

161

When he kissed her she had felt her heart leap up; it was her heart she had felt, not his lips. Her heart had sprung from her mouth like an invisible bird and it circled the room, its fright mocking her. She wanted to put out her hand for it and comfort it, cradling its panicked wings, but she did not know how. She sat there in the candlelight, smiling, speaking in a soft and womanly voice of books and philosophy and music, without her heart, almost without her mind.

"Shall we go back into the library?" She rose, fluffing out her skirts that were the color of fire. "We could sit in the living room if you like, but I prefer the library because it is my own room. All the things I like are in there."

Carlos followed her into the library. She put more records on the phonograph and poured brandy. Only one lamp was lighted. How opulent the room seemed in the shadows, as if she were a rich woman! Leila did not want him to know that she had hardly enough to live on; she did not want him to feel sorry for her. She had been deserted but she was not starving; she could still have a new dress made whenever she wanted one; she could buy Scotch whisky and real French perfume. She knew that girls had been after Carlos for years because of his money, and that was probably why he was so shy, but none of them had ever been able to talk to him as she could. She would be a surprise to him.

"I am writing two papers," he said. He was sitting next to her on the sofa and touching her hand. "They are each so different it will make you laugh. One is an earnings report to my stockholders. The other is a paper on what is wrong with the Brazilian theater today."

"I would like to hear about the second one," Leila said demurely.

"And not the first?"

"If you would like to speak of your business, of course I would like to hear it. My . . . husband often spoke to me about his office."

"I could speak to *you* about my business," Carlos said. "You would understand, I know that."

"Thank you."

"But, actually, I would rather hear myself speak about my paper on the Brazilian theater. I hope to have it published in a magazine. I compare our theater with the vitality of the theater abroad. I think our dramatists have much to learn from the vitality of foreign theater."

She was leaning toward him, looking into his face. He had a half-humorous way of speaking, as if he did not really expect her to think anything he had to say was important. She wondered if that was the way he spoke to everyone, or only to women. He must be so used to having women pretend to understand what he was speaking about and then reveal themselves by some stupid flirtatious remark that had nothing to do with the subject.

"I would like very much to see the American theater," she said seriously.

"Perhaps someday I will take you."

"Really? Imagine! To America?"

"Why not?"

"Oh, you are teasing me," Leila said. She had hold of his hand with both her own, like a child entreating a fascinating adult. "Do you mean it?"

"Would you go with me?" he asked. He had a little half-smile as he spoke.

"Of course I would!"

"Well, then . . ."

"We could travel on a ship," she said dreamily. "It would take nearly forever."

"Your eyes glitter like a little cat's."

"Little cat. My brother called me that." Suddenly her eyes filled with tears and she turned away. She did not know why she felt so moved and full of confusion. She felt frightened, and she was no longer sure whether she was happy or not. She did not know whether Carlos was only teasing her about America; she did not know whether he meant they would go as a married couple or if she would only be his mistress. She did not want to go as his mistress. She did not know what she wanted, and she was afraid to ask him anything too seriously for fear he would stop smiling and admit the whole beautiful scheme had been only a joke.

163

"You are not going to cry?" he asked.

"No." She wiped her eyes with her fingers and laughed.

"I love women because I can never understand them," he said, smiling.

"You understand me."

"Not altogether. I don't want to. You are too charming the way you are." He took her hands and kissed her fingers where they were damp from her tears, and then he kissed her mouth. This time she felt the kiss and tasted her own tears, salty now on his lips and strange to her. It was as if he had taken over her grief, as a man should, and was handing it back to her, impersonal now and no longer painful because he had taken the meaning of it away. Look, his kiss said, here are your tears of a moment ago, and they are nothing; only salt water.

She put her arms around his neck and kissed him several times, and he kissed her. There was nothing wild about their kissing; it was very gentle and romantic and comforting; almost a flirt. In her mind, behind her closed eyes, Leila could see a great white ship, with both of them on it, leaving the harbor.

"I must go now," Carlos said softly, drawing away.

"So soon?"

"I must finish my stockholders' report. I would much rather kiss you all night, but I cannot tell that to the stockholders."

They walked to the door with their arms about each other's waists. His waist was very lean. She was glad that he did not have an old body; he was still a comparatively young man; he would be a good husband. Even, she thought, perhaps even a good lover if I really am reckless enough to make love with him. It did not seem to matter, now that he was leaving her. She felt lonely. If he had stopped at the doorway and said, Be my mistress, I will stay, she would have agreed at that moment, only because the thought of closing the door behind him and being alone made her throat hurt.

"Where are your children?" he asked.

"I have sent them to spend the weekend with some friends in Petropolis. They hate the heat."

"And you? Do you hate the heat too?"

"If I went away for the summer I would not be able to see you," she said.

He smiled. "I am very lucky. Good night, little cat. Thank you for this evening."

"It was nothing."

She watched him as he walked down the hall and then she shut the door. He seemed happy but not eager to get away. As she walked slowly back to the library Leila went over in her mind everything that Carlos had said to her that evening and everything she had said to him. Had she said anything wrong? No, she had been intelligent, interested, solicitous. And he had seemed to like her. He had eaten very much at the table. He had drunk all the wine. He had admired her books. He had kissed her many times. Perhaps he really liked her more than any of the other women he knew. . . .

What he had said to her and what she had answered kept ringing in her head until she had no peace. She wanted to stop going over it all but she could not. Why couldn't there be an answer, so that when a man spoke to a woman he said, I am now making love to you and I mean it because I love you. Or, I am making love to you but it is only a game, so laugh and you will not be hurt. No one spoke that way; you could not expect it. And yet, it was all so new.

She took a book from the shelf but she could not read it. Her mind kept leaving the page and returning to a recital of Carlos' words. She would think of something else. Her children—no, if she thought of them she would worry. Were they homesick in Petropolis, were they crying? Teresinha often cried at night from nightmares when she was at home. Perhaps her older sister would make fun of Teresinha if she cried in bed, perhaps she would not understand. And the boys . . . would they do something reckless, would they get themselves killed? You never knew what boys would do if you didn't watch them. They thought they were so strong, but they were only babies. Leila covered her face with her hands.

She would think of something else; she would remember. She would remember something funny from when she was young, before everything changed for her. She remembered her governess, Madame. Wherever she went she always had to go with Madame, that tall, heavy woman with the tiny eyes. Madame's eyes were so small there seemed to be a useless space between them and around them that was her white face, and yet they were always darting to see that Leila was not talking to a boy or running out of sight. Leila remembered the night of her wedding, her civil ceremony, which took place the day before the religious ceremony, which really counted.

She and João Alberto had been married in the civil ceremony, but even then they were not allowed to be alone with each other, not even to go to the movies. There was a French film they wanted to see, so after the wedding she and João Alberto and Madame and João Alberto's cousin Izabel and Izabel's husband had all gone to the movies together. The two couples knew in advance how they would arrange the trick; they had done it often before.

When they entered the theater there was a great crowd. Everyone was rushing for seats. Leila and Izabel nodded at each other, and then Leila and João Alberto, clutching hands, had run upstairs to the balcony and Izabel and her husband had scampered to the front of the orchestra. Madame, not knowing which couple to run after first, had contented herself with galloping after Izabel because it was easier than running up so many stairs, and besides, Leila and João Alberto were already lost in the mob. They were alone! Leila and her husband of a few hours had sat in the last row of the balcony and kissed and kissed, not even knowing what was happening on the screen.

After the movie was over they walked demurely down the stairs into the lobby. Leila had smoothed her hair. "Oh, Madame!" she cried when she caught sight of her governess breathing fire and looking vengeful, "*There* you are!"

"Here I am, yes. And where were you?"

"We looked all over for you," Leila said innocently. "You must have got lost in the crowd."

"It was a terrible crowd," Izabel chimed in like an angel.

"Tch!" said Madame, but she protested no more, and behind

166

her broad back as they walked home Leila and Izabel exchanged winks, smiling happily.

And the next day there was the religious ceremony, and forever after Leila and her husband were allowed to go to the movies together alone.

Leila stood up now and walked slowly around the library, turning out the lights. She emptied Carlos' cigar ashes into a silent butler. You could not live in the past, and she was not even quite sure now that she wanted to. When she had been a girl running away from her governess to be with her fiancé it had not seemed as amusing as it did now when she looked back on it from far away. It was always easy to say the past was better, but Leila knew it was not, or at least hers was not. Many sad things had happened to her, but she was a grown-up woman now and she was free. She was sure many of her married friends were jealous of her because she had her freedom and could do what she liked.

It was so early; only eleven o'clock. She wondered if Carlos were hard at work on his stockholders' report, or if he had only made an excuse to her and had gone to a *boâte* with someone else. She looked out the window, as if that could help her somehow, but of course she could see only the houses across the street. She looked at the telephone on the little table in the hall and looked away from it, biting at the edge of her finger until it was sore.

Then the telephone rang, almost as if her fierce look at it had caused it to vibrate. For a moment Leila could not believe it was actually ringing. She ran to answer it, pausing for a moment before she spoke in order to catch her breath and still the pounding of her heart.

"Hello."

"Leila? Is it too late? Have I awakened you?"

"No, no, Ricardinho," she said, trying not to let her disappointment show in her voice. She had known Ricardo all her life; she still called him "Little Ricardo," even though he and she were the same age. "I was reading."

"I was at a very dull dinner party at some friends of my

mother's. I thought I might take you to a *boâte* for a drink or two, some place cool. If you are not too tired?"

She almost said it was too late. Then she thought of Carlos. "I will go with you with pleasure," she said. "Come right way."

She combed her hair and powdered her face, humming with anticipation, not as if she were going out with Little Ricardo at all, but as if she were going to see Carlos again.

Ricardo was at her door in five minutes, precise and neat in his white suit, his hair combed back so tightly with lotions that it seemed to be painted on. His smile was bright and happy, as it always was; he loved life, he was happy even to be going to the same night club he frequented at least twice a week, with a woman he had known since he was born. Everything was always new to him, as to a baby. Leila kissed him affectionately on both cheeks.

"You are not with a girl tonight? You have come to take out an old friend? How kind you are!" she said mischievously.

"Ah, I cannot always make love," he said happily.

His car was parked at the curb under a tree and a streetlight, its shiny white paint dappled with the outlines of dark leaves. "Would you like to go to Sacha's?" he asked.

"Let's just . . . drive for a while," Leila said. "I will tell you where to drive."

He drove slowly, glancing alternately through the windshield and sidewise at her. "Where are you leading me?"

"More slowly, please. Turn to this street on the left." She smiled. "It's so beautiful."

"This street is beautiful? More than any others?" He raised an eyebrow at her.

"Slowly!" She was leaning out the window now, counting the floors of Carlos' apartment house to find the one that was his. Those were his windows on the corner; he had told her he had a corner view. One was lighted. She wondered if the window were lighted because there was someone working inside the room or if it were only a lamp left lighted by a servant until someone came home to bed. "*Please* drive by again," Leila said.

168

Ricardo was smiling at her. "You must find this a *very* beautiful street."

"Only as a favor to me, Ricardinho. Please."

"I will drive by this house a dozen times if you ask me to," he said.

"You are always gallant."

"No. I like to help a friend who is in love."

He was circling the block to return. Leila looked at him in alarm. "In love?"

"Aren't you?"

"Of course not."

"Then this is a very late hour to be buying real estate," Ricardo said. He slowed the car almost to a stall. "Slow enough?"

She looked. It was a bright light in the window, the light of several lamps. They were wide, high, modern windows, the curtains drawn far apart. She could see the top of his bookshelf, and yes . . . she saw a figure moving about! "Once more. Only once more, Ricardinho."

"You must be very much in love," Ricardo said.

"No, it is nothing."

They drove around the block again, and this third time Leila saw that the figure walking in the room was Carlos. She recognized him from the color of the suit he had worn at dinner. She sighed happily with relief.

"And now can we go to a *boâte?*" he said.

"With pleasure." But she knew her heart was not in it and she hoped he would not guess from her tone.

"One drink only," Ricardo said. He sounded sympathetic, a little amused, and still happy. "You owe me your company for one drink anyway, in return for my being your assistant spy. Only one drink, I promise."

"I am a little tired," she admitted gladly. "But I am always happy to see you."

"Emotions are tiring, are they not?" Ricardo said. "I'm glad I don't fall in love. I don't think I would like it."

"No," Leila said seriously, "You would not like it. I don't think I like it either. It is very painful, this love."

CHAPTER 11

Some women, even if they never have children, are mothers. They may be childish, immature, romantic, but their attitude toward the people who are closest to them is more motherly than anything else. Perhaps they do not want to have any children; it does not matter. They are mothers to everyone else they touch. Margie Davidow had decided she was one of these, and it seemed to suit her. She knew she certainly was not the sexy type of woman—you had to think about sex or at least care about it to be one of those. She had none of those unconsciously seductive gestures that draw men to a girl who may be completely unaware of what she is doing to them. Margie's femininity was in her way of dressing, her neatness, her point of view, her likes and dislikes, and her manners.

When Mort Baker moved in with her and Neil she was happier than she had been in years. She arranged her large private dressing room for him, the room she and Neil would have used for a baby if they had had one. She put blue sheets on the studio couch and a little vase of fresh flowers on the table beside the bed. She brought a large ashtray (men liked that) and a stack of books from America. Whenever she passed a store window and saw some little thing Mort might like to have in his room, she bought it. She had the maids launder his shirts after he had worn them only once, and if he stepped out of his wet bathing suit and left it lying on the rug making a slowly growing pool of dampness she would wring it out in the sink when he was not around and then hang it back on his bedroom chair. Mort and Neil shared a bathroom. It had just never occurred either to her or to Neil to use the same bathroom and let their guest have his own.

But she could not fuss over Mort in exactly the same way she always could over Neil because he was not so tractable. She had chosen Neil's clothes since they were married because he admitted her taste was better than his. But she knew by instinct that she could never try to dominate Mort Baker.

In a way, she liked this. It made her a little afraid of him. If she wanted to buy him something, give him something important, she always had to do it as a sort of ruse. "We *needed* new towels for that bathroom; the old ones were getting shabby." Or, "I bought this sweatshirt for Neil on sale and he says he hates red. You try it. They won't take it back and it would be a shame for it to go to waste."

All of this attention to his friend only pleased Neil. He knew Margie too well to be deceived by her little ploys, even if Mort was, but he also knew her well enough not to be jealous of Mort. At night the three of them sat up until two and three in the morning talking or playing records. He planned to teach Mort how to play chess, but they never got around to it. It seemed as if there was never time any more to play games; and all of this had happened in only three weeks.

One evening Mort said he would not be having dinner with them; he had met a girl on the beach and he was going to take her out.

"It's about time," Neil said pleasantly. "I was wondering how long you were going to be polite and hang around with us."

"Don't be insane," Mort said.

"I'll give you a key," Margie said. "If . . . you need one." She smiled at him like an ultra-progressive mother who knows her husband has told their son where to buy contraceptives. But she didn't feel like a mother—suddenly she felt strange. "Is she Brazilian?"

"Yes, but she's been living here for a shorter time than I have.

171

She even speaks Portuguese with an American accent. It's funny."

"Well . . . maybe she can be your date for Carnival," Margie said weakly. She didn't know what was the matter with her; she felt as if she should encourage him to have an affair with this nameless faceless girl, and yet she had a sort of pleasant pain every time she spoke to him about it.

"Aren't we all going to go together?" Mort asked. He seemed hurt.

"Of course. But . . . you don't want to be stuck with us."

"Everybody's on his own at Carnival," Neil said. "I'm even going to give you a night off, Margie, if you want. You can buy a mask and go to a ball with Helen and some of your other girlfriends and flirt with all the men."

"And you?" she said, pretending to be jealous.

Neil put his arm lightly around Mort's shoulders. "*We* are going to go to the Married Men's Ball."

"He's not married!"

"That's all right," Neil said.

"Where is it?"

"I won't tell," Neil said happily.

"You'll tell me, Mort! Won't you?" Suddenly it wasn't funny any more; she felt left out. The light pain filled her chest and was no longer sweet. It wasn't that she was worried about Neil's having an afternoon affair at the Married Men's Ball; she almost wished he would. It would make her feel less guilty toward him.

"You can go too," Mort said. "You're married. Just wear a mask so Neil won't know what you're doing."

"She'll spoil all my fun," Neil said.

Margie looked Neil full in the face. "Oh, go to hell!" she said and walked out of the room.

As soon as she was in the hallway she felt ashamed. That was the first time in the entire five years of her marriage that she had ever said an unkind or unfair thing to Neil, even as a joke, and she knew what she had just said was not a joke. She went into her bathroom, locked the door, turned the water faucets full on in the sink and began to cry. What's the matter with me? she thought, standing up with her palms braced against the edge

172

of the sink as if she were about to be sick. She wanted to cry, to keep crying until all the tension was washed out of her, and when she glanced up and saw her contorted, red, ugly face in the mirror the sight made her cry even more.

"I want to go home," she whispered. "I want to go home. . . ."

It was the first time she had said that; it was the first time she had even thought it. Now she had something real to weep about, although she knew in her heart it was not the reason. She conjured up visions of everything back home in New York that could possibly make her homesick—the green trees in Central Park in summer, the crowds rushing to the theater on autumn evenings, parties in winter when she looked down from a high window in an apartment on Central Park West and saw the tiny street-lights twinkling below in the cold like flakes of snow and knew she could turn back in a moment into a warm room where she knew everyone and where everyone smiled on her and Neil with approval. The herd, she thought; it's gone. All gone, everyone who loved us and approved of us and smiled on our marriage because we were both young and healthy and Jewish and well-to-do. My parents were so happy, my whole family too; it was as if I'd joined them as a woman and they were all proud of me. Look at me, Mother and Daddy, I wanted to say. Look at me and Neil! Aren't you proud of what I've done?

And now everyone is far away and we're alone, and I'm afraid.

She opened the medicine chest to find an aspirin and gulped down two from the palm of her hand, without water, as she had trained herself to do since she had been living here in Brazil. It was so much easier than walking all the way into the kitchen. Her safety razor lay on the shelf beside the aspirin bottle. Margie picked it up, more as a whim, really. She didn't really mean to cut her wrists. Why should she kill herself? She had everything— a home, a husband who was devoted to her, good friends like Helen and Bert Sinclair and Mort Baker. She had a glowing tan, she was healthy, she had beautiful clothes. . . . She took out the blade and laid the edge of the naked blade against the inside of her wrist against the thin blue vein. Did people really do this? Did it hurt?

She didn't have the slightest intention of destroying herself, and yet she could not bring herself to put the blade down, not just yet. She really wanted only to hurt herself a little, to nick her skin, as if to give her heart and mind a physical reason for feeling the pain that she was feeling now. She didn't know what was wrong with her. She only knew that she didn't like herself very much and she wanted to hurt herself, just a little.

The cut hurt, but it did not bleed. Margie put the blade back into the safety razor and turned the handle until it was tight. She cut her thumb in the process, and the accidental cut on her thumb hurt more than the one she had deliberately inflicted on her wrist. She squeezed the cut on her wrist until it bled a bit, to disinfect it, and she sucked her hurt finger. I am a damn fool, she told herself. I hope nobody notices.

She washed her face and applied fresh make-up and brushed her hair. When she came out of the bathroom again the hall and bedroom were dark. "Neil?"

Mort was sitting in an armchair in the living room reading a magazine. He had one ankle up on the other knee and he was still wearing his wrinkled khaki shorts with the fringed edges that he had cut from his old Army suntan trousers.

"Where's Neil?"

"He went to the movies."

"*Now?*"

"He said he'd be back for dinner."

"And why aren't you dressed for your date?"

He looked up at her, and Margie saw that his face was rather grimy and he needed a shave badly, and she also saw for the first time a very vulnerable look on his face. He's handsome, she thought in surprise. What a nice face—it changes expression so often you never forget what it looks like and just look at your memory of it, the way you do with most people's. "I thought you might have cut your throat in there or something," Mort said.

"I?" she said. She smiled at him, a calm, secure woman with no secrets; and kept her injured wrist closely against the side of her skirt. "Do you want some iced *maté*? I do."

"I'll get it," he said, standing. "You sit there."

"Sit. You're still a guest even if you are one of the family." She rushed past him into the kitchen and took a bottle of the iced, heavily sugared tea out of the refrigerator. The maids were resting in their rooms before dinner. In the pantry cabinet was the extra liquor supply. Margie poured one tall glass full of iced *maté* for Mort, and filled another tall glass only halfway. She searched in the liquor cabinet for anything that was already opened. There was white rum; that was good. It wouldn't show, and didn't some people make rum punch with tea? She didn't care what she drank; she hated the taste of all of it. It had been a long time since she'd done this, and she didn't even think she could bear the smell of liquor any more. She filled her glass to the top with rum and stirred it with a long spoon.

She brought the two glasses into the living room and sat on the sofa across from him, sipping at her tea and rum and trying to pretend it didn't taste terrible. "I hope I didn't embarrass you a while ago," she said. "If I do scream at my husband once in a while I don't want you to feel like a Peeping Tom. I honestly feel as if you're one of the family, and so does Neil."

"As what member?" Mort asked.

"Just . . . someone we both love." She smiled.

"You've both been too tolerant for too long," he said. "I'm going to cut out soon. The trouble is, Rio is full of tourists now because of Carnival. As soon as it's over and they go away I'll be able to find an apartment and I'll be out of your community housing project."

"You . . . like it here, don't you?" Margie asked softly. "If there's anything you want, just ask me or Neil. And please feel free to go out every night if you want to. You're more than just a guest. I'll have a key made for you in the morning."

"The servants can always let me in. Don't bother, Margie."

"They go to sleep. If I was a man, and free, I'd want a key of my own."

"Don't overestimate the joys of freedom."

"I wouldn't know about them," Margie said. "For me there's always been someone. I don't think I'd know what to do if I ever had to be alone. I guess I'm lucky that there was always someone."

175

"Always someone," Mort said. "What does that mean? I don't even know what that means."

"*You?* The rake?"

"*Rake?*"

"I guess that sounds like a term from the gay nineties," Margie said, a little embarrassed. "I'm lucky I wasn't born a boy. I wouldn't know how to live that way. In a way I envy you. You can just live from day to day, you don't own things, you don't have to pretend anything for other people. Maybe if I'd had to live that way for a while I would have grown up."

"*You* envy *me?*" Mort said. "I always envy you and Neil. No, envy isn't the word. I just like to watch you, without envy, because you're really happy."

"Yes," Margie said. "We are happy." She gulped down the rest of her drink and set the empty glass very, very carefully on the coffee table. She felt as though there was a thin mist in front of her eyes. "We are."

Mort was watching her without saying anything. She smiled at him and lighted a cigarette. "Cigarette?" she asked. He shook his head. "I want you to be happy," she said, trying to keep the words neat and precise. Her tongue felt thick. Half a glass of rum and two aspirins; wasn't it funny how sometimes you could get so high on so little, and other times you couldn't get fuzzy if your life depended on it. She felt a glow of warm feeling toward Mort Baker; he was their friend, hers and Neil's, and she loved him. He was her son, her brother, the old college classmate, the friend of the family, all those wholesome things, and she loved him. She wanted to sacrifice for him to show him how unselfishly she loved him.

"I'm going to have a key made for you tomorrow," she said, enunciating to keep the words clear. "I want you to feel free to stay out all night if you want to, and have lots of 'honeymoons' and be happy. I want only good things for you. I want you to be happy."

"All right," he said. He sounded distressed and he was looking at her in a strange way. "So I'll be happy."

"Aren't you going to get dressed for your girl?"

"She's not *my* girl; she's a girl I met on the beach."

"Where are you going to take her?"

"I don't know."

"You don't know?"

"I just told her I'd take her to dinner. I didn't even think about where we'd go."

"Don't you like her?" Margie asked.

"I don't know yet."

"Yet . . ." she said. She sighed. "What a magic word that is. I don't know, *yet*."

"There's your freedom that you envy so much," he said. "A whole long series of 'I don't know yet.'" He stood up. "I'd better get dressed or I'll never know, because she'll go away."

"Yes," Margie said. "Hurry." She tried to think of something to say to keep him a moment longer, or even half an hour longer, with her. "Yes, hurry," she said again, as if that were a word that really meant "stay." It meant "stay" to her; she said it so frantically and with such feeling that she could not understand how he could not know. "Hurry!"

She stood up and followed him to the hallway that led to the bedrooms. He went into the bathroom that he shared with Neil, and in a moment Margie heard him turn on the shower. She went into her bedroom and sat down on the bed. She was suddenly weak and very tired. The maid had removed the bedspread and turned down the corner of the sheet. Margie pushed her pillow upright against the headboard and leaned against it, lighting another cigarette. It was the loneliest thing in the world to have gotten deliberately drunk because you needed to be free, to be yourself with someone, and then to find you were all alone with your own released feelings. She closed her eyes, feeling her heart pounding heavily from fatigue. She felt at this moment that she could say anything, do anything. She lay on her bed with her eyes closed, holding the cigarette, not smoking it, not moving, until she felt the smoke hot against her fingers, and then she sat up with a great effort and stubbed it out in the ashtray. She heard Mort open the bathroom door and walk to his bedroom.

It was easier this time to move. She stood up, smoothed her hair, and went into the hall. The door to his room was open and she saw him sitting on the studio couch tying his sneaker. He was wearing a clean white shirt with the sleeves rolled up and dark-green chino cloth trousers. With his hair combed and his face newly shaved he looked different again. He looked special. It was that same look that women only achieved after an hour of applying make-up and eyelash curlers and fussing over themselves, and he seemed to have it only because of the expression on his face and his cleanliness. She stood at the doorway.

"You look terribly nice," she said.

He seemed surprised. "Thank you."

She watched him as he tied the laces of his other sneaker and she felt stupid. She was rooted to the floor and she could not say a word. He was even wearing socks. He walked to the dresser, scooped a handful of paper money from the top of the dresser, and put the money into his trouser pocket. He picked up a package of cigarettes, squeezed it tentatively to see if it had enough cigarettes in it for the time being, and put that into the pocket of his shirt. He strapped his watch on his wrist and walked to the doorway where she was standing.

"Goodbye," he said pleasantly. "See you later."

She felt dizzy. "Goodbye," she said.

He was gone.

CHAPTER *12*

In January of that year the *Brazil Herald* reported that São Paulo police had arrested a voodoo witch who was allowing her satisfied clients to pay her for murders on the installment plan. The witch explained: "The system worked beautifully because I did business only with strictly honest people."

A citizen of Nova Iguaçu complained to police that he had been accosted at night on the street by a hold-up man. The authorities explained to him that they knew the dark streets were full of hold-up men, and that was why they had prudently stopped street patrols—so the policemen would not be attacked.

In Rio, a judge complained that a girl of minor age had been unlawfully arrested by police, and dismissed the policeman's charges that the girl had insulted him and behaved in a disorderly way in the jail. "If the detained did not behave well in jail," the judge ruled, "the police could send her away."

The fat, jolly, newly elected King of Carnival, Rei Momo, had his crown stolen from his head by a prankster. A week later there was a minor revolution held by reporters and the city touring department, who decided to dethroné the king because he "behaved indecently at Carnival fetes and got drunk too easily and too frequently." Since they felt that this behavior would reflect poorly on the Carnival events, they elected another Rei Momo, and the dethroned king went back to his year-round occupation as owner of a small shop called The Pastry King.

In anticipation of Carnival the illegal ether bombs in their aerosol cans were lined up on store shelves, even displayed in the five-and-ten-cent store. "Buy your Lança Perfuma early for Carnival," the sign said, in the aisle next to the beach mats and phonograph records.

All the newspapers joined in loud protest about this year's futuristic decorations which the city had put up on the main street of Avenida Rio Branco. One journalist even complained that the "eyesores are apt to frighten away quite some people" and might be responsible for the unprecedented exodus of Rio citizens to the country.

The new Rei Momo returned from a short publicity trip to the United States and said to reporters, "I don't know if many American tourists will visit Rio during Carnival; all what I know is that I personally produced an excellent impression on the Americans."

But tourists were flocking to Rio. The cruise ship *Caronia* stopped at Rio for two days, and the local press described all the passengers as "multimillionaires." This was an index of inflation, since the year before the tourists had only been called "millionaires." The visiting multimillionaires were being provided with "everything necessary to enjoy peace of mind and relaxation, including complete stock-exchange reports every day."

In Recife an unfrocked priest who had killed his bishop got a mild sentence "because victim did not actually die from bullets but lack of treatment."

In Rio the officials of the Federal pawnshop had been working overtime for several days before Carnival due to large public demand.

In the *favellas,* a man named Azevedo, who had confessed to police that he had killed his wife several years before "because I met another woman who could cook much better," was unable to remember the exact spot where he had buried her remains. The police decided that the search for her bones would have to be suspended until the following week, "for being improper at Carnival."

Carnival was approaching, wild and laughing, and all normal activities were put away. Officially Carnival lasted three days and four nights, but there were pre-Carnival balls and parties everywhere. Helen Sinclair bought a Carmen Miranda costume—a Bahiana, with a tight orange and black striped blouse, a bare midriff, an orange and black striped skirt slit up the side, and a great froth of white ruffled cotton petticoat underneath. She had strings and strings of bright glass beads, and a turban complete with piled up artificial fruit and earrings like great white doughnuts. Originally she had been going to buy only a mask. She and Margie went into a small shop in Copacabana, where a man sat at a table sewing stuffed hummingbirds and sequins and paillets on to little masks.

"We can wear evening dresses and masks," Margie said practically. She had been to Carnival before and she was trying to save money. "We'll find something becoming."

"That's right," Helen said virtuously. "We're only going to one ball anyway. It's too expensive to go to everything. We'll just wear masks to be like everybody else."

But even as they were talking they were rummaging through the piles of masks on the tray, holding them up and trying them on, discarding each for a larger, more fantastic one. There were brief costumes hanging tantalizingly on the walls—a cancan dancer, a scarecrow, a Greek boy, a woman of the future complete with fright wig and long black mesh stockings. Every costume was based only vaguely on the theme it was meant to portray. The main purpose was to be as brief and attractive as possible. A red velvet Santa Claus costume had a hat with a white tassel and a strapless dress with a pinched-in waist that looked more like a bathing suit than anything for the obese old Father Christmas, and terminated in a pair of clinging white tights.

"*You* could buy a costume," Margie said. "This is your first Carnival, after all."

"Oh, I wouldn't if you didn't."

"Well, at least try one on. It wouldn't hurt just to *look*."

Half an hour later they each had bought a costume, and they felt guilty and excited and glad. Margie had bought a brief white silk jersey tunic with gold trim, like a Greek boy's. Her tanned legs were bare and she had a wreath of gilded leaves for her hair.

The costume suited her, Helen thought, as Margie turned and postured in the mirror rather shyly. There was something about Margie so . . . neat and childish and . . . unawakened, like the boy-girls of ancient Greece. You didn't notice it when you saw Margie in a dress with crinolines and delicate high heels. She had a façade that was deceiving. But Carnival seemed to bring out the true personality of everyone, even if the person himself was unaware of it.

"I guess I'm a pagan," Helen said, reluctantly folding her costume back into its box. "I'd like to wear that thing right now and every day."

"The men will have to buy costumes now," Margie said. "Do you think they'll be angry?"

"They can wear yachting caps or something."

"I'm *glad* we bought them," Margie said. "Aren't you?" She sounded a little defiant. Helen knew exactly how she felt; she herself felt the same way. Bert would think she was idiotic when he found out how much she had spent for the Bahiana—fifty dollars—but finally he would want some kind of costume too.

"Yes," Helen said. "I'm glad. It makes me feel not like myself any more. I guess that's why people wear them."

"You should see. Nice respectable bankers and businessmen who live exemplary lives all year with their wives and mistresses suddenly take on hidden natures at Carnival." Margie looked around and lowered her voice to a whisper. "You see some of them dressed as Negro women, with complete face masks and complete body costumes, like black leotards, and lots of junky necklaces and padded bosoms and white Mandy gloves and they go around embracing men and screaming in these falsetto voices. People wear so much greasepaint and such complete masks you really can't tell who is a man and who's a woman. And it doesn't help to say the small ones are the women, because a lot of Brazilian men are very short."

"My lord!"

"Oh, you'll see," Margie said. "You wait."

The biggest and most famous pre-Carnival ball was the Baile des Artistes at the Hotel Gloria. For weeks now there had been

182

signs in the streets announcing it. The Gloria is an old, distinguished hotel set on a hill near the center of the city. A long veranda runs along the front of it, looking down on the street. The Sinclairs and the Davidows and Mort Baker met for cocktails first at the Davidows' apartment, and then at eleven o'clock in the evening they started for the ball. The men had been persuaded to wear costumes, to varying degrees. Neil had gone to the store and purchased a white toga and gold sandals so he could pair off with Margie. Bert wore the black trousers from his tuxedo and a white shirt, with a red scarf of Helen's wrapped around his waist for a cummerbund, and called himself a bullfighter. At the last minute he decided it was not enough, so Margie drew a dramatic curving mustache and long sideburns on his face with her black eyebrow pencil. Mort, who had no money and who said the heat in the hall often went up to a hundred and ten, wore his bathing suit.

"But what are you supposed to *be?*" Margie said.

"I'm a member of the *futebol* team that plays on the beach every day."

She laughed. "You'll be thrown out for indecent exposure."

"Not if you aren't."

"No, you have to be somebody else," Helen said. "You can't be lazy and just come as yourself and call it a *fantasea.*" She was being caught up in this now, the whole idea of the Carnival metamorphosis, the costumes that were called fantasies, the greasepaint and masks and disguises. It was important to be somebody else for these few days and nights; everyone in Rio had been waiting for a whole year for this chance to be a dream self, a released self, waited all year for this chance to explode into fantasy.

"You could wear one of your white sweatshirts and we could paint the name of a *futebol* team on it," Margie said. Already she was running into the guestroom, emerging with a shirt, looking excitedly for something to use for the lettering.

He would be a member of the Vasco da Gama team, which was a soccer team of Portuguese players with large black mustaches. Margie drew the letters with laundry ink, and Helen painted a mustache on Mort with the same pencil Margie had used for

Bert's. You had to be somebody else tonight; you couldn't enjoy it if you weren't somebody else.

Neil parked his car across the street from the Gloria Hotel and they joined the line filing in. There was a great crowd of people in the street, watching the rich and lucky ones who had been able to buy tickets. From the opened doors upstairs leading to the veranda there was the sound of the incessant Carnival music, the beat that was like a samba but louder and faster and never stopped, not for one minute, until the dawn. There was the sound of voices singing haphazardly, not following the words but bursting out uncontrollably once in a while with a chorus or an exuberant line. *Vai, mas vai mesmo*—go, but just go. . . . The words didn't make much sense, really, but no one cared. It was the music that made sense, the music that made you dance with anyone who was close at hand or even by yourself. Already, on the stairs, Helen felt herself beginning to sway and tap her feet, smiling, snapping her fingers and clapping her hands, smiling at strangers who were doing the same thing down there in the middle of the dark street.

It took more than half an hour to get into the hotel. As soon as they were through the front door Helen could feel the rise in temperature. It was swelteringly hot. In the corner of the lobby a group of a dozen cows, complete with huge shiny cows' heads and sharp horns and round blind eyes, were posing for photographers. Helen held Bert's hand as they pushed through to the elevator.

Upstairs there was a snake dance going on right in front of the elevator doors, people seemingly welded to one another, running, swaying, perspiring, as if in a trance of ecstasy. Helen, Bert, Margie, Neil and Mort dodged between the snake dancers as if they were on a football field and pushed their way through the crowds to the main ballroom.

There were long tables with white tablecloths on them set around the room. Hanging from the center of the ceiling like a chandelier was a gigantic papier-mâché clown with red electric eyes. He looked like the spirit of Carnival and, somehow, slightly drunken and wicked, swaying and bobbing on his cable. At one end of the room the band played—a blare of horns and beat of drums that was unlike anything Helen had ever heard before. She had heard Carnival songs being played on the radio for several weeks, but it was nothing like the overwhelming noise of this. In the middle of the ballroom, on what must have been the dance floor, was a great colorful mass of costumed humanity, dancing in no space, clamped together and completely alone in abandon at the same time, sometimes bursting out into song.

"Here we go," Mort Baker said. "Now we're going to jump like kangaroos for four days and nights. Good luck." He had already found a drink from somewhere.

Bert looked at the crowd on the center of the floor and then at Helen. "Shall we go in?" he asked, like someone suggesting a dive into a whirlpool.

It wasn't a question of "going in." You stood for a moment at the edge of the gyrating, bobbing crowd, and suddenly you were sucked in and you were a part of it. Helen was filled with a wild happiness. She danced with Bert, she danced by herself when she lost him, she danced with strangers. It was so hot in the room that she felt her hair becoming as wet and stringy as if she had just been swimming underwater. She was not tired. She hopped up and down without knowing the steps and without caring. Neil grabbed her and began to try to samba, but she did not like to dance with him because he was too labored and too slow, as if he still thought the Arthur Murray way counted in an orgy. She waved goodbye and danced by herself.

A boy of about eighteen, dressed like a Turk, with billowing white trousers and a little sleeveless jerkin with nothing underneath, began to dance with her, smiling wordlessly. He leaned closer and said something to her in Portuguese but she could neither hear him nor understand him so she smiled and shook her head. He thought she was Brazilian. They broke away from each other and joined a snake dance that was circling the outside of the dance floor. People were standing on tops of tables now to get a better view, their arms around one another, holding drinks and swaying to the music. It was so hot in the room that when Helen tried to dance with any man who did not have a shirt on her

185

hands slipped off his wet, perspiring skin. You had to hold tightly to your partner to keep from being torn away by the mass motion of the crowd, but the wet flesh was as resisting as if it had been greased. *Torero!* the crowd sang happily. *Torero!*

With relief she found Bert again and took his hands, smiling, too breathless to speak. His entire face was wet from the unbearable heat; he seemed almost to exude a mist. His eyes were glazed, as if he hardly recognized her. They danced together, and Helen put her hands around his arms, moving her fingers against the muscles under his shirt, feeling weirdly that this was not her husband at all but some stranger whom she must touch to recognize. *Copacabana . . . tem agua, tem agua, tem agua!* She didn't even know what it meant, but she sang the words she could make out, feeling a part of the crowd.

"We're going to eat," he gasped.

He led her, still dancing, through the pressed, rocking, flailing bodies until they reached the cooler air of their table at the far end of the room. Margie and Neil were seated, eating shrimps and rice, and Mort was nowhere to be seen. On top of the next table were two girls and two men, their arms around one another's waists, all dressed as harlequins. They were standing on the tablecloth only a few inches away from where other people were unconcernedly eating their dinners. Helen sat down but she could not eat. It was too hot and she was too excited. She found some bottled water and poured it into a glass. The ice was too far away so she gulped the fizzy water lukewarm, glad to have it.

Waiters were pushing their way through the crowd with plates of ice cream, trying to put it on the tables and remove the rest of the food and get the whole thing over with before they were wounded in action. Nobody seemed very interested in food anyway, except Neil, who was devouring automatically as he always did no matter how hot the room was. Margie had withdrawn into a corner and was powdering her face and trying to smooth back her damp hair. For a moment Helen had a pang of conscience, imagining how wet and bedraggled she herself must look, but then she didn't care. She had never felt this way before—so mind-

186

less and happy, like a vessel filled with music and nothing else. She climbed on a chair and stepped on to the table, kicking off her shoes to the floor.

The table was long, rather like a ramp in a musical comedy on which the dancers can go out among the audience. She looked down at the people jumping and rocking below her and she began to sway in time to the music, at first self-consciously because she had never danced on top of a table before and some people were looking at her, and then abandonedly. It was much cooler here on top of the table and she could look down and see everyone in a kaleidoscope of color and movement. She held up her arms and moved her bare feet in her own intricate speeded-up version of the samba, aware only of the music and her own movements. From below, the men who passed by in the snake dance waved at her and called out and some even tried to grab at her ankles, but she laughed at them. Other people were climbing up on tables now, dancing in pairs or alone.

How strange it was! She did not feel like Helen Sinclair, American Housewife—she felt like an anonymous Brazilian dancer, loved by everyone down there on the dance floor, waved at and smiled at and idolized. She waved at them all and smiled at them all. Someone squirted her with ether. It felt icy cold on her bare skin. The sweet, sickly smell of the ether bombs was everywhere in the room, blending with the moist heat. She felt as if she were drowning in flowers, but not bouquet flowers as she had known them; these were strange exotic flowers that grew wildly in the night and intoxicated anyone who breathed their odor.

Behind her a row of men had climbed up on to the table and were dancing too. The table was swaying slightly under their weight and for a moment Helen wondered if it would break, and if it did, where everyone could possibly fall. She kicked aside several empty glasses that had spilled on the tablecloth. The tablecloth was entirely black now, wrinkled, wet, and covered with mud from the pounding shoes. Waiters' hands were frantically tugging at it to remove it from under the dancing feet. Someone stepped on someone's plate of strawberry ice cream. The waiters finally pulled off the tablecloth, and Helen and the strangers were dancing on the bare boards.

Directly below her, between two tables, a man put his hand inside another man's trousers. "Take your hand out of my pants," the second man shouted. The first did not. The second one grabbed a glass, broke off the top of it on the edge of the table, and cut the first man's throat. Hands reached out, taking and holding the attacker and the attacked, taking them away. The music blared on and no one else paid any attention.

Across the room a man, very drunk from liquor and ether, fell off a table on to his head. He bounced once and lay still for a moment, while his friends on the table gasped. Then he sat up, looked around, and stood up, oblivious of the blood pouring down his face. He began to dance again. Helen looked at him, shocked, until she remembered that ether is an anesthetic.

The table was rocking dangerously now and she was beginning to tire. She had only a few inches of space left to dance on anyway, so reluctantly she climbed down to the floor. She drank more water ravenously and looked for Bert. He had disappeared. Behind her was an exit and through it she could see the veranda and the black night sky. She searched under the table until she found her shoes and then she went out on to the veranda.

It was cool outside and the sky was filled with large white stars. There were couples resting against the veranda railing, talking inaudibly. Above the edge of the railing Helen could see the outlines of palm fronds. The street below was lighted by strings of lights and filled with people watching the people on the veranda. The music inside the hotel was less noisy now, pleasanter, almost like a heartbeat. She pulled off her turban and gasped with pleasure as the breeze blew through her wet hair. She imagined herself steaming, the way a hot frying pan does when you run cold water on it. She stood leaning against the railing, her back to the street, looking at the people strolling out of the ballroom. There were a great many couples dressed in Alpine shorts and green hats this year; perhaps because it was an easy costume and cool. But there seemed to be more people dressed as fantastic blackamoors than anything else, with the face masks that looked like a black stocking pulled over the head with little holes cut out for the eyes and mouth.

A tall, beautiful boy with café-au-lait skin strolled by, dressed as an angel complete with halo and huge golden wings. Helen smiled at him because his costume was so exquisitely made, and murmured, "Ah, *lindo*." He glared at her and walked on, and she realized then that he was one of the homosexuals, who sometimes had the most imaginative and lovely costumes of all.

Near the doorway was a group of people dressed as rich Colonial Brazilians. They looked a little like the American southern aristocracy of the Civil War. They seemed different from the other revelers at the ball because they were quieter, more observers than participants, and the women especially seemed very conscious of their elaborate costumes. They talked quietly among themselves and fanned themselves and allowed passers-by to glance admiringly at them, as if they had come to the ball only to discover the effects of their *fantaseas* and then would go home. Surely none of them could dance in those huge hoopskirts on the crowded dance floor. The group turned and walked slowly into the hotel now, except for one of the men, who came toward the railing near where Helen was standing. She did not recognize him until he was next to her because he was wearing a mask and a wig.

"Hello, darling," Sergio said quietly.

"I didn't recognize you," she said. "I didn't think you'd be here." She held out her hand, rather formally, filled with confusion at seeing him so unexpectedly. He kissed her hand and held it for a minute.

"I wasn't going to come with them," Sergio said. "I don't like Carnival. My wife is on the farm, and I was just going to stay in my apartment and go to bed." He smiled ruefully and shook his head. "I say that every year. *This* year, I say, I will *not* go to Carnival. I hate it. I drink too much, and I stay up all night, and I sniff too much ether until I feel sick. It's an orgy; it's ridiculous. But there's something in my blood. . . . I don't know. I say I won't go, I lie on my bed, and then I hear the music coming from the *favellas* on the hill behind my apartment house. It happens every year this way. I listen to that music and I start to writhe on

189

my bed like a snake. And then I put on a costume and here I am again."

"I'm glad you're here," Helen said.

"Are you?"

"Yes."

"You look beautiful. You have a Bahiana!" He surveyed her affectionately and proudly, as if she were a very clever child; she had noticed that look on other Brazilians when they saw an American who was enjoying himself at Carnival as much as they were. She smiled at him.

"It wasn't difficult to buy."

"You should wear it all the time."

"I'd like to," she said.

"Would you like champagne?"

"*Is* there any?"

"Come with me."

He led her adroitly through the crowd in the hot, brilliantly lighted ballroom, through another smaller ballroom, and finally to a room where there was a bar. There were orchestras in every room, playing loudly, pounding out the music that never stopped. In every room people were dancing, bobbing up and down, perspiring, smiling, pushing, until Helen felt as though she were wandering in a labyrinth that had been made to confuse the wanderer because everything everywhere was so exactly the same and so extreme, like a dream.

Sergio bought the entire bottle of champagne from the bartender and took it to a vacant table in the corner. The champagne was cold and on the sweet side, and Helen had two glasses. He drank the rest himself. Helen had never seen him drink so much before. From his pocket he pulled out a gilded aerosol can of the perfumed ether.

"Have you ever tried this?"

"What do they do with it?"

He looked around for an instant to make sure no one was watching. "Don't make a big display," he said very quietly. "It offends some people when they see what I'm going to do." He squirted some of the ether into his handkerchief and quickly held

190

the handkerchief over his nose and mouth, breathing deeply. He was holding his head down so it looked fairly innocent, as if he might be only going to sneeze. "Do you want to try?"

"I . . . don't know."

"I'll only give you a little. It will make you feel drunker, and happy. You must breathe it in immediately after I give you the handkerchief because it evaporates." He squirted more ether on the handkerchief and held it to Helen's nose.

She had a moment of terror, reminded of when she had had her tonsils out as a child and ether on a white piece of gauze had made her unconscious. She breathed in, shallowly and fearfully.

"You've let it all escape. Quickly!" he whispered.

He wet the handkerchief again, and this time she took a deep breath. The damp handkerchief felt cold against her lips and smelled like those same sickly sweet flowers. She breathed it again, closing her eyes.

She felt a little lightheaded, but it might only have been from excitement or from breathing so deeply. She smiled at him. "Give me more. I don't feel a thing!"

"I think you've had enough," he said. "I don't want to make you drunk; I only wanted you to see how it feels." He put the *lança perfuma* quickly into his pocket. "I don't even like it when I do it to myself," he said. "Tomorrow I will feel sick, and I will probably call the doctor to give me vitamin injections. But to-night . . . well . . ." He finished the last of the bottle of cham-pagne and lighted a cigarette.

"Why do you do it, then?"

"I don't know," he said. "I always do it at Carnival. At the same time I'm doing it I'm laughing at myself. Do you want to dance?"

"Yes."

They went into the other room, hesitated for an instant, and threw themselves into the pack of dancers. It was hotter than ever, so hot now that it did not matter any more that it was hot or that there was no longer anyone who was reasonably dry or reasonably sane or whose greasepaint had not run and smeared in streams of glistening perspiration. Helen held tightly to Sergio, her feet moving rapidly to the rhythm of the music, her smile stiffening. Her happy exchange of grins to the other dancers was becoming automatic now and she felt exhausted, her legs beginning to ache. She had been here for hours. She had never danced so fast and strenuously, or for so long, before. At the beginning of the evening the wild dancing had been a release, but now she only wanted to stand very quietly with Sergio and have him put his arms around her.

"It's so hot," she gasped.

"Let's take a walk."

He took her hand and led her through the dancers with the same swift expertise as he had when they had been looking for a drink. They were outside again, and the night air was cool and wonderful. Neither one of them said anything. They smiled at each other and walked quietly to the railing, hand in hand. They leaned against the railing for a moment looking down at the crowds still gathered on the street, and then Sergio turned and put his arms around her. It was what she had wanted him to do. She leaned against him and he kissed her forehead and neither of them spoke.

She could hear the music, softly, and dimly see other couples walking by or standing in embrace. It did not matter; she did not know any of them. She hardly knew herself. She knew only that she felt very much at peace with herself, very quiet inside, as if all this were the most natural thing in the world. She had her arms around Sergio's waist and he had his arms around her; her head was against his chest, their bodies tightly together. She wondered what any of his friends or her friends would think if they came out on the terrace and saw the two of them that way. And Bert . . . But she felt charmed, lucky, as if no one would ever dare to come out on that terrace now except strangers, because she and Sergio were strangers now to the whole world. Neither of them moved or spoke.

Then when they moved they moved at the same time. She lifted her face and he kissed her. Their faces were wet and it was strange—a strange kiss, tender and desperate, the kiss of strangers who have wanted to kiss each other for a long time. They looked into each other's faces, wonderingly at first, as if that kiss had somehow changed them. It was a glance almost of surprise. Then they kissed again, but this time it was a kiss of neither surprise nor questioning but of passion.

She felt the faint brush of other people passing by her on the veranda but she was only dimly aware of them, as if their footsteps and voices and accidental touch were only changes in the current of the air.

Sergio looked at her. "I will take you away after Carnival," he whispered. "Will you come with me?"

She wanted to ask him not to speak, not to make anything real, only to stay there and kiss her. But she felt against her will her lips forming the word *Yes*.

At two-thirty in the morning it was really only the middle of the evening for most of the dancers at the Baile des Artistes. Mort Baker had vanished somewhere with a girl dressed as a black cat. Margie Davidow, exhausted, was sitting on a chair and refusing to dance, looking with admiration at her husband bobbing up and down on the crowded dance floor with first one stranger and then another. Bert Sinclair, who always seemed to be pursued by older women, had found himself in the clutch of a dyed-haired woman of fifty who was dressed as a courtesan of the ancient Roman court and who had one arm around his neck while pretending to eat a bunch of purple grapes from the other hand. Helen came in from the cool veranda and put on her turban again, hot and heavy with its weight of artificial fruit, and she felt as if she were putting on some instrument of torture. She went to Margie.

"Is anyone interested in going home?"

"I am!" Margie said. Her eyes began to sparkle with the first real pleasure they had shown in over an hour.

"Do you think they'll think we're spoiling everything? I'm dead."

"Oh, so am I!"

"Where's Mort?"

"Off with a girl," Margie said lightly. "He'll find his way home—if he comes home at all. I'll get my husband." She climbed up on to the table and began waving and gesturing at Neil.

193

Neil broke away from the dancers and came over reluctantly. "We want to go home," Margie said. "I've had enough."

"What time is it?" he asked, beginning to protest.

"Two-thirty. *Please!*"

Helen had never seen Margie look so tired. She had dark circles under her eyes where her make-up had worn off. But it was not so much fatigue that made her look so limp; it was more a look of hopelessness, a kind of sagging exhaustion. There was something odd going on with those three—Margie, Neil and Mort—and Helen did not know what it was, but it was there. Perhaps Margie resented having the second man in her home all the time—Margie had such a sense of order and such precise, neat ways, and Mort certainly was a Bohemian. Helen remembered Margie's outburst Christmas Eve about her marital privacy. It was always hard to tell what Margie really felt about private things; she covered up so well. You always had the feeling that Margie had some kind of painful secret in her life, but that she was able to keep it to herself because she first of all kept it *from* herself. For a woman that was really the only way to deceive others artfully; you had to convince yourself first.

Helen waved to Bert and he came over to their group. "What are we doing now?" he asked.

"We'd love to go home. If you don't mind."

"I don't mind."

They drove along the beach, and Helen felt the first signs of the exhaustion and muscle stiffness she knew would last for several days. She had never dreamed she would have as much energy as she had shown all night. She put her head on Bert's shoulder and he put his arm around her. He had removed his shirt because it was completely wet and he was holding it out the car window to dry. It flapped in the air from the moving automobile like a castaway's rescue signal.

"I love you," Helen whispered.

"I should hope so."

There was kindness and affection and strength in the way he said it, and if she could have cut out her heart at that moment and handed it to him she would have done so. The minutes on the terrace with Sergio seemed like a bad dream. How could people do such things? She thought of Sergio's wife only in passing, as if the woman were some kind of figure, not a real person. Their relationship in their marriage had nothing to do with her. She thought of Bert, here with his arm trustingly around her, protecting her, and she was filled with pain for him. She didn't want to hurt him, no matter what he might do. She had thought at times that he was sleeping with some woman on one of those long trips he took so often, but that really didn't matter now. She didn't know for sure that he had slept with someone else, and even if he did, if he didn't love the other woman, then it really didn't matter. She didn't want to know any more about it. He was her husband and he loved her, and he always came back to her. Nothing else mattered, or could matter, or else they would not have a marriage. I almost hurt you, she thought guiltily, looking up at his profile shadowed in the dark car. I never will hurt you again, darling, I promise. I promise. . . .

"Do you want to stop off at our house for coffee?" Margie asked. She did not sound very enthusiastic about it.

"You're too tired," Bert said quickly.

"What a bunch of deadheads," Neil said in mock scorn. "Three o'clock in the morning and you want to give up."

"Do you want a dead wife?" Margie asked.

"I'm only teasing you," he said gently. "What does everybody say; should we get tickets for the Copacabana and the Municipal?"

"You mean it?" Margie asked. "You were the one who wanted to save money."

Neil laughed. "I say that every year. Until the first ball is over. Let's go to hell with ourselves and go to all of them."

"It happens every year," Margie said.

"I'd love to," said Bert. "Helen?"

"And can we go into the street one night?" Helen asked, beginning to be carried away by their excitement. "And can we watch the Escola de Samba parade?"

"We'll do everything," Neil said.

"I'm going to buy a *lança perfuma* tomorrow," said Bert.

195

"Bert has to get a real costume," Margie said.

Helen felt warm and happy. These were her friends, and she loved them. And this was her husband, the only man she could ever love. Perhaps she would buy little costumes for the children, and they could have a Carnival party at home before she and Bert left for one of the late-starting balls. She had read in the newspaper that there were some children's Carnival parties in the afternoons somewhere, where there were no *lança perfumas* and nothing was served that was stronger than Coke. She would take Julie and Roger. They were all going to be happy at Carnival; it was going to be special for all of them, the whole family.

Neil stopped the car in front of the Sinclairs' apartment house. "Good night."

"Good night. Thank you. We'll phone each other tomorrow."

Bert put on his shirt and they went into the house. Riding up in the small self-service elevator Helen kissed him. He put his arms around her, and when the elevator doors opened they walked to their apartment with their arms still around each other's waists, and as soon as they were inside their darkened vestibule they kissed again. "I always like to get home," he said.

"So do I. It sounds so wonderful when you say that. Say it again."

"I like to get home?"

"Yes . . ."

They kissed again and she felt the familiar mixture of excitement and tenderness and love that always surprised her because although it was always the same it was always new. She could never bring it back when he was not there, but whenever he kissed her or touched her she felt it again, even though they had been married for nine years. She didn't believe people who said love stopped or changed or became reasonable and placid after several years even if it became deeper in a new way. It would always be this way for her and Bert; she knew it.

"Please don't go away again for a long time," she whispered, her arms around his neck. "Please don't leave me. I miss you so terribly."

"I want you to," he whispered, smiling at her in the darkness.

196

Her eyes were becoming accustomed to the dark and she could see his face.

"You're so beautiful," Helen said.

"Beautiful? Men aren't beautiful."

"Oh, I'm sorry—you know what I mean. I love your face."

"Thank you."

"Don't say *thank you*—" She stopped, remembering where she had heard that, and feeling as she had when it was said to her, and for the first time feeling an acute, unwanted pain. She closed her eyes and tried to put the feeling away.

"The first thing I want to do," Bert said gently, "is something I've wanted to do for the past three hours. Take a shower."

"I don't even want you to leave me for a minute."

"You'll take it with me."

It was like the old days, Helen thought happily, the old days when she and Bert were alone together with nothing but their love. Running the water in the shower at three o'clock in the morning, not terrified that any little sound might awaken a fretful child, not worried about being too sleepy to get up in the morning. This Carnival night had done something for him too; he seemed different, happier, more giving. They dried each other with thick towels, but not any too carefully, and fell on the cool sheets with their arms wound around each other, still slightly damp, everything cool and warm both. Cool sheets, cool skin, cool air from the opened doors leading to the balcony, warm mouth, warm breath, skin that warmed, the scent of soap and the scent of love. She had never loved or desired him as much as she did at this moment, and this was the man to whom she had almost brought pain. Strangely, knowing she had come so dangerously close to hurting him made Helen love him and want him even more.

CHAPTER *13*

Carnival in Rio is a mass explosion, the result of twelve months of frustration, sublimation, hopelessness and hope. At Carnival a beggar can dress as a king. An austere businessman can dress as a clown. A colored girl from the *favellas* who will have twelve or twenty children and live and die in the *favellas* can dress as Scarlett O'Hara, and many of them do. A homosexual can walk about in the streets of the city for four days and nights dressed as a woman. You are who you want to be. There is unceasing music for your soul and unceasing dance for your animal spirits, and ether to make your days and nights a waking dream. There is dancing in the ballrooms for the wealthy and dancing in the streets for the poor. But there *are* no poor at Carnival. There are only the revelers, the transported, the disguised, the dreamers and the orgiastic.

For four days and nights, without sleep, without food, without minds, the dancers jump up and down in a wild, self-hypnotic orgy, together or in a snake dance or alone. At the balls you see old men ready for a coronary attack wetting their handkerchiefs with ether and sniffing at them to get a lift, while holding on with the other hand to the girl in front of them in the snake dance. On the faces of these old men is an expression compounded of ecstasy, agony, exhaustion, and desperation. It is the face of Carnival.

In recent years, of course, as any Carioca will tell you, Carnival has become more commercial. There are television cameras and newsreel cameras and photographers with flashbulbs covering the revelry for magazines. But everything has become more commercial in our day; there are even press agents for wars. The people themselves are the same; the people never change. And the people who say they will not go to another Carnival this year, or that they will only go a little bit, like Sergio Leite Braga, like Margie and Neil Davidow, find themselves involved in the holocaust and happy to be consumed.

On one afternoon of Carnival week Neil Davidow and Mort Baker attired themselves in striped shirts, white trousers, French berets, and face masks, and went to the ball for married men. Actually, as with any of the other balls, it was not restricted to married men and women who wished to meet them; it was merely given the title and held in the afternoon so married men could attend without their wives. Neil had a sense of rising excitement as he walked briskly down the hot street toward the hotel; he was hardly aware of the heat at all. The air was sirupy with heat, and bathers were shrieking on the beach. There were so many people in brightly colored bathing suits that you could hardly see the sand between them. The waves hit the shore wildly, casting up foam like cotton candy ten feet into the air. Neil felt full of energy. He glanced at Mort striding beside him, and although at times he had felt faintly jealous of Mort's assurance and independence, today he was not jealous at all.

The ballroom of the hotel was filled with the unreality of artificial light in the middle of the day, with the curtains at the high arched windows drawn against the heat and sunlight. The air was heavy with the sickly sweet scent of ether. The band blared the same Carnival music, as if it had been imported entire, functioning and unceasing, from every other ball that had gone before. There were girls gathered about the room, alone and together, dressed in masks and head feathers and brief glittering costumes that showed their beautiful legs.

This room was a world in itself, a world of anonymous, willing, giving girls with red mouths and round breasts and tiny waists and long curving legs. Why did all the Brazilian girls have such tiny waists? Neil had been watching them on the beach for years, and they were all shaped like hourglasses. He had never seen such feminine women. He suspected that the ones who did not wear bikinis wore some kind of waist pinchers or girdles under their bathing suits, even when they went into the water. Margie had told him once that next to a Brazilian girl an American girl looked like a little boy.

He wasn't going to think about Margie today. There were long stretches of time during his days away from her when she didn't exist for him at all. Then when he was doing something as ordinary and unrelated to her as lunching at the American Club with some men from the office, suddenly a woman across the room would remind him of Margie—the color of her hair, the way she held her head up—and Neil would put down his fork and be unable to eat at all. He would feel something happen to his breathing, as if breathing were something you had to will and be aware of all the time or it would stop. Margie always held her head up very high when she walked across a room, her chin slightly tilted up, as if she were a little bit of a snob, but she was too short to look like a snob when she walked that way. She only looked like a small girl trying to appear taller, and there was something touching about it, or at least Neil found it so. Everything about her was touching; an accidental gesture of her hand, the look of fright that came into her eyes, even her complete, absolute, immobile frigidity. He felt like a deformed beast when he touched her, not like a man or a husband or a lover, but like some abomination from a Jean Cocteau movie. The enslaved beast, disguised, with the lonely heart of a man. Neil felt only that he had never been able to give her anything, and that unless he could . . . But he wasn't going to think about Margie today. He was at the Married Men's Ball with four hours to himself and he was going to get slightly drunk, just to have an edge, and then he was going to make love to a woman.

"Every man for himself," Mort said, looking at him. "All right?"

"We'll meet here later," Neil said without conviction. He was being the proper husband with no seriously bad intentions, but he hoped Mort would protest. Mort did.

200

"Well . . ." Mort said, and for some strange reason he sounded slightly embarrassed. "*I* have nothing to do later. Maybe you won't see me. But I'll see you at eleven o'clock tonight, in time for the Copacabana. Okay?"

"Sure." Neil patted him on the back, although the gesture at that moment seemed false. "*Te logo.*"

Mort held up his hand like an Indian saying "peace" and was gone in the crowd. Neil stood there for a moment listening to the music and watching the girls. Then he looked for the bar.

He bought scrip and then he had three straight whiskys rapidly in a row and then a whisky and water for a chaser. He began to feel relaxed. It was going to be a good party. The people seemed nice, the music was good, the whisky was not bad. He finished the whisky and water, put out his cigarette at the bottom of the paper cup, and went off to dance.

He would dance for a while and then he would repair to the bar for a drink, and if he was dancing with a girl who was attractive he would buy her a drink. He had the feeling that he shouldn't try to press it, that this afternoon was a very important one shot, and there was a lot of time left today to pick a girl he would really like. Every time he found one who seemed particularly attractive and he was on the verge of asking her if she wanted to leave and find a drink someplace better he would reconsider and decide this girl was not good enough. Her legs were too thin, her mouth too small, or she seemed too silly. He wanted a particularly voluptuous girl, even a rather dirty girl, the kind of girl the guys used to call a "pig" at college. The drinks he had had were making him think in slow motion and it was pleasant. Today was going to be an important afternoon. I want, Neil thought pleasantly, the kind of girl you can drown in, the kind you want to tear apart. A great, round, wild, silky, resilient, fleshy girl, *but not fat;* with long, long hair and slightly smeared lipstick, the sort of girl who looks slightly messy *before* I mess her up, a girl who moans, a girl who . . .

"Neil . . . ?"

The girl standing in front of him at the bar had a timid, slightly thin voice, and she was neither fleshy nor resilient-looking. She was short and slender, and she was wearing a black and white striped tiger costume which covered her from the top of her head to the top of her thighs. It had a cap with two perky ears, and it covered the entire upper half of her face. The costume even had a long tail. She wore black mesh stockings and high-heeled black shoes, and she had the kind of legs you see on an Apple Blossom Queen—nice but not particularly sensual.

"Do I know you?" he asked.

She giggled. The giggle was unexpected. "You don't know me?"

The voice was completely familiar, and if he had not had so many whiskys Neil was sure he would have recognized it in a moment. She had the slightest of Brazilian accents, almost imperceptible. "Say something else," he said.

"I have loved you since the moment I saw you." She put her arm through his, to show she was teasing, and peered into his face.

"Something more."

"I have loved you for years, and you don't know I'm alive."

Neil looked at what was left of his drink, and then swallowed it. "Keep going. This is nice."

"I would like very much to kiss you. Will you kiss me?"

"My pleasure."

He put his arms around her small waist and pulled her close to him. Something about the feeling of her body was both familiar and strange and he suddenly felt very much aroused. He kissed her mouth hard and kept holding on to her.

"You've had quite a lot to drink," she said. She did not sound reproachful, only surprised.

"What would you like to drink?"

"Could I have a Coca-Cola?"

"No."

"I can't drink," she said. "I have a bad liver." She smiled at him. "Don't you really know who I am?"

"Christ, how should I know who you are?"

"Good." She kissed him again, lightly, and this time Neil really could not let go of her. He kept his arms around her tightly and

202

forced her lips open with his tongue. She was trying to get away from him now, but subtly, squirming a little. Her movements only made him more excited, and he suddenly hated her. He remembered whom she felt like with that tiny waist and that slim mobile body; she felt like Margie. She turned her head away from him.

"Let's have a drink," she breathed. Her voice sounded frightened. Neil wanted to choke her.

"What the hell do you think you're doing?" he said angrily. He was really drunk, he knew, because her face kept getting blurry and he had never spoken to a woman in this way before. "Damned little cock-teaser! Who do you think you are?"

"Oh . . ." she said, very softly. "Oh . . ." Suddenly, surprisingly, he saw that she was crying. "I didn't mean to make you angry. I thought it was a joke," she whispered. She reached up and pulled off the tiger cap and mask so that she could wipe her eyes.

When he saw who she was he became almost sober. The mysterious girl with the supple body, dressed as a tigress, his drunken memory-image of Margie, and the prosaicness of who this girl really was—a secretary in his office—all blended into one improbable girl. "For God's sake, Gilda," Neil said. He tried to make a joke of it. "As they say in the movies, I didn't recognize you without your glasses, Miss Jones."

"And then she's always Lana Turner," Gilda said. "She's not just me." She wiped her tears away with her fingers and Neil handed her his handkerchief. She smiled. "I think I could use that drink now," she said. "The hell with my liver."

"No," he said. "I wouldn't dream of it." He slid some more scrip across the bar to the bartender. "Double whisky and a Coke."

She was an odd girl; he really didn't know her very well. She was from an old, rather social, Brazilian family, and she had been educated in the States. In fact, she had even gone to Radcliffe, giving it up after two years and coming back to Rio and getting a job. Office work paid almost nothing for these girls, but Gilda's parents had money and she lived with them. Her way of dressing, her speech, her manners, were all more American than Brazilian, and in a way Neil had felt sorry for her around the office because she seemed lost. She wasn't feudal, or dependent, or unthinkingly passive like other girls from her background, and yet she had to live here in Rio and behave like everyone else. He had sometimes wondered what kind of boys she went out with.

"What are you doing at a party like this?" he asked her.

She straightened the seam of her black mesh stocking. "I don't know. I was bored. You know, I haven't been in Rio at Carnival time for six years, and before that I was too young so my parents used to ship me off to my grandparents in the country. This is really my first Carnival. So I thought I'd go to everything."

"Including parties where married men pick up girls?"

"If you're worried that I'll remember, I won't. You'll find this ball is as secret as the confessional. A friend of mine was in love with a man who she thought was at the Married Men's Ball last year, but when she begged everyone she knew to tell her if he was there, they wouldn't answer. Not that anybody *does* anything. But not telling adds to the mystery."

"It does," Neil said. He was beginning to like her, and his anger had all ebbed away. He felt a little embarrassed. "I'm very drunk," he said, by way of apology for what had gone before.

"Everybody is."

"Are you here alone?"

"Entirely."

"And are you having fun?"

She shrugged. "In a way. I think I'm crazy—you know? I hate Rio and I love it. I hated sitting around the *piscina* all day drinking orangeade, so I got this job. And do you know I don't even make enough money to buy myself a new dress? If I bought three dresses a year I wouldn't have a penny left for anything else. I figured it out. And sometimes when I go to a party where there are a lot of girls I grew up with, who are all married now and have babies, I catch them looking at me as if I'm some sort of a freak. I even think they're sorry for me. They think I'm an old maid."

"How old *are* you?"

"I'll be twenty-one next month."

"Terribly old," Neil said. "Disgraceful."

"The worst of it is, I have nothing to say to them any more.

And they have nothing to say to me. They tell me how nice it is to be married and have babies. And then there's a long silence."

"Not so different from in the States."

"Oh, it *is* different!" Gilda said. "I love the States. There are so many men to go out with. And they treat a girl like a person, not just a wrestling partner. At Radcliffe I went out every night. Well, I don't know why I'm telling all this to you."

"Because you've loved me ever since the moment you first saw me," Neil said.

"That's right! How could I have forgotten?"

They both laughed. Neil wanted very badly to put his arm around her, but this time he felt foolish, like the older man, the executive, the boss chasing the secretary behind the filing cabinets. "Put your mask on again," he said softly. "Please."

She did not ask him why, or even look puzzled. She merely slipped the tiger mask and cap over her head and tucked in the stray wisps of hair. Neil put his arms around her.

"I can feel your heart beating," Gilda said.

"Are you always so candid?"

"It's a defense."

"If you can say so, it isn't."

"If I say it to you it's the truth."

"Yes," Neil said. "I believe you."

"Do you want to dance?"

"No," Neil said. "If I start knocking myself out in there I'll sublimate."

"You frighten me a little."

"*I do?*"

She smiled. "Because I like you. Does that make sense?"

"Yes," he said.

"Carnival is crazy, isn't it?"

"You're a funny girl."

"I'm a freak," she said lightly. But she stiffened as if he had hurt her.

He put his chin on the top of her head. "You're a *little* girl."

"Wouldn't it be nice if I were still growing? Maybe I am."

"Wouldn't it be nice if we *all* were," Neil said thoughtfully. "Do you mind if I keep my arms around you?"

"If you take them away I'll fall apart like a jigsaw puzzle," she said very quietly.

He was touched. He looked down at her face, but all he could see was her pink mouth, with the lipstick smeared where he had kissed her savagely a while before. The smeared lipstick made her look vulnerable. Not sexy and dirty, the way he had pictured his dream pick-up an hour ago when he was drunk, but only vulnerable, and not unattractive either. She had a young mouth, not really finally formed yet, like a little girl's, and her teeth were very white. He wondered if she was a virgin.

"I have to go to the Copacabana Ball tonight," he said, "but I wonder if you would be willing to have dinner with me now. I mean, I'd like to get out of here."

"I never eat dinner until ten o'clock."

"I'm not hungry either. But we could have a drink. Or, I could."

"Rio is a very small town," Gilda said. "Everybody talks. You and I couldn't get far in these clothes, even during Carnival."

Her transparent attempt at evasion amused him, and at the same time made him rather angry again. "Are you afraid of me?"

She took a deep breath; he heard it and felt it. "No."

"That means yes."

"My mother always used to say that a girl is never afraid of a man unless she's afraid of herself," she said lightly.

"I didn't invite your *mother* to dinner, I invited you."

"That's what I'm afraid of!" she said. She smiled at him, and then Neil could not decide if she really was afraid of him or not.

"Let's go," he said. "We'll take a taxi to the Barra de Tijuca. That's at the end of the world." He took her hand before she had time to reply and began to lead her through the crowd and out of the place. The music was blaring, and all the dancers were dripping with perspiration, as if this were a giant musical Turkish bath. Gilda's hand was small and cool.

Near the doorway he noticed Mort Baker dancing with a tall, red-haired girl dressed as Pierrette. Neil turned his face away and walked more hurriedly, so Mort would not see him. He did not feel guilty or nervous, and this reaction rather surprised him. It was only that he felt a need to keep this evening private, whatever might happen. For some reason he felt happier than he had in years. It was this feeling of secret happiness he wanted to keep to himself, not the intrigue of sneaking out to the beach at Tijuca with a girl who worked at his office. It was the odd happiness . . . He looked down at Gilda walking beside him and he noticed that she held herself very straight, her head high, her chin up, almost a snob. It reminded him of the way Margie walked, but it didn't hurt; it just reminded him. And then Neil forgot about it, and they went outside into the warm, still-bright evening to find a cab.

CHAPTER *14*

Cidade Maravilhosa . . . coração de meo Brasil. . . . There were lights strung along the Rio streets at night and bands playing everywhere. You would come upon one of them unexpectedly or it would come upon you; you would turn a corner and there it was, people marching and singing, people dancing in the street. You would be sitting in a *churrascuria* eating dinner and suddenly you would hear the music of a street band, so you would throw down your napkin and run to the doorway to watch them and perhaps even give in to their invitation to come along. You would turn a corner in the twilight and suddenly the air would be ten degrees warmer from the massed body heat, and young couples would be dancing in an area set off from the rest of the sidewalk by strings of ragged colored streamers. There would be chaperones lined up on the periphery of the group, watching, because this was a dance for the young. Lights bloomed above the streets during the hot, bright days, and people wandered about squirting one another with ether, dressed in half-naked costumes and sweat-streaked make-up; the old and the young and the in-between, even babies in their father's arms, too young to walk or talk but not too young to be dressed as a black cat or a harlequin with round circles of rouge on their cheeks.

Marvelous city . . . heart of my Brazil. . . . The people pushed against one another in a solid mass for hours to get through the doors of the Copacabana Palace Hotel the night of the Copacabana Ball. "Stop! Wait!" Margie Davidow cried to her friends, trying to stoop in the tightly packed mob. "I've dropped one of my contact lenses!" Wherever it had fallen, feet had ground it to dust. Policemen tried vainly to keep the line orderly.

At the João Caetano Theater the seats had been removed and the Baile des Pederasts was being held. There were the usual yearly protests from some of the Rio citizens that it was immoral for men to disguise themselves as women in such an open way. But a high-ranking city official said firmly, "Somewhere these people have to divert themselves at Carnival."

At the Iate Clube there was a Roman orgy. Most of the women came as Cleopatra and most of the men disguised themselves as Nero. There was much eating of grapes, reclining on couches, drinking of wine, and much kissing.

At the Hotel Gloria, where the Baile des Artistes had been held, there were now other balls, less extravagant, less expensive to get into. The music was as loud and unceasing, but the costumes were plainer, some of them not really costumes at all. Everything seemed less bright, the air was hotter, the revelry a little sad. Somehow, revelry in its natural state without the glittering trappings of make-believe is always a little sad, not because it is different from first-class diversion but because you can see more clearly what it is.

There were balls for children, in the afternoons, with chaperones and soft drinks and elaborately bejeweled, feathered, sequinned costumes that made their tiny wearers seem like midgets, not children at all. On the solemn, beautiful faces of these parading child-midgets you could see the expressions they would be wearing in years to come when they were adults competing for most unusual costume at the adults' Carnival balls. There were Roman warriors, and knights, and butterflies, and fairy princesses. Leila Silva e Costa's children attended, and Helen Sinclair's children, and Mil Burns's children. The children had a wonderful time, eating too much, dancing until they were exhausted, showing off. Their mothers, watching them, felt a little sentimental and sad. On these child faces, covered with rouge and lipstick and varicolored paint, smiling and shy and excited, was the look of the future that would come all too soon, and the look of a different past that would never come again to their mothers, who watched them and remembered.

The afternoon that Neil Davidow and Mort Baker went to the Married Men's Ball, Margie Davidow and Helen and Bert Sinclair took a streetcar downtown to the center of the city. There were handles along the outside of the streetcar and a narrow running board to stand on when all the seats were occupied. The Sinclairs and Margie stood along this running board, pressed against the side of the trolley, squinting happily against the wind, drawing back whenever cars whizzed along too close beside them, Helen and Margie laughing nervously when the streetcar shot through the tunnel. There was a colored samba band on the streetcar, playing the whole time, and whenever the car stopped for a traffic light the people clinging to the outside would jump off and dance in the streets, running to jump back on again when the car started to move. Children standing on the sidewalk aimed their water pistols and *lança perfumas* at the passengers on the outside, and the passengers shook their fists at them.

On the sidewalk an elderly man dressed as a Bahiana, with rouged cheeks, flounced quickly along, swishing his ruffled skirts, his head held high, looking neither to left nor right, anticipating taunts and yells and pretending to ignore them. The ice-cream vendors were out in full force, and there were stands set up along the street where men sold hot foods. In some streets there was no traffic at all, only people strolling or dancing or gaping at the others. Some of the people had been out in the street for three days without stopping to sleep.

Some people slept, sometimes. They went to bed at half past eight in the morning when the sun was bright and other people were soaking out hangovers on the beach. They slept fitfully in hot, darkened rooms, the air faintly perfumed from their damp, ether-soaked costumes that had been dropped on the floor or flung across chairs. They awoke to twilight, or to nighttime dark, breakfasting at dinner time, feeling like inhabitants of a nightmare world, putting on their soiled costumes again—or perhaps new, more imaginative costumes—and setting out for another ball.

No one, anywhere, went to work. Sometimes, miraculously, mail was delivered. More often not. A mailman, bending under his sack of undelivered letters at four o'clock in the afternoon, suddenly straightened up and tossed all the letters into the gutter. Another mailman, neater, burned his. It was inhuman to think of making anyone work at Carnival. Rei Momo, the king of joy, was sovereign in the city.

One night there was the parade of the Escolas de Samba—the samba schools—who had been practicing for this great night all through the months before. New songs had been written for the occasion, songs that had already swept Brazil with their rhythms, played by orchestras at all the balls. The costumes for the parade would be hand-made, and fantastic, the product of a year of planning and work and unexpressed dreams. First there would be floats. The parade would go on all night, and from the provinces the poor came to watch, bringing their children, older children and babies who slept peacefully on blankets spread out on the sidewalk of the main plaza. There were benches for early-comers to stand on, but they were all occupied by the morning before the parade. The plaza was paved, and there were little trees growing on it. There were twenty-five-foot-high painted wooden figures that had been erected for Carnival—a pirate, a Bahiana, a clown. The bases of these figures were hollow wooden rectangles, twelve feet high, and people helped each other to climb up on top of them, clinging precariously, to watch the Escolas de Samba parade from above the heads of the crowd. At the foot of the wooden figures were entire families, mothers with five or six children, some of whom had taken the bus from villages as far as a day away, and who had been sitting there surrounded by ragged blankets and parcels of food for as long as ten hours. For them this was the event of the year, the one night of magic and beauty, the only Carnival party that was entirely free.

Every samba school from every district near Rio was represented, parading slowly by, each dressed entirely in its own chosen color: pale green, violet, red, blue. They did not march, they danced. They were all Negroes, the men dressed as wealthy Colonials of a period of feudal history not long past, with lace cuffs and satin jackets, powdered wigs, costumes compounded of history and fantasy. Reality, even tinged with nostalgia, had never been this beautiful. The women wore huge hoopskirts, pale satin with lace and glitter, white wigs, flowers, glass jewels. Some played instruments, all danced, all who did not play an instrument sang. *Levanta Mangueira* . . .

The onlookers stood on each other's shoulders, leaned against strangers, supported each other, gaped and cried out in wonder. "Look!" Helen said, pointing. "That Bahiana must weigh a hundred and fifty kilos!" The enormously fat Bahiana whirled by slowly, a great tray of fruit on her head, her bright pink hoopskirts bordered in lace, looking somehow all dignity and not ludicrous at all.

The greatest ball of all, the climax, was the Municipal. Most tickets had been bought long in advance. It was in the vast Municipal Theater, the seats had been removed, there was a movable catwalk high above the theater floor for the parade of contestants for most beautiful costume. Costumes had been in the making for an entire year. Some of them cost ten thousand dollars, dripping in real fur and jewels. Later when the magazines published photographs of the winners the captions would all state the cost—fifty thousand cruzeiros, a hundred thousand cruzeiros. A huge ramp had been erected leading from the street to the front entrance of the Municipal Theater. The ramp was guarded by rails and police and lighted by floodlights. Below, in the streets, the poor people gathered, waiting to see the show of arrivals. There were television cameras and newsreels. If you were a celebrity you could buy a ticket to a box. The President had a box, so did the generals of the Army, so did the visiting movie stars from Hollywood who had been brought to Rio to add to the Carnival glamour. There were other boxes, ranging in importance according to their position around the ballroom. Below on the theater floor were the people who wanted to dance, or mill around, and those who had only been able to buy a

212

"walking ticket," which meant you had to push your way about all night with no place to sit and not even a glass of water from the harried waiters. Ether bombs were forbidden. Of course they were there.

The Sinclairs, the Davidows, and Mort Baker had purchased walking tickets. They had hesitated at first, knowing it would be an ordeal, but finally Carnival excitement had won out. The Municipal was the climax of everything. Anything that came afterward was anticlimactic: you rested and licked your wounds. You could not miss the Municipal; it was the most beautiful ball of all.

Margie, holding Neil's and Mort's hands, watching Helen and Bert, trying to keep the group together, felt like a mother hen. She didn't like to see anyone get lost, especially at the Municipal, because if you lost whomever you were with you never saw him again. She smiled when she noticed the expression on Helen's face; Helen was speechless with bliss and amazement. For herself, Margie was already tired. She had been to other Carnivals in Rio, and somehow she never seemed to find that same abandon at any of them that Neil and their friends found. She glanced fondly at Neil. He had been different somehow at this Carnival— happier, younger. It seemed funny to say that Neil was younger; after all, he was only thirty-one. But he had more energy and exuberance this week than she had seen him show in years. She had almost forgotten how handsome he was until this week, and suddenly it struck her with remembered pleasure. Neil had a wonderful smile.

She had never thought of Carnival as either an end or a beginning, although she knew that to many people it was one or the other. Before, Carnival had been only a public orgy to try to enjoy, to get through, to watch and try to participate in. Margie was not much for mass letting-loose. She tried. But she hated to feel so hot that she was bathed in sweat, to feel her clothing shrinking and clammy, to know that her hair was dangling like limp string and her mascara was making black circles under her eyes. The discomfort of Carnival and the constant jumping and hopping, the pressure of strange bodies, the unexpected bruises that appeared the next day on private places of her body, were all a strain for her. She smiled whenever Neil looked at her; she tried to pretend she was one of the group, but secretly she was so tired she wanted to cry. Her legs ached, her back hurt, muscles she had never known she possessed pained and stiffened during the week of Carnival. She really went to Carnival because Neil liked it. But next year, she kept hoping, we will go away to Porto Allegre, or Preto d'Ouro, and stay there all through this madness, quietly and alone.

How happy everyone looked! They looked as if they were drugged. Margie smiled, she put her arms around Neil's neck and hopped up and down in the dance with him, trying not to lose her sandals, trying to keep her gold wreath from being knocked off by someone's elbow, breathless, smiling, thirsty already in the hot, bright room, trying not to be wrenched out of Neil's arms by exuberant, heedless strangers. It occurred to her suddenly that she did not simply dislike Carnival: it terrified her. For the first time she admitted that to herself. And having admitted it at last, Margie felt a wave of hopeless exhaustion. Why am I so different from all the others? she thought, looking at them. They seemed to have superhuman strength and endurance; they did not feel heat or thirst or physical pain. Someone's shoe ground against her bare instep and she winced. She had a cramp in her side. Are they the crazy ones or am I?

She saw Mort standing in one of the *camerotes* on the theater floor. Trust him to know someone who had a box. He was talking to a girl with bleached blond hair and he was drinking a high-ball with a lot of ice in it. Margie tugged at Neil.

"Look! Maybe Mort will hand us out a drink."

Helen and Bert had already vanished. Margie stood on tiptoe at the edge of the mob trying to find them. Then she saw them, rushing by, bobbing up and down, only their heads visible, like a couple who have been drowned in a great wave and are momentarily revealed on the surface of the force that has destroyed them. She tried to wave and cry out to them, but they did not see her, and then they were gone. She turned and leaned on the edge of the *camerote*. There were people standing on the railing

214

already; she had to push past someone's bare legs. No one seemed to mind.

"Mort!"

"Hi," he said. He handed out a bottle of imported Scotch. "Here, quick. Take a drink."

"Isn't there any water?"

"*Water?*" He walked around in the box, looking for water among the half-filled glasses people had left on the small table near the wall. There was a silver platter of something that looked like chicken croquettes, getting cold and congealing in their white sauce. There was some limp lettuce and a bowl of melting ice cubes. A man dressed as a scarecrow and a girl dressed as a stripteaser the moment before she vanishes behind the curtain were kissing each other passionately. Mort walked around them as if they were a pillar and reached for a glass. He sniffed at it.

"Here," he said. "Water. I think."

"I'll take the Scotch," Neil said.

Margie drank the water and sat down on the edge of the railing on a man's feet. He moved and apologized, and then when he looked down and saw who he was apologizing to he tried to kiss her. He was a middle-aged man, slightly drunk, very happy, and when she pushed him away and scowled at him he looked bewildered. He apologized again and turned away. A moment later he turned back, leaned over her, and asked hopefully, "Will you dance with me?"

"No, thank you."

"Some whisky?"

"No, thank you."

"Some champagne?"

"No, thank you."

"Some food?"

"No, thank you."

"You are American?"

"Yes."

He looked at Neil. "Your husband?"

"Yes."

"Very fortunate man," he said gallantly, gave a little bow, and turned away, this time for good.

Mort came over to her. "What did you tell your admirer?" he asked, grinning.

Margie took Neil's hand and smiled. "I said Neil was my lover and very jealous," she said. She touched the back of Neil's hand to her cheek.

"I am," Neil said. He tilted the bottle of Scotch and took a long drink.

"Do you know what I would like more than anything in the whole world?" Margie said.

"What?"

"A cold bath, and then to go to bed." She realized, of course, as soon as the words were out, that both of them misunderstood. They thought she meant really Bed, not to sleep. She tossed her head and tried to pass the whole thing off, looking slightly wicked. Back home in New York, young wives had made comments like that all the time, and their husbands had said much worse, and no one had thought it particularly offensive to talk about one's private life while playing bridge. Perhaps, Margie thought now, some of them had been lying too; crying wolf and talking big so that no one would know everything was not quite kosher at home.

"Let's watch the people from the second floor," Neil said, taking her hand.

They went out of the ballroom and up the stairs, inching their way past the people who were thronging the narrow corridor. Outside, on the floodlighted ramp, people were still arriving, the ones with such elaborate costumes that they could not dance and could barely walk; they would arrive only for the judging and to show their *fantaseas* and then they would go home. One woman wore a dress with side panels that opened into a huge silver fan when she held her arms out stiffly to the sides. The ends of the fan were attached to her wrists and she walked slowly and posed for photographers, smiling, her arms held rigidly out all this time as if she had been crucified.

216

"How can anyone have *fun* like that?" Margie asked, but her question was drowned out by the music.

They made their way to the second floor and tried several of the doors to the boxes until they found one that was unlocked. Margie had a moment of panic. She did not know these Brazilians or, indeed, any Brazilian, and she had no idea what surprised and hostile group they might find on the other side of that door. She glanced at Neil. "I'm afraid."

"Come on!"

He was smiling, he was so happy, he was like a little boy. She could not think of anyone she would rather go to a party with than Neil. And yet, sometimes, she felt he went too far. . . . They opened the door and slipped in. All the occupants of the *camerote* were sitting or standing against the rail, leaning out to see, and none of them even turned around when Margie and Neil invaded their box. There was an old matriarch watching the dancers with tolerant amusement. Neil found a straight-backed chair and pulled it toward the front of the box for Margie to stand on.

"No," she said, "Really, no."

A man dressed as a harlequin left his place at the railing and went to the small table near the door to pour himself another drink. He smiled at Margie, thinking she and Neil were friends of someone else's. She stood on the chair. Below there seemed to be several thousand people. She saw the bright colors of their costumes and their upturned faces. There was no separation among them or even a pattern; it was only an undulating, moving mass of humanity, bobbing, swirling, almost frightening. There was no longer such a thing as an individual down there. The music played loudly, as if its persuasive beat would continue to give strength to the dancers long after their muscles had given way. Even from this high above them she could see the sheen of perspiration on their faces and the fixed bright smiles that made some of them look like Esther Williams emerging dripping but smiling from under water in one of her movies. People were standing on tables at the side of the room, dancing alone or with others on the white tablecloths, and people were standing

217

solidly side by side on the railings that edged the ring of boxes around the main floor. If someone were to faint and fall, Margie thought in horror, there would be nowhere to fall; he would simply be carried along on the wave, borne along unconscious on the merriment of the others. Some of the dancers looked up and waved happily. The people in the second-floor boxes, who were lucky enough to have chairs, waved back and squirted the dancers with their golden aerosol cans of perfumed ether.

"I want to get down now," Margie murmured.

Neil put his arms around her hips to help her jump off the chair, and when she was standing beside him he did not open his arms but slid them up to her waist and held her against him.

"What's going to happen to us?" he whispered. "Margie?"

She shook her head; she couldn't speak. She was too hot, she was perspiring, she was tired, and she suddenly felt such a constriction in her throat that she could not have answered him even if she knew what to say.

"After all this is over," he said. "Then what? We have to wake up some time, don't we?"

She didn't know what he was talking about, but there was genuine suffering on his face. For the first time in all the years they had been married, she suddenly realized, she had not the faintest idea what was in Neil's mind. "Of course," she whispered, not sure whether or not that was what he wanted to hear.

It seemed it was not. "Yes," he said dully, and he let go of her at last, his arms falling heavily to his sides. "Let's go find the bar."

They pushed their way into a room which had a bar in it and fought through the crowd until they were standing againt the bar. Neil bought whisky for both of them. She drank hers as quickly as she could, as she had in the old days, and she noticed he had done the same.

"Let's get drunk," she said. "Let's get plastered together."

"I'll match you."

She felt happier after the second drink and she wondered why she had needed it. Neil looked rather grim. She had thought it would be fun to match drinks with him, sort of in the party

218

spirit which she seemed to be so lacking tonight, but from the desperate way he looked he did not seem to need her to keep him company at all. She smiled at him. "Good luck."

"Same to you." They drank.

"Health."

"Happiness." They drank another.

"This," Margie said, rather fuzzy now, "must be what they call Togetherness."

"To togetherness."

"Never apart." They drank.

"Perfect couple," Neil said.

"Perfect young couple. Isn't that what they say?"

"That's right."

She tried to keep the words precise, although her tongue seemed to refuse to say what her mind told it to. "Such . . . a . . . lovely young couple, Margie and Neil."

There was a stirring now among the crowd and cries that the costume parade was about to begin. Neil tipped the bartender and helped Margie to follow the other people back into the main ballroom. She saw the backs of the people in front of her as if through a mist, but with the colors very bright. Her eyes felt hot and she realized with some gentle surprise that she was crying. She was not exactly sure why she was crying because she did not feel very sad, only very drunk. From far away she heard herself speaking, and she was not exactly sure whether she was speaking out loud or only to herself.

"I hate them all," she was saying. "I hate them."

"Who?" Neil said. "These nice, lovely people?"

"No," she said. "No, those other ones. The ones who call us a perfect young couple. Those are the ones I hate. I hate them."

"Don't hate them," Neil said. He patted her shoulder. "Don't hate them."

"Can't I?"

"No. No percentage."

"They're far away," she said. "Why can't I hate them?"

"Ignore them."

There was a small space between two girls who were standing

on the railing of a *camerote* and Margie was able to squeeze her way up there too. They put their arms around her in a friendly way to help support her and smiled at her happily. Neil stood in front of her and she leaned against his back a little and looked up to where the movable catwalk had been lowered so that it made a bridge across the room, up high, for the contestants to parade across. She wondered why they were neither afraid nor airsick.

A man was announcing the title of each entry in rolling, resonant tones, through a loud-speaker, with over-enunciation. First there were the groups. "Ar-le-cam," he enunciated. "Ar-le-cam."

A group of harlequins, shiny with satin stripes of many colors and tinkling with little silver bells, rushed across the catwalk, bobbing their heads and whirling gaily to wave at the people on both sides far below them. There was applause.

Then there were scarecrows, shaggy and fantastic and identical, and then there was a group of men dressed as Far Eastern temple dancers. After each group there was applause. Then there were the single entries.

"Dragon of Gold," the announcer intoned. "Dragon of Gold." As if we didn't have eyes, Margie thought. But the dragon was impressive. It was a young woman, her dragon's body covered entirely in stiff, gleaming golden scales. Her head was a dragon's head, rather like a golden prehistoric monster from the Museum of Natural History, with an open mouth showing a red tongue. The eyes were green and lighted up. The tail trailed behind for at least six feet, and on the ends of the fingers were golden claws. There was applause from the crowd. A devil came out then, dressed in red, with a wicked grin. He bowed and swirled his cape, and tossed handfuls of gunpowder on to the catwalk, surrounding himself with small explosions and puffs of gray smoke. He ran by so fast Margie wished he would come back and explode some more gunpowder.

A blue and white clown paraded across the catwalk, bowing to the people. "He had that costume made in Paris by Jacques Heim!" one of the girls exclaimed to Margie, nearly pushing her

220

off the railing in her excitement. "He came to Rio just to wear that costume to Carnival!" Everyone was much impressed by the cost of the Parisian costume and there was wild applause.

"Chinese Merchant. Chinese Merchant." Very small, skimming lightly and whirling across the catwalk, the Chinese Merchant came, his head entirely shaved and his face and head covered with shining gold paint. His hands, too, were painted gold. On his shoulders was a bamboo pole, and hanging from it were an exquisite birdcage with bright-feathered birds in it and a basket of flowers. His gown was thickly embroidered in wondrous colors, all glittering, and from the bamboo pole were fluttering scarves of chiffon in pale shades of every color, pink, blue, green, yellow, violet. There was so much applause that he had to walk across the catwalk twice.

"Every year he is a Chinese Merchant," the girl said. "But each year he is dressed even more beautifully."

There was a woman who called her costume Ninotchka, dripping great, silver fox tails, dozens of them, even a headdress of fox furs, like the rays of the sun. "That *fantasea* cost a hundred thousand cruzeiros!" the girl said, smiling as delightedly as if the owner were planning to sew all the fox tails together afterward and present them to her.

"It must be very hot," Margie murmured.

"Ah, but how beautiful!"

There was a woman pretending to be a bird of paradise, covered in a brief costume of bright feathers, feathers springing from her head, her bare legs entirely painted silver. She stopped in the center of the catwalk and posed with a bird attached to her wrist. Everyone applauded.

It was over. The catwalk was raised slowly and disappeared into the shadows of the ceiling; the judges were deliberating. Margie's heels hurt from trying to keep her balance on the narrow wooden railing. She jumped down and rubbed her foot. The judgments were confusing; it seemed as if everyone had won something or other. The first prizes were a trip to New York and a trip to Paris. I wonder which one I'd like, Margie thought. I think Paris. I'm so far away from home now, nothing else seems strange. I'm going to feel this way for years and years—maybe for the rest of my life.

"Let's go and beat the crowd," Neil said. The people had begun to dance again, but many of them were leaving, evidently with the same idea Neil had, and the mass was visibly thinner. Margie looked for Helen and Bert and finally saw them looking for her. None of them really wanted to go, and yet they did not want to stay and dance any more either. They all knew this was the climax of Carnival, the last and greatest ball, the last night they would be caught up in this madness. There would be other things; parades, die-hard parties, street dancing, the dwindling smoke of a firecracker, but this had been the explosion. They were exhausted, their costumes were soiled and damp and even torn, Helen had lost a string of her beads, but they were somehow reluctant, now that it was all over, to take off these rags and say it was over for good. These were still not quite rags; they were still the clothing of a Bahiana, a bullfighter, a Greek athlete, a Greek boy; and until they were actually in the hand and flung away they still carried magic.

They looked for Mort but he was gone. Margie wanted to stay a little longer until they found him, she felt that everything would be spoiled if he was not there too.

"Oh, come on," Helen said. "Mort isn't a little boy. He can take care of himself."

Margie felt a stab of resentment. How smug Helen was! Everybody in his own place, according to his own function, two by two, Noah's Ark. And Mort the bachelor off with a girl somewhere, perhaps in an all-night café, if there was one during Carnival, or perhaps even on the beach making love. She wondered if he would be making love to a girl, on all that gritty sand, and if it were a girl he had known for a long time or one he had met only tonight.

Neil drove to the Sinclairs' apartment house and parked his car alongside the beach. The sky was already light. They all got out and stood there watching the sunrise, streaks of pink and gold above the blue line of the sea. There was no one on the beach at all, not a soul, nor on the sidewalk. The sand looked very pale and clean. There were the goal posts for the *futebol* team on the sand, and in the distance the glowing outlines of the hills. The sun hit all the windows of the apartment houses on the long crescent of beach. A milkman came by with a wooden wagon drawn by a brown horse. He took some bottles of milk into an apartment house.

An ancient taxi struggled up to the curb behind the milk wagon, and Mort jumped out and reached in to pull out a slender girl dressed as a tigress. She was shaking her head.

"Look," Mort said, pointing at the milk wagon. "There's breakfast."

He ran to the milk wagon and helped himself to two bottles of milk, carrying them in his arms fondly as if they were newborn twin babies. He came over to the others smiling a big smile. "Good morning."

"Good night," the tigress girl said in Portuguese. "I don't have your strength."

"This is Lucia," said Mort. "Helen and Bert. Margie and Neil. Lucia doesn't speak English."

Neil was looking fixedly at the Brazilian girl, a sad, tired expression on his face. Then he smiled at her. "That's a pretty *fantasea*."

"Thank you."

Mort opened the milk and began drinking it and passing it around. "First-quality water," he said, "with a new flavor thrill: *milk* flavor. Guaranteed to contain not over two per cent milk. Especially recommended to allergic patients, Hindus, Brahmins, and untouchables."

A policeman, dressed in khakis and a sun helmet, emerged from the alley between the two apartment houses and looked at them suspiciously. Then he made a decision and marched resolutely over to Mort.

"Did you steal this milk?"

"Steal?" Mort said, his eyes opened wide in innocence. "I was going to buy it." He took a handful of paper money out of the pocket of his shorts. "I am waiting for the man to come back."

"I will take the money," the policeman said.

223

"Oh, no. I will give it to him. It will be too much trouble for you."

"No trouble, Senhor."

"Thank you, no, Senhor. It would be very sad if you lost it."

"I will not lose it."

"You might. I will put the money on top of the wagon, here, so the man will find it when he comes back." Mort put the two empty bottles on top of the paper money so it would not blow away.

The policeman backed up a few paces and looked at the money with the empty bottles on top of it. Then he looked at Mort. Mort waved at him and smiled. The policeman glared at him. Mort walked back to the others on the beach and then he turned to look at the policeman. The policeman was fingering his gun and he looked as if he could not decide whether or not to arrest Mort, and if he did arrest him what he could arrest him for. Mort smiled innocently and sweetly.

"He's angry because I won't let him steal the money," he said.

"Look at the sunrise!" Helen breathed. "Oh, Rio is so beautiful!"

It was very quiet. The only sound was the thudding of the waves on the shore, and once the milkman's horse stamped his hoof. The sound rang out in the quiet street like the fresh clang of a faraway triangle. Margie felt she could sit here on the sand all day, never moving, watching the white surf and listening to it. But already the sun was becoming hot. The milkman came out and drove down the street.

"Good night," the girl named Lucia said. She started to walk away.

Mort jumped to his feet. "I'll walk you home."

They watched Mort and the girl walking down the deserted street. The girl was walking very quickly, almost like a real tigress, her step light and silent. She looked very slim and long-legged and stealthy, an animal of the night who knew all these winding streets by heart, and to whom no real harm could ever come. Margie didn't like her.

"We have to go home," Helen said. "I'm asleep." She stood up, shaking the sand out of her shoes.

224

"I guess it's all over," Bert said.

Margie stood up too, holding on to Neil with one hand while she brushed the sand off her clothes. Then she brushed the sand off him. She peered into his face. "Look at my poor husband. He's so tired he's getting depressed. Don't look so sad, love."

Neil gave her a weak smile. He did not say anything.

"I'm going to sleep for a week," Helen said.

"That's what you think," said Bert. "Wait till the kids come in about two hours from now."

"I'll bet you forgot for a while that you *had* them," Margie said, smiling. "The party's over."

"And the circus begins," said Bert. He was trying to look long-suffering but he really looked proud.

"Good night."

"Good night. Thank you."

"Thank *you*."

"Good night."

CHAPTER 15

There is a grayness that settles down over a city after a holiday is over, no matter what the season of the year. In America, after New Year's, everyone who is rich enough goes away to a sunny place for a winter vacation, to escape. Those who cannot, wait longingly for the sun to come to them. February is the shortest and the longest month in any hemisphere. In Rio, when Carnival is over the city settles down for the grayness of Lent. The people who work in São Paulo and other cities, who came to Rio for Carnival, go home again. In São Paulo the offices open at seven in the morning. It is not like Rio; it is the city of business people, of one-hour lunches, of bars and restaurants that close at ten.

In Rio, after Carnival, the poor return to their slums and their memories. The new middle class of white-collar workers return to their offices, waiting for hours in the early mornings for over-crowded trolleys and *lotações*. The *cafegistas*, who lie on the beach all day and sit in the cafés all night, call their doctors for vitamin injections or get one at the drugstore, and then they feel strong enough for the beach again. The American wives go back to the Golf Club. The Brazilian wives go back to their dressmakers, their hairdressers, their games of cards. It is very hot.

After Carnival was over Mort Baker found a furnished apartment and moved into it. Margie and Neil Davidow decided to have separate bedrooms, as they had planned before Mort came

226

to stay with them, and Neil moved into the vacated guestroom. Leila Silva e Costa and Helen Sinclair went back to the *favellas* to visit their protégée, Maria, and found themselves confronted by an angry priest. The priest told them he had discovered all about Leila's sin of giving birth-control information to Maria, and they were never to be allowed to come to the *favellas* again. Leila had brought with her a large box of food and clothing for Maria and her children, including her own children's discarded Carnival costumes (Maria could use the material to sew something else). She gave the box to the priest to give to Maria.

She was neither ashamed nor angry nor embarrassed; she was philosophical. She shrugged and smiled. "I only wanted to help," she said, as she steered her car down the difficult road away from the *favellas*. "I am sorry it's over."

"I am too," Helen said. She felt subdued. The result of the whole incident was so extreme, it wasn't fair. She wondered what would become of Maria and her children, whether anyone else would befriend them and bring them food, whether they could get along all alone. "I need a drink," she said. "Let's go to the Golf Club."

Leila opened her purse and tossed a small package out the car window. "I think I will go home now," she said. "Perhaps Carlos will call me. I told my maid to tell him I had gone to the *favellas*. Will you come with me?"

"My children are at the Golf Club. I'll call you tomorrow."

"All right. I'm sorry about what happened."

"I am too."

Leila drove her to the gateway of the Golf Club and they kissed each other on both cheeks, very formally but warmly. Helen waved until the car was out of sight and then she walked down the driveway that led to the clubhouse. Julie and Roger were in the swimming pool, with Mrs. Graham watching them from a canvas chair. They waved at her and splashed about vigorously, showing off for her.

"I'll wait for you upstairs and we'll have lunch when you're ready," she said.

Mil Burns was sitting at a table on the veranda with a middle-aged woman. Helen had not seen Mil for a long time and she found herself quite happy to see her.

"Come over and meet my mother," Mil said.

Mil's mother was a large, formidable woman, an image of what Mil would be in thirty years. There was a strong family resemblance, but next to her mother Mil looked somehow rather delicate, and much younger than usual. They were both drinking whisky sours. "My mother, Mrs. Penny. Helen Sinclair," Mil said.

"How do you do."

"How do you do," Mrs. Penny said. "Have a whisky sour. What is it you're not supposed to drink in this place? Ice? They have no ice in them." She gestured at the waiter. "Well, how do *you* like Brazil?"

"Very much," Helen said, sitting down at their table.

"You'll change," Mrs. Penny said. "I've been here only two weeks and I hate it. It feels as if it's been two years. That Carnival —my God!"

"It isn't always that way," Helen said.

Mil's mother drained her whisky sour. "We're going home, thank God. I'm taking my daughter out of here."

Helen turned to Mil in surprise. "For a visit or for good?"

"My mother's a little drunk," Mil said. She smiled weakly. "I thought I'd go home with her for a couple of months. It'll be good for the kids."

"My grandchildren are going to grow up as good, wholesome, hundred per-cent Americans," Mrs. Penny said firmly.

The waiter brought new drinks. "It will be a relief to get home," Mil said. "I miss it. That wonderful Chicago snow! I've had enough of the Good Neighbor Policy."

"And the cockroaches!" Mrs. Penny's face contorted in outrage. "*This* big! The first night I was here there was one in my room. All those legs—you should have seen it. Disease carriers, that's what they are. I chased it with a copy of *The Ladies' Home Journal,* but it ran under an armchair and I couldn't get at it. I was so frightened out of my wits I couldn't sleep. Damned thing. It came back the next day. I got kind of used to it, the damned thing. I named it Hercules. But I fixed Hercules." She smiled mirthlessly. "I used to put a little bit of food inside the waste basket every night so the cockroach would go in *there* instead of climbing up my arm or something while I was asleep and biting me to death."

Helen laughed. "Hercules!"

Mrs. Penny drank her whisky sour. She lowered her voice and looked around carefully. "Did you ever notice those Brazilians, how sneaky they are? You can't do business with them without a contract. In America all you have to do is shake hands. But not here. And they all have mistresses."

"You learned all that in two weeks?" Helen said.

"Oh, I knew it in two minutes. I can always size up a person by looking at his face. I've been around, you know, fifty-seven years. I wouldn't trust one of them. What do you expect? It's hot all the time. Something happens to the mind when you're in tropical heat all the time."

"It gets quite cool here in the winter," Helen said.

"I knew she was miserable," Mrs. Penny said, ignoring her. She put her arm around Mil. "I knew it from her letters. I don't care how old she is, she's still my baby. Aren't you?"

Mil smiled shyly. "We don't have to discuss it now," she said softly. "We'll talk about it later."

Helen had never thought she would see Mil Burns so gentled and changed. It seemed as if when she was away from her mother, her mother lived on in her, but when she was face-to-face with the dynamic original the imitation simply faded away. "What about Phil?" Helen said.

"He can just shift for himself," Mrs. Penny said airily. "I ask you, what kind of a man brings his wife and little children out here in a barbaric country like this? There are plenty of good jobs at home. So he won't be a millionaire. So what! A million dollars is going to do him a lot of good when he's a hopeless invalid for the rest of his life with dysentery."

Mil smiled, a smile compounded of embarrassment and sympathetic approval. "Helen likes it. Don't disillusion her, Mother. She'll find out."

"I just think you're all wrong," Helen said.

Mil's mother leaned forward and touched Helen's hand. Her voice when she spoke was kindly, in a mother-knows-best way, but there was steel underneath. "Do you think you can ever cure dysentery once you've got it? It stays forever in the alimentary canal. I read that in a magazine."

The waiter came past their table and glanced at them, but Mil shook her head. "We're not going to have any more drinks," she said. "We're going to have lunch now."

"I haven't felt well since I got here. I don't know, I just don't feel well."

"Would you like to have lunch with us, Helen?"

"I have to have lunch with Julie and Roger alone today," Helen said quickly. "I promised them."

"Just wait until your children stop speaking English," Mrs. Penny said darkly. "Just wait until they're ashamed of you because *you're* the foreigner. You tell her, Mil."

"I'll chance it."

Mrs. Penny rose heavily to her feet. "I'm going to the . . . what you call it . . . *balnerio.* You can order me a cheese sandwich, baby."

Mil looked at her mother with concern until she had disappeared into the main dining room. Then she brightened and seemed more her old self. "Don't mind Mother. She's a little disillusioned."

Helen wanted to say something about prejudice, but she was afraid of getting into an argument. What would be the use? She felt suddenly sorry for Mil, and for Phil Burns, and even for the mother. "What did you tell Phil?"

"He thinks it's only for a visit," Mil said. "I had to tell him that. I might really come back in two months—I don't know."

"Don't go," Helen said. "I know it's none of my business, but please don't go. If you go you'll plan to come back but somehow you never will. I just know it. I don't know how or why I know it, but I just do."

"I know," Mil said quietly. "You're right." She smiled, but surprisingly there were tears in her eyes. "Listen, it's not easy to leave your husband."

"And for what—for *snow?*"

"For me."

"For you?"

"For *me*," Mil said. "For *me, for me.*" She was jabbing at her chest with her thumb as if the real essence of herself, whatever it was, were an organ inside her something like her heart. "It's different for them, for the men. They have something—their work. They have friends. They *do* things. But what about me? I can't sit here for the rest of my life and watch my kids starting to speak English with a foreign accent, wanting to settle down here when they're grown because it's all they know. We have only one life to live. I don't want it to be here where I don't belong. I want to be home, in my *real* home. I don't want to play cards all day in a place where you can't get an American book until it's eight months old. I have to take care of myself and my kids. If he won't, then I will."

Why, it's almost as if she's not talking about her husband at all, Helen thought in surprise. It's not as if he's someone she really knows and loves at all, but just someone she once made a bargain with: you do thus-and-such and I'll do this-and-that. Love, honor and cherish, and a house in the suburbs. In sickness and in health till a cockroach do us part. There must be dozens of wives, Helen thought, who think all the things that are advertised in the bridal magazines are an identity. And they're perfectly happy as long as they have everything that everyone else has, or perhaps a little better. But as soon as it's different they feel deserted, cheated. . . . But maybe I'm being unfair. After all, maybe there's something between Mil and Phil that she'd never mention to me. Maybe it's something personal. I don't know. We know so little about our friends' private lives. They tell us so much, but they tell us all the wrong things. We never really know *why*. Maybe it's because so many of them really don't know why themselves.

"I'll sit with you until your mother comes back, but then I have to go," she said. "Julie and Roger will be starved."

"We don't see each other much lately," Mil said. "It's a shame. And now I'm leaving. What do you do with yourself all the time?"

"Well, there was Carnival."

"Oh, before that. And lately. You haven't been to the club for weeks."

"I go to the beach quite a lot. And my children like to go to the beach every few days as a change, and then they have lunch at home. The days pass."

"I always thought you and I would be better friends," Mil said. "We have a lot in common. We're certainly brighter than the average, we both went to college, we could discuss things. You go around with Margie Davidow a lot, don't you?"

"She's my best friend in Brazil."

"Oh, she's sweet. She's a very sweet girl."

Helen smiled. "That means you don't like her."

"Oh, I like her. I just don't see you two together. Why, you two wouldn't even have ever met if you were back home in New York."

"Then I'm glad we're here," Helen said. If there was one thing she disliked it was someone who told you that you and she ought to be good friends because you were both so much more intelligent than anyone else.

"Well," Mil said wryly, "nothing ever turns out the way we want it to. But we try, don't we? We try damned hard."

She had that faintly superior look on her face; the Iowa State Corn Queen for ever and ever, with a sense of humor as a bonus and a diploma to go with it, and don't you ever forget it—and yet, for the first time there was a crack in the façade, as if Mil Burns were on the verge of learning that it is possible to laugh at oneself without having the whole room join in the chorus.

"I guess we do try," Helen said wistfully. "But half the time we do the wrong thing." She was not talking about her abortive friendship with Mil now, and she knew Mil wasn't either. For herself, she was thinking with a growing disturbance about Sergio, because lately from time to time the memory of him kept coming back whenever she was alone. It frightened her. During Carnival she had been sure he was out of her life for ever. She felt as if she had lost her mind and found it again in one climactic week. But now that Carnival was over, and she was

232

rested, and the whole week seemed as if she had imagined it in a fever dream, she was right back where she had been before. It was Sergio she thought of, things he had said, the way he looked, and no matter how much she hated herself for it she could keep the memories away only by sheer effort. She wondered how it could be possible for a woman to be in love with two men at once in different ways. Men, of course, could manage it, and did. But women? Women weren't supposed to be like that; it was unnatural.

"Do you feel better, Mother?" Mil asked. Mrs. Penny sat down heavily in her chair.

"I have to leave now," Helen said, rising. "Goodbye, Mrs. Penny. I hope the rest of your stay is better than the beginning."

"I can't wait to go, that's all."

"I'll call you before I leave," Mil said. "So long."

"Thank you for the drink."

Mil's mother did not seem in the least reluctant to see Helen go, in fact, she seemed rather glad. She leaned closer to Mil and took her hand. "Now when we get home . . ." she was saying happily. Helen did not hear any more as she walked away quickly to see the fresh, lovely faces of her two children.

CHAPTER *16*

As February came to an end Helen Sinclair remembered the tag ends of other Februarys in other places, and how she had felt. It seemed as though every end of February was the turning point of the year, the ebb when nothing could become colder or gloomier or more miserable, and from then on everything was better. She remembered slush in Westport, dangerous roads, the children at home cranky with colds and tired of all the therapeutic educational little games she had invented for them, the floors of their rooms constantly littered with cut-out colored paper, their hands on the quilts sticky with library paste, their noses running, their voices shrill with petulance despite their hoarseness. And then she herself always caught whatever cold the children had, but much worse, and being the head of the household during the day she could not allow herself to go to bed. She would have a headache and sore throat and feel ugly, and there was always something: the oil burner broke down one February, Julie's Siamese kitten was killed by a car driven by a twelve-year-old boy with no driving license, and one February their substitute cleaning lady (the regular one had the flu) disappeared, taking with her, of all improbable things, considering the jewelry and heirlooms in the house, their portable television set. But the children considered the loss of the TV a much greater tragedy.

It seemed as if every February Helen had offered up a little prayer to no one in particular, to herself perhaps. "If I can just

234

get through *February* everything will be all right." Then small green shoots would appear through the frozen crust of earth, and the deathly silence that held the land would be broken by the music of water running in brooks and children shouting at play in front and back yards all over the farm country of Connecticut; the barns that were decorated now with nonobjective art and rewired antique lamps and Swedish-glass martini pitchers.

In Rio Helen did not have that late-February feeling at all. How could you? The sun was hot, the beach was crowded, every day was exactly like every other day. Her friends and family at home sent her envious letters. She sent them cheerful ones. But she had a strange feeling inside, as if something were going to happen, and although she knew it was she who could prevent it she was not at all sure she wanted to.

She had taken Julie to the dressmaker to have two new bathing suits made. She had finally persuaded Julie that little girls *had* to wear bathing suits with tops, even if on top they weren't different from little boys. It was funny, because Julie genuinely liked to dress up in full-skirted flowered dresses with crinolines and sashes with bows. Helen thought she still might be a little jealous of Roger. To compromise and make the entire prospect more glamorous she told Julie she could have a bikini, and had a matching one made for herself. Children, she thought secretly, were really the only people who could wear bikinis without looking dreadful, and yet she remembered the way she had felt in the swimming pool that night of Baby Amaral's party, when she had worn the borrowed bikini and had met Sergio. It was really Sergio she was thinking of when she had the bikini made, because for some reason now she wanted to do and wear everything that reminded her of the times with him. Surely there wasn't much harm in that—it was a small, private aberration. But when she came home from the dressmaker the maid said a man had telephoned and left no name.

"He called for Senhor Bert, you mean."

"No, Dona Helen, he called for you."

It could have been anybody. Or, more likely, the maid had made a mistake. But Helen knew it had been Sergio, and she

235

could not help her feeling of excitement that overrode the resentment she felt at his having been reckless enough to intrude on her home. She had a strange double feeling about him. He was unfair, he was too confident, he did not care if he caused trouble and embarrassment if the maid had told her about the phone call in front of Bert. And yet she was sure he must miss her a great deal if he took the chance, and knowing that made her feel a wave of tenderness toward him.

"He was Brazilian, not American," the maid went on helpfully.

"Thank you."

"Is nothing."

Helen started to walk away.

"All your friends who telephone, I can not understand them when they speak. Their accents are too bad. But this man spoke very well. He was Brazilian."

"Thank you."

"Is nothing," the maid said, pleased. Sergio had evidently made a great ally out of her.

"Please write messages *down*," Helen said. "Don't *tell* me."

"You *know* I cannot write, Senhora. It is not necessary to write. I remember everything."

"I'm happy."

"Is nothing."

Helen went into Julie's room. Julie was sitting at the small table next to the window working on an enormous jigsaw puzzle from America. Helen's mother had sent one for each of the children as one of their Christmas presents, but between Helen's parents and Bert's parents, all of whom evidently thought they were doing missionary work among the natives, there had been so many Christmas presents that Julie and Roger were just now getting to use the last of them.

"Hey, Mama . . ." Julie said. She called Helen something different every month, this month it was Mama, the month before, Mother, the one before, Mom.

"What?"

"Can I sleep in your room tonight?"

236

"In my room? Why?"

"I just feel like it."

"There are two people in that room already, Daddy and me. What's the matter with your room?"

"I just feel like it. I can sleep in your bed."

"And who on the floor?" Helen sat down at the table next to Julie and kissed her.

"There's room. I'm little."

Helen kissed Julie again and smoothed her hair. "Come on," she said. "Spit it out. What did I do?"

"Nothing!"

"When we moved into this apartment you wanted the biggest room. You said, 'I want a big, big room, all to myself.' And then when you found out Mrs. Graham was going to sleep in here with you instead of with Roger you were furious at me, remember? You said, 'I'm a big girl, I want to sleep alone.' Now you want to sleep with *two* of us, in the same bed even. How about that?"

Julie was bent over her jigsaw puzzle, concentrating furiously. She was trying to find the place to put an odd-shaped piece and did not answer. Helen guided her hand to the hole where the piece would fit. "I just do," Julie muttered finally.

I did something, Helen thought. What did I do? She thinks I don't love her, she wants to be a baby again. My God, I must be a terrible mother—what did I do?

"That's no reason."

"Well . . . you'll think I'm a baby if I tell you."

"I don't exactly think you're a middle-aged woman," Helen said tenderly. "I'd certainly be worried if you didn't act like a little girl sometimes."

"Well, Roger doesn't care. He isn't afraid."

"Afraid of what?"

Julie held her hands out to embrace an invisible object at least a foot long. "Of Hercules the Cockroach. Tony Burns says his grandmother told him there's a cockroach in her bedroom *this* big, and at night it climbs up people's sheets and eats people."

"Oh, my Lord!" Helen said. She was so relieved she began to laugh, but at the same time she felt like crying. "That's just a story. Tony Burns's grandmother just made it up. The day you ever see a cockroach even half that size you tell me right away and we'll sell it to the horror-movie people in Hollywood and make a million dollars."

"Do they want big cockroaches?" Julie was beginning to look pleased.

"They'd want anything *that* fantastic."

"Well, she said it was true."

"All right. And I say it isn't. It's absolutely not true. You've seen the cockroaches they have here. You're the one who picks up bugs and bees and God knows what in your bare hands—I'm not. You're not afraid of bugs, and there's no such animal as Hercules the Cockroach."

"Hey, Mama . . ."

"What?"

"Are you always right about everything?"

"No. But I'm right about a stupid story one of your friends tells you. I'm right about this. Other things—well, I'm older than you and I know more, and I'm your mother so you have to listen to me. I'll tell you everything I know and then when you grow up you can go on from there and you'll know more than I do."

"Do you know more than your mother?"

Why do children always know so well how to put you on the spot, Helen thought, admiring and a little exasperated. "Some things," she answered bravely.

Julie looked pleased. Then she became serious again. "Did you tell her?"

"Tell her what, pigeon?"

"That you know more than she does?"

Helen thought for a moment of lying and saying yes, and then she stopped herself. She only lied to Julie in cases of emergency, and hoped they would always be few. "Those things don't matter so much between grown people—who knows more than who," she said finally. "It doesn't matter as much as it does between grownups and children. When grownups think differently about the same thing they each just try to go their own way."

"Oh," Julie said. She picked up another piece of her puzzle and

238

stared at it with concentration and then carefully fit it into its place. "Do you want to do one, Mama?"

"Thank you." She picked up a piece shaped like a heart.

"When I'm grown up," Julie said, "if I know more than you do, I'll tell you whatever you don't know."

"Yes? Thank you. Meanwhile, for a few years anyway, *I'll* tell *you*."

They worked on the jigsaw puzzle together for a while in silence. Then Julie looked up at Helen. On her soft, eight-year-old's face was a comical look of what Helen recognized as a first attempt at grownup sophistication. "It's nice once in a while to have a talk together like this," Julie said. "Woman to woman."

There was too much time to think. Helen had trained herself to block everything out of her mind but the pleasure of the warm rays of the sun on her body while she lay on the beach, but still, after the first ten or fifteen minutes, thought came anyway. There was a new fad now: splashing Coca-Cola on your skin in order to get a deeper suntan. It would seep into her straw beach mat and collect sand; then she would have something else to think about. But not for long. A few minutes in the surf, toes and heels digging into the shifting sand to keep from being pulled along by the powerful undertow, a short, reckless swim, and she would be cool and clean again, and the thoughts of Sergio would come back. Bert was going away at the end of the week to the Interior. He would be gone at least a week. She knew what Sergio was going to ask her: to come away with him then, at least for a few days.

She was missing Bert in advance, as she always did when he went away, and at the same time she was thinking with forbidden and guilty excitement what it would be like to spend two whole days alone with Sergio. She could say she was going to São Paulo for some shopping. Wives did that at least once a year; the stores there were bigger and better and you could get all the things you couldn't find in Rio. The children could stay with Mrs. Graham, and Margie could look in on them every day. Margie adored the children. But even as she was planning this imaginary thing Helen was rejecting it, telling herself it was nothing more than a mental exercise. How to run away with your lover. The whole idea was ridiculous. Sergio was not even her lover. But of course he would be if she went anywhere with him. . . .

Helen had thought about this more and more as the days went by. What frightened her, what really terrified her, was the certainty that if she and Sergio ever became lovers it would not be merely a fling for her to get him out of her system for once and for all, but a bond that would tie her to him for longer than she dared think about and make her love for him inescapable. She was sure now she was in love with him. Even a little bit in love— the thing he had told her would not satisfy him. But could you be a little bit dead? She felt like a schoolgirl. When she thought about him or pictured him she missed whole sections of conversation that was going on around her. When the telephone rang she jumped, her hands shook and became cold, and when it turned out not to be him at all she felt so disappointed she could hardly speak.

She felt independent, almost disassociated, from the rest of her daily life. She did things now by ritual. The only times she felt alive were when she was with the children or with Bert, because then the warmth of her love for them filled her and she became a part of whatever they were doing at the time. But alone she was like a sleepwalker. She was unable to come to a decision either to put Sergio out of her mind forever or to admit him into her life, because secretly she knew what she was going to do and she was afraid to face it. It must be like the last moment before you dived off the high tower into an icy swimming pool for the first time. You saw the space between, you imagined the feeling of falling and the shock of cold, you contemplated retreat. But if you had not intended to jump, why had you climbed up to the tower in the first place? You couldn't climb down without completing the act. But you kept putting off the moment. You knew that one more step, one graceless involuntary movement of the body, and you would have no choice. If you were going to do it, you might as well dive well, with as much style as you had. You couldn't fall protesting and struggling into a love affair; it was ridiculous. You had to enjoy it or not do it at all.

I've changed, Helen thought. We've been away from home almost a year and already I'm planning my life as if home didn't exist, as if among strangers I'm anonymous. Is that why some people travel, why they rush to Europe with those terribly juvenile comments about "finding" themselves? Maybe those ideas aren't so juvenile at all.

"Telephone for you, Senhora."

She walked to the telephone with her heart pounding heavily, and for a moment she hesitated before speaking into the receiver. Her voice was almost inaudible. "Hello."

"Mrs. Sinclair?" A woman's voice, slightly shrill and nasal, with an American western twang.

She had a moment of actual physical pulling-away, of shrinking from that probing, friendly voice, and she could not answer.

"Hello? Helen Sinclair? Hello?"

"Yes, I'm here. The connection must be bad."

"Oh, aren't the telephones the limit! This is Honor McVitty, from the Book Club. I'm in charge of getting the members shaped up, and I notice from our lists that you haven't been to the meetings for months. Is there some reason?"

"I've . . . been busy."

"Well, we're all *busy*, Mrs. Sinclair. All of us are married women with husbands, and most of us have children to take care of. But we all feel that our intellectual lives can't be ignored no matter how busy we are. Don't you agree?"

"Yes," Helen said weakly.

"Now we need all our members present at our bimonthly meetings so the discussions will be interesting. And we need the money, too, to buy the books. Now if you're too busy to *read* two books a month, Mrs. Sinclair, you don't have to actually *read* them. You can just listen to the discussion of the other members who *have* read them, and then you can decide whether you want to read that particular book or not. Quite a few of our busy members do that."

"I see," Helen said.

"If you're worried about the cost, Mrs. Sinclair, I can assure you that chipping in with twenty-five other members to send for these books from the States is really not expensive at all. We all have to watch the pennies, you know, all of us. But we feel culture has no price. And we always get best sellers, right from the best-seller list of *Time* magazine. So you don't have to worry about *that!*"

"It was very nice of you to call," Helen said, "but actually I've found that I like to do my reading on my own. I'm just used to doing it that way. Thank you anyway."

"I suppose you think we're not intellectual enough for you," Honor McVitty said. She was pretending to be modest and a little amused, but actually her tone revealed genuine resentment. "I want you to know that most of us are college women, Mrs. Sinclair, and very intelligent. I'm sure you won't find us lacking in intellectual companionship for you, if that's what you're thinking."

"I didn't say that at all."

"We have to keep up our cultural lives here. If you won't help us, Mrs. Sinclair, how do you expect us to get along?"

"I'm sorry," Helen said. "Really I am."

"Then come this Thursday afternoon. Two o'clock."

"I'm sorry. I can't."

"You know what I think?" Honor McVitty's voice rose in indignation. "I think you're a snob! You should talk to some of our women, you'd see how intelligent they are. Some of them even had *jobs* in the States before they came here with their husbands."

"Look," Helen said, "*I* didn't graduate from college. *I* never had a job except as a homemaker or whatever you intellectuals are calling it nowadays. But I happen to like to read by myself, and think about books by myself, without twenty-five women telling me what it all means before I even get a chance to figure it out. Reading alone is just a private vice I seem to have, and I plan to keep it."

"It's women like you," Honor McVitty said shrilly before Helen let the receiver drop back into place, "who give the American colony a bad name!"

Helen went into the living room and lighted a cigarette. The call had disturbed her more than she thought it could. It seemed

242

as though the badly filtered voice of that woman from the Book Club had come from outer space somewhere, from another world. *Shape up,* wasn't that the phrase she had used? Did she think they were all in the Army? Perhaps that harmless, touchy woman, with her dog-eared passed-around novels and community discussion, was only trying to save herself, just as Helen was doing, just as they all were, Bert in his mines, Margie going to the same movie day after day during those bad secret months. They were all trying, in their own way, to save themselves, because the world that had saved them before, with its train schedules and sinkfuls of dirty dishes and children home with colds and parents and aunts and uncles and friends, was gone. It was far away, far, much farther than the voice of someone named Honor McVitty calling lost American housewives to arms, to shape up, to keep up, to keep the faith.

We're alone, Helen thought. We're all alone. Love one another, my children, or ye shall die.

Two days before Bert left for the mine Helen gave a small farewell dinner for Mil Burns. She had been putting it off because she knew that Mil was going to leave Phil for ever, and Phil did not, and giving a going-away party for Mil's "temporary departure" seemed not only heartless and hypocritical to her but also made Helen feel a little like an accomplice. But how could she ignore Mil's departure completely? Mil would feel hurt, rejected; and the Burns's had entertained the Sinclairs at their home, so not to give a farewell dinner would be rude. She invited Margie and Neil, three other couples, and of course Mil's mother, and then as an inspiration to prove to Mil and Mrs. Penny that there really were charming, lovable Brazilians, she called Leila and invited her, and told her to bring Carlos or anyone else she wanted to escort her.

Leila said she would be delighted to come, she was looking forward to it, she would certainly love to meet Helen's interesting American friends. She never showed up; nor did she call to say that she could not come. At ten-thirty, when everyone was starving and making indignant remarks, Helen served dinner, and made up a lame lie that she had told Leila the wrong night. She felt like a fool. She knew this sort of thing sometimes happened, and her household was flexible enough so that one couple more or less never disturbed a party very much, but she could not bear Mil's I-told-you-so look right next to Phil's innocent smile. She felt that inadvertently she had made things even worse for Phil, when she had only wanted to help.

When the last guest had left at a quarter to one Helen was relieved. She had a headache but she was too nervous to go to bed. She carried a glass of brandy out to the balcony that led off her bedroom.

"Darling, don't go to sleep. Come out and talk to me."

"It was a nice party," Bert said. He leaned on the balcony railing next to her and she knew that he was only making conversation because she wanted him to stay out here with her.

"It wasn't a nice party and you know it, darling."

"Why wasn't it?"

"Leila doing that to me, and everyone being so pointed about it, and Mil getting ready to sneak out of her husband's life for ever unless he comes trailing after her all repentant and housebroken. . . ."

Bert laughed. "What have you got there? Brandy?"

"Have some. Have it all."

He sipped at the brandy thoughtfully. "Maybe she has another guy," he said.

"Who has? *Mil Burns?*"

"What's so unbelievable about that? She's a little too fat, but she's still an attractive woman. Some men like broad broads."

"I don't mean she can't get a man," Helen said. "I mean she wouldn't want to."

"Why not?"

"Well, she just wouldn't. She's . . . I mean, she wouldn't think of it."

"Helen!"

"What do you mean '*Hel-en*' like that? What am I missing? Am I the only one around here who doesn't know something?"

Bert ruffled her hair, looking amused. "I don't know a thing,

244

and if I did, I would tell you. It's just that you're very naïve for a woman who's been married ten years."

"Nine!"

"Nearly ten."

"That's like saying a woman's nearly thirty when she's only twenty-nine," Helen said, putting her arms around him. "It's just something that means different things to men and to women. We have been married exactly nine years and four months, and that is *not* nearly ten years. But I'm glad for every minute of it."

"That's because I'm away so much," he said cheerfully. "You can't get bored with me."

She knew he didn't mean it, so she only made a face at him. She wanted to say, I wish you didn't go away so often, but she couldn't, because she knew he had to go. It wasn't that he *had* to go for business; she had discovered that a long time ago from some inadvertent comments one of his associates had made at a dinner she had given; but Bert wanted to go away because of some need inside himself, and therefore he had to go. It was the same thing. She didn't really understand it: why he felt he had to leave her from time to time, why he never could discuss it with her, but she was afraid to mention it to him for fear of making something big out of it. Some men did much worse than simply take a semi-business trip for a while. They had affairs or, the worst thing of all, one big affair that meant more than their marriage. She was glad that she did not have to worry about other women, and she never considered it strange to be glad instead of merely confident. She knew those things happened too often for you to be confident and smug, but you could be confident and glad.

"What do you mean I'm naïve?" she said.

"Are you back at that?"

"Well, you said it."

"All right. I guess this isn't just you; it's the difference between the way men and women think. And this has absolutely nothing to do with Mil and Phil; it's an abstract. It's just that when two people are having trouble, or, better example, when a man is seen very often in the company of an attractive girl not his wife—

say, Neil and the pretty Brazilian secretary from his office—a woman *wonders* whether or not they might *possibly* be having an affair, and a man just assumes they are having an affair and waits for it to be over."

"Neil *Davidow?*"

"I just used him as an innocent example."

"Well, you must have meant him if you said him."

"I don't know," Bert said calmly. "Theirs is a perfect marriage if anyone's is. Actually, I guess to mention Neil and the secretary was the most farfetched example of all. But I meant anyone."

"Even me?"

He looked at her, but with neither suspicion nor surprise. "You mean if you were seen going around with a man?"

"Just suppose."

"I'd probably think it was just the interior decorator. Until you told me differently."

"You keep contradicting your theories."

"I suppose because the way I feel about them is contradictory. I don't care what anyone else does."

"But me?" Helen said. She was surprised to hear how pleading her own voice sounded in her ears. What she really wanted him to say, she knew, was that he would kill her if she ever slept with another man. She wanted her husband to make the decision for her, and she knew that if he did, at this moment on the balcony in the darkness, by three short words—*But not you*—then it would be the law, and she would obey it happily and lovingly for the rest of her life. "But me?" she said again, and she could not understand how he could not notice that her voice trembled.

"If you wanted to have an affair with someone I wouldn't stop you," Bert said.

"*Why?*" She was near to tears; she was so angry she almost hated him.

"I'd want you to be happy. If you felt happiness was with someone else, then I wouldn't want to feel as though I kept you a prisoner."

"Then you'd leave me?"

"I guess so. It would depend on the circumstances. Let's get some more brandy."

She took hold of his sleeve. "Please, not now. If you go into the living room and get more brandy we'll get off the subject. And we'll never get on it again."

"That would be all right with me," he said.

"It . . . hurts . . . doesn't it?" she whispered. She could feel the pain, in her own throat.

"No," he said. "I just think it's silly."

She felt almost nauseated. She had already forgotten how the discussion had started. She only knew that she did not want it to end this way. "If you hadn't met me when you did, if you had met me five or six years later, I probably would have had a lover. Maybe I would have had several. Would you have married me anyway?"

He smiled. "If you and I hadn't gotten married and if you had met someone else five or six years later, then you would have had me for a lover."

She had to smile too, remembering, and she felt better. She put her arms around him again. "We were practically married then. I felt as if we were married. Didn't you?"

"Yes."

"*That* won't change for us ever, will it? Making love? Everything else changes but that won't change?"

"Of course it will," Bert said calmly. "Everything changes. Do you think we're the same as we were the first year we were married, or even the first few years? Everything changes a little every year and neither of us is really very aware of it."

"I don't like that," Helen said softly. "I know you're right, but aren't there *some* people whose marriages never change?"

"No. Of course not. There are only the people who waste time regretting it and the people who are sensible enough not to."

"I see," she said.

"What does that mean?"

"Nothing," she said lightly. "I see. You're right. I'm just one of the nonsensible people. But then, as you told me before, I'm terribly naïve for a woman who's been married ten years."

"And sentimental," he said. But he looked at her as if he were remarking on a featherheaded little flaw and not something that might be rather rare and good. He left the balcony with the brandy glass in his hand, and even though Helen knew he was going to be in the same apartment with her and then the same room and then the same bed for the rest of the night, she felt as if he had deserted her.

She felt ugly. Not just ugly inside but ugly outside as well, as if her face had changed in these few minutes to something drab and unlovable. Something compelled her to trail Bert into the bedroom to continue their discussion, to flog it on until it came to some sort of conclusion. She did not know what she meant to prove. She was aware that she would be annoying him if she brought up the subject again, and that if she did, eventually he would fight with her. In a way, she wanted him to fight with her. At this moment, when caution and secrecy and prudence were essential to keep everything in her marriage as unspoiled as ever, she felt reckless, leading herself into danger and not knowing either why she did or how to stop herself. It was as if she wanted him to see how ugly she was, how she had been planning to deceive him, so that he would make some strong gesture to prove to her that he loved her too much to allow her to destroy herself and their love. If he could have done that, right now, she could escape from her love affair while there was still time.

"Bert . . ."

"What?" He was sitting on the edge of the bed, taking off his shoes.

"Do you think we have a good marriage?"

"Don't you?"

There was a flicker of warning. It ignited her. "I asked you."

"Yes, when you don't keep me up in the middle of the night having philosophical discussions about it."

"Well, I don't see you during the day."

"What do you expect me to do? Stay home from the office?" He dropped his shoes to the floor and began to unbutton his shirt.

"Very funny."

He didn't answer for a minute and she thought she really had made him angry and she circled him warily, looking into his face. She waited. "That's part of a good marriage," he said finally. "Loving my work. If I didn't love my work I couldn't have a good marriage either. You're touchy because I'm going away again, aren't you?"

"No. I know you have to go."

"Then what is it?"

"I just started to think about things."

"At one o'clock in the morning?"

"Maybe I'd better set aside special hours for thinking. Say, four-thirty in the afternoon? Four-thirty to four-forty-five. Can I make an appointment with you?"

"You're pretty funny yourself."

"That's nice. I always think there has to be humor in a marriage."

He had taken off his clothes and now he put on his pajamas. Somehow, for no reason, it annoyed her that he was standing there naked and then putting on his pajamas as if she were invisible, as if the fact of taking off his clothes in her presence had lost all its romantic significance. She might as well have been a salesman in a men's shop. Because, even to this day, whenever she dressed or undressed in front of him she was aware of how she must look to him, of her body before his accidental gaze; none of this had lost its significance. Perhaps it was because as a girl she had been brought up to be more modest than he was, so that nudity in the presence of a man, even for the functional purpose of changing clothes, was meaningful to her.

"Good night," he said, and got into bed.

"Good night," she answered. She said it coldly. She waited for him to say something or even glance at her in response to her tone. He said nothing and appeared to be almost asleep. She suddenly wanted very much to kiss him and ran to the edge of the bed and sat down beside where he was lying. "Kiss me," she whispered, almost pleadingly.

He opened his eyes and looked at her and then he raised himself on one elbow. Helen put her hand on the back of his neck and kissed him on the lips, not just a casual kiss good night but a longer one. She held the kiss, waiting for him to respond and feeling herself respond, and finally, what seemed a long time later although it could not have been very long, he reached up and pulled her down on top of him, over the sheet, and kissed her deeply, as if he really meant it, as if he really wanted to kiss her, not because it was a formality more informal than a pat on the head.

She did not really think at first of making love right now; she had only thought of kissing him good night. She knew he was tired. But once she had begun to kiss him she did not want to draw away, and then when she did not draw away Bert's arms tightened around her and she knew that he was thinking of it. There was a moment when she still could have stopped without having stopped anything, but she could not bear to lose him to sleep when they were so close at last to each other, and so when he began to feel for the hooks at the back of her dress she helped him.

She dropped her dress, inside out, on the floor, and he peeled off his pajamas with as much desperation and distaste as if they had been a badly fastened strait jacket. "Wait," she whispered. "I'll close the door. Wait . . ."

She closed and locked the door, remembering the presence of the children, and walked back to the bed quickly on bare feet, smiling with love and excitement, conscious as always of how she must look to him walking naked toward him this way, hoping he still thought she was beautiful. He took her into his arms immediately and kissed her again very hard twice and then entered her so quickly that she was startled. He was not looking at her; he seemed to be looking over her shoulder at some vision of pain that made his face so grim, and then he closed his eyes.

"Darling . . ." Helen whispered, but suddenly it seemed only a word, uttered after the fact, for no real reason except to mask disappointment and to pretend that something had happened to her too, because it was over. She did not know what to do. He tried to leave her but she shook her head. "Please," she whispered. "Don't go away. Stay here just a minute."

250

"I didn't want to do that," Bert said grimly. "Why did you make me do it?"

"*Make* you do it?" Her hands slid limply off his back and she stared into his face, not quite believing what he had said.

"I was too tired," he said. He stood up and put on his bathrobe quickly and walked out of the room to the bathroom.

Helen lay on the scarcely wrinkled sheet with her hands opened flat beside her, reaching and empty, and she looked at the lamp on the dresser and the dresser itself and the mirror above it as if she had never seen these simple things before. She felt as though Bert had hit her. If he had actually struck her, slapped her or done something impulsive and regrettable out of anger, she could have borne it. But she was filled with terror now because what he had done had been much worse. She heard Bert running the shower in the bathroom and she had the devastating feeling that he was trying to wash off the touch of her love-making.

She sat up with a great effort and walked slowly and weakly to the mirror. She looked at her face very closely, and then took a step back and looked at the upper half of her body. Suntanned shoulders and arms, white breasts, then tan again to the waist where the dresser obscured her view. Was she still attractive, or not? She didn't know, she couldn't know now, and she wondered if she were still attractive to him. She might as well have been looking at the body of a stranger for all the pitiless scrutiny she gave it. She was nearly thirty—she would be thirty in a year and a half—and she had never before thought of this as a milestone. She would be thirty years old with a husband she knew well and two children who were growing up to be wonderful human beings. Despite what she had said jokingly to Bert, thirty had not been anything to view with alarm, but simply another year. She stepped back another few feet and looked at the rest of her body. The stretch marks on her stomach from carrying the children had always been almost imperceptible, but now she ran her fingertips over them and peered at them critically. They said you could tell a woman's age from her legs. She had always had nice legs. Now she looked at them doubtfully. Did they reveal something she could not see?

She turned quickly when Bert came back into the room and put on her silk robe, belting it tightly around her and putting the collar up. She felt as though she could not breathe. "I'm . . . sorry," she said.

"Well, so am I." He smiled, and she smiled at him, and she wondered why they were smiling at each other. She put her hands on his chest and looked up into his face. His smile vanished and into his eyes came a trapped look. That inadvertent look, as if he thought she wished him harm, as if he really thought she would try to pull him beyond the limit of his endurance for her own selfish reasons, hurt her more than anything he might have said. She put her hands quickly into her pockets.

"I love you," she said.

His voice was tense. "I know," he said.

"It's late," she said lightly. "We'd better go to sleep."

His damp bath towel was hanging over its rack in the bathroom and the air smelled of dampness and steam and faintly perfumed soap. The bath mat was kicked into little ridges. She looked at her face again closely in the mirror over the sink. She looked tired; there were little lines under her eyes, but perhaps they were only lines from the sun. She whirled and almost violently turned on the water in the shower. The sooner she washed away the memory of this night the better, although she knew it was not over with or forgotten, because neither of them had said anything more.

When Bert had been gone for a day and a half Sergio telephoned. It was early: nine o'clock in the morning. So this was how it happened. If she could have imagined how the moment of decision would be, it would never have been like this, at nine o'clock of an ordinary morning, in her calm household, with the sun shining through the windows and the maid clearing away the breakfast dishes from the dining-room table. But the moment she heard Sergio's voice the everyday world disappeared, and Helen was alone with the receiver cupped in her two hands, listening to his voice, her face as alive as if he could see her standing there. He had to go to the farm unexpectedly for business the following morning. He had to leave very early, so they could drive through the hottest part of the city before the day became too unbearably hot. He would be gone overnight and the next day, and drive back at night. Could she go with him?

Helen hesitated, but reluctance now was a slow, lovely pleasure, the last instinctive wile of woman, not a thing of conflict and indecision. She knew she would say yes, and hesitated now only because it made the final acceptance more of a relief to herself.

"The farm? Is it far?"

"Six hours by car," he said. "Five if I drive fast. Don't you want to go?"

"Isn't your wife . . ."

"She is in Rio. She came here for a week to have some new dresses made. I . . . please come with me. If you want to." His voice was gentle, almost diffident.

"I do want to."

"Good! Can you be ready at seven o'clock?"

"Seven?"

"I usually go at six. But I will go at seven for you. No later. It gets very hot."

It seemed so strange to be talking about time and transportation and weather this way, as if she were actually going to the farm only out of curiosity about what a Brazilian *fazenda* looked like. "All right."

"I wait for you in a taxi at the corner in front of your apartment. It is safer. You look for a taxi."

"Yes."

"And then we take the car. Does it sound like a spy melodrama?"

She laughed, relieved. "Yes."

"I love you."

"What?"

"I tell you tomorrow," he said. He hung up.

Helen stood there motionless for a moment and then replaced the receiver slowly. She felt happiness illuminating her face, as if she were giving off light or endless energy. *I love you.* It was not something to analyze or to doubt or to argue against. He loved her now, and he would love her tomorrow and the day after. He would make love to her with love. Love always changed, she had learned that now, but this was new love, and fresh, and freely given, so that even for the moment it mattered and was important. Sergio would never love her only a little; he had told her that when they had first met. I love you too, she thought, realizing even as she said it to herself that it was the first time she had ever dared to think those words. The feeling of love rushed through her, making her feel strong and alive again. How bright the floors were here in the hallway in the sunshine, polished and rich and clean! How beautiful everything was in this room, as if she had noticed it all for the first time.

Julie came trailing down the hall, wearing her new bikini, carrying a partly deflated rubber beach ball for her mother to blow up for her. Helen knelt beside her and put her arms around her child's small, compact body, filled with love for her, and kissed her cheeks and forehead and silky hair.

"Oh, Julie, you're going to be so beautiful when you grow up!" she said. "So beautiful!"

CHAPTER *17*

The small plane was airborne at eight in the morning. It was already a hot day; the night mists that were left at the rim of the land burned quickly away. There were six other passengers on the plane, and it would make three stops. Bert was not sleepy at all. He lighted a cigarette and looked down out the window at the last markings of city and civilization disappearing under the wing and he felt the first, free exhilaration that always hit him at this moment, as if suddenly they were flying into rarer air.

He had with him a canvas flight bag filled with rough, worn clothes, his boots, a carton of American cigarettes, and a fifth of good Scotch. The seat next to his was unoccupied, so he took his bag from under his own seat and put it on the empty one so he would have more room to stretch his legs. He yawned, moved his ankles back and forth until he felt the faint crack, dragged on his cigarette, and felt fine.

Below was an ocean of trees. He looked down at it, seeing only the beauty and endlessness of it; and then he reminded himself of what was really down there, awakening in himself the slight fear, the prickling knowledge of danger, and liking that feeling more than the awareness of beauty. Those trees were enormous, ancient, joining their leaves to block out the sky. Below them it was dark and damp, filled with the screeches of unseen wild creatures, the clicking and clacking of life unknown, gibberish and howls, and sometimes sudden silent death. A man dropped

255

into that jungle, a plane downed there with survivors, would be lost forever. There was no way out; the vastness of that leafy, vine-choked land prevented it. You could run until you had to walk, walk until you had to crawl, reduced to the level of the animals who were your sole companions, and finally, unlike those animals, you would pay for your weakness and superiority by dying. But animals died too, down there. The constant chain of killing and eating went on; kill to eat, eat to live, live to die and nourish, nourish so that he whom you nourished would grow into rich food for another stronger claw and fang that would then devour him, you, all. There was death in the jungle, but there was never nothingness, for whatever died, fed, even if it fed only those strong vines thicker than a man's arm, those deep roots sturdier than his body.

Between the trees there were sometimes rivers, like thin threads, yellow or brown. Miles, miles, miles of trees, on and on, punctuated only by those occasional rivers, and nowhere was there man. After several hours of flying there would be a town, and then the jungle again, with no way in between but the air. The amethyst mine with its mining town was at the end of this trip, a remote and vigorous world where Rio was an image, a name, nothing more.

Bert felt happiness and contentment seeping through him as though they were drugs he had taken. Flying into the sun there was a small sun on the glass of his window, golden, sending off sparks. The plane throbbed like a heart. How far he had come from the past, only nine years ago, and paradoxically how much farther from the years that followed directly after!

He remembered those years of the past dreamily now, with benevolence and a touch of poignance, although he knew (and this was perhaps what made the poignance) that he never wanted to go through all that again. Smiling now, he remembered himself as he was in those lost days, striding to work on the first fall mornings of his first job. The city seemed his city then, and the office buildings of New York seemed very clean and bright against the blue autumn sky, their windows catching the sun. He would emerge from the gloom of the train tunnel and join the people of his city, the others who were out to conquer it too and the ones who had long since given up hope, and he felt as though he would outstrip them all. It was a secret belief, and one he would have felt embarrassed to confide to anyone, even to Helen.

He and Helen were first married then, and he knew she was still in their tiny apartment in Riverdale, cleaning the place. He would think of her fleetingly for an instant, but his thought was mainly a mind picture of an unmade bed and a table with coffee cups on it, and the machinations that women perform to alleviate all this disorder before sundown. It was not his world back there in that apartment, although it was his home. It was more like his chrysalis, from which he had emerged the way a bright, vigorous butterfly does, leaving the shards behind. This was his world, the morning city, and the offices full of ambitious people. I am doing it all for her, he would tell himself sentimentally, because he was in love; but at heart he knew this was not true. He was doing it for himself. It was his life force, as if his strength and youth entered and interreacted with the receiving life force of the working world, thrusting, straining, giving, and finally at the end of each day withdrawing, spent. Being young and intelligent and full of enthusiasm and vigor, he was always successful, so that although he was tired at the end of the day it was the kind of tiredness that only needs a night of deep sleep to be gone.

Once Helen had said to him, laughing, "I really think you're having a love affair with your job." He had been surprised and had pretended to be offended. "Honey," he had said, looking put upon and unappreciated, "I'm trying to make a life for us and the children. I'm knocking myself out for you."

"I know, darling," Helen had said quickly. Then she was the one who tried to cover up. "I didn't really mean it."

Every Christmas, during those first years, he became nervous and tense, because he knew the raises would be given out. It seemed almost as though Christmas should have been called the Season of Reckoning; the bills came in and so did the raises, and you knew then what you had wondered and worked for all year— whether or not you were worth what your spending said you thought you were. It was not that he and Helen were extravagant, or even extraordinarily materialistic. Helen, especially, like many girls who have been brought up in good families who have never known either extreme want or extreme waste, adapted very well to the stringencies of living with a young man who was just beginning to earn a living. She liked to save money for him. But still, it was Christmas, and there were the children, and he loved his wife, and you couldn't be a piker. Money was a symbol, Bert liked to think. It was a symbol of whether you were appreciated. It didn't matter whether you agreed with the system or not. You might despise it. But still, if the boss thought he didn't have to give you a raise this year, then five years from now he might not think he had to give you a promotion, and twenty-five years from now you would still be slaving in the same underpaid job, doing other people's work, and all you would have to show for it would be a gold watch.

During those pre-Christmas days, when the streets were filled with the music of tiny bells, and fat and thin Santa Clauses cried out by their multiplicity the falseness of the legend, Bert would walk to work with his face set grimly, looking as if he had never heard of Christmas spirit. If I don't get the raise I asked for I'm going to quit, he would mutter to himself. It's the only way I can keep my dignity. I'll leave and find another job. It's the only way. And then, finally, he would get the raise. He always did. But it never mattered; every Christmas the tension would be the same, because it had to be proven to him that he had done well; it had to be *shown*.

After the first two years the autumn-morning streets did not have that same new feeling about them, except on certain mornings when something about the angle of sunlight striking a windowpane or the sweet bite of the air reminded him of how he had felt every day. Then he would walk a little faster and hold his head up, breathing deeply and even smiling. It was still his city; he still had freedom and the future. Less frequently too, then, he would think of Helen as he had left her in their apartment in Riverdale, but this time his mental picture would include Helen holding Julie in her arms, and Julie waving her arms and her sticky hands and smiling lovingly, and putting Pablum in

258

Helen's hair. I am doing it all for them, he would say then, but even then he knew in his innermost heart that this was not true. There was something almost martyrish about saying you were doing all this, giving of your youth and strength and vigor, for two other people. It sounded lofty, but it wasn't true, nor was it even entirely right that it should be true. You could not give these innermost things, these important things, only for others. You could not give away your very life. He was doing it, Bert knew, because it was his way of life, and his reason for life, and, most of all, his *feeling* of life came from this work. He wondered sometimes why Helen did not seem to have the slightest idea of the intrinsic importance his work had for him. Sometimes when he had to stay late at the office and came home tired she would put her arms around his neck and say, "Poor thing!" as if she actually thought he had suffered. But somehow, when he tried to explain, he always discovered that it was much easier to pretend that he *had* suffered rather than to try to explain. Explanations made him lose it, made the whole idea seem rather high flown and corny. It was almost as silly as trying to explain the feeling you had when you were in bed with a girl you loved, making her happy and making yourself happy and even rather proud in the process.

Although that first, vigorous feeling which composed his happy early memory became dissipated during the years, and almost disappeared into grinding exhaustion during the years of commuting from Westport and back, when he took his family to Rio he felt again as he had on the first job. Rio was a new city, a new future, when he already had the experience to promise success in it. He would look at the suntanned faces along the streets as he left the place where he parked his car and walked to his office building, and they were entirely different-looking faces from the ones he had seen in New York. They were lethargic, cheerful, devil-may-care. He remembered a story one of his colleagues had told him about a recent revolution—that the entire revolution had been temporarily halted so everyone could go out to eat lunch.

"Oh, yes," his Brazilian secretary had exclaimed, "I remember that! I was in a night club one night when we were having a revolution. I didn't even know anything was happening, except that when we went out on the street we couldn't get a taxi."

The other American men Bert knew didn't really take the Brazilians very seriously in business. No Brazilian was in a hurry, no one seemed afraid of what might happen if they didn't stop to drink a *cafezenho* every time someone stepped into the office. *Cafezenho* first, business later. An executive with a mistress—whom he usually called a fiancée, even if he were married—would leave the office for an entire afternoon if the "fiancée" telephoned. Love first, business later. Even the telephone system seemed against any show of urgency. There were not enough telephone lines in Rio to service the number of telephone instruments, so from two until four in the afternoon you might have to wait over an hour to put in a business call to an office which was within walking distance. You could purchase any kind of new telephone; the modern one that was only a handle with the dial on the base, in a variety of pretty colors, but you might as well purchase a toy telephone for all the good it would do you. You can't call today? You can call tomorrow, or after tomorrow. You Americans, the Brazilians said, are always in a hurry. That's why you have heart attacks. We don't have heart attacks. Liver, yes; terrible. It's our climate. But heart attacks, ulcers—never. Those belong to the American business world.

Some American businessmen in Brazil got ulcers because they could not cope with the aggravating slowness and casualness with which they were forced to conduct important business. To Bert Sinclair, this national business apathy seemed a stroke of luck. If the others wanted to play grasshopper and sing and play all summer, then he would play ant. The morsels belonged to the provident ant, who stored them away for the harsh winter, but in Brazil it was always summer, in a way. Winter would be back home, where he would return one day, but he would return secure. These mornings, going to work, Bert often thought how content he was in this rich, fertile, growing land full of promise. It was a primitive land in many ways, with flaws and lacks you never could get used to even though you learned to tolerate them just below the threshold of irritability.

260

He knew just how primitive Brazil was whenever, as now, he went into the interior to the mines. Actually, as a gemologist, he need never have gone to the mines if he did not want to. He had never told Helen that. She thought he was indispensable to the mines in some way, as if he had to tell their owners whether the stones the miners hacked out of the rich earth were fabulous fortunes or useless chunks of mineral. It was in the mines that Bert felt a true resurgence of the old, autumn-morning feeling.

The mines meant more to him than he almost dared to admit to himself. Each mine was different, with its own secret wealth hidden in its dark layers. First you would strike away the earth with heavy, sharp tools, to the rock, and then reveal the first layer of mineral, the one that told you by its composition what was hiding beneath. The aquamarine, the amethyst, the citrine, or the tourmaline, clung back to back with the poor, coarse mineral, like a beautiful young Brazilian virgin with her chaperone. You would pry away a chunk of this twinned solid mineral from the side of the mine pit and then you would spit on your finger to moisten it and rub it on the stone. From the moisture a bright color would emerge. Not so pure and bright a color as would later be revealed when the stone was cut and polished as a gem, but enough to substantiate what your practiced instinct had already told you. It *was*. . . .

The first mine he had ever seen in Brazil had been this same amethyst mine in the State of Bahia, to which he had first been invited as a guest by a friend. It was such a richly giving mine that rough amethysts lay on the dusty ground all over the floor of the pit. Dullish purple, some as small as gems and others like chunks of coal, and some larger than your clenched fist, their octrahedron crystals so perfectly formed it seemed as if some divine stonecutter had cut them that way before he hid them in the earth for men to discover. Some of them were inferior-quality amethysts taken from nearer the surface of the pit, but even knowing that, Bert was speechless for a moment at the wonder of this profligate richness. Nearby some Brazilian workers, dirt-poor, were preparing to eat the midday meal their wives had packed for them to take to the mine. The food had been put in round tin pots, stacked one upon the other. Bert watched one man gathering rocks and bits of wood to make a fire to heat his food. And then he saw a sight he never forgot. Another miner, lazier than the first, merely squatted on the ground and scooped up a small pile of amethysts, which he used to hold up his tin pot of *feijoada*. He made the fire within this cradle of purple amethysts, as if in their abundance they had been no more than rocks.

It did something to Bert to see that. It was as if suddenly he had been shown a vision of *possibility*. Anything was possible in this land—wealth, success, valor, discovery. That was when he had begun to be drawn to the mines. The men began to know him. The owners liked him because he took a personal interest and was always available for consultation when they thought they had struck a new vein. Sometimes, so many times, you would find two different kinds of valuable gem stones in the same pit. The owners didn't really need him, because they were usually trained minerologists themselves, but they liked to have him there because he was a specialist and so willing to go, and so *simpatico,* and eventually Bert became so *simpatico* that the owners began to think they actually did need him. *Call Bert Sinclair. What does Bert Sinclair think? Bert Sinclair, the American expert, agrees with me.* It was a good life.

A good life? It was more, much more. It was a special life. The pale, resigned faces of those men who did not like their work, who stepped toward it every morning like automatons, were something he wanted to put away from his memory forever, as if he had accidentally looked upon the faces of the dead. Someone had written once, "If you do not love your work you would do better to sit as a beggar at the gates and accept alms from those who do love their work." It was a good thing not too many people took that advice seriously.

The plane dipped and climbed down to the tiny airfield in the Interior that was its first stop. Two men got off and another got on. The air that came through the opened door was hot and moist. Bert closed his eyes contentedly. If he could drop off to sleep, even for an hour, it would make his arrival seem sooner.

The plane put down at his stop at a little after two. A bare air-

262

strip carved out of the jungle. A few wooden buildings, reassuring with red and white advertising signs extolling a pill for stomach acid. Bert took off his jacket, but by the time he had walked across the air strip his shirt was already sticking to his back as if he had gone swimming in it by mistake. His friend Hector Adolpho Moreiro Oliviera was at the edge of the field beside his jeep, and when he saw Bert he ran to meet him halfway.

They embraced each other. Hector Adolpho was the owner of the mine, a wiry man in his early forties, taller than most Brazilian men, very tanned from the sun. He was a trained minerologist and he spoke several languages. With Bert he spoke English.

"How was the trip?"

"Good."

"We'll go to the hotel. You can wash and we'll have lunch. The Mayor and some other friends will join us there. Are you too tired to go to the pit?"

"No," Bert said. "I want to."

"We found a new vein last week. That mine gives on and on. But that's not why I wanted you to come, of course. I wanted you to see the secret. If it is what I think it is—" Hector Adolpho's face lighted up with the hope of it and he held up his crossed fingers. "I believe," he said. "But I want you to see too."

He started the jeep and they drove toward the town. Neither of them said the word *emeralds*. But each of them knew, hoped, thought it, and were aware of all it could mean. There were no emerald mines in Brazil. If it were true that a new vein had revealed the companion minerals of emerald, or if any bits of emerald itself had been found, it was not only a valuable secret but a dangerous one. The vein would have to be explored further— how abundant were the emeralds, how good was their quality? It could mean a fortune, millions—dollars, not cruzeiros. When they were sure of what they had, the mine would have to be temporarily closed, sealed off, with guards and machine guns posted on top of the wall, while Hector Adolpho negotiated to buy all the surrounding land, pretending he wanted it for farming. There were rich emerald mines in Columbia, but some experts thought they were becoming exhausted. If this were so, then the discovery

263

of an emerald mine in Brazil would be much more valuable. This new mine would be the only source of emeralds in the hemisphere; the only other place was Africa. There were economic factors: price, demand, supply. There were human factors: publicity, skepticism, belief. A small bright green stone for some lady to wear at her throat, for a ring, a gift, an eventual heirloom, for vanity, for sentiment, for lust—fortunes could be made or lost on just this.

"What are you thinking?"

Bert patted his flight bag. "I brought some Scotch."

"Good."

"For right away. Before lunch."

"Better."

They drove into the town, a dusty cluster of white-painted buildings set around a dirt-paved square, with a fountain and statue in the center of it. The town's only hotel was a four-story wooden building with ramps instead of staircases, surrounded on three sides by a rickety veranda. Bert's room, one of the largest, finest ones, was clean but had neither screens nor windowpanes. Flies buzzed sleepily around the flowered chintz cover on the double bed. There was a bathroom with a shower down the hall, but since only one of the other rooms was occupied the bathroom was nearly private. Bert washed his face and put on the clothes he always wore at the mines—the faded tan shirt, the khaki trousers, the leather boots—and took the bottle of Scotch downstairs with him to the bar.

He and Hector Adolpho spoke Portuguese because the Mayor and his two friends did not speak English. A waiter brought soda and doubtful ice, and they drank the Scotch at a long table in the empty room. There was an electric fan in the corner, and the barroom opened to the veranda, so it was cool. One of the Mayor's friends was the banker, the other owned the general store. Both the bank and the store had been closed for this occasion, their doors locked and windows shuttered, while Bert answered questions about America, about business, politics, Latin-American friendship, and Marilyn Monroe. They drank several times to friendship. When they finished the Scotch the waiter

brought platters of meat cooked in sauce, rice, *feijoada*, broiled
filet mignon, and a bowl of raw onions and tomatoes chopped up
together to put on the beef. There were white rolls and half-
rancid butter, and huge steins of frosty Brazilian beer.

They finished lunch at five o'clock in the afternoon. There was
one movie theater in the town, showing an American film, and
none of them had seen it. It was too late to go to the amethyst
mine; it would soon be dark. As they all walked across the square
to the movie house the proprietor of the rival general store saw
them, waved, and said he would go too. He locked his doors and
ran after them, putting the key into his pocket. Sunlight made
the dusty street golden, and it was quiet. A dog slept underneath
a dusty tree. The owner of the filling station stood outside his
establishment, looking under the hood of a 1939 Ford. Some little
boys stood outside the combination bar and candy store, watching them curiously.

When they came out of the movie it was almost dark. Bert
and Hector Adolpho crossed the village square to the bar. On a
high tree a loud-speaker was playing tinny-sounding radio music,
the music of the evening promenade. The young were out walking, the pretty girls, the unmarried men, the chaperones. Around
and around the square in the casual watchful promenade, with
nothing else to do—and nothing that seemed more important than
this prelude to pairing. In the bar Bert and Hector Adolpho drank
beer and watched the people outside in the square and talked
quietly of the mine, each pretending there was no point in being
elated so far in advance. Tomorrow they would know more. . . .
But Bert knew that Hector Adolpho already knew. He did not
need Bert to corroborate his judgment. If there were emeralds,
this man knew it.

Bert felt a secret pride that he had been chosen to give his
opinion. It meant a great deal, not only professionally but because
it was a sign of friendship. This man was not asking; he was
showing.

They decided to meet at five-thirty in the morning in the hotel
dining room for breakfast and leave at six. Bert would have been
willing to go even earlier. It was a nine-hour trip by jeep over

rough jungle roads to get to the location of the emerald mine. Nine hours today, but perhaps several years from now the road would be opened wide and there might even be a town.

They shook hands warmly at the top of the ramp that led to Hector Adolpho's room. "Until tomorrow."

It was only nine o'clock, but Bert felt tired and good. The beer on top of the aftereffects of the Scotch had made him sleepy. Through his open windows he could hear the loud-speaker with its scratchy music, far away and somehow pleasant. He took off all his clothes and got into bed naked. The mattress smelled of mildew, but the sheets were clean and smelled faintly of soap. He put citronella on his arms and face to chase the mosquitoes, and turned off the light. The scent of citronella always brought back his childhood—summer camp. He slept, still hearing the music faintly in his dream.

He dreamed of the mine, of tomorrow, of great mountains of emeralds, green as grass, Kelly green, shiny and already cut. Strangely, it was not the Brazilian emerald mine at all, but the stone quarry where he had hiked as a boy at camp. The great piles of stone were no longer granite, gray, but emeralds and green. No one seemed aware of it. He was the only one who knew and he wanted to tell someone, his counselor. His counselor was handing around a bottle of citronella to chase off the mosquitoes, because it was evening and they were going to sleep at the quarry that night under the stars, with sleeping bags. When Bert tapped his counselor on the arm, the man turned around and his face was the face of Hector Adolpho, tanned, lined, handsome and shrewd. Bert smiled at him, suddenly stupid with adolescent admiration. If Hector Adolpho didn't notice the emeralds, who was *he* to say anything?"

"I thought I would help you," Bert said in the dream. "Is there anything *I* can do?"

The face of Hector Adolpho disappeared and so did the emeralds; the boys were all sitting on the floor of the quarry where the ground was flat, and someone had lighted a campfire. There were about a dozen boys, all singing. The black sky was dotted with lonely stars. It was a foreign-sounding song, and somehow he didn't know the words, so he moved his lips and pretended.

They were all happy and sleepy and very good friends, so no one seemed to care. They swayed to the tune of the song and watched the hot fire. Bert knew that the summer was almost over, this was the last hike of the season, the long three-day hike, and he felt nostalgia and sadness filling his throat so that he could not sing any more. I'm going to come back every year, he thought loyally. Every year until I'm too old, and then I'll be a counselor. I'll never leave my friends. I want to stay here forever. But even saying that resolutely to himself, he knew it would not come true. It would all vanish, all of it, the night, the campfire, the friends who swore to remember. All this good feeling would be gone. The gang would be gone. It made him sad, as if he had no human insides at all but only something bitter and black.

The tiny alarm on his wristwatch went off like the buzzing of a hornet. At first Bert did not know where he was; then he sat up in bed and looked around, shaking off his dream. The huge wooden dresser loomed up at him, then the dark square of the opened window, lightening now to gray. It was five minutes to five in the morning and he was in the hotel. He found an opened pack of cigarettes in the pocket of his shirt and lighted one, and then dressed. He washed in the bathroom down the hall but did not bother to shave. When he went down to the dining room at five-thirty the sky outside was already blue.

They ate sliced rolls with jam, and coffee with condensed milk, and took along a package of food and several bottles of beer and soda for the trip. Hector Adolpho was wide awake; he said he had been up since four.

The two of them took turns driving the jeep. The jungle seemed tamer on either side of them, conquered and familiar. It was not the jungle Bert had looked down on from the plane, and yet a short time ago it had been exactly like it. "Look at this road, that jungle," Bert said. "Eventually man conquers everything."

"Don't be too sure of that," Hector Adolpho said.

After an hour and a half of driving they passed the road that led to the amethyst mine, but they kept going and did not turn off. There would be plenty of time for that in a day or two, on the way back. Amethysts were only bread and butter now. The sun was very bright.

267

They reached the new pit at a little after three in the afternoon. It was a deep, narrow valley, over a quarter of a mile long. The land around it had been cleared and was flat and treeless. Dusty and ugly—and beautiful. There were Brazilian and Indian workers and guards, but the digging had been halted just at the point when Hector Adolpho's assistant had told him he suspected the existence of something entirely different from what they were looking for. They greeted the men casually, as if this were only an inspection trip. Bert climbed down into the pit and felt his tongue sticking to the roof of his mouth. He had been stiff from the long hours in the jeep but now his tiredness vanished. His breath came in gasps that hurt his chest. Even his eyeballs felt dry, painful to move from side to side. His hands were trembling.

His sharp tools were attached to his belt. On the wall of the pit there was a serpentine vein of black mica, a yard wide—the biotite in which emerald crystals should be embedded. He hacked at it, going deeper. As he chipped into the formation there were crystals embedded—greenish—bigger and greener as he cut deeper into the vein. He chipped off a tiny piece of one and kept it in his closed hand as he climbed back up the side of the pit.

"It's very hot here," Hector Adolpho said, taking his arm. "Let's have a beer in the shade."

They walked back to the jeep, the dust stirring around their heavy boots. Bert opened his hand and looked at the tiny bit of greenish mineral.

"Well?"

"It's emerald," he said. "You can test it, but I'm sure now."

"Yes. I am too."

They looked at each other for a moment and neither spoke. Bert moved the piece of rough emerald between his thumb and finger, feeling it, looking at it. Deeper into the vein the emeralds would be loose, lying in caves of white powdery-looking albite, gem-quality stones, valuable, hard and bright. He looked at Hector Adolpho.

"This must be a secret," Hector Adolpho said. "Don't tell anyone. No one."

Bert nodded. "No one. You can rely on me. Besides—" he smiled —"who could I possibly tell?"

268

CHAPTER *18*

Four hours by car from the city of Rio de Janeiro, toward the city of São Paulo, there are miles and miles of highway cutting through the rich hills and leaving gashed red earth on either side, land so rich it seems to bleed like a living thing. The green grows above the red earth, thick and moist, and far away the hills dip into purple shadows. The sky is very blue, flat, with long white clouds that look dry in the bright light of the sun. It was eleven o'clock in the morning.

Helen sat next to Sergio in his car and they did not speak often. He held her hand. There were very few other cars on the highway, and once the Rio–São Paulo bus, the *Cometa,* came streaking by, honking, and disappeared over the next hill. Sergio drove steadily, and fast, but completely effortlessly. He had made the trip many times. Every once in a while he glanced at Helen to make sure she was all right.

"I feel as if you belong to me," he said. "Isn't that strange? Do you feel that way too?"

"Yes."

"Right now I adore you more than anyone else in the world. There *is* no one else in the world. Whenever you and I are together, and alone, from now on, it will always be this way, but every time it will be better and better."

She said it to him now for the first time. "I love you."

"I haven't even made love to you yet."

"I know."

"That's strange too, not to touch you for such a long time, and to want to so much."

"I'm glad you didn't. I was afraid to before. Now I want you to."

He held her hand very tightly. "We will be something together, won't we!" he said softly. "I know it."

She heard his faint accent that revealed itself whenever he was intense or excited and she realized again how different he was from her and from any man she had ever known, out of a completely different world. She had never wondered about his other mistresses, other affairs, and even now she did not, but there was that experience about him, that emotional intensity, which drew her to him and frightened her a little at the same time. She felt very naïve beside him, completely passive and innocent. She had never in her life gone to bed with any man but her husband, and her thoughts had never been whether or not she was a passionate woman but, rather, how she reacted in relation to Bert. She and Bert were good together—or, they *had* been. Her life was changing minute by minute now, and she did not know what she would have to think of next. She felt shy.

"When we get to the farm," Sergio said after a while, "my father will be there. And maybe my cousin. I will be a little formal with you when they are there, but I don't want you to mind. You will stay in the small guest house right next to my father's house. It's very pretty. I stayed there with my friends when I was growing up—*boys*, that is." He smiled at her. "Not girlfriends. But later I will stay there with you."

"Why are you taking me where your family is?" Helen asked. She looked at him, shocked, and felt so unnerved that she almost pulled her hand away from his, as if his father were already there watching them. "I thought we'd be alone."

"It's so beautiful there," Sergio said. "I wanted you to see the place where I grew up. I have always loved it more than any place I have ever lived since. You don't have to be afraid of my father. He loves life. He has a sense of humor. He's almost seventy years old, but the only thing you'll have to be afraid of is that he will probably try to take you away from me."

"I'll chance it."

"I wanted to take you to a special place this first time," he said. "I didn't want to make love to you in a *garçonier,* or in a hotel room. Do you remember that hotel where we had lunch upstairs on the roof? You can walk down the stairs from there, without taking the elevator, and go right into a room. People reserve the rooms in advance, you know. In case. I couldn't do that with you. We may have to do that some time; but later on, when we trust each other enough so that it doesn't make any difference where we are."

"Trust each other?"

"You think that's a funny word to use? You think two people trust each other just because they are lovers?"

Helen smiled. "No, I guess not."

"I know that we will make each other very happy, and also sometimes very unhappy. Whenever you love someone he has the power to make you suffer, only because you love him, not because he is better at tormenting than anyone else is."

"I know . . . very well."

"That's why lovers don't trust; they fear that pain. It's so easy to give. But, even so, the ones who fear it so much they are afraid to love at all—those are the ones I feel sorry for. They might as well not be alive. Actually, they're not alive."

She felt he was right. She had never felt more intensely aware of everything around her, and everything inside her mind, and of her body itself, than she had ever since the morning before when she had finally decided that she and Sergio would become lovers. Even now, with him in the car that was taking them to his *fazenda,* there was an air of unreality about the whole incident, but it was an unreality she recognized from years and years ago, the unreality of first love. Why should he love me, me of all people in the world? He, *he* loves me. She was special to him and therefore special to all the world, she knew it, as if the feeling and knowledge of being loved by this special man shone out of her and made her lovely. Despite her shyness about what to do with her first lover, her first stranger, Helen felt a warm sense of security and strength. She was not even apprehensive about how

271

to behave when she met his father. She felt that even though she would be forced to pretend and perform away from Sergio, she would only be away at arm's length, watched and cherished and safe. She was even enjoying the idea, as a challenge.

At eleven-thirty Sergio pointed to the right side of the highway and said, "Look, the farm begins here."

There was the flat land and the hills beyond, the trees and the blue sky, for miles and miles, exactly as it had looked for hours. "Where?"

"This is only the beginning. We will get to the house in three quarters of an hour."

"How big is it?" Helen cried.

"Twenty thousand *alcares*—that's about eighty thousand acres, more or less. This isn't a very big farm; there are many much bigger."

"It's big enough for me," Helen said. "I have to admit when you first said farm I pictured a few chickens, some vegetables— you know . . . like home."

"But land is so cheap here," Sergio said. "Believe me, eighty thousand acres isn't something extraordinary." He pointed. "Look there. Eucalyptus trees. We use them to make paper. I'll take you to see the paper factory. And we have a sugar-cane factory too, where we make liquor out of our own sugar cane. All the workers live on the property. See there—a restaurant and stores for the workers. This farm is really more like a town."

"The man who owned a town. It sounds like the title of one of those tycoon novels."

He seemed embarrassed. "See the cattle?" he said. "Over there."

"It looks like an ocean of cattle! How many are there? And if you say a million I won't be surprised."

"Only twenty-eight hundred head," Sergio said. "This isn't a cattle farm. What are you smiling about?"

"I can't help it, darling. It's only that it strikes me funny, your saying that. 'Twenty-eight hundred. This isn't a *cattle* farm.' I never expected any of this. It's not that I'm laughing; I'm just kind of shocked silly."

He gave her an amused glance and turned the car off the high-

272

way on to a smooth dirt road. There was a white wooden sign nailed on two tall wooden posts which made an archway under which they drove. On the sign was painted a kind of insignia and the word *fazenda* in black paint. The road continued and was bordered on both sides by a forest of sweet-smelling eucalyptus trees. The trees were tall and blackly leaved against the sun, and beneath them it was cool. They drove on under the trees for what seemed like miles.

"These are the trees that make paper?"

"A certain kind of paper, yes," Sergio said. "Rough paper mostly, wrapping paper, corrugated paper. Not stationery. We don't have the facilities here to make special things like stationery. This is only a—"

"Small farm," Helen finished, interrupting him. They looked at each other for a moment and then they both laughed.

"Gringo," he said.

"I am, aren't I."

He skidded the car to a stop in a cloud of dry dust and pulled Helen close to him and kissed her so hard he hurt her, and then he kissed her gently. There was no one on the road, no other cars, no houses, only the dark wall of trees on either side. It was very quiet.

"I'm so afraid I'm going to say something to hurt you," Helen said. "And I won't even know I'm doing it. I *am* a foreigner, we *are* different, you and I, and I'm so afraid I'll say something you'll take the wrong way and you won't tell me. You have a terrible pride; I know that. Promise me you'll tell me if I say something wrong. Promise me you won't keep it to yourself and stop loving me."

"I promise, of course," Sergio said lightly, but she knew she had been right.

He took his hands away from her with an effort, as if they had been glued, and started the car again. "I don't think I had better let any of the workers find me taking off your clothes in the middle of the road," he said.

"No. They might be shocked."

"Of course they'd be shocked. They do it with their clothes *on*."

273

He smiled at her with that look that had seemed so mysterious to her that night at the swimming pool and now had become very personal and dear.

"It's so strange to be looking at somebody and wondering what he's like and if you'll ever in your entire life get to know anybody like him, and then such a short time later to find that he loves you," Helen said.

"I felt that way about you too. The blond American." His voice became tender. "Scared to death to be standing in the swimming pool in a bikini with a strange man looking at her stomach."

"I wasn't!"

"Yes you were. I liked that."

In the distance was a huge house, painted white, with a red tile roof. There were several smaller houses grouped around it, one perhaps for servants, one a garage, and one the guest house Sergio had told her about. Next to the main house Helen could see a swimming pool bordered by weeping willows, and then a wide, smooth, bright-green lawn with patches of flowers and umbrella-shaped flamboyant trees with their brilliant orange-colored blossoms. At the edge of the lawn there was a row of palm trees, and beyond that she could see a lake glittering in the sunlight. Sergio drove up to the main house and parked in the driveway.

There was a veranda at the side of the house, shaded by the sloping roof, and on the veranda Helen could see small tables and large chairs and a hammock with someone's feet protruding from it. A male voice was singing an American song in an atrociously bad accent. "'You must remember this, A kiss is still a kiss . . . a sigh is still a sigh . . .'"

"My cousin is here," Sergio said. He took Helen's overnight case from the car and led the way into the house.

The main hall of the mansion was dimmed against the sun and cool with the trapped cool stillness that a great house has in the summer when all the shutters have been closed in the early morning to keep in the coolness of the night. The floors were dark polished wood, and scattered on them were the skins of cattle and steers, made into rugs, white and tan, white and black. They bore only the outlines of the cows, but they made Helen shudder just the same. A cow rug wasn't like a bear rug or a lion-skin rug.

"From our own cows," Sergio said rather proudly.

"They're very pretty."

A butler emerged from the shadows, dressed in a black uniform and white gloves. "Good morning, Senhor Sergio. Your father is having his massage," he said in Portuguese.

"What would you like to drink, Helen?"

"Gin and tonic?"

"Is the liquor locked or unlocked?"

"Locked, Senhor Sergio."

Sergio looked annoyed. Then he shrugged and looked at Helen with a little smile. "My father keeps the liquor cabinet locked and he keeps the only key. It's a . . . habit of his. We'll have to wait until he comes down. Would you like some iced tea?"

"Of course. That will be fine."

"Two iced *maté*, please. Tell my father I have taken my guest to the little house."

The butler bowed and disappeared. Sergio picked up Helen's overnight case and led the way out into the bright sunshine again. "I'll put you in here and you can put on a bathing suit and we can swim before lunch," he said. He was suddenly very formal, as he had said he would be. He opened the door. "Here is your bedroom, the larger one. It's quite cool. The bathroom is there. Have you enough hangers? Will you be all right?"

"Yes. Thank you."

"I'll meet you at the swimming pool when you're ready. Hurry up."

"I will."

He stopped, with his hand on the doorknob. "I hope you didn't mind about the liquor," he said. "I forgot to tell you before. I'm sorry."

She wanted to run to him and kiss him, but she thought a maid or a butler or perhaps the mysterious cousin might come in at any moment, and, besides, the strange house awed her. She compromised by touching his arm rather timidly. He immediately put his arms around her and put his lips against her hair, and she

275

almost began to cry with relief. She wished they had gone somewhere alone instead of here. She felt like two different people: the fascinated houseguest-tourist being polite and *simpatico,* and the woman in love who only wanted privacy with her lover. Her morality could not yet cope with both selves at once; it was too much of an adjustment even to be one. How much I have to learn, Helen thought.

"I want you to be happy here," Sergio said. "You like it, don't you? I'd like to stay here forever. I wish you could stay here with me forever."

"It would be wonderful . . ." With his arms reassuringly around her she really meant it.

"I hate the city. You and I could be happy here together for the rest of our lives." He sounded sad.

"I know . . ."

"Put on your bathing suit," he said abruptly, releasing her. "I'll meet you at the pool." And he was gone.

Helen looked around the huge bedroom, seeing it for the first time. It contained high twin beds with lace-trimmed sheets that seemed to have been hand-embroidered, a tall, heavy old-fashioned armoire for her clothes, a small dressing table and mirror, and a night table with a lamp on it. Except for the elaborate heirloom sheets the room was almost spartanly furnished, but immaculately clean. There was a straw rug on the floor. It was a real summer house. White-painted wooden shutters covered the large windows and shielded the room from the sun. Helen opened one shutter and looked out. There was a beautiful view of the lake, and a little to the side of her window, near enough so she could reach out and touch it, was a tree with wild purple orchids growing up the trunk. She reached out and snapped off a spray of the tiny orchids and put it on the bare dressing table, and then she opened her overnight case and laid out her cosmetics and comb and brush beside them. It made her feel more at home.

She walked into the bathroom. It was as huge as the bedroom. You'd need roller skates to get from the sink to the toilet, she thought, and ran around in delight. There were twelve narrow windows, with vines curling in from outside, and a tiny lizard

276

walked down the tile wall. The bathtub was set on a kind of platform with three steps leading to it, like the bath of a Roman emperor. The floor of the entire bathroom was made of golden marble and on it there was a large oriental rug. Brazilians evidently had greater respect for bathrooms than Americans did.

There was another door, leading to the other bedroom. It was smaller than her bedroom, and furnished almost the same. Then there was the hall, with a smaller room and bath at the end of it, which must have been the governess's room when Sergio and his friends had stayed here as children. She wondered if his children stayed here now, in this house, when they were at the farm. Perhaps not, because there was no sign of children now, no forgotten toy lying anywhere, no pencil marks low down on the white walls, no little shirt or bathing suit or dress left behind in her armoire. The children of Sergio and his wife probably stayed in the main house with their grandfather, who was old now and liked to have children around him. Helen was glad there was no trace of them in this house where she would sleep tonight with their father. It made it easier to pretend that she and Sergio were both free, so that when he said to her, "You and I could be happy here together for the rest of our lives," it would not sound so make-believe and sad.

When she came down to the pool Sergio's father and cousin were there. The father was a thinner, older version of Sergio. There was something grayish about his face, and Helen suspected he was not in good health. His hair was gray streaked with white, and worn rather long, and he wore a white linen suit and a white shirt and a red silk tie. He did not seem to be bothered by the heat. He sat on a white filagreed metal loveseat on the lawn beside the swimming pool, all in white, with his thin grayish face and white and gray hair, and he looked as if he were going to die before winter. Helen thought Sergio must be his youngest child. She realized that she had never asked Sergio how many brothers and sisters he had, or if all of them were living; but at her age and his those things were so unimportant. The last time she had been courted by a man information about members of his family had been part of the expected earliest conversation, but now, years

277

later, when you fell in love with another grown person each of you tried to be separate and important as yourself, without any past. But she wondered now if Sergio had known his wife since childhood, as Leila had known her ex-husband.

The cousin, Guillerme, was about twenty-two years old, almost as short as Helen, and he had light-brown hair bleached blond on top from the sun, and a healthy tan. He eyed Helen with open delight and covetousness.

They all spoke Portuguese. It became evident to Helen immediately that Guillerme could not speak any English at all, except for the words to the popular song he had been singing, which he had apparently learned by rote, and that Sergio's father could speak only a little English but preferred to speak none at all.

"It has been years since I have spoken to an American," Sergio's father said in Portuguese. "I go to France every year, and often to Germany for the health baths. I speak French very well. I apologize to you for my English."

"I apologize to you for my Portuguese," Helen said. They both laughed politely, sizing up each other.

"Come sit here next to me," the father said.

She sat beside him on the hot iron bench beneath the sparse shade of the weeping willow tree and decided she liked him. She tried to think of something to say.

"Are you comfortable?" he asked. He put his arm around her.

"Yes, thank you."

He gave her a little hug. Then she wasn't quite sure whether she still liked him or not. He was smiling at her, and the look he gave her was not fatherly at all. Sergio was sitting on the grass at his father's feet, and he and his father began a very rapid conversation about politics and inflation and what the inflation was doing to the prices of their liquor output. The cousin Guillerme lay on the grass under the tree with his arms under his head and sang quietly to himself: " 'Saturday night is the loneliest night of the week . . .' "

The butler came to them with a silver tray of cold drinks—tea. Sergio's father looked at Helen. "Would you like gin instead?"

"No, thank you," she lied, because an icy gin and tonic was

exactly what she would have wanted after their long hot drive to get here.

He seemed pleased. "We will have wine with lunch," he said, and turned back to his discussion of politics with Sergio.

" 'I don't mind Sunday night at all,' " sang Guillerme, " 'Because that's when my friends come to call . . .' " He sat up. "Do you know Frank Sinatra?" he asked Helen in Portuguese.

"I know who he is. I like him very much."

"Is he your friend?"

"I never met him. I mean, I like his records very much."

"Oh." He flopped down again on his back. "I have all his records," he said, waving one foot in the air like a baton. "I know all the words. If you meet him, tell him I like him."

"All right."

He looked at her, with that openly acquisitive look. "Do you have a boyfriend?"

"No."

"A fiancé?"

She was beginning to feel uncomfortable. "No."

"Let's go swimming," Sergio said, rising quickly to his feet. "There isn't much time before lunch." He walked to the pool and dived in, and Helen followed him with relief.

She and Sergio swam toward each other and met in the water. "What did you tell them?" she whispered.

"What?"

"About me?"

He shrugged. "You are my guest." He disappeared under the water and bit her toe and she screamed and headed for the shallow end of the pool. Sergio followed her, disappearing and our facing again, teasing her and darting about in the water like a child. Helen wished then that she could swim well. She wanted to meet him in the cool shadowy intimacy of the bottom of the pool, under the water, secluded from the eyes of his family, but she had never in her life swum underwater. His skin was silky with water and tanned from the sun. He surfaced, blowing water, like a sculptured Pan on a fountain, his wet hair curling down over his forehead in tendrils. He was very beautiful.

The father arose from his bench with effort and stood upright. He held up one thin hand. It was the signal of authority. "Eat," he said, and turned and started slowly across the lawn to the house, Guillerme hovering beside him trying to support the old man without being obvious about it.

Sergio swam quickly to the edge of the pool in a shower of spray and climbed up. "Hurry," he said. "You have to dress for lunch."

"A dress or slacks?"

"It doesn't matter."

He held out his hands to pull her up to the side of the pool, thrust a dry towel at her, and then they were running breathlessly to the house. Helen had the strangest feeling that she was a young girl again, that they were both only in their teens, dating and in love under the considerate eye of the family. The whole household, silently, seemed dominated by the presence of Sergio's father. It was not anything anyone had said; it was simply the way Sergio looked at him and he looked at Sergio and at her.

She felt it more clearly at lunch, when all the conversation through the entire meal was directed to the father and for him. He sat at the head of a long, polished, wood table, with beautifully hand-embroidered linen mats at each place. Sergio sat at the foot, and she and Guillerme across from each other at the middle. There was a large space between each person at the table, which necessitated speaking in a rather loud voice. It was a long, enormous meal, with course after course, most of them unfamiliar to her. With each course the father turned to her and said proudly that the food had been grown on their own farm. Even the cheese came from their own cows. There was a light, delicate Brazilian wine. The butler who served all this was still wearing the white gloves, and Helen wondered if he were very hot.

"He has been with me for fifty years," the father said, gesturing at the butler, who continued walking around the table with platters while they talked about him, as if he were entirely deaf. "He came here as a child of five. He was brought as a companion for my younger brother, who is dead now. They were exactly the same age. Have you these same companions in your country?"

"Many years ago . . . yes, I think so."

"It is very good. A poor child has a good home, then stays to work for the family. I was in the United States in nineteen twenty-six."

He smiled, remembering. "I went to many speakeasies."

"It is much different now."

"What else is different?"

"Oh, everything," Helen said. "The buildings. The old buildings are gone, many of them, and new buildings have been built."

The father nodded politely but he did not seem very interested. For a while he concentrated on his food. Helen wondered how such an old man could eat such a heavily spiced, large meal every noon in the heat of the day, particularly when he already looked so white and frail. "I like to go to the Riviera," he said. "I take my servant there with me every year. We go to Paris, too. Do you like Paris?"

"I have never seen it."

"No?" He seemed horrified. "You come to Brazil and never go to Europe?"

"My . . . husband works here."

"Ah. Very good. I understand."

"These plums and pears come from our own trees," Sergio said. "Eat them with cheese, Helen; it's good that way."

She gave him a weak smile and tried to eat, for him at least, if not for the father. She pushed the food around on her plate, trying to make it look as if she had eaten a great deal, when actually she had been able to force down almost nothing. She sipped some of the wine.

Sergio and his father began to talk about the management of the paper factory. Helen was relieved that she did not have to say anything any more. Guillerme kept looking at her across the table as if he were trying to figure out to whom she belonged, and that made her nervous. She dropped her fork on the floor. The butler immediately brought another one, on a small silver tray with a white doily on it. She felt as if the meal were going on forever. Guillerme said nothing at all, but looked at her, and gorged himself, mixing all the food together on his plate as chil-

281

dren sometimes do. She had never seen a family that liked to eat so much; they seemed to devour everything with an intense loyalty, because it came from their farm (they kept mentioning it to her) and because they thought it was the best in the world, and because indirectly they had created it themselves and therefore it had to be eaten and appreciated and complimented upon and brought back for second huge helpings. Actually, it was all delicious, but she was almost ill with nervousness and the dining room was very hot.

Finally the butler brought tiny china cups half filled with sugar and poured the strong black Brazilian coffee into them. Helen drank her coffee without stirring it, quickly, hoping she could get at it before all that sugar melted. Even so, it tasted like sirup.

"You don't have a spoon to stir your *cafezenho?*" the father asked, concerned. He glanced at the butler, who sprang to attention.

"Yes, thank you. I like it this way."

The father looked at her as if she were crazy, and then smiled indulgently and chose a long cigar from a silver box. The butler lighted it for him. Then the old man stood, with obvious effort, the butler at his side. The lunch was over.

She had thought she would be alone with Sergio after lunch but instead the old man insisted on taking her on a tour of the house. "The doctor says I should take a rest after lunch," the father said, "but I don't listen to him."

"You should," Sergio said.

"Ah." He put his arm around Helen's waist. "I'll rest in heaven."

"That won't be for a long time," Sergio said quickly.

"Did I say it wouldn't?"

The house was built on two floors, but it was very large. There were corridors with room after room leading off them, a white breakfast room separate from the dining room where they had had lunch, an office, a library, the living room, another living room, six large guestrooms, which had formerly been rooms for the old man's children, and before that rooms in which he and his brothers and sisters had grown up. His other brothers and sisters, Sergio's uncles and aunts, were either dead or traveling in Europe, except for one brother who lived on and operated a neighboring *fazenda*.

"At Christmas the whole house was filled," he said. "All the grandchildren, and friends. Parties every night. What a noise!" He gave Helen's waist a squeeze. "You must come back when there are more friends here. It will be more amusing for you."

"Thank you."

Sergio's father occupied an enormous suite. It had the best view in the house, looking over the gardens, and it had evidently been reconverted from several rooms. Helen felt a moment of pity for him, as it must be for him now, taking over rooms that other people had gone away from forever, converting loneliness into solitary luxury. She wondered why he had never remarried.

"This is my bedroom," he said. There was a huge, old-fashioned double bed, with a canopy. All the furniture was of the dark, heavy, carved, antique Brazilian kind that she had seen once in the museum in Petropolis. "How do you like my paintings?" He pointed with great pride at four water colors that hung on either side of the bed. They were of young girls, naked to the waist, with enormously overblown and uptilted breasts and shapely legs in black mesh stockings. They had the faces of twelve-year-olds, with innocently pursed lips, rosy cheeks, and flowers in their hair. They were even worse than calendar art.

"This one is called 'Beautiful Hawaii,'" the father said. "See the lei around her neck? Do you like my little girls?"

"They're . . . lovely."

In one corner of the room Helen noticed a font for holy water, which seemed to have been intricately fashioned out of solid gold. Next to it there was a large oil painting of a nude woman reclining on a sofa, the kind you used to see hanging over the bar in a Western saloon. On the opposite wall was an oil painting of a saint with a gleaming halo, his eyes piously upturned to sacred thoughts and away from the nudes. Beside it there was an ivory crucifix, with the figure of Christ on it.

The dresser, which was as long and heavy as a coffin, bore an assortment of prescription bottles, liquids and pills, and glasses

283

and spoons. And beside them, as casually put there as any decoration you might see on anyone's dresser, was a small bronze pornographic statue portraying a goat doing something to a nude woman that was only suitable for him to be doing to another goat. Helen looked away from it quickly, but not before the old man saw her eyes.

"Do you like my statue?" he asked, and began to guffaw. "Isn't that funny? A friend sent it to me for my birthday."

"His seventieth birthday," Sergio said, but he looked at Helen earnestly, with apology in his eyes. She did not know whether his feeling for his father was awe or respect or pity or love, or perhaps a painful emotion compounded of all four. She did not know what she would do if she had a father like his, whether she could accept his senile eccentricity with such filial loyalty that she would even bring someone she loved to be a part of it. It was all very new to her. She moved away from the father's encircling arm and sat in a chair far away from them both. She felt very much alone.

"You have to rest," Sergio said firmly to his father. He guided the old man to the high bed and helped him climb up on it. He removed his father's tie and shoes.

"Don't help me," the old man said. "I'm not dead yet." But his voice was much weaker than it had been during lunch. "I want this beautiful girl to help me, not you. Go away." He smiled weakly at Helen, a pitiful effort at a lecherous grin, and closed his eyes. Next to the clean white pillowcase his face looked a soiled gray.

"Let's go," Sergio whispered in English.

They walked quickly and quietly out of the room, down the silent corridor, and out into the bright sunlight. The sunshine was a relief; Helen felt cleansed. Birds were chirping and calling and singing from trees everywhere, and the hot air sang of its own heat. There was life in the thick grass, and insects crisscrossing in the air. A gardener was putting red and white striped canvas cushions on the tiles beside the swimming pool.

"I hope you weren't offended," Sergio said. "I forgot about that statue."

"It's all right." She leaned down to take off her shoes, and felt the live grass under her feet. "I guess people have to hold on to life in their own way."

"You are a tender woman," he said. "You will always make someone happy."

"You?"

"Me. Others too. Whoever loves you."

"I'm not so sure about that," Helen said.

"It doesn't have to be forever. One day is a gift. You saw that with him. All he has now are days. They told him months ago he would die. There's something wrong with his blood."

They walked on for a while in silence. "I'll take you for a tour in the jeep," he said.

They drove on the narrow road around the lake, and Helen saw ducks swimming on it, and several small bridges, and a canoe pulled up to the shore at the water's edge. Then they drove down another road past green *en tout cas* tennis courts, immaculately kept and deserted, their white tapes gleaming in the sun. Farther on there was a soccer field with bleachers.

"The *futebol* field is for the workers," Sergio said, pointing.

"For the workers!"

"They have to do something with their spare time. Do you like horses?" He drove up a bumpy side road past flower gardens, and Helen saw stables and a few horses wandering about in a large enclosure. Sergio stopped the jeep outside the gate and they walked through. The horses were in their stalls, each stall with a plaque with the horse's name on it. *Emperor, Sultan, King, Omar Khayyám, Vizier, Pasha, Mahmud.* And at the end a stall with a white pony in it and a plaque that said: *Roy Rogers.*

"My son's," Sergio said. "He's crazy about America."

"So funny. And your father's practically never heard of it."

"Is that so different from the generations in your country?" He took her past another row of stalls. "Polo ponies." He patted one horse's nose and spoke to it. Then he took her back to the jeep. "We can ride tomorrow morning if you like. Do you like to ride a horse?"

285

"I haven't done it since I was a child at camp. I wasn't made for the feudal life, I guess."

"That's all there is to do here. Eat, swim, ride horseback, play tennis, walk, play cards, sleep. My father and Guillerme's father manage the farm, and now they are teaching Guillerme to do it. I think he will do it well."

They drove past the paper factory, an old-fashioned building with tall smokestacks, and then through some fields where sugar cane grew. The land stretched out on either side until there seemed to be no end to it except the sky. No planes crossed the blue sky, no cars appeared on the long dusty road; it was like a land out of another time. On one side of the road there were rice paddies, and then later there were little hills where lettuce and beans and tomatoes grew, and farther on there were miles of coffee bushes with the small green coffee beans on them. There were fruit trees: pears, plums, oranges, papaya, mango, avocado and banana trees. Every tree that did not give fruit was a tree that could be cut down to make paper from its wood. Everything on the *fazenda* could be of some use.

Then the road led past what seemed like a housing development, with small private houses surrounded by gardens and wooden fences. There were chickens, and small pigs in pens, and children playing in the front yards and on the road, who looked up to wave respectfully when the jeep drove past.

"These houses are where the workers live."

"They're so pretty. I wouldn't mind living in one myself," Helen said. "That pink one, for instance."

"I'll take you to the liquor factory."

It was the strangest feeling; she felt like someone out of *Gone with the Wind*. The closer they came to the distillery the more people there were near the road, and every one of them knew Sergio, or at least recognized the jeep, and every one of them greeted him the way a peasant greets a feudal lord. They drove through a small village square with a chapel, a post office, a general store, a bar and a movie theater. There was a horse-drawn wagon standing in front of the post office. Sergio stopped the jeep while a priest came out of the chapel leading a line of children.

The priest and the children looked up at him, smiled and called greetings, and walked on across to the other side of the village square.

"What town is this?" Helen asked.

"It's no town. It's just part of the farm."

The chapel bells were ringing when they drove out of the square, and when they approached the distillery Helen could smell the heavy sweetish odor of crushed sugar cane. She had never seen a distillery, but this one looked more like a still from Prohibition days than what she had imagined. Everything was very primitive. There was a large shed made of boards, where great piles of cut sugar cane were stored, and in front of this shed two oxen stood patiently attached to a wagon while flies bit at them and circled greedily, attracted by the sweetness of the sugar juices and the live flesh. Barefoot workers brought armfuls of sugar cane to the wagon, and the wagon brought it to another shed, where it was apparently crushed in some machinery. There was an overhead system of tubes that transferred the juice to a huge vat standing outside another shed. The air was heavy with the sweet-sourish, slightly spoiled smell of fermenting sugar cane juice that would eventually make *cachaça*, the firewater white liquor of the poor.

The vat had been decorated with all sorts of odd pictures cut from magazines and comic books and pasted on, and even with some old whisky bottle labels. Evidently the workers had some affection for it. Inside this last shed there were tables set in rows, where young barefooted girls and a few very young boys, really only children, were pasting labels on sealed bottles of the colorless *cachaça*, and packing them carefully in excelsior-lined crates. The young girls nodded shyly when they saw Sergio, and a few of the older ones stared and then giggled and looked down at their packing, pretending to be very busy. Evidently he bore the status of young lord of the manor even with these adolescent girls, who were at the hero-worship age and seemed to have long-distance crushes on him.

"Did you ever taste *cachaça*?"

"No. Can we try some here?"

Sergio reached to take a bottle from the table and then stopped. "We'll get some at the house. I forgot, all the bottles are counted. My father will think one of the girls took it."

"Well, can't you take it and tell him?"

"You forget, darling, this is a business. There's plenty at the house."

Yes, Helen thought; locked up. This was a strange family, stranger the longer she knew them. If not a millionaire, the old man was as close to it as anyone wanted to be. But whisky, which came pouring out of the cane of his fields, was locked up in his own home and doled out as if it were either precious or dangerous. In many ways, ill and old, he was already slightly dotty, but to his grown and mature children his word and will were law. She knew it was only she, the outsider, who remarked on this. His children and grandchildren accepted him. But the outside modern world had already started to come into his ordered, protected life and take things away, just as she the outsider had driven up this morning in a car with his youngest son. The polo ponies stood patiently in their stalls, the tennis courts were rolled every morning and then stood all day in the sun untouched by anything but insects and butterflies. The canoe rested on its side on the shore of the lake. The ducks swam. The servant put out the red and white striped cushions at noon and then took them away again at dark. His children traveled by ship and plane and soon by jet. The priest in his long black coat and flat black hat walked slowly across the square in the village that was only part of the old man's farm, followed by a line of village children, while the old man's own children traveled to Europe and America to gape as tourists at the priests and children of other villages.

Roy Rogers stamped in his stall next to Omar Khayyám. Guillerme, who was learning to be a feudal lord of all this land, parroted the slang of love songs that had been written by a people whose unchaperoned dating habits he was probably already beginning to copy. The old man, who was the past, changed only with the unpredictable personal quirks of the old and ill. Whatever odd thing he did, Helen realized she could understand it. But it was Sergio, here with her, the man she loved, who was

288

really the difficult one to understand, even though he seemed so much more simple.

Sergio, who had married wisely and well but not for love, stood here now beside the woman he would love wisely and well but never think of marrying. He spoke of love to Helen in her own language so skillfully that she often forgot that he thought about her in his own language, which contained not only different words but an entirely different meaning for their meaning. He was the one she would have to try hard to understand, because he deceived her by seeming almost every moment to be so much like herself.

They walked out of the packing shed to the jeep. Sergio nodded to some workers who were outside loading crates on to a truck. They greeted him respectfully and looked at Helen curiously but with their respect for him carried over to his companion, whoever she was. She pretended to herself, in this fairy-tale setting, that she was his wife. What would it be like to be the lady of this great feudal settlement? She could live here all year round, she told herself, and only go into Rio for occasional shopping trips or visits with friends. She would ride about the miles and miles of property on horseback, under the vast blue sky, and vegetate, and love every minute of it. They could have ten children, to fill all the empty rooms of that great house, to laugh and run about in the silent gardens, swim in the pool, fight over whose turn it was to take the canoe out on the lake. And Roger and Julie would be beside themselves with ecstasy in a place like this . . . it was all a dream. She would never marry Sergio, she would probably never even allow herself to think about it again. It was a momentary fantasy. And yet, how lovely it would be! A strange place like this, different from anything she had ever seen, made Helen feel that anything might be possible for her now; she could even change her life. She pictured herself learning about crops and trees, becoming gracious and lazy like a rich Brazilian housewife, making a tour of the estate her entire daily diversion. She even pictured herself in some anachronistic long-skirted dress, riding sidesaddle; it was an amusing thought. If she was ever lonely she could invite Margie to come for a week or two. Look how my life has changed, she would say to Margie, still not quite able to believe it herself. Look, Margie! Would either of us have imagined all this?

"I have to make a telephone call," Sergio said. He headed the jeep back toward the square where the post office was.

"Here?"

"There are no phones at the house. My father won't allow it. For a long time we couldn't get one—you know how hard it is to get a phone in Brazil. And then one of my cousins got a job with the government, and he said we could have all the telephones we wanted. But by then my father was used to it this way and he refused. In a way, I like it. It's peaceful."

The one telephone at the back of the post office, which was actually the one telephone on the entire *fazenda,* was an old-fashioned wooden boxlike affair with a crank and a black outside bell. It looked like the kind of thing Helen's Westport friends had used for candy dishes or rewired lamps. It took ten minutes of cranking and shouting to get the operator. Then they waited fifteen minutes, and finally the operator called back and said there would be a delay of an hour and a half to get the call through to Rio.

"Peaceful?" Helen said. "It would make me nervous to have to scream into that thing."

"I don't want to make you wait here," Sergio said. "I don't even want to wait myself. But this call is important; it's to my father's specialist." He paced about the small back room, looking tense and angry. "I have an idea. Maybe I can get São Paulo. I know somebody who is going to Rio tonight. He can call the doctor when he gets there." He cranked for the operator again, looking nervous but no longer angry.

Helen lighted a cigarette. How dreadful it would be if there was ever an emergency, she was thinking. You could die here before you would ever get word to the outside world. For the first time she realized how isolated, actually, they were here.

There was a great deal of shouting and repeating in Portuguese from Sergio to the operator, and finally he seemed to be talking to someone at an office. He lowered his voice to its normal tone.

290

He was one of those people who smile and react facially when they speak on a telephone, even though they know the person at the other end cannot see them. She watched him and felt a sudden tenderness. He was so handsome when he smiled—that wolfine grin, a combination of charm and sexuality and a sheer lucky formation of features. And he never seemed to be aware of how handsome he actually was. She had always instinctively disliked people who smile at you while they are talking because they know they look attractive that way and want to bewitch you. Sergio's face was always a reflection of his reactions to the other person; it was the most perceptively responsive face she had ever seen.

"There was a great deal of flooding because of the rains in São Paulo," he told her. "I was afraid the lines would be down. It's all right. We can go now."

She passed him going to the door and they both stopped at the same instant and stood still, looking at each other. Sergio glanced at the closed door that led to the main room of the post office and then he took hold of her shoulders and drew her to him very slowly, looking into her face.

"You look lovely now," he said. "You should see yourself."

"I was thinking that about you. When you were talking on the telephone."

He smiled. "We're two beautiful people—to each other, anyway."

"That's all I need. I don't want to take a poll."

"If we took a poll you wouldn't have to be afraid. You'd win. I'm not so sure about me."

"*I'm* sure about you."

"Kiss me."

She kissed him, feeling a momentary instant of shyness at having to be the one to move forward first, as if it were the first time she had ever kissed anyone. But Sergio's response was so instantaneous and urgent that she felt as though whatever she could give him, he would return it a hundredfold, so that no matter if she hinted or initiated any gesture of love-making she would always be the recipient and the one who gained the most.

The feeling of having been humiliated that had stayed with her since that terrible night with Bert two days ago began to slip away. It was something that had happened to someone else, years and years ago.

"We go to the house," Sergio said softly, his arms still around her, his lips on her neck. "We lie down for a little while."

He made it sound so companionable, so full of mystery and promise, that it was almost as if they might be going to lie down together on a bed to rest after all. She could not even remember when she had last made love in the middle of the afternoon instead of waiting for any planned and special time of isolation in her own unprivate household. Sergio had suddenly made the thought of the act of love seem as new as if she had not done it for years. She felt herself trembling in the hot sunshine as they drove in the open jeep, trembling inside and outside as well with a combination of anticipation and shyness and need. She felt as though nothing could make her stop this delicate shaking except the entire weight of his body on hers to keep her from flying apart.

He drove the jeep to the driveway of her small guesthouse. It was so still outside in the sun that Helen could hear the buzzing of the bees and the crack of someone hitting a golf ball on the lawn in front of the big house. When the golf ball whizzed across her driveway in a white blur she looked at it as unrecognizingly as if it had been a missile from outer space.

Guillerme followed it, running, shouting, waving his arms and his golf club. "I have been waiting for you!" he shouted. "Where have you been?"

"Play golf somewhere else," Sergio said nastily. "You'll break a window and Uncle will break your stupid head."

"I'm bored." He gave Helen a milky smile.

"Make him go away," she said softly in English. "Please."

"Get out of here," Sergio told him. "Disappear. Kill yourself." The words were sharp but he looked in control of himself again; he was even smiling to soften their unkindness. "I want to talk with my *noiva* alone. Go away."

"What's *noiva*?" Helen asked.

"Fiancée."

She looked down at the path, taken with embarrassment.

Guillerme swung his golf club, cutting off the heads of flowers at the edge of the path. "Nobody lets me bring my girl friend here," he said sulkily. "Do you think I like to be here? All the time with cows and horses. I wish I was in Rio with *my* fiancée."

"You'd better not have a fiancée," Sergio said. "I know what kind of girls you take up to that empty apartment. The janitor gives you the key. Ha! I know all about you. Go away and leave the grownups alone."

Guillerme smoothed back his sun-streaked hair with one hand. He tried to look winning. "Helen likes me," he said pleadingly, more to her than to Sergio. "You like me, Helen, don't you? Let's all go and have a drink together."

Sergio gave his cousin a not unfriendly push. "I know what I'm going to do for you if you're so lonely," he said. "I'll talk to your father next week. He has a very nice, dull, fat girl for you to marry. A rich girl. Someone like Glorinha."

"No!" Guillerme howled in mock horror. "Not Glorinha!"

"She would *love* to marry you. Your father likes to play cards with her father, so I'm sure he would approve. She'd make a good wife for you; she's just out of the convent. I'll tell your father—"

"I wouldn't support that fat cow," Guillerme said. "One dress would cost me a year's pay for the material alone."

"Listen to the millionaire! She could support you."

They were smiling at each other now and roughing each other up, Sergio giving his cousin a light punch and Guillerme fending it off and feinting a jab in return. Helen felt odd: everything was so open and unserious now that in one more minute Sergio would probably announce that he was going to go to bed with her and take her through the door. She didn't feel like herself, she felt like some stranger, some casual girl who says, "Excuse me, I'm going to go make love now," as if she were going off to the powder room.

"Let's go and have a drink," she said, interrupting them. Her voice sounded strained. "All three of us."

They walked back to the house, Sergio in the middle. Guillerme swung his golf club and chattered happily, almost triumphantly, one arm linked through Sergio's. Sergio was holding Helen's hand. He glanced at her from time to time and his eyes were troubled. Guillerme ran ahead to see if he could cajole the key to the whisky cabinet from his uncle.

"He's jealous," Sergio said.

"That's not much consolation for me."

"I know, darling. What shall I do—kill him? Gun, sword? You tell me how."

"Poison."

"All right. In the drink. No, then he couldn't marry Glorinha. I wouldn't want to spare him that."

"Would you really make an arranged marriage for him?"

"It would be good for him," Sergio said. "But he won't do it. He'll marry someone he's known all his life, but at least he'll pick the one."

"Did . . . you?"

"I chose her myself," Sergio said, almost defensively.

"I mean, did you know . . . her . . . all your life?"

"Yes."

"Now I know," Helen said lightly. "I don't know why I asked, because knowing that doesn't really make me know anything anyway, does it?"

"You mean, do I love her? I told you before. Don't talk about it here."

"Can I ask you one more thing?"

"Her name is Mariza," Sergio said.

Sergio's father was enchanted enough at the presence of a young female in his house that he opened his liquor cabinet and allowed each one of them a small glass of *cachaça*. It tasted sickly sweet and much too strong to Helen, who choked over the first sip, but she felt honor-bound to drink it if it killed her, if only so that the old man could not pour it back into the bottle. Dinner was to be served early in order to give them all time to go to the movie at their own theater. The doctor had told Sergio's father not to go to bed late, so he was having the movie shown at seven. There was one movie theater on the *fazenda*, and whenever any member of the family planned to attend, word was sent out with one of the servants and the picture was held up until the family arrived.

His afternoon rest seemed to have revived Sergio's father. During the dinner, which was slightly less long and complicated than their huge midday meal, he leaned forward often to speak to Helen alone, made private jokes which she could not understand but which amused him, gave her alternately coy and covetous glances, and in short behaved as if the sight of her had convinced him that he could still use a girl instead of a hot-water bottle in his bed. He was always chivalrous about it all, never crass or outright, but there was something about his eyes—twinkling at the corners with patriarchal amity and probing from their depths with proprietary lust—that made Helen acutely uncomfortable.

The light chilled wine was delicious, and the evening air had become less muggy. There was the same cheese before dessert, followed by fruit and then a sweet creamy custard with caramel sauce. Sergio continued to discuss conditions in the outside world of Rio and São Paulo with his father, never including Helen since she was only a woman and knew only about dressmakers and hairdressers. It was as if she were already a member of the family. The butler walked silently about the table, bringing and removing plates with his deft, white-gloved hands. Guillerme mixed up all the food on his plate, as he had at lunch, and devoured it indiscriminately. Helen thought he would be a wonderful person to have to get rid of left-overs, since he didn't seem to know what he was eating anyway once he had destroyed it.

It was so easy to imagine she belonged here. Even the father's changing attitude, his growing intimacy, showed that he had accepted her. Everyone obviously knew—or believed—that she was Sergio's mistress. No one seemed shocked. The old man was, after all, Sergio's father, not his wife's father. The children were not here. The tight, family air of the *fazenda* was dissipated this holiday and had been replaced by the spirit of fun. She wondered what the meals were like when Sergio was here with . . . Mariza. She remembered his wife only vaguely from the swimming pool: a chic, cool woman with a frighteningly knowledgeable look in her eyes. A woman who knew by instinct when her husband was becoming interested in someone else. Or perhaps knew from experience. . . .

"What is the movie tonight?" Helen asked.

"Who knows?" Guillerme said. "An antique, of course."

"It will be amusing for you," Sergio told her.

When they finally rose from the table a light rain had started. Helen could hear it outside on the leaves. Everyone seemed happy about the rain, because they were farmers. Sergio went to get the jeep and drove it under the overhang of the front porch so she would not get wet.

She drove with Sergio in the jeep, with the top up, safe and dry, while he whizzed down the unlighted dirt roads he had known since childhood. His father and Guillerme had gone in the father's chauffeur-driven limousine, an ancient black Mercedes-Benz. The movie theater was a small yellow stucco building set on the edge of a village square of its own. Beside it was a general store with an open front, inside which Helen could see bolts of rough cotton materials stacked on shelves, huge sacks of rice and beans and flour open at the top and containing large tin scoops for measuring, and a wooden counter with glass jars of hard candies. On the other side of the movie house was a bar with swinging doors. A short distance apart from them was a small gasoline and repair station.

Workers were already gathered on the narrow, crude sidewalk in front of the movie theater, taking shelter under the overhang of the roof. The rain dripped off the edge of the roof into the dirt road, making puddles. Sergio drove the jeep up on to the sidewalk and let her out.

The workers looked at her and greeted her with respect. Some of them had women with them, their wives or perhaps fiancées, and many of them had brought their young children because the movie was early tonight. The children ran around playing tag and teasing one another, dodging the bicycles which many of the workers had used for transportation and which were now parked in a great clutter of wheels and chipped painted handle-bars under the small shelter from the rain.

296

It was twenty minutes past the time the movie had been scheduled to begin, but it had been held up until the family should arrive. Helen and Sergio waited outside until the black Mercedes-Benz drove up, and then the four of them walked into the theater, together, a little like a royal procession, with the workers in their faded clothes parting and bowing slightly on either side.

The inside of the theater was painted a dull yellow, with stucco walls decorated with ancient movie posters, some of them American, which were beginning to come away at the edges from the wall. Helen remembered some of the movies from years ago —she had seen them when she was in college. Some of them she had seen later on television. The family had a box upstairs. Actually, they had the entire balcony, but it was a small one, with straight-backed wooden chairs set in three rows. They all sat in the first row. Below, Helen could see rows and rows of removable chairs, more like a schoolroom than a movie theater. When the family entered their box everyone in the theater looked up at them, as if they had seen visiting celebrities. She almost expected an unseen band to strike up the national anthem.

The lights went out and the film began. It was as much of an antique as Guillerme had said; flickering, scratched, and accompanied by a tinny soundtrack. She could hear the projector whirring in the small projection booth above them. It was almost impossible to follow the action of the film. Everyone spoke very rapidly in Portuguese and jumped up and down and broke into song and dance at odd moments. It was evidently a musical, set in a slum, with men playing music on instruments made of washboards and tops of garbage pails, and a hyperthyroid bleached blonde with a pompadour and blue jeans apparently saving all of these slum dwellers from losing their homes to a wicked landlord. The audience roared appreciatively at all the jokes, but Helen could neither hear very well nor understand the Portuguese slang. There were, of course, no subtitles. She felt completely out of it.

She glanced at Sergio beside her. He looked bored and he was glancing at her too. "Do you understand it?" he whispered, taking her hand.

"Some," she lied.

"We'll go out soon," he whispered guardedly.

The old man kept falling asleep. Every now and then his head would nod, then fall forward on his chest as if his neck had been broken. But whenever Helen squirmed on the hard chair and turned to look longingly at the exit the old man would wake up again and give her a large, eager smile. He was so pleased that he had his own movie theater, he wanted her to like it. Guillerme was smoking a cigar and watching the movie avidly.

The pompadoured blonde in blue jeans was shaking everything, as if she were trying to shed a skin. The jerky hopped-up action of the film on the projector only emphasized this, so that her gyrations were something superhuman. Helen found a perverse fascination in this.

Sergio, in the darkness, put his hand lightly on her breast. She wondered why they were here at all. The shock of his touch traveled pleasurably through her whole body, and when she turned her head to look at him they were so close their lips almost touched. She looked at his mouth and she wanted so badly to kiss it she had to bite her lip and draw away. "We'll go," he murmured.

He leaned across her, with his hand on her thigh, lightly, as if it were only accidental, but she knew he was as acutely conscious of that touch as she was. He spoke across her to his father, in a loud whisper.

"We're going to leave now. Helen is tired from the trip."

"Good night," the father said, smiling at her, crinkling up his eyes at her, giving her a pat. "Good night. See you tomorrow."

"Good night," she whispered.

Guillerme pouted at them around his cigar, his elbows leaning on the railing in front of him, looking like a large, angry baby with a pacifier in its mouth. "Sleep well," he said nastily.

Helen and Sergio scrambled around the empty chairs and made their way out of the box and down the stairs to the now empty lobby. She could hear the audience laughing happily at some unintelligible joke. Outside, the rain had stopped. It was a cloudy night, heavy with mist, the stars invisible. The moon was full and white, split across the middle by a shred of cloud. Neither of them spoke.

Sergio stopped the jeep in front of her house. "I go put the jeep in front of my house," he said, helping her to climb out. "Then I come back to you and stay all night."

"All right."

He hooked his finger in the front of the waistband of her skirt and pulled her close to him. "Don't go anywhere," he whispered with a little smile.

"No."

He kissed her then, with passion, and suddenly Helen felt a curious resistance in herself, a reluctance and a kind of pride. Who do you think you're fooling by moving the jeep? she wanted to ask him, and she felt hurt.

"I tear you to pieces," he was murmuring, holding her tightly. "You are the most beautiful—wait for me."

He was gone, driving the jeep off in a wild shower of rainwater in the muddy driveway. Helen walked slowly into the guesthouse and she felt almost disconnected, lightheaded but with her arms and legs very heavy. The maid had turned down the covers of one twin bed in her bedroom and left a lamp lighted on the table beside it. The shutters at the window had been closed to keep out the rain.

Helen pushed open the shutters, all of them, and leaned out, breathing the cool, heavy air. She was trembling again, as she had that afternoon when she and Sergio had been on their way here to make love, but this time it was more of a shuddering. She felt very cold, and frighteningly lonely, as if a stranger she had never met before was coming here tonight to rape her.

I could let him, she thought, and I would like it as soon as I got used to him. She realized with terror what she was thinking. This was not the passionate, uncontrollable coupling of two people who were hopelessly in love with each other; it was a lay. That was all—a lay. I feel like a whore, she thought, and bit into her knuckles, hardly feeling the pain, wanting to feel it, wanting to feel something besides this overwhelming disgust with herself.

She had had an intimation of this feeling; she had sensed it coming this afternoon. She had known at dinner but she had forbidden herself even to recognize it. At the movies when she and Sergio had excused themselves with the blessings of his father and the jealous farewell of his cousin, she had known. She was his mistress, his woman, and everybody knew it. So what, they thought. He's lucky. I'd like to get a piece of that myself.

He wanted it to be good for us, he wanted it all to be beautiful, she thought, and she began to cry. The tears spilled out of her eyes before she even knew that she was crying. Her throat closed with the held-in, unspoken sounds of weeping. He doesn't know me at all, he doesn't understand me, nor I him. I can't do it, this way, I can't. Oh, Sergio, I can't do it. It's all gone.

Was it because of Bert? She thought of Bert, as he had been that night two days ago when she had almost hated him, as he had been all those other days and nights when she had loved him very much. She still loved him, but it was a deep part of her, a quiet thing, not like her heart, but like . . . her spine perhaps. Bert had been right; their love had changed. But whatever it was, quiet or unquiet, she loved him more. She was simply attached to him by something more than emotion or words or even love itself, whatever that was. She was attached to him by a life. As long as she lived Bert would be part of her whether he was with her or had left her forever, whether he loved her or was indifferent. Even when she forgot him, as she had all this long day with Sergio, she needed him. Bert was still there.

Oh, Sergio, she thought, and she still wanted to kiss him, but in a different way. It was no longer with passion or even hope of passion, but with tenderness and regret. For the first time, knowing she no longer loved him, if she ever really had, she almost loved him just for that. She was almost afraid to look at him again, because his face and body were beautiful to her, because they would still stir her, but only lightly, hopelessly, as dead leaves stir in wind, as that old man in the great house with his pictures of young girls might be hopelessly and weakly stirred by the sight of beauty he could no longer want. If we had only gone off somewhere sordid and secret, she thought, wiping the tears away with her hands. There were tears between her lips;

they were salty. He had kissed her, he had touched her, and she had wanted him. I could have done it secretly and hurriedly in some hotel room, with guilt. Am I crazy? I would have *liked* doing it guiltily, secretly. I can't do it this way, openly. It's all wrong.

She heard Sergio's footsteps on the driveway outside and she felt weak with fright. She didn't know what to say to him now.

He came into the bedroom, and he had such a happy look of belonging on his face that it frightened her more. She felt that he was not the outsider here; she was. She realized for the first time how strong he was, that his gentleness and tenderness had been for her and their love. It had never been a sign of softness but only of the attitude a man displays toward the weakness of woman. He was carrying a bottle of champagne in his hand, the green glass streaked with water drops from the cold place where it had been chilled. In the other hand he carried one champagne glass for them to share.

"Where . . . did you get that?" she asked, for lack of anything else to say except the truth.

"I took it from the liquor cabinet when we were having cocktails." He smiled with the delight of a romantic conspirator. "I put it into the refrigerator for us until now."

He brought a small hand towel from her bathroom, wrapped it around the bottle, and deftly loosened the wires that held the cork. Helen watched him, hugging her elbows, her fingers clutching her flesh. Sergio loosened the cork with his thumb and it sailed to the ceiling with a small explosion. The champagne fizzed over the neck of the bottle in white foam. He let the champagne waste itself, delighted with his own profligacy, and when it had stopped foaming he poured the glass full to the top. He held the glass up in a toast.

"To you," he said. He looked at her. "You're so far away. Come here."

She took a deep breath and could not say anything. She walked to him slowly, her heart thumping, and let him hold the glass of champagne to her lips. She tasted it and tried to smile.

"Why were you crying?"

"For . . . for you," she whispered. "I . . ."

"My darling . . . my love." He put away the encumberments of the champagne and glass in an instant, he had his arms around her, he was stroking her and kissing her, and Helen suddenly knew that he thought she had been crying for him and their love, for the romantic hopelessness of it, for its poignancy, and that being able to comfort her this way only made him feel this moment was more painfully their own. She tried to get out of his embrace.

"Please listen."

"I will let you cry for me, but only in love. Never alone. Never from any sad thoughts." His hands on her body frightened her more than they aroused her, and his words that a few hours ago might have made her cry again for gratitude now made her shudder. He was kissing her neck, her ears, biting her with tiny, soft bites, licking her skin.

"Beautiful," he said, looking at her. "Beautiful . . ." And suddenly his voice was the voice of his father, saying, "Beautiful Hawaii," glancing with old, wicked eyes at the pictures of young naked girls on his wall. "Beautiful," the voice said, Sergio's voice and his father's, and it was no longer a compliment or a gift but an amused prelude to the taking of pleasure. Bert's face rose up before her closed eyes, his humanness, his loyalty to her, and he seemed at that moment the only thing in that room that was beautiful at all. She pulled away from Sergio's arms.

"Please listen to me!"

"What is it?" Quickly all the expression on his face withdrew from her; it was a mask of controlled waiting. She had no idea what he was thinking.

"Please don't hate me. Please understand. I . . . I can't. I just can't. I can't."

"*You can't what?*"

She felt like a tease, worse than a whore, and she looked desperately into his eyes searching there for any understanding, even though it might be more than she deserved to expect. "I have to go home," she said.

302

He smiled then, and she almost fainted with relief. "You're afraid," he said softly and wonderingly. "Why?"

"No," she said, "It's not that. I'm afraid, but not of you. Oh, everything I'm going to say is going to sound so pompous, so banal, as if I think I'm virtuous or better than anyone else, and I don't think that. I think I'm worse. I don't even know myself any more. Don't you think I *wanted* you to make love to me? Oh, God, I did want to, and I still do. But I can't, I *can't;* in the middle of it I'd think I was a prostitute. I'd lie there looking at myself from somewhere else, like two people. I can't do that to you."

"You are crazy," he said calmly. But the light of his eyes had withdrawn from her and they looked very hard and black. She had never noticed how dark his eyes were; she had always thought they were light.

"Maybe I am crazy. I don't even understand myself. But I have to go home to my husband."

"To him? Why to him? He isn't in your house. He's away somewhere with his girlfriend; what do you think, he sleeps with his hand on his cock?"

"Stop it!"

"You are a stupid woman," Sergio said.

"Let me go home," she said. Her voice sounded dead.

"I don't care what you do," he said. He picked up the glass of champagne and drank nearly all of it in continuous swallows. Then he stopped and looked at the little that was left in the bottom of the glass. He held it out to her. "Champagne?"

She nodded, unable to speak, and he handed her the glass at arm's length. She drank the champagne quickly and it tasted like vinegar.

"That's all you get," Sergio said quietly. "The left-overs. That's all you get from life. You know why? You don't want anything better. You want to live this way? Go ahead. I tried to give you something better. I would have given you something beautiful. Now I don't want you. You are a dishonest woman. You cheated me, and your husband, and yourself. What are you going to tell your husband? That you and I played cards here all night?"

"I told you the truth," Helen said.

303

He poured the glass full again with champagne and drank it. He left a little for her again at the bottom of the glass, but this time she refused it. He smiled and finished it himself. "I feel pity for you," he said.

"I really loved you, Sergio. I know you don't believe me, but I did love you very much until . . . I hated myself so much I couldn't love anybody any more."

"*Love!* That's your word for everything. If you knew love . . ." He turned away from her and finished the champagne without looking at her. "I take you home tomorrow."

"I want to go tonight. Can you take me to where the bus stops?"

"I go to the house and find out the bus schedule."

"Thank you." She looked at him for some sign of friendliness, but there was nothing. He looked at her as dispassionately as if she had been some worker woman on the farm who had suddenly gone harmlessly insane.

At the door he stopped. "You want to sit up all night on an uncomfortable bus? Perhaps you won't get a seat. You could sleep here and I will take you to the bus in the morning."

"I want to go, Sergio."

"I suggested it only to be kind to you."

"I know. I . . ." She tried to say something light and ironic, at least to make him laugh at her instead of this icy politeness. "Wouldn't it serve me right if I were attacked on the bus by some strange man, instead of staying here comfortably with you!"

Sergio glanced at her with distaste and his voice was cold. "Nobody has to rape anybody in Brazil," he said. And he was gone.

The bus stopped outside the gate to the *fazenda* at a little after ten o'clock. It was an old bus, not the *Cometa*, and not air conditioned. It rocked from side to side like an old ship. Sergio helped Helen climb up the steps and handed her overnight case to her. She wanted terribly to say something meaningful to him, something that could make them part as friends, at least. She wondered if he would think all Americans were like she was, all the wives unsatisfied and searching, and running away at the last moment because they were confused and guilty. It seemed paradoxical to her to be thinking of foreign relations at a moment like this, when she should be thinking of her own with her ex-and-never lover, but Helen felt as if her own self had vanished during this night. She did not even think she was a hypocrite; she felt empty. She missed Bert and her children and their apartment so passionately that it made her feel emptier than ever.

"Please say goodbye to your father for me," she said to Sergio. "Tell him I said thank you. I've never seen such a beautiful farm. Tell him I'm sorry I couldn't wait to say goodbye."

"I will."

She held out her hand, expecting him to shake it. Instead he lifted it quickly to his lips and kissed it. It was an automatic salute; his eyes above her hand were already disinterested in her.

"Goodbye," she said softly.

"Goodbye."

The doors closed, and she went to a seat near the front of the bus. The bus was nearly empty, most of the passengers sleeping fitfully. The bus went swaying and rumbling down the rough road, turned on to the highway, headed toward Rio, a clumsy creature lighting its own way through the dark night. No one paid any attention to her. She knew that the bus would not get to the city until nearly four in the morning. It didn't matter. Time didn't matter any more. She needed more time to think than she could ever have on this bus, even have at home in Rio again. Relief to have escaped filled her with happiness, but through it she felt the emergence of a new kind of fright. Nothing was really settled. She knew now she could not run away from Bert and their marriage, but the things that had made her run away were still there.

CHAPTER *19*

On a hot afternoon at the end of February Leila Silva e Costa and Mariza Leite Braga, the wife of Sergio, were at the dressmaker's together. In the friendship cycle, which was more peculiar to Rio than to most small towns and colonies, the two women were currently very close. Everyone always had one best friend and confidante, but with the boredom and petty gossip and intrigue of small colony life there was often an emotional argument followed by an estrangement, the loyal merging with another best friend, eventually followed by a breaking off and a resumption with the first best friend. Feuds and finishes never lasted long. X might be heard to say that Y was disloyal, immoral, too possessive, or deceitful; she might continue by stating that she would never allow Y into her house again; but a month or so later X and Y would be observed behaving like loving sisters. So it was with Leila and Mariza.

Mariza was a year older than Leila and they had known each other ever since they could remember. They had never been particularly friendly until both were married; then they became very close. Part of this was because Leila liked Sergio. She found him charming and amusing. She had never considered him even remotely as a lover for herself, but she liked him in a sisterly way, and this warmth extended to her feelings for his wife. Mariza was extraordinarily chic. She wore clothes well, she was very thin, and it meant a great deal to her (and to everyone else in Rio café society) that she was often named as one of "The Ten Best

Dressed." Her hair was bleached to a fashionable grayish blond, she had beautiful jewels, she never wore a dress more than twice in public and then she gave it away to her maid. She looked more French or Italian than Brazilian. There was a local magazine that interviewed a debutante in each issue and asked the girl, among other questions about her schoolwork and hobbies, who was the woman she would most wish to be like. Madame, the President's wife? A cinema star? Most of the debutantes answered: Mariza Leite Braga.

Now Mariza was standing in front of a tall mirror wearing her nearly finished new dress, holding herself stiffly to avoid being stabbed by the straight pins that bristled out of its tight bodice. The dressmaker knelt on the floor at her feet, making adjustments. The dress had a complicated skirt, in a series of drapings, a copy of a Grés from the latest *L'Officiel,* and Mariza was a perfectionist.

"Do you like it?"

"Very beautiful," Leila said, considering it. "You can wear this; I can't. I'm too fat."

"You're not fat. You're perfect. Do you like this material?"

"Very much." Leila was leafing through a copy of the spring issue of *Elle.* It was already falling apart from too much handling. "I think I will have a little coat made," she said thoughtfully. "Something in white. I was at the hairdresser this morning looking at the new *L'Officiel,* but already people had torn out half the pages. It's disgraceful! If they can afford to go to that hairdresser and to a dressmaker, why can't they buy their own magazine?"

"Maybe they're just afraid someone else will copy that same dress," Mariza said with a little smile. "I tear pictures out myself sometimes."

"Oh, no!" They both laughed.

"Light me a cigarette."

Leila lighted a cigarette and put it between Mariza's lips. "When are you going back to the farm?"

"In a few days. Why don't you come too, and bring the children? We have no one there these days."

"I might do that," Leila said. "It depends on my Spanish. I'll see what he wants to do."

"Who is this famous 'Spanish' anyway? You tell all your friends about your handsome Spanish, but none of us has ever seen him. I think you're afraid someone will steal him."

"Maybe," Leila said, grinning mischievously. She opened her eyes wide.

"You could bring him to the farm when you come. I won't steal him. The children won't steal him."

"You will meet him one day."

"How did you ever find a Spanish in Rio?" Mariza turned around slowly, until she was facing Leila. The dressmaker had a pair of scissors and was snipping little threads and repinning one of the drapes. "He lives right here in Rio and I've never seen him? None of us know him? I'm beginning to think you don't like me, Leila. You could at least tell *me* the secret."

"If I tell anyone it will be you."

"Then tell me. I promise I won't steal your famous Spanish. Maybe I can even help you."

"All right," Leila whispered. She hated to fool her best friend, and besides, she was so pleased with her cleverness that she could not resist telling at least one person. She sat forward on the couch, hugging her knees, smiling with delight. *"He doesn't exist!* Everyone is talking about my Spanish and wondering who he is, but I made him up! You know how much gossip there is in Rio. I hate it. Especially because I am divorced; all those hypocrites pretend to be so virtuous, but really they are jealous because I have my freedom. Everyone was always telephoning me: 'Oh, I saw So-and-so's car parked in front of your apartment house. Was he visiting you?' I couldn't stand it any more. Now they all think I go out with this Spanish, and so I can go out with anyone I want to and they won't know."

"You clever little thing," Mariza said, but she sounded disappointed. "No Spanish at all."

"No. You mustn't tell anyone."

"You can trust me." Mariza slipped out of her new dress with the dressmaker's assistance and put on the beautifully made

308

slacks and shirt she had arrived in. She combed her hair and put on more lipstick and rimmed her eyes with more pencil. There was a lengthy arrangement with the dressmaker about the time and date of the next fitting, but finally it was arranged, and Mariza and Leila went out of the small apartment to the creaking, doubtful elevator.

"You told me something, now I'll tell you something," Mariza said, putting her arm around Leila's waist. Her voice was matter-of-fact, but Leila could feel the tenseness in her body through the thin silk shirt, like the subtle vibration of electricity through a wire. "My husband has a new fiancée," Mariza said.

"Oh, I am so sorry. How terrible men are!" Leila put her arm around Mariza, and holding each other that way as they walked out of the elevator into the bright sunlight they looked like two very attractive young matrons exchanging delicious secrets. "Has this been going on long?"

"Since before Carnival, I think. They have been seen together quite openly. You know how Sergio is. It's all right for a *man* to have an affair, but if I ever did anything he would kill me."

"Men are so cruel," Leila said sympathetically. But she was really thinking more of herself than of Mariza. Mariza was strong, she would get along, she always did when this kind of thing happened. She wished she could manage to be as independent as Mariza. "Is she someone we know?"

"It's a blond American."

"An American! A tourist?"

"She lives here. My friends say they have seen her husband around for a year."

"Ah, but it won't last," Leila murmured. "Sergio needs someone like that to give him confidence in himself, but he will be tired of her soon. I read all about that in one of my books. It was called 'The Don Juan Complex.'"

"What has a complex to do with Sergio?" Mariza looked insulted and dropped her arm from around Leila's waist.

"It's something to do with sex."

"A sex complex? Sergio isn't crazy." Mariza smiled. "Why in

the world are you reading a sex book at your age, after a husband and four children and probably several lovers?"

"It's about the *psychology* of sex. It tells you how men think. Not how they *think* they think, but how they *really* think in their unconscious minds."

"That must be really confusing," Mariza said. She laughed, her good humor restored, and opened the door of her car. They climbed in and she headed the car efficiently into the stream of traffic, avoiding the wild *Lotaçãos* and the jaywalkers. "You must lend it to me when you're finished with it."

"I will."

"He told me he went to the farm this morning," Mariza said. She lighted another cigarette, one hand on the wheel. "I wonder if he really did, or if he went somewhere to spend a few days with her. You'll notice he ran off to *the farm* the moment I came back here. This must really be a passionate love affair." She inhaled deeply, with obvious need, but the slim hand that held the cigarette was steady and her voice was more ironic than troubled.

"I know a blond American," Leila said thoughtfully.

"Who is she?"

"But she's not really blond. She's not blond like you. She has sun streaks in her hair. I suppose someone might call her a blonde."

"Is she beautiful?"

"Oh, she's a housewife," Leila said, trying to avoid the answer. "She adores her husband and children."

"Is she after Sergio's money?"

"I think her husband is rich."

Mariza began to hum. "Do you know this song? It's French. It's cute.

> *Si tous les cocus*
> *Avaient des clochettes*
> *Des clochettes au dessus*
> *Au dessus de leur têtes*
> *Ça ferait tant de chaut*
> *Qu'on ne s'entendrait plus.*"

"If all the cuckolds . . ."

"If all the cuckolds," Mariza said, "had little bells over their heads, that would make so much noise that no one would be able to hear themselves any more."

"Bells instead of horns?"

"Bells attached to their horns. Who knows? It's true, though." She began to sing the song again, ironically, driving very fast through the crowded street, and Leila hummed the tune beside her, smiling.

"You must teach me the words."

"With much pleasure. We can sing a duet and dedicate it to the husband of the blond American, whoever she may be. And also dedicate it—" she smiled thinly, and glanced sideways at Leila with kohl-rimmed eyes that were very bright—"to my dear husband."

They rode for a while in silence, each with her own thoughts. "I wish *I* had a lover," Leila said finally.

"Someone more real than your famous Spanish?" Mariza laughed.

"Yes."

"Rio is full of handsome men."

"I know. But most of them are dull. What do you think . . . what do you think, for instance, of . . . Carlos Monteiro?"

"Carlos? Don't waste your time on him," Mariza stated flatly.

"Why not?"

"Oh, I've heard stories."

"What kind of stories?" Leila cried desperately. She was almost in tears.

"You know everyone has a story about everyone. I have heard several about him, that's all. *Why?* You weren't thinking of *him,* were you?"

"But I love him!" Leila cried. It was out before she could restrain herself. And once she had said it, she was relieved, because now Mariza knew, and perhaps Mariza could help her.

"Oh, you poor child," Mariza said, reaching for Leila's hand. Her voice was still light and ironic. "Don't you know anything? Do I have to take care of you all your life? I see that I do. Carlos

—my dear little girl—Carlos is, first of all, the dullest man in the world and, secondly, the most proper and, third, he would never, never, *never* marry a divorced woman. He's madly in love with one right now, and he's told all his friends he can never marry her. Don't you get started with him."

Leila tensed. She could feel her world slipping away, and her heart hurt terribly. Mariza's casual words, *madly in love with one right now,* crushed her all the more because of the way they had been dropped, completely unthinkingly, as life dropped deathly weights on one without even a moment's warning or thought. Her eyes filled with tears. "But Carlos has been taking *me* out nearly every night. Who can she be, this other woman? Is she someone young? She can't love him as much as I do. He talks to me about books, about music, about everything . . ."

"It's you, you silly little girl. It's you, of course. Who else could it possibly be? You should have confided in me a long time ago." Mariza shook her head in mock despair. "You and Carlos, you both, with your secrets. He is so proper and chivalrous, keeping the name of this divorcée a great, dark mystery. You with your little ruses. Tell me—" her voice was suddenly serious, business-like—"tell me, has he made love to you yet?"

"He . . . kisses me very much."

"I thought not."

"But I know he loves me. I can tell. A woman can sense those things."

"I'm sure he does," Mariza said, "in his way. Tell me, what would you say of a man who is forty years old, handsome and healthy, with all the money any woman could want, and who has never had either a wife or a mistress?"

"He has never had a mistress?"

"Never."

"Well, perhaps . . ." It was unthinkable, but it was better than what she was already beginning to think. "Perhaps he goes to one of those houses."

"Never."

"Well, all those other women must have been too stupid for him. He likes to discuss books with me. Carlos is an intellectual."

Mariza sighed. "You had better go back and read some more of your books to find out about Carlos."

"I can't believe it," Leila said weakly. She wiped her eyes. "You have made me terribly upset. I am going to ask him."

"Excuse me, Carlos, are you a homosexual? Well, I was simply wondering; some of my friends said you were."

"*What shall I do?*"

"Keep on talking about books," Mariza said kindly. "And forget about marrying him. I wouldn't let you marry him even if he was cruel enough to ask you. Sergio knows all about him. You just go out with Carlos and have a good time. Someone will come along for you. Perhaps a *real* 'Spanish.'"

"I'll never get married again," Leila said softly. "I know it. All my life I've had bad luck. I'll never get married again."

"Of course you'll get married. You're still young. And very beautiful."

"There's no one for me in Rio. Why do the hard women, the vulgar ones, not even attractive, not even young some of them, why do they always find other husbands? Some of them find three or four. Why isn't there anybody for me?"

"It's a very small world, our Rio, yours and mine," Mariza said gently.

"But it's where I *live!*"

"I know," she said. "I know. And we always will."

Mariza drove Leila to her apartment house and they kissed each other goodbye, on both cheeks, warmly. Leila took Mariza's hand in both of hers; it was the hand with the wedding ring, and Leila looked at the ring and then at her friend's thin, stylishly delicate face with its too-bright eyes. "Sergio couldn't get along without you," Leila said.

"You're a good friend. I love you."

"I love you too. I'll telephone you later tonight." Leila ran into the lobby of her apartment building. *Was* it Helen Sinclair, she was wondering, *was* it Helen? She felt such guilt at having unwittingly brought Helen and Sergio together that she could not face Mariza's eyes another moment. As she rode up in the elevator she composed herself. Even if it was, it wasn't her own

fault; Sergio might have found Helen anyway. They would have met sooner or later.

She had not talked to Helen for over a week, not since the day Helen had called to invite her to dinner. It couldn't be Helen and Sergio—could it? Everything was falling apart today. She was sorry she had gone out of the house at all. *Carlos, oh, Carlos.* How could she believe such a terrible thing about him? Her apartment was empty; the children were out somewhere. Leila felt loneliness closing in on her, as if the walls were sliding closer and closer. Carlos would never marry her, Carlos *could* never marry her. She wondered if homosexuals could marry and reform. The love of a good wife might save Carlos. No one had ever said he was in love with a man; perhaps he was only very intellectual. A man had a right to wait until he was past forty until he made love to a woman.

But even thinking this, Leila knew in her heart Mariza was right. Mariza knew all about men. She had a lover now, someone whom she kept very secret, but Leila knew there was someone. Mariza had a way of keeping her own secrets even while she inveigled you into telling her yours. Leila felt duped. She had told Mariza everything, even that she and Carlos had never made love. But Mariza had never told her about her own lover. Was this entirely fair?

She felt a little less guilty. After all, it was Sergio who had requested to come to the Macumba when Leila had told him she was going with Helen. He had insisted. Sergio always liked to have fun, to go wherever there might be a party or some adventure, so how could she have suspected? It was certainly not her fault. She felt grieved for Mariza, but still Mariza had someone, and Sergio would never leave her, so Mariza really had two. Even now, Mariza was having her massage—or was she? Perhaps Mariza was actually with her lover. Leila smiled to herself. After her lover, or after her relaxing massage, Mariza would look glowing either way, so who could tell the difference?

But it is I who am always lonely, Leila thought sadly. It is I who am always being left. It was close in the apartment, it was hot, it was too quiet, and she was afraid. All her life there had

been people: her family, her husband, her children. Today she was alone, and she was lonely and afraid. This is the way it will be when I grow old, she thought. When I am too old and ugly to go out dancing with men, when no one wants to invite me to dinner. My children will be married and I will be alone. My babies will be married. . . .

She felt tears begin at the thought of herself growing old and withered, but she fought them back. Carlos might call her, and she would have red eyes. The telephone tempted her, there in the hall. She dialed Carlos at his office but then replaced the receiver just as his phone began to ring. Let him telephone her, if he really had told all his friends he was madly in love with her! Her fingers darted nervously over the numbers on the dial as she tried to remember Helen's telephone number.

"Is Dona Helen there?"

"No, Senhora. She is away for two days."

"When did she leave?"

"Early this morning. Very early. Is not here."

"Where did she go?"

"Don't know, Senhora," Helen's maid answered cheerfully. "I forgot."

"Did she go with Senhor Bert?"

"No. She went alone. Senhor Bert is not here."

"Thank you," Leila said.

"Is nothing."

Leila hung up, feeling lonelier than ever. She was sure now that Sergio's mistress must be Helen. How curious to find out these things about your friends! Life was full of ironic surprises. She had a lump in her throat when she thought of what Mariza had told her about Carlos, the same sort of bewildered ache she used to feel when she was a child and she had been left alone at night in the dark. But at the same time she felt lightheaded. Her cousin Izabel knew Carlos, and Izabel was a worldly woman. Perhaps Izabel could help her, advise her on what to do. And Izabel would be speechless with surprise when she heard about Sergio and his new affair. And her friend Vera; Leila had not telephoned her for two weeks. Vera must be angry at her by now.

315

And her friend Gilda, who had given such a nice dinner party the same night as Helen Sinclair's. Leila should call to *thank* Gilda, at least.

She dialed the first number quickly, and when she heard Izabel's maid going off to call Izabel to the phone Leila felt the lump in her throat begin to dissolve. The pain softened away, and she felt the light fluttering beginnings of excitement again. "Oh, Izabel!" she cried happily, smiling at the reassuring sound of her cousin's throaty voice. "I have not spoken to you for such a long time! I have so much to tell you!"

CHAPTER *20*

In five years of marriage Margie Davidow had become less naïve about everyone's marriage but her own. If she was not quick to notice the sign of a restless or unfaithful husband she at least accepted the secondhand information with a knowing nod, and said, "I'm really not surprised," or, "Yes, I suspected something like that." She never considered a scandal shocking or disgraceful, even when it happened in her own country club to people she had known well; it was as if unfaithfulness and adultery and ugliness never actually touched her in any way. It was all abstract, and being abstract she was able to accept it with a knowing womanliness she really did not possess.

She had always known that Neil was attractive to other women, but she had always thought of it more as the attraction to a handsome man, not a sensual one. He was her clean-cut, good-looking husband, and when they walked in to a party together Margie noticed with pride when other women looked at him or tried to meet him, but she never thought any of them actually wanted to have an affair with him. Perhaps it was because he did not have that effect on her. She knew he was a normal man, she did not think he was a masochist or a saint, but she had never really thought about the future. If Neil had been anyone else's husband, occupying his lonely bedroom, Margie would have been immediately alert to trouble. But the walls of her own home surrounded and lulled her, reassured her, like a symbol:

317

home, the magic circle, like a wedding ring. She knew that Neil had been staying later and later at the office in the evenings, sometimes even going briefly back there at night, but she thought —well, if she thought anything she thought rather shamefacedly that he was sublimating through overwork.

One evening at the end of March he said something strange. They had finished dinner and were deciding whether to call some friends, go to a movie, or play chess. Lately they were seeing people a great deal, they seemed to go nowhere alone together, and on the few evenings that they stayed in their apartment alone they played furiously concentrating games of chess in which nothing was said for hours while each one tried to win. But tonight Neil seemed nervous.

"You know," he said, from nothing, out of the clear blue sky, "if either of us decided to marry again, he'd have to admit it right away."

"Marry who?" Margie said, and she smiled at him. "Who'd marry me?"

"*Either of us*," he repeated, rather sharply.

She looked at him, her smile fading, and she felt cold for a moment in her throat, as if she had swallowed an ice cube. "Of course," she said then.

"If you wanted to marry again I would give you your freedom. And if I wanted a divorce the same would hold true. Don't you agree?"

"You sound like a lawyer."

"Let's go to the Ricamar," he said. "They have an American movie."

They went to the film, they sat side by side, but Margie hardly saw any of it. She glanced at Neil's profile from time to time, but he was staring straight ahead at the screen, his jaw tensed, and she wondered if he were really seeing the movie either. No one forgot himself at a film when he bore a look of such obvious effort at concentration. She supposed it was silly to get herself worked up about their conversation. Divorce was not such an outrageous thing to mention in the abstract; it was quite possible that someday one of them might . . . She didn't want to think

318

about it. But it was true they had to mention it, just in case someday . . .

A week later he brought the subject up again. It was a Sunday morning, and they were having a late breakfast together. They always liked to eat breakfast together on weekends, even though they awoke at different times, and so whichever one had eaten first would sit at the table again and have a second breakfast with the other. This day it was Neil. He had been awake for hours; he was even shaved and dressed. It was only ten-thirty. Margie felt the coffee pot, decided the coffee was not hot enough to be the way he liked it—he could scald his throat, that crazy man, he never seemed to feel it—and she sent the maid back to the kitchen to heat it up.

"You're not eating anything, darling," Margie said to him. "Did you have the figs I bought for you? And I bought Catupiry, a fresh one, here." She held out the white, soft cheese in its round wooden box, so he could see how good it looked.

"You should be a wife," Neil said, softly and sadly. "You should always be a wife."

"I *am* a wife."

"And you should have children, lots of children, all around you. Babies for you to mother until they're grown-up babies."

His tone frightened her. It was too wistful to be a compliment; it was more of an epitaph. "What?" she said, very gently. She put her hand over his on the blue tablecloth, gently too. "What, Neil?"

"I told you before . . . if we didn't last . . . if we—" The maid came in with the pot of newly hot coffee and put it on the table, and Margie and Neil sat facing each other silently, her hand on his, until the maid had deposited the coffee pot and left. "I want a divorce," Neil said.

She kept on looking at his face and she was too stunned to cry or even feel anything beyond a sickening falling sensation. There was no pain, only the falling. "Divorce?" she said stupidly.

"I have to do it this way."

"Why?"

He slid his hand away from under hers as if he felt too guilty to continue touching her while he said these dreadful things that were going to destroy her life. Or perhaps, Margie thought suddenly, because he could no longer bear touching her at all. She felt for the first time as he must have when she could not let him touch her, and for the first time tears came to her eyes. "Why?" she said again. "Why?"

"You know I'd never leave you all alone if there wasn't someone else," he said. "You know that, don't you? I'd stay with you, no matter what happened between you and me. But I can't stay with you now, because there *is* someone else."

"You mean there's a girl?" She didn't realize how stupid the words sounded until they were out, and then she had to smile at them and Neil smiled too, and then she began to cry. She put her hands over her face and tried to stop crying, and after a minute or so she did. "I wouldn't have cried," she said, gasping, "if I hadn't started to laugh."

"I don't know what to say," Neil said.

"Well, tell me who she is."

"She's a Brazilian girl."

" . . . *Brazilian?*"

"She works in my office. She's a secretary. You don't want to hear any of this, do you?"

"Yes, I do," Margie said. "What's her name?"

A change went over his face—emotion, then fright, then resolution. That girl, the intruder, hadn't been real until this moment, but as soon as he said her name she would be, unremovably real. "Her name is Gilda."

"Is she beautiful?"

"I think so. She—it's funny, she looks a lot like you."

"Oh, Neil."

"I want to marry her," Neil said.

Margie looked at her hands. She looked at the food on the plates beside them. It looked like garbage. It was odd that her knuckles were so white under her tan because she couldn't feel her clenched hands at all. "Are you sure?"

"Yes. I'm very sure."

"Are you having an *affair* with her?"

He didn't answer for a moment. For that moment, which seemed very long, Margie dared to think that he had not slept with this Brazilian girl, that she was forcing Neil to marry her because it would be the only way that he could sleep with her. But then she knew he would not make the same mistake twice. She could see his idea of chivalry toward this girl and his loyalty to herself warring in him; she had never seen him look so unhappy. "Yes," he said finally. "Of course I am. What did you think?"

"I'm glad," she lied.

"No, you're not."

"Yes, I am!" She was almost shouting, she glared at him. "It's good, isn't it, with this girl?"

"Yes."

"Well, I'm glad," Margie said, but her voice broke.

"Margie, I *love* her," Neil said. "She's a very sensitive, intelligent, kind of a sad girl. She thinks I'm the most wonderful person who was ever invented." He smiled wryly. "And I need her. I want to be with her all the time."

"Oh, why are you so moral?" Margie asked. "Why do you have to *marry* her? You don't have to marry her, do you? You could just go on this way. I would let you."

"I can't go on this way."

"She's pregnant! Is she?"

"No, of course not." He smiled. He wasn't angry, simply amused at her ridiculous idea that this might be a shotgun wedding and not a love marriage at all, and then for the first time Margie felt real pain. She felt it, it was like fire, all over her whole body, but she was cold at the same time. "I can't go on this way," Neil said, "because I need a life. Not half of a life, like you and I have, or two separate halves of a life, the way I would have with you and with her. I need a whole life."

"I guess she wants to marry you," Margie said.

"Yes."

"But she's *Catholic!* Isn't she? She can't marry you if you're divorced, and—" she was beginning to feel a little better, and her voice rose in excitement—"and did you tell her you're Jewish?"

"We went through all this. She wants to marry me. And I want to marry her. Period. Finished?"

"Your mother will kill herself," Margie said faintly.

"Not if she knows I won't be there to revive her." Neil smiled. "You know, the ironic thing is that if you and Gilda had ever met each other you would have liked each other. You would have liked each other very much."

"Don't plan anything perverted like having us become friends," Margie said.

"You'll never meet."

It hurt her, the way he said that, so sure of himself, already protecting this girl and his relationship with her, as if she were some delicate special flower. Margie poured a cup of coffee for herself and one for Neil, automatically, because if she did not go on now doing the everyday things she thought she would scream or strike him or throw herself out of the dining-room window. She tasted the coffee and it had become cold.

"The coffee's cold again," she said.

He was looking at her carefully, to be sure if she were all right or if she were only pretending. She tried very hard to make her face look as if she really cared whether or not the ridiculous coffee were cold, as if she could ever care about those things again. She wondered what the girl looked like. Like herself? Dark? Darker than she was? Small? Neil picked up his cup and gulped down all the lukewarm coffee, completely oblivious for the first time in his life to the fact that it was almost undrinkable.

"It's *cold*," she said.

"I didn't notice."

"Do you want some toast?"

"I could eat some toast."

"One piece?"

"Thank you."

"Does she speak English?"

"You don't want to talk about that any more, do you?"

"They always give the condemned a last request."

"*Margie*—I'm not going to walk right out of your life. I *love* you, in a way, and I always will. There'll never be anyone who means the same thing to me in the same way as you do. I can't throw away five years of marriage. Don't you know how much this hurts me too?"

"Yes. Does she speak English?"

"She went to college for two years in the States. Radcliffe, as a matter of fact."

"Oh, my God!"

He dropped the toast, untasted, on to his plate and tossed his napkin on top of it. He lighted a cigarette, and both the cigarette between his lips and the match between his fingers were shaking so much he could hardly do it.

"I guess I should go home," Margie said. "I don't want to stay here. What do you want me to do?"

"I want you to do exactly what you think you should do."

"I can't think. I don't know what to do."

"First of all, I'm going to move out," Neil said. "I have a little apartment at the other end of the beach, a sublet. I'll leave tomorrow."

"A *garçonier?*" Margie said. She smiled, although there was nothing amusing about it; she smiled because now she remembered that it was Neil who had told her about the *garçoniers* married men kept when they wanted to have affairs. "You've had this planned for a long time, haven't you!"

"No, I haven't. I only rented the apartment on Friday. I think I should leave because it will be easier for you."

"I can't think."

"I know," Neil said. "I know. If you don't want me to leave tomorrow I won't. I'll wait as long as you want."

"Forever?"

"I mean a week. I think it's better, Margie."

"Do you love her?" she said. "*Do you love her?* Do you really love her?"

"Yes."

"But how do you know?" Suddenly she wasn't Margie the rejected wife any more; for a moment she was Margie the mother, and this was her Neil who needed to be taken care of. "What makes you so absolutely sure?"

He caught the change in her tone, the warmth of it, the sign that at last Margie was becoming recognizable to herself again, was returning to life. He leaned forward and his face opened up to her, all his feelings: romance, hope, confidence, hope of happiness. He looked softer. She realized then that he was really only a very young man hiding forever against his will behind a mask of placid rightness, and her heart went out to him in the old kind of love she had always had for him. They were still tied to each other, always would be in a way, even though they were separating now and that parting would be irrevocable.

"Oh, darling," Margie said, "you don't have to tell me. I know."

He stayed on with her in the apartment for three days, and in those three days Margie realized he had been right: it *would* be easier for her if he left altogether. Whenever he made a quiet phone call she felt ill. She walked past the telephone on some pretext, only to know if he were talking to that girl, telling that girl everything had been arranged, would be all right for them now. The calls were always business, and after each elaborately casual walk past Neil and the phone, when she realized he was not lowering his voice or trying to hide anything from her, Margie would feel a small shock because she had been wrong about him. It was at these times she realized how truly far apart she and Neil had grown during the past months, for her to have become so suspicious now and so wrong about his motives.

He tried to pretend nothing had changed, but of course everything had changed. Even his need for her as a friend, as a comforter and guardian, had changed. He needed that other girl now. It was obvious in the little things, the way he neither noticed nor complained when something in the house went wrong, as if Neil were now only a polite and grateful houseguest instead of her husband. When, one morning, Margie discovered that the laundress had torn a large hole in one of Neil's sheets, and that he had been sleeping on the torn sheet, with his feet tangled in it, for almost a week without mentioning it to her, she sat on the edge of his bed and cried. The tears poured down her face, she shook with sobbing, but it was not because of this alone but because of everything. She could not do anything for Neil any more, she could not help him, and what was much worse, he did not want her to. Perhaps, she thought, he had not even noticed the sheet was ripped and twining around his restless legs like the rag supplied by some third-rate hotel. He went to bed satiated, relaxed, rich with love. His body was drugged from happy love-making; his mind raced ahead with plans and then slowed peacefully to sleep. There was nothing more his wife could give him.

Outside, the autumn rains had begun, in torrents. The inadequate drainage system clogged up immediately, and some streets were flooded. Someone reported seven meters of water on the highway leading to the airport. People who left to visit other cities remained there for days, floodbound. The waves shot up into the air, and the beach was deserted, the red flag whipping back and forth in the wind. In many parts of the city there was no telephone service. Margie hardly noticed any of this. There was no one she wanted to speak to and nowhere she wanted to go anyway.

Neil tried to pack secretly, to spare her. This only hurt her more, because she still wanted to take care of him. She felt deserted and suspicious, and whatever he tried to do to make things easier she mistook for signs of surreptitiousness and rejection. She thought perhaps she was losing her mind. Neil had taken off his wedding ring; she noticed this the morning of the day he finally left. The flesh of his finger was slightly swollen from the years-long pressure of the gold band, and there was now a band of white where the sun had never touched the skin. He was still bearing her mark; he was tattooed with her existence. She saw him rubbing the swollen place absent-mindedly and she took that as a rejection too; it almost made her heart stop, because she felt that Neil was trying to smooth away everything that was left on him of her.

She thought vaguely every day of home, of when she would leave, of how she could close this apartment and get rid of the furniture. It seemed too drastic a step, like the cremation of a body that was actually only unconscious; an irrevocable tragedy. One part of her mind told her everything was over, she might as well think of the future if there was any, but she knew she could not think of a future when the present still seemed so unreal. Her parents' home seemed both a haven and an insupportable embarrassment. She had not had the heart to write to tell them. What could she tell them? She did not even know how to begin. She and Neil had always been the ideal young couple, and the truth could never be explained. Margie wondered now if she herself had ever known the entire truth. Had she and Neil ever loved each other as much as they thought they had, or had they only loved the idea of being married to each other, of joining the stream of life?

How could she not love him? She might as well not wish well for her own self, her own face and body. You could look into the mirror critically and say, I hate this and that, or you could analyze your spirit and say that you were selfish or dull or too lazy, but you never really wished yourself ill. You had to love yourself to stay alive, and that was how she felt about Neil.

When he left, with his suitcases, unexpectedly he kissed her. It was a brief kiss, on the mouth, with his lips open. They had not kissed this way for months. There was a strength and confidence about Neil in that sudden kiss that startled her. But she knew it did not mean reconciliation. It meant only that now, for the first time, he was truly free of her. She did not know how she knew it, but she knew.

"I'll call you," he said. "And please, please call me, whenever you want something. If you feel lonely, if you only want to talk, please call. Any hour, Margie; I mean this. You have the number at my apartment, and at the office, of course."

"If I call you at . . . home, she'll be there."

"That doesn't matter."

"All right," she said, biting her knuckle with sharp teeth she could hardly feel.

"You can use any money you want in our joint account. I'll put in a deposit this week for your plane ticket."

"All right."

"I'm not going to say goodbye," he said. "I'm still here. Remember that."

"I guess I said goodbye to you a long time ago," Margie said.

He was gone. She stood in the doorway after he had left and thought absurdly that he should not have gone out in the rain like that; he would be soaked to the skin. He should have waited another day or two until the rains stopped. He must be in a hurry, she thought dizzily, he must . . . because it's raining so hard out and he'll get so wet.

It continued to rain almost every day for two weeks, but Margie stayed inside the apartment the entire time even when it was not raining. She had always cared for her appearance, had gone to the hairdresser at least twice a week, but now she did not. Neil called her every afternoon. He sounded friendly on the phone, almost paternal. Now it was she who needed the care. He talked about money, he asked her plans, he told her amusing little anecdotes about the office. He was always in a hurry. "I called to say hello," he would say, his voice light and kindly, pleasant, and she could never decide if it were a duty call or if he missed her. Then, after two weeks, he didn't call any more.

She did not see anyone but Helen. Helen came over every day and tried to make Margie come out of the apartment, but it was useless. Several times Helen brought Julie and Roger, and Margie liked that. The children made her happy for a while. She wondered if she and Neil had had children if he would ever have left her then. They're right, she thought bitterly, those women who have babies right away, get pregnant on their wedding night; then their husbands can't leave them. The ones who have a lot of children are even smarter; then the husband can't *afford* to leave. In a way she even resented Helen now, for having two lovely children and a husband who would stay with her. She knew this was distorted, that Helen was her best friend in Brazil, and if she began to resent Helen's happiness she would have no one. But she could not help feeling jealous.

Then one morning she woke up and felt as if she had come out of an illness. She was neither unhappy nor happy. The sun was out, it was a good day, and she thought she might go to the beach. She looked in the mirror carefully for the first time since Neil had left and she was startled to see the thin wildness of her face. Suntans faded as quickly as they came in Rio, and her skin was a pale yellowish beige. There were circles under her eyes. Her hair looked frightful; it was the unkempt, unwashed mane of an invalid. She had not bothered to wear lipstick for so long that her lips had become as pale as her face.

"What a beast you are!" she told her reflection, and she took a shower and ate a large breakfast and then she telephoned the *cabellereiro* to have her hair and nails done. "A man wouldn't look at me," she said, not unhappily. "Not even a blind man."

When she was finished at the beauty parlor she walked over to see Helen. The noontime sun in the streets felt good, like a new skin to cover exposed nerves. "I'm alive," Margie said, when Helen followed her maid to the door.

"You look pretty," Julie said, sounding rather surprised, because children get used to anything in several weeks and begin to think it was never any other way.

"Julie!" Helen said, and then added. "You *do*."

"If you want to buy any of my furniture," Margie said, trying to be casual, "you have first call. I'm going to make a list. Neil says he doesn't want any of it."

"Sit down and have some coffee first."

"I want to keep busy," Margie said, and for the first time that morning her voice was unsteady. She was alive, but none of this was going to be easy. She had changed twice, she realized, in a few short weeks. Once when she discovered you could not count on life to remain the same while you grew different, and again when she realized no one was going to take care of her any more. It was going to be strange, this new life alone. Stranger still because it was happening to her for the first time at twenty-five. She wondered if she was going to be able to manage.

CHAPTER *21*

It was a month now since Helen had gone to the *fazenda* to begin a serious affair with Sergio Leite Braga and had left him before it had begun. In this month, for the first time since she had come to live in Rio, she did not feel that her life was suspended, or that she was apart from the daily things that happened to her. The guilty secret of what she had almost done to Bert was with her always. Although her routine went on almost as before, she felt everything very strongly: loneliness, a sense of uselessness, of waste, homesickness, and timid hope for a future that was several years away. She wondered if she and Bert could have another child. Somehow the idea of having a baby to care for made the idea of the next several years seem less mysterious and frightening; she had brought up two babies to the age of childhood and at least in that area she knew what to expect. For everything else in her life this moment she felt only fright, for the first time, because for the first time she had to admit to herself that she and Bert could not reach each other any more. She wanted to confess, she could not confess, they could not even speak together.

She had never before realized how much she had depended on the outward signs of peace and security in her friends' households to add stability to her own. When Mil Burns had left Phil and gone home to the States it had upset Helen out of proportion to the friendship she had felt for Mil and Phil. It had shocked and repelled her, as if in all other marriages she saw her own. And now Margie and Neil Davidow—the happiest marriage in the world—was all over.

She came every day to Margie's apartment, smiling, comforting, often bringing one of her children, but the entire time she had to conceal from Margie her mounting panic. She saw the light go out of Margie's face, the glow of a loved woman fading as visibly and quickly as the golden tan left her skin. Without being loved, Margie was no longer pretty. The change in her hurt Helen very much, not only for Margie herself, whom she loved, but because it seemed an omen. If Margie and Neil could separate, then anyone could. Helen knew now that whatever had been wrong between Margie and Neil had not been a sudden thing; it had been hidden from her and their friends for a long, long time, and that was even more frightening. From the look of paralyzed bewilderment in Margie's eyes Helen knew that Margie Davidow had done such a good job of hiding her dissolving marriage from all her friends that she had ended deceiving even herself.

Although it was spring in the States and fall in Rio it was not much cooler yet. At night Helen had begun to dream again of home, and during the day she sometimes thought of it so longingly she felt as if she were a child again at camp crying secretly the first two nights, with her head under the khaki blanket of her cot so no one would discover what a baby she was. It was funny how quickly one could lose patience with all the little things that had seemed so enchanting: the casual uncaring, the tomorrow or next week attitude, the provincialism that had seemed cozy and now was so boring she wanted only to be alone. But to be alone for what? She wanted to confess; she could not confess. When she was alone with Bert she noticed now for the first time how he constantly occupied himself with things; reading a new book, an old American newspaper, a magazine, attending to work he had brought from the office, teaching the children how to play cards, complaining about the car. The car had been giving him trouble lately, and when he was alone with her he spoke about it all the time—how he had tried to obtain a new part, what might be wrong, what went wrong with automobiles in tropical countries, the unpleasant personality of his repairman, and so on. She had heard about other couples who were united during the dark hours of early evening by nothing more than a car or a washing machine, but now she knew it had happened to her.

She in turn spoke about Margie. What could she say about Margie? What was there to say? The only definite clue Margie had given her was the admission "Neil and I hadn't slept together since Christmas Eve." But even that was really not an answer, because Helen knew by now that sleeping together was not always a bond; it was sometimes only a habit. It had become only a habit between her and Bert since that night before she had gone away with Sergio. Perhaps it was more to Bert, but not to her, not now. Bert never mentioned the difference. Helen wondered if he cared.

She went to the club several times, and the women were very anxious to hear from her all the details of the Davidows' separation. She said she knew nothing about it. Two or three of them said, "Of course you do!" and persisted. "Tell us! You know if anyone does. Is it that girl in Neil's office?"

"Why don't you mind your own business for a change?" Helen said. "Or is it too boring?" After she said that she was ashamed. The women probably thought she was a bitch. Well, she felt like a bitch. Of course their own business was too boring. If Margie hadn't been her best friend, if she didn't love Margie, she probably would have been asking those same nosy questions; the only thing that stopped her was not virtue or self-control but the fact that she knew now how real the pain of the answers was. It was not abstract gossip any more for her; she had come too close to it in her own life.

The only one she said any more to about it was Mort Baker. She met him on the street one day at the end of March, the same day Margie had come to visit her looking alive again. Mort's new apartment had no telephone and he seemed to have disappeared from everyone's life after Carnival. He looked very suntanned and good.

"Why don't you go to see her?" Helen said. "It would cheer her up."

He nodded without replying, just nodded slowly twice, still

looking stunned from her news. At first she thought he was either just stunned or had many other plans which a visit to Margie would interfere with, but then she saw a secret, withdrawn look on his face and she recognized it as an expression she had sometimes seen on Roger's. It was the elaborate casualness that masked excitement.

"Well, I'm going to split now," he said, and gave her a half wave of his hand. He disappeared into a café on the corner. It was a sidewalk café and there were several people seated at tables drinking beer or waiting for people. But he went into the back room where the bar and telephone were, and Helen felt pleased. Mort was a good friend. He was slightly crazy, but he was a good friend.

That night Bert went out to dinner with some business people from São Paulo. He told her he would not be home late. At eight o'clock Margie telephoned.

"Can you come to the movies with me?" Margie asked.

"Didn't Mort Baker call you? I met him on the street today. He said—"

"Yes," Margie said. "He wanted me to have dinner with him but I was too tired. Please come to the movies. I don't want to go alone." Her voice sounded odd.

"All right. I'll pick you up in fifteen minutes." She left a note for Bert saying, "Going to the movies with Margie. Love, H.," kissed her children good night, and drove to Margie's in the car which was temporarily in running order. She was glad to get out of the house herself.

There was no film that both of them had not seen except something in German with Portuguese subtitles about a beautiful blind girl who needed an operation. Neither of them cared, so they went to see that. When the film was over they drove to Bob's and ate American ice cream at the counter on the sidewalk and they talked casually about things that did not matter.

"I'm going to have dinner with him tomorrow," Margie said finally.

"With whom?"

"Mort. It's funny, we know him so well, but I feel funny about going out with him alone. It's sort of like a . . . date."

"That's why you didn't go with him tonight, isn't it? But you can't go into *mourning*, Margie. You have to see your good friends."

"I know," Margie said softly. "But it's different now. I don't know why. All of a sudden I'm scared of him."

"Of Mort? Why?"

"I don't know," Margie said. Her eyes filled with tears. "I don't know."

"Let's drive around," Helen said.

They drove along Copacabana Beach with the windows lowered to the warm air and the sound of the surf. There were lovers on the beach, dark humps that sometimes moved a great deal and sometimes did not move at all. "I was sick all evening," Margie said. "I couldn't eat dinner and I kept shaking. Feel how cold my hand is."

Her palm on Helen's arm was damp and cold. "If it makes you that sick you really shouldn't go out with him," Helen said.

"But I want to," Margie said. She looked out the window as she spoke and the breeze almost blew her words away because they were so quiet. "I was so happy when he called. We haven't seen him for such a long time. I realized how much I missed him. I almost said, 'Come right over this minute if you have nothing to do.' But then he beat me to it; he said, 'Can you have dinner with me tonight?' And I started to feel sick."

"Why, Margie? *Why?* Think about it. Why? There must be a reason."

"I don't know," Margie said again, her head back against the back of the car seat, her eyes closed, tears showing at the corners of her eyes. "I don't know. Stay with me for a while. Come up and have some coffee. I don't want to go to sleep."

When Helen arrived home it was a quarter past twelve. All the lamps in the living room were out but one, glowing dimly at the entrance. The room was shadowy, the curtains drawn against the windows for the night. It was very still. She felt rather than heard the presence of someone in the room, although she saw no one; it

was as if the waves of air that crossed invisibly from wall to wall
had stopped and flowed around a vibrating human body rather
than an inanimate piece of furniture. She felt a tension that stiffened her and crept up the back of her neck like breath. Then
she heard a breath, from the corner next to the curtained windows, the intake of breath from between clenched teeth. Bert was
standing there and he was holding on to the wall with one hand.

"You're home," he said.

"Why are you standing there in the dark?"

He took two steps to the table, pulled the cord that lighted the
large lamp, and flooded the room with light. He was still leaning
on the table with one hand and he had accidentally pushed a
bottle which had been on the edge of the table ever farther
toward the edge, so now she watched with frozen surprize as the
bottle tilted and then fell to the floor. It did not break or spill
because it was empty. She realized then that Bert was very drunk.

"Did you have a nice time at the movies with your friend?" he
asked, trying to enunciate very clearly to cover his slurring speech.
The effect this gave was one of enormous held-in rage and sar-
casm.

"Not very. She was upset. And the picture was dreadful."

"What did you see?"

"It . . . I forgot the name. It was German."

"Oh, really?"

"It was about a girl who was blind, and a doctor said he could
cure her but her mother didn't want her to have the operation."
She ended the description limply, realizing suddenly that he
either did not believe her or was no longer listening. He had been
holding a glass in his other hand and now he held it up to the
light, saw that it was nearly empty, and drank the rest in one
gulp. "I know it sounds silly," she said.

He walked toward her, slowly. He was wearing the trousers to
his dark silk suit and the same wrinkled, damp white shirt he had
worn all day at the office and then out to dinner. He had removed
his tie and shoes. It upset her to see him so drunk and quietly
menacing, and instinctively she drew away a little.

He smiled, a tight smile utterly without humor, and walked

334

closer. With that thin-lipped, slit-eyed grimace, he looked like a giant tiger or cheetah. "What did you do in four hours and five minutes?" he said. "How many *movies* did you see?"

"Did you get this drunk at dinner?" she accused weakly, backing away. He reached out and took her wrist. His fingers did not close tightly enough to hurt her; they were simply an unbreakable band. She smelled the whisky.

"I didn't go to any dinner. I came home at eight-thirty. I just wanted to give you time to get out. I knew you'd go. You haven't had a night alone with *Sergio Leite Braga* for a long time, have you!"

She was drowning. She felt blood in her eardrums like the sound of the sea thundering over the head of a struggling swimmer, her heart pounded until it strained and hurt her, and she could not speak. Bert said something else but she did not hear him and then he put his fingers around her neck. She hardly felt them and waited in panic for them to close out the air from her throat entirely, and then she realized that the reason she could not feel Bert's fingers was that they were cupped very loosely around her throat. He looked at her.

"I could kill you," he said.

The pounding of her heart turned from shock and terror to excitement. His eyes were very close to hers, completely open and filled with grief, his lips were closed and very white. Helen sagged against his cupped hands, allowing him to hold her up, feeling at that moment as if he might strangle her accidentally and for one mad instant not caring at all. She had never felt so weak, nor that Bert was so strong. Unreasoning physical love filled her, weakened her, made her feel faint. His fingers were no longer steel bands around her throat but human flesh, and she could feel his pulse through his fingertips. He had known for a long time, perhaps even weeks, and all these nights that they had sat together in this living room pretending to talk about the car and dull household things he had known. He had known, and he had felt this agony she saw now, and he had not known what to say to her.

Go ahead, she wanted to whisper, kill me; but she could not

bring out a word. Her eyes were wide and fixed on his, and what she meant to say she said through them and he heard her. She knew, she saw his face change as he looked at her, and he opened his hands. She put her arms around him to keep from falling to the floor, and then she held to him more desperately because he was trying to get away from her. He reached behind his waist and took hold of her wrists to pull them away from him. Then, with his hands on her wrists, he stopped, and his hands slid around her arms and up to her shoulders, and then tenderly touched her face. Neither of them said anything.

"I haven't seen him for a month," she said finally. "It's all over. I'm never going to see him again. I never even think about him."

"How long were you sleeping with him?"

"Never. I never did." She saw that he didn't believe her; he must have heard gossip, perhaps even about the *fazenda*. "I . . . went away with him. The last time you went away. I was going to . . . do it, but I couldn't. I ran away. I know that doesn't mean anything, because if I went away with him it was obviously because I *meant* to go to bed with him. But I didn't do it, and when I decided that I knew it was all over too. Maybe that means something—just something—to you?"

"Something," he said. "Go on."

"It was nothing. Lunches; we kissed. I never loved him. I thought I did for a while, but it was only because he knew what to say to me when I felt as if nobody cared for me."

"That I didn't?"

She couldn't look at him. "Yes."

"Why didn't you tell *me* you thought I didn't love you? Did you have to tell *him?*"

"I tried to tell you."

"When?"

"That . . . night after the party I gave for Mil Burns. On the balcony. And . . . afterward."

"God," he said. He didn't touch her any more; he sat on the sofa and lighted a cigarette. Helen knelt on the floor at his feet. From below, his eyes were dark and shadowed so she could not tell what he was thinking.

"And other times too," she said timidly. "It's much more my fault than yours. I never could tell you really what I was afraid of, or how I felt, so how could you know?"

"You tried to tell me," he said. He sounded quite sober now.

"You told me once you wouldn't stop me if I wanted to have an affair. I didn't want you to say that. It made me feel like the ugliest woman in the world. I wanted you to tell me you would act the way you did tonight."

"Didn't you know I would?"

"How could I know?"

"Don't you think I have pride?"

She didn't answer for a moment. Then she said slowly, "I don't think pride like that should matter between two people who love each other. Not when one person's pride matters at the moment more than the other's."

"I don't know if you and I will ever get together," Bert said.

His words hurt her so much that she felt dizzy again. She imagined herself arguing and struggling with him through all this long night and only becoming farther and farther removed from him. She had never loved or needed him as much as she did at this moment when she was most in danger of losing him.

"If you mean that," she said, "then you might as well really kill me. I don't want to live without you. I can't."

"Would you ever have told me about Sergio Leite Braga?"

"I don't know. I never had to live with something that terrible before. Every minute I wanted to tell you, but I was afraid."

"Afraid of what?" Bert said ironically. "If you thought I wouldn't care if you had an affair?"

"I was afraid you'd leave me anyway. That would be the worst; you not caring but leaving me anyway out of pride or distaste or principle, or—"

"Or absolute human agony," he said. "Leaving you because I couldn't look at your face any more. I know the way your face looks when you love, and afterward, and every time I looked at you I thought that someone else was seeing that private look too and then you were coming home to me with it all smoothed out. That isn't pride, darling. That's much more."

337

"Why is it," she whispered, and her voice caught in her throat, "why is it that people only say beautiful true things like that to each other when they're saying goodbye?"

"That's when they're free, I guess. An exit line is easy. You can walk out and close the door. And they feel they owe it."

She couldn't bring herself to ask the question; she was too afraid of the answer. She had to fight now, for him, against him, perhaps both. She had never before suspected the true depth of his pride and she felt now that she could say anything, humble herself completely, beg him, if that would change the way he felt now and make him want her again. The balance of love was so tricky; it was as if you were an aerialist walking on a taut wire above a net. The net was there to save your life, as the marriage itself was there, but what good was it to sprawl humiliated and helpless on the net of marriage because you had failed the important thing, which was to walk grandly and skillfully across the heights of love? They could live together now in sullenness and acceptance, remembering. They had the children, and she and Bert could say, It's for the children's sake. Or they could say that they had been married for a long time and they were used to it. Or that alimony and child support were expensive, and Bert could not afford it yet, and that adulteresses (did he still think she was?) did not deserve to live alone and free and be supported. It made everything ugly to accept and be sullen and not speak out anger, to pretend to forget and never forget, to pretend to understand and never forgive. It would be better to break off entirely—and yet, she could not bear even to think of it, she could not lose him entirely and go on.

"Why didn't you ask me, when you knew?" Helen asked. "Why didn't you tell me you knew?"

"I don't know."

"Why didn't you?"

He got up then and walked away from her, looking for another bottle. He found one, opened it, and then looked at it and put it down. He walked to the wide windows and pulled the cord of the draperies, opening the room to the lights of night. The sight of any world outside this room startled Helen. She wanted him to

338

close the drapes again and leave her here with him in their private purgatory. Even the night sky and the street with cars and people on it seemed too much to think about. She bit the edge of her finger, ripping at the skin with her teeth until she tasted blood, watching Bert and wondering what he would answer, but he did not answer anything.

"Maybe if the same thing had happened between you and . . . a woman you thought you loved, I wouldn't have said anything either," she began, fighting for him. "I don't know what I would have said if I thought *you* were. I would have been afraid. Not that you'd lie to me, but that you'd say you were glad I'd brought it out in the open so you could get rid of me. We never lied to each other before. I guess people have a right to lie to each other sometimes; they don't want to know terrible things. We never had a confess-everything marriage. We never felt forced to give up our own private lives completely, did we? I always hated the kind of marriage where two people get to look like twins, they say yes-dear, no-dear, they never have a single individual thought. I always wanted you to feel free. But secretly I didn't want to be free, *I* didn't. I wanted you to care what I did and what I thought. I *wanted* you to be jealous. I wanted you to *care* more about me. I'm not old," she went on breathlessly. "I'm very young. But we've been married so long—it's not fair, it's not *fair* to me to say that we've been together so long it isn't the way it was in the beginning. Oh, Bert, I know it isn't the way it was in the beginning, but we're not middle-aged either. It's not fair!"

"Maybe you're bored with me," he said tiredly. "Do you want to go home?"

"*Home!* Oh, God," she said, "where's that?"

"He's attractive and rich and sophisticated, they tell me. You could have done worse. At least I'm not insulted."

His cold tone cut her. She could almost believe him. She felt her throat close and she was afraid she might cry, so she waited tensely until the feeling passed away and then she said, "Don't be sarcastic."

"I'm not. I'm tired and drunk and I'm beginning to get a hang-

339

over. It's a shame to get a hangover in the middle of the night. I should at least wait until morning."

"I thought for a minute you were going to kill me."

"You would have enjoyed that, wouldn't you? It would have been dramatic."

"Dramatic! Oh, please, please—stop it. Please *talk* to me; don't just say things to hurt me." But he was right. She knew suddenly he was right, and she turned her face away so he would not read the confession in her eyes. She had wanted him to do something conclusive, something to show her without any doubt that he had been touched and changed and that he needed her enough to be driven to do something totally unlike his sensible, rational self. She had been driven to do that; to go off to sleep with a man she almost did not love, only because of some terrified search for love that had made her give it a face and voice of its own. She knew now why she had thought she loved Sergio. It had nothing to do with his wooing. It had been her own form of violence. And yet, there had been a time when her feelings for Sergio had seemed all tenderness, all gentleness and gratitude, the soft, incongruous under-feathers of the hawk.

She looked at Bert. "What's wrong with me?" she pleaded.

"Why?"

"I can't look at myself any more. The things I see get worse and worse."

"Such as what?"

"My feelings toward you. Toward myself. Toward . . . him."

"I'm not sure I want to know about them."

"You're right," Helen said very softly. She felt drained. Everything was gone. "You're right."

Bert poured a drink and stood looking out the window, drinking slowly. It was straight whisky but it might as well have been water or ginger ale. He drank steadily and calmly and did not look at her. "You were with Margie tonight," he said finally.

"Yes. That's true."

"I know."

He didn't say anything more for a while, and Helen waited, afraid to speak, afraid of what he might say, feeling crazily that

340

everything would be all right, *had* to be all right. She knew him too well, he was the man she had lived with and loved for a third of her lifetime, and yet, they had not known each other very well after all. . . .

"It's strange," Bert said. He sounded as if it were an effort for him to say the words. "Delusions. It was like a nightmare in which you know you're asleep and that it's a nightmare but you can't wake up. And all the time you believe it, even though you know it isn't happening. I'm glad it's over. It *is* over."

"*Everything?* . . . Me too?" She stood up and stood there stiffly, with her arms at her sides, speaking quietly but feeling as if he were very far away from her at the end of a tunnel and could not hear her. She wanted more than anything to run to where he was and touch him, make him say that it was not over, that it had instead never really happened, but she stood there without moving and watched the walls of the room moving away from her, her husband moving away from her, the world opening out and falling away.

"No, the other is over," he said. "It's finished. Tonight when I was alone I didn't know what I was going to say to you. I knew I had to say something. All right, I thought, if this has to be the end this is it. I even divided up the children. I got Roger, you got Julie. It was all simple. It wasn't simple at all."

"Oh, Bert . . ."

"How can people think it's simple? I can't leave you. I can't let you leave me."

She ran to him then and put her arms around him. "Tell me," she cried. "Tell me, *tell me!*"

"I'm too involved with you," he said in a strange, choked voice. "Not just a marriage or our children, or time; I mean involved with *you.*"

"I am too, with you," she whispered. She had her arms tightly around his waist, her face against his shirt, and in the warm room she felt that his shirt was cold and wet. She felt that she wanted to shield him from anything that could happen to him, from all bad things, from illness, from human frailty, from her own tormented selfishness. After only an instant she felt his hand come up gently to stroke her hair. The fear, the tenseness, ebbed away, and in its place came a wonderful calmness, the lifting above pain that comes when a fever breaks. She felt she could stand there forever, guarded and guarding, leaning against him. Only a few minutes ago she had thought her affair with Sergio had been a form of violence; now she realized how distorted it was even to imagine that. It had been stupidity perhaps, or desperation, but not violence. Filled with this wonderful calm she saw herself again clearly, and everything was real. She felt as if Bert had given her something she had lost. How fragile the line was between reality and delusion! Bert had seen it tonight in himself, waiting for her, and she had seen it too, only tonight, waiting for him. She knew then what Bert and his love had given to her again. He had restored to her herself.

CHAPTER 22

Dressing to go out for dinner with Mort Baker, Margie Davidow remembered many things. The night was warm and humid. As she chose jewelry to go with her dress she remembered that her gold charm bracelet had been given to her by her parents for her graduation from elementary school, started for her then with the tiny gold diploma that hung from it, and then every birthday and Christmas afterward another charm was added. A tiny gold book with the Ten Commandments printed inside in letters so small you needed a magnifying glass to read them, and the Star of David on the cover, a gold heart, a tiny tennis racket with a pearl for the tennis ball, a wedding ring and an engagement ring with a diamond chip in it—these rings had been given as a bit of whimsy when she was sixteen, long before she met Neil. She put the bracelet back into her jewel case. It made her feel guilty toward her parents, who would be receiving her air-mail letter in five days, the letter she had finally made herself write last night after Helen had gone home. She felt guilty toward them, for the shock and grief they would feel, and she even felt in some obscure way a guilt for herself, for that young Margie who had received the charms for this bracelet and dreamed of a life that had turned out so differently. She knew it was not entirely her fault, but she felt as if she had betrayed her childhood.

The triple-strand pearl necklace had been given to her by Neil's parents for an engagement present; she certainly couldn't wear that. It had a diamond clasp and a three-strand bracelet to go with it—she remembered how overwhelmed she had been when she first saw them. She picked up an old-fashioned pin that had belonged to her grandmother. She couldn't bring herself to put that on either. There was an aquamarine ring Neil had bought her here in Brazil, and a plain gold bracelet he had given her for an anniversary. Her gold wristwatch had been given to her by her parents when she was graduated from high school—her father had said it wouldn't be a graduation if you didn't get a gold watch. There was nothing here that had not been given to her by someone else who loved her; she could not make herself wear any of it.

You should be a wife, she remembered Neil's saying. She had always been a wife, or a daughter, always a member of a family, always belonging to someone else. She wondered if people who had always belonged to others, or with others, looked different than people who had lived alone. Did it show? Ever since she had been alone she felt as if the front half of herself had been sliced away, replaced with glass, revealing all her feelings and vulnerability.

She finally ended by wearing no jewelry at all. There was a bowl of fresh flowers on the living-room table and she picked a red rose from it and pinned the rose to the lapel of her dress. She tried not to think about Mort getting dressed to go out to meet her. She remembered that evening when he had lived with them and had dressed for a date. She recalled it clearly. Tonight all over the city people were getting dressed in clean nice clothes to meet one another, as they were in New York, in towns, anywhere. Years ago she had thought this when she fussed over her clothing before it was time for Neil to ring the doorbell of her parents' apartment. Strange . . . the cycle continued. She had not gone out on a date for six years, and many things had happened to her, but here she was again with the same feeling of excitement and chilliness, going through the same motions for someone else.

She mixed a pitcher of martinis, six-to-one, the way she liked them, and drank one very fast. The first one always stung and

made her cough. For a minute she always thought it might come back up. Afterward it was easier. She had another small one and then stopped and chewed a piece of peppermint gum. She waited for the lightheaded feeling, it came, and the chilliness left. She remembered that Mort Baker was funny, and he liked to talk, and that he had always liked her very much. They had all been happy together, the three of them—she, Mort, and Neil. There was no reason to be afraid. She and Mort had lived under the same roof for weeks, they had known each other for nearly three years, they had always been special to each other. Still, she wondered what she would say to him for conversation.

She ran to answer the doorbell herself before the maid could get to it. Mort came in fast, smiling, but he did not shake hands or attempt to touch her. He had gotten a very good suntan while he was away from them and Margie supposed he had been spending part of every day on the beach. His teeth looked very white. He looked extremely neat and fresh, clean blue oxford cloth shirt with a button-down collar, open at the neck, clean tan chino pants which were not faded and perhaps brand-new.

"How have you been?" he asked; and without waiting for an answer, "You look beautiful."

"We haven't seen you for ages. You ought to be ashamed."

"I am," he said, but he smiled when he said it and Margie thought he hadn't been ashamed at all or even thought of them. Here today and gone tomorrow, these bachelors. "Are you hungry?" he asked.

"Yes." If she could get one bite down, she thought, she would be lucky. And then she realized suddenly she was hungry after all.

They drove along the curve of beach toward Ipanema and beyond, up into the hills. The sky was streaked with pink and blue and purple and gold. The water was blue and white. Mort talked constantly as he drove, as if he had been away on a long trip and was filled with news for her. She realized that while she had been worrying about what to say to him tonight she had completely forgotten *him*, who and what he was, and had been planning dialogue with a stranger. Now that she was with him she felt cheerful, she laughed, she felt as if she were on an

entirely different level of her existence: outside of herself and much more aware of everything around her, but as if none of the things she saw and knew could give her pain; they were only more interesting.

There was a sort of market and barbecue in a clearing at the side of the road, on top of one of the hills that overlooked the sea. Mort stopped there. "We can get *hors d'oeuvres*," he said. There was only one other car parked by the barbecue stalls, and some dark, ragged children were playing and watching.

In one stall a man broiled bits of filet mignon on a long sharp stick, on a grill there were small sausages, and in a huge barrel there were ears of corn boiling. There were exotic fruits with bright lumpy skins piled on a counter, breadfruit, mango, papaya, pineapple, bananas, and something she did not know the name of. There were watermelons split open, red and wet with juice.

Mort bought filet mignon for both of them, broiled on the thin sharp sticks until it was juicy and rare, then rolled in the *farofa* that tourists called "sawdust" and seasoned with spices. They ate four sticks apiece.

There was an Italian restaurant nearby on the hill and they drove there and sat outdoors on a terrace festooned with brightly colored lanterns and drank martinis, looking out at the last of the sunset over the sea. There were small islands in the distance, in the shimmering water. Margie wondered if anyone lived on them.

"I'd love to have a yacht and sail to one of those islands," she said. "I'd like to stay on it. Never have to think of another thing."

"A friend of mine has a yacht. I'll take you next week. But you'll think, all right. You think *more* when you're on an island."

"You must have a hundred and fifty friends."

"A hundred and fifty-one. They're not friends. I know them, that's all. Sometimes I don't see anybody for weeks. By choice."

The way he said it, with neither self-pity nor striving for effect, made Margie feel slightly envious of him. She felt left out, because he was so self-sufficient. "Do you ever think about certain people when you're not with them for a long time?" she asked.

"Some people."

346

"Us, for instance? I guess you were pretty well tired of us by the time you left."

"I should think it would have been the other way around."

"Oh, no!"

Neither of them said anything for a while. Suddenly Margie felt nervous again. She kept her hands in her lap so she would not tear her cocktail napkin into messy little pieces. She looked into Mort's face and tried to guess what he was thinking.

"It's hard to get over something like that," he said finally. "Traumatic. You keep thinking *we* when you have to start thinking just *me*. I couldn't believe it when I first heard about you and Neil. I guess you never know what people are really feeling. Nobody ever wants to give it away. Everybody has secrets. I was always pretty hung up on you, but I never let myself think much about it because I thought if there was one marriage that would last it was yours with Neil."

"Me?" she said. Her voice sounded too shrill in her own ears. She ripped her cocktail napkin in half.

"Some men are born to be married and some are born to be bachelors. The ones who are born to be bachelors can go on all their lives having affairs and loving every minute of it. They never want things to be any other way. I was born to be a bachelor, but then I got to know you well and after a while I began to hate being alone. Sometimes there's one woman who changes everything. Am I making any sense?"

She nodded, staring at him. She felt too numbed from everything that had happened to her to register quite what he was trying to say.

"Before I picked you up tonight I kept asking myself, Should I take her to dinner and make jokes for about three hours and *then* will that be the conventional time to propose? And how *do* people propose anyway? I never really thought about it. I never thought I would ask anybody to marry me." He stopped nervously and looked at her almost unhappily. She realized that now he was waiting for her to say something, to fill in for him, to say she understood, to accept or say no, to say anything, but all she could think was *He loves me*, me. *Why should he love me?*

347

"I can't ever get married again," she said finally.

"I should have waited. I'm an idiot. I don't even know how much you like me. It's just that I've wanted to marry you for such a long time that I thought I'd tell you so anyway."

"Oh, it's not . . . Neil. It's not that I'm going to carry my grief to my grave. I'll get over that. And I . . . I've always liked you more than anyone we . . . *I* know." She smiled at him, feeling less numb. "I said *I*, did you notice? Not *we*." She looked down at her hands on the table top and realized that she had torn her cocktail napkin into bits, like confetti. "I want to tell *you*," she said softly.

"You can tell me anything," Mort said.

She looked at him then and she realized that she could, not just because Mort Baker was the person who some people thought was eccentric and more people resented because he did exactly what he wanted to do and said exactly what he wanted to say and had life the way he wanted it to be. She knew he was the only person she could tell because he would understand, and he would know why she had to tell him. For the first time, telling someone else about her and Neil wasn't a betrayal. She felt very close to Mort at this moment, and less tense, but still it was hard to begin to speak about it after so many years. She wondered if she would even be able to find the right words. He waited and did not say anything.

"I guess you want to marry me because you've always thought of me as a wife," she said. "No, don't interrupt me, wait. I mean . . . you knew me when I was already married and you lived with us and always thought we were happy. You said so yourself. What you fell in love with wasn't just *me* but a happy marriage. I can just see how it happened." Suddenly she choked and she could not say any more because, ridiculously, she thought she was going to cry. She felt an intolerable sadness, as if everything that was sweet and gently loving was going to fade away from her, the happy ending that you cry over because it happens to someone else, never to you.

"That's not what you wanted to tell me."

348

She shook her head. "Don't you think it was just our happy marriage you liked?" she whispered desperately.

"I've seen a lot of happy marriages and they only bored me," Mort said.

"I'll tell you about ours." She told him then, as briefly as she could. When she started to explain about how she had at first not liked Neil to make love to her and had finally at the last become almost ill when he tried to touch her, it seemed at first as if she were talking about someone else. Had all this really happened to her? How much worse, how almost gruesome, it sounded when she told about it in this calm way. She hoped frantically that Mort would not think she was telling him as some sort of come-on; she remembered that someone had told her married women told stories of this kind when they wanted a man to go to bed with them. That my-husband-never-gave-me-an-orgasm kind of story, from a hypocritical woman trying to be pathetic with a lecherous gleam in her eye, and off to a hotel room to help the poor wife find happiness. But he was leaning forward, listening with sympathy and great calm. Not too much sympathy, which would have frightened her, but with understanding rather than inspiration to action.

She felt better then, telling him; she felt very close to him. She felt a pang of guilt only at how little shyness she felt at talking to him about her most intimate life; there was an excitement in telling him that made her confide on and on. "I'm never going to make that mistake again," she said.

He drank all of his martini, and Margie realized that what she had just said to him sounded rather like a proposition. Well, perhaps it was. She could hardly believe it herself, and yet, why not? Her fingers, ripping the bits of napkin, shook.

"I don't know what to do," he said.

"I don't either. I don't know what to do with my life. I've never been so mixed up. I wish I'd never gotten married. No, I don't wish that at all. Part of our marriage was perfect. But you don't know what it's like to be getting a divorce. It's the most terrible thing in the world. It's just terrible. I never knew . . ."

"I can't even ask you how you feel about me right now," he said. "You don't know how you feel about anything."

"No . . . I'll tell you."

"I want to know."

"I feel two different ways about you. You're an old friend and something else that's even more special. I think I could fall in love with you very quickly. That should make me feel better, but somehow it only makes me feel worse."

"I know the feeling," Mort said. "I had it about you for the past year. For different reasons, but it's the same sensation. You don't want to think about it."

"But for once in my life I want to be *responsible* for what I do. I never was before. Things just happened to me. I never really knew what I was doing."

"Would you like another drink?"

"No. That's the first thing. I want to know *why* I'm doing things."

The waiter was at the other end of the terrace. That was one nice thing about Brazil, Margie thought, the waiters didn't hover. In fact, they didn't care. She wondered what it would be like to live here with Mort instead of going home to the States. Certainly it would be different from living with Neil; it would almost be as if she were discovering Rio all over again. All the mysteries about Mort, the way he lived, the things he did when he was alone, would be things he would be sharing with her. She tried to remember what she had thought about Neil when he was a bachelor and she was thinking about marrying him. There had been a mystery there too. But it had been a mystery about *men, husbands,* not so much about Neil himself. Neil had seemed the virile representative of all those unknown men, Orpheus descending to rescue her and take her to the place where other people lived together and were happy. But when she thought of living with Mort she only thought about being with him alone.

"I don't know how to put this to you," Mort said. "I don't want you to think I'm asking you on just another 'honeymoon.' I remember how you used to talk about that. I don't want you to think I can solve anything for you. But I love you, and maybe we can go away somewhere together. Would you do that?"

As soon as he said it she realized she had been thinking tentatively of it herself, and yet the spoken words gave her a small shock. If she were her dream self, her brave self, she would go. And yet, what would be the good?

"I might," she said.

"I have a friend who has a house on the beach at Cabo Frio. At Buzios, really, and it's more of a shack. He's never there during the week and I can use it. It's very primitive—no electricity, kerosene lamps, right on the sand, and nobody around but fishermen. Buzios is the most beautiful place you ever saw."

"How many girls have you taken there?" Margie asked, smiling.

"None. What did you think?" He looked angry—no, hurt.

"I just wanted to make sure."

"You have it in your mind that I'm some kind of a great lover," he said. "I'm not taking you off for a seduction or an orgy or a wild weekend and then goodbye. I want to go someplace where we can be alone for a while."

"I have to think," Margie said.

"We'd have five days completely alone at first. And after that we could stay on as long as we want to."

"Let me decide later. I don't know."

"We ought to have dinner," he said reluctantly. "Where do you want to eat?"

"I don't know that either," Margie said. "I've just been proposed to and propositioned, both in one evening. I don't think I could manage to eat dinner too." But she smiled when she said it and she felt surprised at how happy she was. She felt restless and confused and she wanted to be alone to think things out, but she knew that tonight when she went back to the empty apartment and was alone she would not feel lonely or afraid. "I'd like to be alone. Is that all right?"

He waved at the waiter. She thought it was typical of Mort that after four years of living in Brazil and speaking perfect Portuguese, he still didn't hiss at the waiters as everyone else did. "Are *you* all right?" he said to her.

"Yes, I'm fine. I'm happy. Isn't that funny?"

"Kind of," he said. "I am too."

He drove her home and took her upstairs, and said good night to her at the door to her apartment, standing two feet away from her and not even attempting to shake hands. She remembered the last moments of dates she had had when she was young: the instinctive knowledge of which boys were going to sneak up to you, which ones were going to grab you in a rush, and which ones had no intention at all of doing either. She knew if she stood there for an hour talking, stretching out the last minutes of good night because she had something more to say to him, because she was reluctant to be alone at last, he would not misunderstand her delaying.

"I always go to the beach in the morning," he said. "It's my project. Do you want to come?"

"Yes."

"Ten o'clock. I'll pick you up."

She laughed. "You're turning into a *cafegista.*"

"It's a mood I'm going through." He gave her a big grin and rang the bell for the elevator.

"Where are you going now?"

"Home to sleep."

Neither of them said anything more about Cabo Frio. It was not necessary for her to mention it; she thought of nothing else. Mort waved his hand at her and was gone.

She walked into her apartment slowly, like a sleepwalker. She felt different. Yesterday she had wondered if she could ever make a life for herself; tonight she saw one ahead. She had only to accept it. No, it was not so simple. She was through with accepting things. Accepting things as if whatever people wanted you to do was your acknowledged destiny, was like keeping a present even though you would have to make enormous inconvenient changes in your life just to use it. She looked at the clock in her bedroom. It was ten-thirty. She wondered if Neil would be home so early.

She had forgotten his new number or, rather, had deliberately prevented herself from memorizing it so she would not be able to telephone him when she became desperate. It was written

352

on a slip of paper in the top bureau drawer, the same paper he had written it on. His handwriting gave her a sad feeling. She didn't want to call him; pride prevented it, the pride of a kind of last-chance feeling that she had to make this decision about her life by herself. But I *can't,* she thought. I never decided anything without Neil.

The first time she dialed a wrong number, and when a woman's voice shrieked at her in Portuguese she thought at first it was that girl of Neil's. She sat with the receiver in her hand, terrified and embarrassed, until she realized that the number the woman was shouting was not Neil's number at all.

"Pardon, Senhora. Wrong number," she murmured, and the woman hung up indignantly. Perhaps it was a warning, an omen. She hadn't spoken to Neil for a long time. Maybe he didn't want to hear from her, perhaps he was right in the middle of . . . making love . . . to that girl. Then he doesn't have to answer the phone, that's all, Margie thought in sudden indignation. She redialed Neil's number carefully.

She listened to the telephone ringing and imagined it sounding in his empty apartment. She had never seen that apartment. She wondered what it was like. Was he there often? Did he have a maid to keep it clean? Was that girl living there with him, or still with her family, like a nice Brazilian virgin?

"Hello," Neil said. He sounded breathless.

"It's Margie."

"Wait just a second, I have to close the door. I just walked in." He put down the receiver and for a panicked moment Margie thought he was not going to come back. "Margie, how are you?" he said, sounding warm and concerned.

"I'm all right. How are you?"

"Fine. I was going to call you tomorrow morning."

"You're busy. You can call me tomorrow."

"No," he said. "I'm not busy at all."

"Are you alone?"

She thought he hesitated. "Yes."

She tried to sound casual. "No, you're not. You'd better call me tomorrow as you planned."

"What is it? It's something important, I can tell."

"It is!" she said suddenly. "I *have* to talk to you. I can't tell you on the phone. Can you come over, just for half an hour? Please!"

"Of course. I'll come over now."

"Can you? I mean . . . is it all right?"

"Of course. I'll be right over." He hung up without saying goodbye.

She realized he was on his way over, might be there in five minutes—she didn't even know really how far away his apartment was. She ran to the bathroom and peered into the mirror at her make-up. Her hand was shaking so much she could hardly put her lipstick on straight. She wouldn't have time to wash her face and put everything on from the start. She felt grimy. It was so hot tonight. Neil might have forgotten how she looked, he might think now that she was less attractive than he remembered her, he might tell himself he was glad to be rid of her. She put on more powder and ran a comb through her hair. She should have brushed her teeth *before* she put fresh lipstick on; now she was getting lipstick all over the toothbrush. God!

When the doorbell rang she started. Neil wasn't using his key any more; he was just like a stranger. She put on more lipstick and ran to the door, running her tongue over her front teeth to be sure there was no lipstick on them. On the way she turned out one of the lights.

Neil looked pale. He had hardly any color at all. It was she, Margie realized, who was surprised and disappointed in him, not he with her. He glanced at her admiringly. She smiled at him, and felt a warmth and security. But there was something missing too. She felt . . . lonely with him. She felt there had to be a great deal of talk between them before she could get back that *whole* feeling she had always had when she was with him. But she had needed to talk to him; that's why she had called him and made him come here.

He sat on the couch and crossed his legs. He was completely and immediately at home.

"Would you like some coffee? A drink?"

354

"Some Scotch maybe. Not strong. You?"

"I'll do it." She mixed the two highballs at the bar, feeling acutely Neil's eyes on her back, the hostess in her own home, not their home but hers now alone. She made her drink stronger than his.

They sat side by side on the couch with a space between them. Neil leaned forward to light her cigarette. She smiled at him. "I'm glad to see you," she said.

"I'm always glad to see you."

"Are you happy?"

She saw the happiness arise in his face, just at her mention of it. She knew then that he was, and that whatever she and Neil had between them was now deep and loyal friendship, but that alone. It made what she wanted to say to him easier.

"Yes," he said, trying to sound tentative so as not to hurt her more.

"I'm glad. I am. I'm glad. You deserve to be. Are you still going to marry her?"

"Yes, of course."

She looked at her fingers. "Mort wants to marry me," she said.

"*Mort Baker?* Why, that . . . *well!*" Neil said. The shocked look on his face gave way to pleasure, because he genuinely liked Mort, and then to puzzlement. "How do you feel?" he asked.

"That's what I wanted to ask you."

"Well, you don't have to ask me if you can get married."

"No, it's not that. You know."

He took her hand gently between both of his. "I'm going to give you a lecture," he said. She looked up at him, frightened. "No, listen," Neil said. "I had it in mind to tell you this a while ago, but I didn't think it was the right time. You know I love you, Margie—in our way—you know what I mean. You're so sweet and innocent, and I never want you to become tough and, well, a slut like some married women are. They're always looking for new affairs, new lovers. Or they go from husband to husband, always looking for something, because they're conventional enough to get married in order to sleep with the guy but not too

355

conventional to get divorced if it doesn't work out all right. I want you to be happy."

"Tell me what to do," Margie said. "*Tell* me, Neil."

"I never thought I'd be telling any girl this, particularly not you," Neil said. "I've changed my thinking a lot in the past few years. I think both of us made a mistake. But I don't want you to become tough. I couldn't stand to see that. I want you to promise me something. If you love Mort and you think he'll make you happy I want you to marry him, but first I want you to go off and live with him for a while. Promise me that."

"I will," Margie said softly. She sighed and moved closer to Neil and put her head on his shoulder. She felt a great relief, as if for the first time in her life she was loved by many people with a love that demanded nothing—no perfection, no artifice, no dependency. She felt love springing out in return, out of gratitude and a sense of her own freedom. Perhaps everything would be all right for her. "I love you, Neil," she said, without embarrassment.

"I love you too. I wish you had been my sister."

"I wish so too. Maybe we can adopt each other."

"Do you love Mort?"

At the mention of his name her heart began to jump and she felt odd. She drew back and smoothed her hair. "I think so," she said thoughtfully. She wanted to say more then, she felt braver, she wanted to say *yes*. "It's all been so quick. Maybe it's only infatuation or shock."

"It doesn't take long for things to work out," Neil said.

She smiled at him. "I know."

He stood up. "I have to go back now. I'll talk to you tomorrow, late in the day."

"Thank you for coming over."

She walked beside him to the door. There they both stopped. She wanted to try the words out on her tongue while he was still there to listen to them, to force honesty out of her. She wanted to hear what the words would sound like. Perhaps then she would know if they were true. "I think I'm . . ." she began, and then she couldn't say it. It wasn't because the words were not true. It was only that if this growing excitement and longing and tender-

ness she was beginning to feel toward another man was real, she
didn't want to talk about it to Neil. It was so different from the
way she had ever felt about him that she felt as if she had
cheated him.

In Buzios, at the tip of Cabo Frio, there is a hill where you can
stand at a certain hour of twilight and see on one side of you the
setting sun and on the other the rising moon. For a long time they
both float high in the sky, one on either side of the hill, both the
same size and shape when the moon is full, one white, one orange.
Then the sun goes into the sea, and for a while the edge of the
blue water is streaked with orange. At the top of this hill is a
small church, painted white with blue doors. Below are the scal-
lops of coves and beaches, some edged by a line of the square
shacks of the fishermen's families. The grass of this hill is scrubby
and stiff, buffeted eternally by warm, salty winds.

Standing silently on the top of the hill you could believe that
your luck would change. All your life you were told—and you
believed—that you could not have the sun and the moon both;
you had to choose. Yet here they were, both, equal. Not one rising and the other quickly disappearing but hovering together
motionless and suspended, larger and brighter and more beautiful
than you ever imagined either could be. In the magic and silence
of this place you feel sure that everything will be different for
you from now on.

The sun goes into the sea, but it is not very dark because of the
moonlight. And then you think, No, *I* was wrong too; you can't
have either one. Not to keep, not to hold, not even to touch. And
if you could take hold of them, what would you do with them?
They are thoughts to make you shiver, because you always want
too much, you always pretend, and you really know all the time
that it isn't your luck that has to change but your dreams.

Margie Davidow stood at the top of the hill with Mort Baker
and looked at the sky and the sea. Below on the beach the fishermen were boiling their nets. The nets were very large and brown,
the color of old kelp. The smoke from the troughs rose up into
the branches of a big sea grape tree that arched above them. In

the two troughs was some sort of brownish dye to keep the nets from rotting and tearing apart in the sea. When the sun went down all Margie could see was the dim smoke rising and the cool, silvery curve of the sand. The fishermen were singing. Mort's car parked there looked anachronistic. It was not cold but she shivered.

Next to the ocean or a lake she always felt closer to the meaning of life. It was simply that the ocean overwhelmed her; it was so much nature, so old, and so strong. She wondered if people who had not been brought up in a city like New York felt this way. The sound of the water touching the beach went on and on, very lightly and quietly. The sky seemed immeasurable and she felt cold. Her own life seemed so small to her at this moment, and yet she knew at the same time that she was with someone who cared very much what she would do within the next days because it might mean to him a change in the pattern of his entire future. Her life might be small and virtually meaningless when she stood here overlooking the ocean and thinking about the world, but she had learned in the past weeks the feelings of loneliness and need, and of pain that could neither be explained nor shared away. Whatever happened to her *was* important; she could not escape that by philosophy or stoicism or by trying not to think about it at all. Her destiny seemed so simple: to love. To give love; not even so much to receive it, but to be able to give it freely when it was needed. It was the destiny and meaning of a woman—so simple, and yet for her so fragile and so perilously almost out of reach.

In the night winds that rushed all about her on this hill her private suffering, the ache of loneliness in her throat, the fear that made her heart begin to pound almost audibly, seemed washed away so that although they were not gone they were less. The pull of the wind and the sounds of the sea and the fishermen's voices seemed more important because they were eternal. And what of me? Margie thought. To live dully the endless days without loving, and finally curl up and die with all that ungiven love still withheld and dying too?

The week before she had come here she had gone to the beach

358

every morning with Mort and to dinner with him every night. Neither one had touched the other, not even with a tentative gesture. He seemed so easy about it that it was almost like the old days when she and he and Neil were all together. And then she began to feel the slow, straining pull toward him, the longing that seemed not something new but mysteriously, something experienced before and forgotten. And then the night they had made their plans to leave for Cabo Frio the next morning, Margie had suddenly remembered what it was. She was almost astonished at the sly duplicity of her own feelings that had deceived *herself*. Suddenly free, suddenly about to be alone with him and far away from Rio and all their friends, she remembered. This was the feeling she had always struggled with and hidden from herself when she was with Mort and he had been living in their apartment. She was free to touch him now, to do anything—but free? The word was ironic, for her, and she did nothing. She was still the complex creature of desire and ignorance, and so she waited for the morning and the trip to Cabo Frio, and gave him no sign, and she wondered what would become of her.

She knew only one thing. She was beyond the stage of coming away from this emotion fresh and untouched; she was committed. If they left each other now, if their week at Buzios failed, if they could not reach each other, it would leave a wound that would be a long time healing. He had already reached her. There was no turning back, but she wondered if she could go ahead to an ending where they both were free to love.

Then, early that morning she and Mort had driven to the ferry that took them from Rio to Niteroi across the bay. She stood by the rail and watched Rio growing smaller, white buildings in a haze of heat. Seagulls flew above the choppy water and there were things floating: rolls from a picnic, white and bloated from the water like tiny dead bodies. The cars on the ferry were steaming hot in the sun. Mort bought Paulista grapes from a man who had two wooden crates of them on the ferry and they ate the grapes standing side by side on the prow and tossing the seeds into the wind. From Niteroi they drove the car to Cabo Frio and then to Buzios, arriving in the afternoon. Even before they came to the beach house, while they were still driving along miles of endless tan dirt roads where cows wandered in front of their car and the foliage was low and dusty, Margie felt as if they had come to the end of the world.

Mort's friend's house was a white stucco box set in the middle of a sand dune. You could see the water from all its windows, and when you opened the gate beyond its tiny sand-choked garden you had to run only a few feet down to the edge of the surf. The wind banged all the shutters open and closed. Some flagstones had been set into the sand in the garden, making a terrace. There were white wooden chairs and a table with a red umbrella, seashells for ashtrays, and some old, curling society magazines weighted down by stones so they would not blow off the table. The house had a living room, a kitchen, a bathroom, and two bedrooms. One of the bedrooms had a double bed.

He had been right; it was a romantic place. The nearest house was a fisherman's shack far down at the other end of the beach. There was a cove with gray rocks for sunning yourself. It was three o'clock in the afternoon when they arrived, and hot. Mort put her suitcase in the bedroom with the double bed and dropped his suitcase on the floor of the bathroom. All he had brought with him was a dark-blue plastic Varig airlines bag. It was filled with bathing suits, men's toilet articles, books and magazines. As soon as she had been in the house five minutes Margie realized that, as she always did when she went to the beach, she had brought too many clothes.

The door to her (their?) bedroom had an old-fashioned hook and catch. She locked it and put on her bathing suit very quickly, hoping that she would be all dressed and the door opened again before Mort had an opportunity to discover she had locked it. She felt very self-conscious and foolish for being so shy, and her hands shook so much she had trouble tying the knot of her bra.

They swam in the water that was cool but not too cold, and lay on the gray rocks in the sun. A Portuguese fisherman came by once in an old canoe with a little naked boy. The little boy jumped into the water from the canoe and paddled around like a puppy, his black hair streaming into his eyes.

"You never see the fishermen's wives or daughters swimming here," Mort said. "They aren't allowed to wear bathing suits; it's supposed to be shocking. But the children wear nothing."

"You mean the girls can't go swimming when they grow up?"

"Some do now. The city people came here and changed everything. A few years ago they would have been shocked to see you in what you have on. But by now they're getting used to it."

"How awful to live on the edge of the sea all your life and not to be able to enjoy it," Margie said.

"The water doesn't mean the same thing to them that it does to us. It's just the places where they work."

She had found a smooth rock, just long enough for her to lie on it, and she was lying on her back in the warm sun. She closed her eyes. So here we are, she thought, and the sunlight was not hot enough. That morning before they left a cablegram had arrived from her mother, who had just received her air-mail letter about separating from Neil.

YOU OLD ENOUGH MANAGE OWN LIFE, the cable said, at a dollar a word. DADDY AND I SORROWFUL BUT REALIZE MANY DETAILS UNWRITTEN. OLD SAYING EVERYTHING WORKS OUT FOR BEST. HURRY HOME. WE LOVE YOU. MOTHER.

The cable was folded in her purse. It had made her feel homesick, but through all the rush of memories and pictures of her parents, her childhood home, the two people who would accept her back again and love her because she was their daughter, she did not want to go home. She wanted to be here. And here she was. It frightened her. Here she was, of her own choice, and it was her own gamble. She could imagine her mother's horror, her father's fury. Some men think that any divorced woman is fair prey, she remembered her mother saying indignantly about someone else, a forty-year-old woman, hardly an innocent child. Margie opened her eyes and glanced at Mort beside her on another rock, stretched out in the sun, his eyes closed, almost asleep. Fair prey? She felt such a wave of affection and attraction for him that she reached out and touched his bare chest. He opened his eyes immediately.

"You're a lovely man," Margie said.

But when they came back from the beach she took a shower with the bathroom door locked and dressed in the bathroom. He had warned her that there was a shortage of water, and of course no hot water at all, so she could not stand under the shower for long. The shower water was pleasantly cool and she rubbed all the sand off with soap quickly and rinsed the salt water out of her bathing suit. Even though during water shortages all water had to be brought from the town in huge metal tanks, there was a shiny new white porcelain bidet and a large white sink beside the stall shower. It was like a garden made of plastic flowers.

The beach house came supplied with an Indian servant, who slept somewhere behind the house in a garagelike shack and arrived at mealtimes to cook and serve. He was a thin, dark little man with a beaked nose and a very sweet look in his eyes. Mort had brought the food from Rio. There was filet of beef, *feijao* and rice, squares of boiled pumpkin with melted butter, salad, chilled Spanish wine, cold Brazilian beer, crackers with three kinds of cheese, tiny cups of strong black coffee, and brandy. There was too much wind to eat outdoors on the terrace so they ate in the living room beside the huge glass sliding doors that looked out over the beach and sea. It was still light.

"I want to take you to see something before the sun sets," Mort . . . so after they ate nearly all of the food and drank all of the . . . d beer, they took the bottle of brandy in the car with them . . . we to the place where there was the hill with the church o. . . . and you could see the sun set and the moon rise at the same time.

So here we are, Margie thought again, and she still could hardly believe it. On the hill, in the moonlight, she shivered. The fishermen's voices were soft and rough, like the smoke that lifted softly into the leaves of the dark tree. She could no longer see the tree, but she saw how the smoke fanned out and separated into the blue-black sky. There were thousands of low, glittering stars. She could see the shape of the constellations but she did not know where one left off and the other began.

"There's the Southern Cross," Mort said. "You can't see it in the States."

362

"Where?"

"There, where I'm pointing. See the big star? And the next one?"

"I see it!" She felt excited, like a child seeing the mystery of the heavens for the first time. She had seen the stars and tried to trace the shapes they made many times before, at camp, on her honeymoon in St. Thomas, but they had never seemed so near or so brilliant. She could even see the little far ones, the pinpoint ones, scattered in between the large ones in hundreds of thousands. "You can't *ever* see the Southern Cross in America? Never?"

"No. The curve of the earth gets in the way."

"The curve of the earth. . . ."

He gave her the bottle of brandy and she drank some from the bottle. It burned her throat a little when she swallowed it, but it was very fine brandy and after she swallowed it the taste it left was good. It made her feel warmer.

"Let's go back," he said. "Otherwise we'll break our necks going down the hill in the dark."

The fishermen had taken their nets out of the troughs and spread them on the beach to dry. The sand was hard and smooth and the air was warm. Mort held Margie's hand going down the rocky ledges from the hill and he kept holding it until they got to the car. She sat next to the window, far away from him. She felt such a combination of excitement and reticence, such a timid going forward and a panicked withdrawal, that she was completely without any words to say to him. If he had asked her at that moment such a simple and ridiculous question as what day it was or how much were one and two, she would have had to think stupidly for five minutes before she could answer him. She stared fixedly ahead through the windshield all the way back and did not look at him.

They drove over a rough road through a tiny community, only a group of boxlike houses really, with no streetlights and no glass in the windows. She could see people sitting inside their homes in the yellow light of the kerosene lamps: thin women with dark, lined faces and shapeless, faded cotton dresses, men in groups talking together, children dressed in scraps and shreds of clothing, more naked than not, playing with bits of wood for toys or standing staring out the window at the lights of their car, little girls with strange, beautiful faces, mulattoes with golden hair. With the concentration of the desperate, Margie saw every detail. She wanted to say something to Mort, something about these people, those children, but thoughts swirled inside her mind and disappeared deafeningly unsaid into her own brain. How loud her thoughts were, how meaningless! They seemed to scream back at her, like the cries of someone in a tunnel shouting and hearing his voice rocketing off the walls into his own ears. The only thing that meant anything was the thought she tried to put away, safely away, and she concentrated on the gibberish shrieking inside her mind with the fixed catatonic intensity of an insane person.

Their house was fluttering with shadows. The Indian had lighted a kerosene lamp in every room, turned the wicks low, and disappeared into his own dwelling. There was the bitter, smoky smell of kerosene, and through the opened shutters on their glassless windows the gentle sound of the surf.

"I want to go swimming," Mort said. He seemed to have sensed her distress all through the car ride home, and he looked so pleased with the idea of swimming in the middle of the night that she felt slightly reassured. He knew, after all, everything about her. There were no secrets between them. He was not her husband: the disappointed, the teacher, the hurt and loving. He neither had to prove anything to her—nor take anything from her. The look he gave her was solicitous and affectionate. Margie wondered suddenly with a stab of jealously if he had gone swimming at night very often with other girls, and if afterward those girls had been accomplished and wild in bed. Without knowing any of them she hated them all.

"Yes, lets!" she said, and ran down to the beach in her clothes, without even bothering to take a bathing suit. She felt reckless there in the dark, free, and light on her feet in the softly blowing wind. She kicked off her shoes. The sand was as cool as water.

She saw him unbuttoning his shirt and she could not look

away; then she pretended she wanted very much to run down the beach for the sheer joy of racing in the dark. When she saw his head appear in the water and heard him splashing she ran back to where he was. There was light glowing around him in the black water; wherever his hands or feet broke the surface there was a shower of greenish light.

"Look!" he called out to her, "It's phosphorescent!"

The water was alight with tiny moving lights. The surf touched the shore with dully gleaming greenish bubbles. Where tiny fish moved out in the dark sea they left a swift, zigzag line of light. His upraised arm as he waved at her was green and glowing, like the arm of a pagan idol. He did not even seem human.

She unbuttoned her shirt and folded it neatly before she laid it on the sand in a dry place. She unzipped her slacks, stepped out of them, and folded them to keep the crease in place. It was so dark here in the moonlight that all she could see was the white of her bra and pants; the rest of her body was suntanned to invisibility. Instinctively she rolled her underwear into a tiny ball and put it under her slacks and shirt where it could not be seen. She looked out at the endless water and she felt chained, trapped by her own compulsive neatness. It seemed so ludicrous here, but it was the way she was, and she wondered if she could ever escape from herself.

She stepped into the edge of the surf. The water was at first cold, then warmer than the air. Phosphorescent greenish bubbles spumed around her ankle; her feet in the shallow water set tiny concentric circles of light shooting out around them. She ran a few steps and dived in.

Wherever she swam the lights moved with her; she seemed to control them. She laughed aloud with pleasure and swam to Mort; his leg when she touched it with her foot underneath the water seemed warm. They swam side by side creating whirlpools of fluorescent green. They splashed each other, laughing, like magicians throwing off sparks.

"Look what I can do!" she cried breathlessly. "Look! Look!"

In the deep water far out he swam in a circle around her, encircling her with a trail of light. It seemed to her at that moment that they were both supernatural, creating their own elements.

They swam to shallower water where they could stand. "*We* did it," he said, moving his hand to send forth lights. "It's ours."

"Here," Margie said, holding her arms apart to embrace the cool fire that had no feel, that disappeared and reappeared, to follow her as often as she created it. The water rocked her, moved her to and fro without will to resist. She brushed by him again under the water, or he brushed by her, she did not know which, his leg against her side. He was warm, he was all warm under the water, and for the first time they put their arms around each other and twined their bare legs together and kissed, moving and rocking in the motion of the water. Margie felt dizzy.

She could not breathe, she thought she might faint and drown there in the shoulder-high water, she could neither break away to save herself from the warmth of his body nor stay to lose herself to it. She gasped and he opened his arms and legs and she floated and swam away as if she had been released from the bottom of the ocean. She swam to the shore and ran onto the beach.

She was all a glowing, silvery green from throat to feet, covered with a veil of drops of light. She stared at herself, so shaken with surprise and joy that tears came into her eyes. Even the tips of her breasts, standing out in the cool air, were shimmering with this greenish light like the breasts of a statue. Now it was she who was the pagan idol; she had no name, no past, no identity beyond the miracle of this moment. She held out her arms to him and he ran to her across the sand, green like herself, alight and miraculous.

His lips were warm and tasted of the salt water. He was very strong. She felt as if she were trying to destroy him, her lips, throbbing, could not let his go and within his parted lips she felt his bright animal teeth as if they were her own. She felt so dizzy and faint with want of him that she did not know how she suddenly discovered herself lying on the cool sand, feeling it on her skin and in her hair. The sand was gritty and damp, it was tangled in her hair, and when she moved her head from side to side her hair thrashed in the damp sand and became entangled in it more. She hardly noticed it. She smelled the sea and a gentle musk in his skin, and in her own, and the air above them was pure oxygen.

In the one instant that she had to be gentle to receive him she was suddenly aware of herself again. Margie felt all the wildness slipping away from her as she lay there, and the instant was long enough to think, Now it starts. She saw the black sky above Mort's shoulder and the sea beside them. Her mind went blank with the agony of reality. Now, her mind thudded the words down, you can't fail him. She had lost the feeling; it was all lost. She stiffened with fear and loss and could not move or even breathe. If I don't breathe, Margie thought, despising herself, perhaps I will die this minute. She hardly noticed what he was doing to her, and yet, his touch was so gentle and persuasive that slowly she felt a new feeling—that it did not matter if she hated herself or not, if she responded or not, it only mattered that he not stop, never stop, no matter what happened.

She wanted to give . . . to give . . . love. She heard the words whispered on her own breath: I love you. She did not know if she really spoke them or if she only felt them. I love you. She wanted to be closer, to give, and, for the first time, to take. She strained against him and held him tightly and moved, and suddenly she was making love to him.

Afterward they lay together for a long time and neither of them spoke. Margie knew he knew everything she wanted to or could say, and anything he could say aloud would not sound the way he meant it. What kind of comment could either of them make? He had given her a miracle. Not just that sweet agony on the sand but much more; he had led her to himself and she knew him now. Margie wondered if that was why they used the word *knew* in the Bible—"he *knew* his wife." She knew Mort and she knew herself. She felt as if they were already married.

Living in that beach house was like living in a doll's house, it was so small and clean and always filled with little toy things like shells and bits of driftwood they had collected and which had meaning only to them. They were completely alone. The Indian, in the wonderful way of Brazilian servants, kept himself nearly invisible except when they needed food, and then the food appeared in an instant and he disappeared again. He never spoke; he might have been deaf, but he understood whatever they said to him.

Margie and Mort wore bathing suits all during the day, and nothing as soon as it was dark. They swam, they lay in the sun, they talked, they made love a great deal. Margie thought how surprising it was that although they had known each other for nearly three years there was so much about herself and her life she had never told him; she wanted to remember and tell him everything, so that by telling him she would forever make him a part of it, as if he had been there when it had happened to her.

"I never thought my life was interesting until I started telling it to you," she said. They were lying on the sand in the sun.

"The Life Story. The oldest form of social communication. Every time people fall in love they tell the same story again—it's always new."

"Did you . . . tell it to all those girls?"

He smiled. "Selected excerpts."

"I can imagine!" She laughed at him.

"This is the last time," Mort said. "No more life stories to anyone. No more stories at all, not derring-do stories, not bedtime stories, nothing. Just us, nobody else, ever."

"Nobody else," Margie said.

He kissed her hands.

They drove to other beaches sometimes, along the edge of the arm of land, beaches that were at times as deserted as their own. If the wind ruffled the water of their cove so that it was not good for swimming there was always a peaceful cove at the other side. They went to one beach at night. It was long and wide and very white in the moonlight, and completely deserted. Mort told her that penguins had been seen there in winter, marching out of the sea. The sand dunes were as vast, high, and unmarked as temples made of marble. On the smooth sand ahead of them they saw their own shadows, huge, swaying and joined. The moonlight was so bright you could read by it. They wrote messages to each other on the sand with their fingers.

When the weekend came, Mort's friend did not appear, so they stayed on, and stayed the following week. This is the first time in my life, Margie thought, that I have done exactly what I wanted to do without thinking what anyone else would think about it. It gave her such a feeling of freedom that she hardly recognized herself. There was still something in her of the girl on the beach all green from the phosphorescent water.

They made plans, because they knew they could not stay at the beach house forever. It seemed easy now to think of disposing of furniture, moving out of the apartment, going to the States for the divorce. She knew that when she walked into her apartment again it would not be so easy, there would always be too many memories, but at least now she did not feel dismantling them was destructive. She was not destroying her former life, she realized now; she was only moving it farther into the past so she could begin to build a new one. Mort was going to come with her to the States while she waited for her divorce, and then they would be married there and come back to Brazil to live as long as they wanted to stay. He wanted to travel, and she wanted whatever he did.

She wondered if she was going to become pregnant from that first night on the beach. Afterward, of course, she had been careful. In the old days she had hated all the paraphernalia of being safe; it had seemed as though it was all a messy invention to make going to bed at night even more to be dreaded. She had missed being single when she could just go to bed and go to sleep. But now none of it bothered her at all. She thought once that it would be ironic if at last, having learned to be grateful for the things, it was too late. She counted. The possibility was very remote, and yet, she felt a giddy delight. She had never wanted a baby so much. She felt neither ashamed nor frightened; all she felt was this joy that flickered within her as if it were already a formed and created life. She wanted to miss nothing that could bring her and Mort closer together, she wanted to miss nothing that there was to being a woman—and perhaps that was what this flickering was, not a specific life but the awareness of life itself.

CHAPTER 23

In the States, in the fall, Margie Haft Davidow was married to Mort Baker in Las Vegas, Nevada, by a Justice of the Peace who wore a thin leather thong for a tie. Her mother wept—whether tears of happiness or sadness, no one knew, least of all herself. Margie was so beautiful and vulnerable looking . . . thank God she and Neil had had no children . . . young people today were so smarty and independent . . . they could at least have had a rabbi. . . . Etta always cried at weddings. Margie's father, who was still annoyed at his wife's impetuous insistence that they fly down here at the last minute for this foolishness, choked back a few tears himself. Margie looked so dark, so sunburned, like a *shvartza*, and so many things had happened to her all alone in Brazil—the separation, this new boy, but she still looked so young it was as if this were her first wedding day six years ago. How small her hand was, he thought, as he pressed a folded check for a thousand dollars into Margie's palm.

In Rio, newcomers came: Americans and Italians and Swiss and English and Germans and French; the traveling, the dispossessed, the wanderers, the hopeful, seeking excitement and their fortunes, seeking escape and peace, seeking familiar faces and the accent of home. Helen Sinclair sought out and met all the new Americans, most of them people as new and frightened and anxious to be liked as she had been long ago. They blundered, they complained, they admired, they asked questions, they were quick with answers, they mistrusted differences, they trusted too much what they took to be sameness. She saw it all as if she were watching her own self being played by another person.

She and Bert had been living in Brazil for nearly two years, and they probably had only another year here. *Only* another year! What a short time it seemed, and less than a year ago, at Christmas, she had been thinking two more years was an eternity. She loved it here, she didn't want to go, but they were a moving family.

She had become used to new friends and to people leaving. Some of them went home and never came back, like Mil Burns. Some of them went home and came back quickly for a new life, like Margie and Mort. It seemed strange for a while to think of Margie-and-Mort instead of Margie-and-Neil, especially with Neil still here in Rio, but very soon Helen was used to it. And some of the people, like Neil Davidow, came here to stay, and changed. It was apparent by now that Neil was never going to marry his Brazilian girl; he hardly even saw her any more. He had discovered that he liked being free. Since his divorce Neil had become one of the town's most determined bachelors, and one of the most popular.

"It's ironic," Helen said to Bert, once. "Neil always liked and admired Mort so much. It's as if now he and Mort have sort of changed places. Now Neil is the big lover. And Mort is so faithful and happy to be good. I wonder if one of the reasons the two of them were such close friends is that each one really wanted to be more like the other than himself."

As small as Rio was, some people managed to vanish without a trace. Helen had never seen Leila again. She had meant many times to call Leila, invite her for lunch, but so many things intervened. There were so many things to do, for the children, for the apartment, for herself, to return invitations, and you grew so lazy and apathetic. . . . She thought of Leila sometimes, and she wondered if Leila were thinking of her. The thought almost seemed to suffice as communication, or at least the good intention did. She knew they would run into each other someday soon, and it would be as if they had seen each other only a few days before.

Eventually you always saw everyone, even people you hoped you would never see. Helen had seen Sergio twice again, from a distance. Both times she had been with Bert. Once he had been walking into the Bon Gourmet for dinner as she was walking out. They brushed past each other and did not nod or speak. At first Helen thought Sergio did not see her. Until he was past them she had not even realized it was he. It all happened so fast. Sergio was with a woman and another couple, all of them laughing and talking and gesturing. She had never realized how much he gestured when he spoke. She was filled with emotions when she saw him: with surprise and shock and fear that he might turn back to speak to her, and with embarrassment, but not with love. She wished she could forget her affair with him, the words they had said to each other, she wished none of it had ever happened.

The second time she saw him was at Sacha's. She was on the tiny dance floor with Bert, and it was, as usual, very dark and cool. She did not see Sergio until he was right next to her. He was dancing with a girl, a very young girl, perhaps eighteen at the most. The girl was wearing a white lace dress and she was bosomy and curvaceous to the point where in one more year she would probably be too full-blown. But right at this moment she had a wild prettiness. The girl and Sergio were kissing each other.

This second time when she saw him Helen felt a subtle wistfulness that was almost painful. She did not desire him, she did not love him, she had only contempt for him for so openly kissing a girl in the night club where all his wife's friends liked to go. And yet, there was always some bond that lingered between a woman and a man who has kissed and touched her—for the woman, not for the man. Sergio looked full at her and pretended not to see her, and Helen looked away. She knew he had seen her. She was ashamed to feel this poignance about a man she did not want, while she was in the arms of the man she wanted for ever. What was it? Perhaps only that she had been freely herself with Sergio, and had let him look into her heart, so that now when he kissed a stranger there was something of herself lingering on his lips, so in effect she kissed that stranger too. The

372

thought made her shudder. It must have been the same for Bert, she thought, but so much worse. And for the first time Helen knew how it had been.

It was spring here . . . fall—what was it? Sometimes Helen became confused. You wanted to give yourself over altogether to one kind of life and thinking, you wanted to give up the effort of comparing dates and seasons, the dual existence—and yet you kept going out of your way to keep your identity, your loyalties, the little things you suddenly remembered and missed and tried to duplicate here. But no matter what season it was, during the day the sun shone, and at night the stars shone, and there were lovers on the beach.

One night walking home from a dinner party at Margie's, Helen stopped still on the mosaic sidewalk in the moonlight and looked at Bert. "Let's walk on the sand," she said.

He jumped off the high sidewalk to the beach and held out his hands to her. The sand was deep and soft where they walked in it, and the breeze ruffled Helen's skirt. It was a lovely feeling to be walking along the beach in a party dress. She was holding hands with Bert and swinging her shoes from her other hand. She looked up at the apartment buildings across the street. A few blocks farther along was theirs, with the balcony where she had stood looking down at the lovers on the sand.

"Let's stop for a minute," Bert said. He looked at her questioningly, and at her chiffon dress, but she sank down immediately onto the sand, her skirt billowing all around her, and pulled him down too, and laughed.

"Look at them," she whispered. "We won't have to give the children a serious lecture in the library when they get a little older. We'll just take them for a walk one night."

The couple twenty-five feet away from them, their privacy interrupted, got up and moved farther away down the beach. "Poor guy," Bert said. "We shouldn't have bothered them."

"Serves them right."

"Put your head back. The buildings are upside down."

"It makes me dizzy." She lay flat on the beach with her head on Bert's shoulder. He put his arm around her. It was very comfortable and peaceful on the sand, cool, the sand very soft against her bare legs. Once in a while she heard a car drive by, but otherwise it was very still. "I used to watch them," she said. "Those people. I wondered who they were. People with no homes? Kids running away from chaperones? Clods with no need for privacy or romance? Utter romanticists?"

"Two of each."

A beggar, dressed in torn shapeless pants and a fluttering rag of a tan shirt, came shuffling along the beach looking about for someone who seemed rich. He was middle-aged, unshaven for a week, as thin as an old chicken, and slightly drunk. When he headed for them Helen stiffened with alarm. He stopped in front of Bert and looked down at them both.

"I only want some money," the beggar said in Portuguese. He swayed above them. Helen had the sudden thought that he might do something violent—even kill them. She glanced at Bert.

Bert took some cruzeiros out of his pocket and handed them to the man. The man took them but he did not leave; he stood there swaying gently, looking at them.

"I only want some money," the beggar said again, thickly. "It is very bad, the inflation."

"Oh, Bert!"

Bert looked calm, even slightly friendly. "Go away," he said in Portuguese. "I have no money, and we're in love."

A great black-toothed smile came over the beggar's face. "In love?" he said. He hunched his thin shoulders, put his hands into his pockets, and reeled away quickly over the sand. He turned around once to look at them over his shoulder, and he still had that resigned and beneficent smile. "Okay," he called back to them in English. "In love? *Okay!*" He disappeared into the darkness.

They laughed and lay back in each other's arms. It was midnight in Rio, and ten P.M. in New York where Helen's mother and father were, and nine P.M. in Chicago where Mil Burns was, and only seven in Hollywood, California, where Guillerme's movie stars were living their celluloid lives. In the States, summer had ended; cities were coming to life again from the torpor of heat and hibernation; it was the first weeks of fall. In Brazil, winter had ended; spring was here and soon summer, soon again Carnival, the season of folly and liveliness. One continent cool, one hot; both newly stirring and aware of the new season; neither aware of the other—the curve of the earth got in the way.

ABOUT THE AUTHOR

RONA JAFFE, *a native New Yorker, is twenty-seven years old and a graduate of Radcliffe College. Her first novel—the best-selling* The Best of Everything—*was published in 1958.*